THE
ANESTHESIA
GAME

10-12-15

For Maryjane,

with best wishes,

rea nolan martin

REA NOLAN MARTIN

Cover & Interior Layout Design: VMC Art & Design, LLC

ISBN: 978-0-9910322-2-8 (Paperback Edition)
Library of Congress Control Number: 2015909160

WIAWAKA
PRESS

For Zach,
who played the Game and won

Our birth is but a sleep and a forgetting:
The Soul that rises with us, our life's Star,
Hath had elsewhere its setting.
And cometh from afar...

— William Wordsworth

Hannah

HANNAH CHANDLER AWAKENS WITH a start from the same weird dream. Her head jerks forward, striking the bottle of estate reserve pinot noir clutched loosely in her left hand. Slightly stunned by the impact, she stares into the neck of the open bottle for a few seconds before upending it and polishing off the last mouthful. How she loves a good pinot.

Pushing herself up to a sitting position, she tries to shake the dream—the giant birds, the chaos, the raging fire and an unidentifiable spectral character, probably from the shopping channel, warning her about...whatever. She really doesn't know what the message is, if there even is one, since every time she has this dream she wakes up before the creep with the wagging finger can finish. *"Don't come looking..."* is as far as it gets. Looking for what, though, Hannah wonders. Trouble? She doesn't have to look for that. It's the default location on her GPS.

The realization of her deteriorating life burrows into her head like a nest of snakes. She curls her long, slim body on the elegant sunshine-yellow couch, her head buried in perfectly manicured hands, still clutching the bottle. She has squeezed into many a tight financial spot, she knows, but this one is so cramped she can't tell her head from her poppy-red toenails. She must be a contortionist to have crammed in this far, but not really, since she doesn't know how to get out. A contortionist would know. "Face it," she tells herself, "you're broke."

Her words echo into the neck of the empty bottle and back out through a decade of indiscreet spending, maybe more. Just looking at her or her impressive rural estate, nobody would ever believe it, but there it is—the bald truth. Where it all went she doesn't know. Or she might know, but in the end, what difference does it make? It's gone. No amount of petty ass, line-item analysis of this gold bracelet or that organic wrinkle cream will bring it back.

She doesn't have much to show for it either. It's not as if she's hoarding rooms of museum-grade furniture or gilded, hand-painted tiles surrounding gold-leaf sinks. She hasn't been greedy or delinquent. That isn't what happened. She just lost track of her divorce settlement because she always thought she and Jonah would get back together. Even though she was the one who sent him packing, but still. Why didn't he come crawling back?

She shifts positions, placing the bottle on the floor and facing the empty fireplace at the end of the room. One arm braces the back of the couch that rests against the grand picture window to her left. A swooping raptor catches her attention and she turns. Turkey vulture maybe or red tail, hard to tell in the dusky gray sky. She's only seen an eagle here once. Whatever it is snags a tiny creature in its claws and takes off. Hannah follows its flight path above the rolling fields, twirling her stylish, chin-length mop of auburn hair nervously around both index fingers. What must it feel like to be snatched like that? Just plucked out of your life for a snack. *Good God!*

The raptor disappears, but Hannah keeps staring. She stares and shivers because it's chilly outside and a little bit inside. The chilliest January she can remember. She'd light a fire if she weren't so lazy. Or not so much lazy, really, as mentally exhausted from all the stress. She could use a valet right now— somebody to fetch a sweater and light a fire. Shake a martini. She used to call that a husband, but not anymore. Husbands are too much trouble and they tend not to come back when you kick them out.

She leans down, retrieving another bottle—her spare—from the floor and sips. She should really buy a new coffee table or end table or something to put things on. Or a tray table for God's sake, anything. *Did Jonah really have to take the tables?! Why the tables?!* As soon as she gets her bills paid she'll buy some new ones. She sips again and replaces the bottle on the floor.

This is all so dreary and tedious, but she can't ignore it. She's not a coward. Or is she? Maybe she is. She drags her body back to a hunched sitting position, draping both arms across the back of the couch and staring out. Frost covers the languid fields and the barn roof in the lower paddock, not to mention her entire future. She could lose everything. After all, who's going to save her now? Nobody. She's commando. The only way it ends well this time is if e-Harmony hooks her up with a Saudi prince or she manages to write a prize-winning novel. *Huh.* She straightens up.

The novel has merit.

Not any novel. To be worth her while it would have to net at least $1,000,000 and a Pulitzer or a Nobel, or any of the other elite literary prizes du jour. Who cares which one, as long as it pays the bills and endows her with enough celebrity to launch a reality show? It's not the first time she's thought about it, but maybe the time is finally right. Nobody in her pedestrian book group can figure out how these prize committees pick winners, but Hannah might have an idea. She's read the books, and there's a random kind of cryptic formula to them. You can't just empty a barrel of ordinary words onto piles of paper and expect to win. It has to be something inventive, but completely true. And bizarre, nearly incomprehensible, but again, true. But dangerously close to not being true. Something like what's become of Hannah's entire life, not that she would ever write about that. *Although.*

Not that she's completed a story in a long time, or rather, constructed one from beginning to end; she hasn't. Just snippets. Since she was twelve years old she's been scribbling these genius snippets on receipts and sticky notes, whatever's available, and burying them anywhere—drawers, closets, file cabinets, book flaps and magazine margins. Heirloom seeds just waiting to germinate into prize-winning classics. She's been doing this her entire life; it isn't new. It's who she is.

Snippet #1 from this morning: "*Her social networks were the last to die.*"

Snippet #2: "*She supports the earth with the middle finger of her right hand, twirling it to show off at parties.*"

Right?

Her gift is 100% authentic; she's not delusional. It all came down twenty-six years ago in Loudoun County High School when she was paid $50 by the Daughters of the Confederacy for an autobiographical essay she'd composed beginning to end in a single twenty-minute sitting. She made it all up, of course—a frenetic and unfaithful assortment of childhood stories she'd pieced together about Irish forebears and how they'd settled in the wild hills of Shenandoah County. How they fought against alcoholic black bears for the rock gut whisky leaking from the volatile stills hidden in the wooded piedmont. How the bears were as soused as her fake uncles. How her whole family wouldn't even be here now if the bears hadn't been beaten into area rugs and lap blankets that still grace the bedrooms of her ancestral cabin.

Original!

Not that any of this childish reminiscence will put money in Hannah's pocket. Money she needs to pay the stack of bills currently fanned out like a raven's wing on the dining room table. Money she now imagines arriving dressed in a black-tie literary prize with enough celebrity to keep the hang dogs from feeling sorry for her and her niece, Sydney. Not that Sydney lives with Hannah; she doesn't. But she should. She lives in Connecticut with her mother, Mitsy, Hannah's big dull sister. Not to be unkind.

To be clear, Sydney lives in Connecticut with Mitsy and her super-fly rock-steady reliable dad, Aaron, when she isn't in the hospital ICU or clinic following endless treatments for some kind of disorder no one will identify. Not that Hannah wants to know the exact name of the disease; she doesn't. She's not very medical. Besides, it's all too painful to think about since Sydney is more like Hannah than Hannah. And even though Hannah didn't want kids, if she'd had one, it would have been Syd. Not that Hannah sees her niece that much, she doesn't, but she would if they lived closer. Or if the girl's mother wasn't such a nutcase. Again, not to be unkind. *But.*

Hannah cocks her head, listening. Is that her cell? The ringtone is muffled. It could be her cell phone or a SETI signal from space, it's that remote. Maybe she's hearing things. But no; there it goes again. She searches her pockets, the cushions, but no-can-find. Hanging upside down, she flips the couch skirt to see if it fell underneath, but no. While she's down there, she tips the bottle and sips more wine. Or guzzles, really. Guzzle-sips to be accurate. There should be a combo word for people who prefer to drink out of bottles. 'Gips' or 'suzzles', maybe. Not that Hannah gips or suzzles every day, just when there's no one to clink with. She supposes she could just fill two glasses and clink on her own, but in the end that seems a bit pretentious, not to mention dishonest. You can't get much more honest than suzzling straight out of a bottle.

She hears the faint ring tone again, and from the sound of it, it's in the kitchen, so the hell with it. The last thing she needs right now is to get up. It's probably one of her creditors anyway—Bloomingdale's or Neiman's or wherever she bought the Donatella gown for Syd's Make-a-Wish hospital gala. Those stores are all about you when they think you have money, but get in over your head for a split-second and you're a whack-a-mole at a fold-up carnival. Or maybe it's her sister, Mitsy.

Quite frankly, Mitsy is more than Hannah can deal with right now, anyway. She's needy, true, but so is Hannah. She has to get her own house in order first, or farm, really, before the bloodthirsty mortgage hounds catch the fox. The fox is Hannah, of course. Foxy, yes, but not just in the sexy way, as she's oft been told, even though she's well into her thirties. Okay, early forties. She's outsmarted her creditors so far, and she's not giving up now. Why should she? She has a prize-winning novel in her that will blow their illiterate minds. They'll beg her to wear their designer gowns at the award ceremony in Stockholm. And God knows Hannah can rock a sheer, snug designer gown—the more cut-outs the better. She'll pay her goddamn bills, all right, and it won't be with scratch-off cards.

She stretches back out on the couch, leaning over for the bottle. She lifts; sips; replaces; lifts; sips; replaces. And repeat.

One more time—it's a long way down. What she needs is a compelling opening line. Something like: "By the time you read this, I will be dead." A line nobody can put down, walk away from, or ignore. She sits up and adjusts the vintage denim jeans on her long slim legs, absently pulling at one of the holes until it shreds straight across at the knee. It's a fabulous tear, actually. She couldn't do it again if she tried. Once in a lifetime tear. If she knew where her cell phone was, she'd snap a knee selfie and post it everywhere. No one would believe it. On ebay alone it would fetch thousands.

Chilled, she reaches behind her for the homespun turquoise velour blanket she picked-up at the Whistle Stop last week, and wraps it around her shoulders. *So luxurious!* Expensive, true, but after all, it's important to support local craftsmen or they'll move to Charleston or Savannah. It happens all the time. Another sip of wine and she's back to the window, mesmerized by what looks like a huge barn owl on the gazebo roof. Nose to window, she squints. Can't make it out. Daylight is disappearing—*what time is it?*

Used to be Hannah gazed out this window at 35 miles of undulating hills across highways and high-wires all the way to the Godfrey estate. Miles of undulating hills dotted with brick-red barns, prize-winning cattle, glossy thoroughbred horses, and perfectly stacked bales of hay. Not anymore—thank you, unscrupulous politicians and voracious developers. Now her eyes rest on treeless miles of bland colonials decked-out in acrylic siding in a hundred shades of taupe, not to mention the ubiquitous fake-stone facing. What's next, Tupperware houses? Little transparent, oxygen-deprived houses where people's moldy little lives are on full display? *Plant some trees, people!*

Thinking of the devaluation of her own farm—her only remaining investment, Hannah fantasizes about actually killing herself and leaving the brilliant first line of her prize-winning story as a suicide note for Jonah, who probably wouldn't even finish it. *"By the time you find this…"* and already he's bored. As if he'd ever given a shit about anything she wrote or said or thought. And still…she loves him. Oh God, she thinks, dropping her head, where's the gun?

She collapses her torso dramatically backwards on the foam pillows, rolls to her side and dips down for the bottle. Suzzles thoughtfully. Back to her prize-winning story. The old reviews still tickle her: *"Genius!"* the reviewer had written in the *Loudon Times-Mirror*. *"This writer will go far!"* Well, she could have lived up to their remarks if she'd wanted to. If she hadn't acquired two self-righteous (ex) husbands and a sprawling farm. Not that they farmed anything but hay. Not that she'd actually had anything to do with the hay. But just the stress of looking out the window at all that work, season after season. And anyway, at this point she needs a hell of a lot more than a $50 award from the Daughters of the Confederacy to pay that stack of bills. God, she's hungry. She hauls her ass off the couch, shuffling across the mahogany-stained floor on stocking feet for a fat pile of empty calories.

Standing in the middle of her barn-beamed kitchen a la rustica, she surveys the near-empty fridge: a yellowed log of dried-up goat cheese, a loose spray of shriveled mint, four bottles of chardonnay, and a cell phone. *A cell phone!* No sooner does she stuff the phone into her back pocket but it rings again. Shit. Thinking positively though, maybe it's Dr. Kevorkian. She slams the fridge door shut with her hip. Mitsy's number flashes on the screen. Well, fine; she'll answer it. Not exactly an upper, but Mitsy needs her. When someone needs you, you answer once in a while.

"Hey," Hannah says.

"Hi, Hannah." Flatline.

"Hold for a sec?" says Hannah. She lays the phone on the counter, opens the drawer and rummages for snacks. Popcorn will have to do. She trots the bag back to the living room where she can despair in comfort. She drops anchor on the couch, suzzles from the pinot bottle on the floor and tosses a few kernels into her mouth. *Crunch*.

"Okay, I'm back," she says, chomping. She waits. Nothing. No one. She swallows. "Mits?"

Mitsy sighs, but that's the only sign of life.

Nothing about these phone calls is easy, which is why Hannah limits them. She has a limit. She pushes through the utter stagnation. "Everything okay, Mits?"

"Sure. Well, you know. As much as can be expected."

Hannah burrows into the corner of the couch. What can she really say about any of this? Mitsy doesn't realize how difficult it is to talk to her these days. You need a crow bar to open every sentence. "I told you I'd help out if you needed me," Hannah offers noncommittally. She might as well offer; Mitsy will never take her up on it anyway. Everyone thinks Hannah's unreliable.

"That's kind of why I'm calling," Mitsy says.

"What?" Hannah coughs up a kernel.

"Are you okay?"

"Yeah, just…dinner," Hannah says.

"I wondered if you could come up and help out for a couple of weeks," says Mitsy.

"Weeks?" Hannah croaks. She runs her greasy fingers through her hair.

"I'll pay you, Hannah. I know you can't just up and leave everything without pay."

"That's not the point."

"To me it is. Sydney would rather have you up here helping out than a stranger, and I uh, well. I…have a few new challenges of my own."

"What challenges?"

"Sorry to tell you this way, but."

"You haven't told me anything." Hannah puts her whole hand in the new knee tear and expands it. "Out with it."

"They ran some tests," Mitsy says. "I have a…situation. Autoimmune. It's manageable, I guess, but I have to get it under control first. A couple of weeks or so and I'll be back on Sydney's schedule. No sweat, I swear. Just need you for the gap." She heaves a sigh. "I *need* you, Hannah."

"A 'situation'? Where? What is it?" This is insane. One thing after another. What the hell has happened to Hannah's life?!

"I would just, I don't know…rather tell you in person? I'll be fine, is what they say. I believe them. So should you."

"Believe who about what?" Hannah grabs the bottle. "Don't be so obtuse, Mits."

"I have my way of dealing with things," Mitsy says.

"Like all that yoga and mystic woo woo? You're too soft with all that stuff. That's probably what got you sick in the first place. You're so damn soft. You need to toughen-up; get pissed off. Go mental. Pick up a car and throw it at somebody."

"It's not like that," Mitsy says softly. "It's okay. It's a spiritual world, Hannah, whether you know it or not. Whether you believe it or not doesn't change what it is."

"Spoken like a real charlatan." Hannah shakes her head. "Eegadz."

"Pandora is not a charlatan," Mitsy says. "She's the real thing. You could benefit from her. She's the reason I'm not crazy."

"Right," Hannah snorts. "Whatever." *Just the name!*

"So you'll come?"

Hannah sighs, defeated, running her fingers through her hair, trying not to pull it out of her head. "Maybe. I don't know. I'll try. I've got some things to work out first." She hesitates. "I can't promise anything." *In other words—no!* "And anyway," she says, "What about the hubby? I'd just be in the way."

"Aaron will be in and out of town. He's got a new project in Austin a couple of days a week, but…" Total mental traffic jam shuts down the verbal highway.

"But what?" Hannah pushes.

"But I don't know," Mitsy finally says in her generally depressive manner. "I can only deal with so much at once. And in fairness to Aaron, it's a bit much for him to take care of both me and Sydney, not to mention the job and the traveling." She pauses. "If you don't come, we'll hire someone anyway. I'd rather hire you."

"Money isn't the point," Hannah repeats emphatically. Although in a way it is. Not Mitsy's money, of course—how much is Hannah really worth as a caretaker, anyway? It's the award money she's worried about. Could she actually write a prize-winning novel in the middle of all that chaos? It was a long shot she'd have to think about, because after all, there are bills to pay. Not to mention an entire estate to manage. How can she go, *really?* She absolutely cannot. "Okay, Mits, I'll get back to you soon, how's that?"

"You'll think about it then?"

"Yeah, sure, why not? I'll think about it."

Hannah ends the call, grabs handfuls of her hair and pulls it out straight from both sides. "Aaaaaaaa!" That conversation was insane! What does Mitsy expect from her, anyway? Hannah has a life, for God's sake. No way she'd ever survive that insanity. *No effing way.*

All at once, shadows descend, and the night sky envelopes the farm, the house, and Hannah like shrink wrap. It's suffocating.

She snaps on a few lights, but still…a familiar kind of slow tension crawls up her nerves and accumulates. *Threatens*. How will she keep it at bay tonight? She grabs the TV remote and plops back down, absently flipping through fifty-plus channels before landing on QVC. A few minutes in and she's trading a potential full-on nervous breakdown for an amazing flameless rosette candle complete with timer that would certainly be helpful on lonely, dark winter evenings like this. If only she had one now.

She trots into the kitchen for her purse and credit cards and grabs a bag of pretzels to go with the popcorn. If you put them in your mouth at the same time, it's a veritable explosion of flavor—popzels or pretzcorn. She's surprised none of the food giants have caught on to this. Her ideas are platinum. If she could unscrew her head she could lease her brain and make a fortune while she sleeps.

Back on the couch, she wraps herself in the velour throw with her food bags, and orders the candle. At $65 it's such a bargain that the instant she hangs up she regrets ordering only one. After all, they're flameless. You don't even need matches. She calls back and orders two more.

The next display of QVC panic-busting merchandise is jewelry, not that she intends to order any. But wait, look—a magnificent 14k gold medallion of that new pope everybody likes. Francis. Very interesting heirloom-like piece at a reasonable price. And maybe lucky, too, since he's obviously a popular man. She could use some good luck, who couldn't? She dials 1-888-… etc., numbers she could recite in her sleep. She orders the medallion before she loses interest. You have to stay on top of these items or they're gone. Only a QVC novice loses a good piece. You can't get all overconfident and wait. And look here—a set of insulated polka-dot travel mugs. Save her a ton of money on Styrofoam and paper. Prevent her and every other environmentally-responsible buyer from destroying the earth with refuse. 1-888-...ordered. But that's it; no more. She's done.

Satisfied that her evening is now worth something—*$735.55 to be exact*—she relaxes back into the couch and searches for any of the Housewife franchises, polishes off the popzels, and washes them down with estate reserve. She's lucky she knows how to deal with issues like a sick sister and sicker niece without completely bottoming out. It isn't easy to clear a conversation with Mitsy from your head. It takes a QVC village and a winery, at least. That entire conversation was like...*what?!* Like the horrible tedious job Hannah had at the hospital that whole week one summer. What was it again? Oh yeah, medical transcription. A conversation with Mitsy is like twelve hours of transcribing people's colonoscopies while you're in the middle of the worst hangover ever. *When will it end?!* She tips the bottle back. She might as well earn the hangover.

The next day the sun rises above the horse barn in the lower paddock, burns through the picture window, and singes the fog at the edges of Hannah's brain. Her mouth is a latrine. Her eyes are stuck together with sleep and eyelash glue, and her lower back aches. Where is she? She reaches up and pulls one sticky eyelid apart, then the other, only to find herself staring into the intoxicating crème de cocoa eyes of her ex-husband, Jonah.

Shit!

She hikes herself up on her elbows. "What are you doing here?" she mumbles. Oh *God*, how her head pounds.

"Good afternoon," he says drily.

When she doesn't respond, he says, "Party of one?" as he

dangles two empty bottles of wine over her. He shakes his pious head. "Is this what it's come to?"

She winces from the dagger in her right temple. *Ooooph.* "I had a little party last night," she says to no one, to the couch, trailing off as she collapses back to sleep for a minute or a week. But not long enough, apparently, to change the station, because Jonah reappears when she opens her eyes. His substantial 6'4 frame is perched on the edge of the couch. He nudges her awake.

"Here," he says not unkindly, toting a glass of water, two aspirin, and a giant mug of steaming coffee.

She swallows the aspirin, hands him the glass and takes the mug. Two sips of coffee later, she comes to her senses. "I'll be right back," she mutters, shifting and pushing her way upright. *Everything aches!* She lays the mug on the floor. Two credit cards fall off her lap as she rises, and she kicks them under the couch.

Staggering carefully across the room to her right, she balances her gait against walls and furniture, dodging the love seat and the antique jelly cabinet on her way to the front stairs. "Don't leave," she says under her breath. "I'll just be a minute."

After an arduous walk up the front stairs, she arrives in the master bath, steadying herself against the sink. Easy does it. She splashes cold water on her face and neck, pulls off the bent lashes, and brushes her teeth vigorously. Gargles. She tames her expertly highlighted auburn hair with a wide-tooth comb, swipes her armpits with deodorant, and wanders back to the bedroom closet. Flipping desperately through a poorly organized, department store-size inventory, she settles on a sexy, sheer, ruby silk sweater with a sparkly hexagram for Love stitched on the front. Not that Jonah will know what the hexagram means, but subliminally maybe he'll get the message. *Two days later he's hers!*

She pinches her pale cheeks, and checks the full-length closet mirror. *OMG the eyes!* Her signature crystal green pools are now surrounded by wild tributaries of blood red. Back to the bathroom, she squirts Visine in both eyes, blinks, and blots the tears. *You can do it!* she tells herself as she ambles downstairs, carefully balancing her head on her shoulders. Nothing is automatic. Everything is a carefully constructed illusion. But she won't let on. This was not a one-woman party as far as anyone is concerned. It was a frat house blowout, and too bad he missed it.

She rounds the corner to the living room, and there's Jonah, all Paul Bunyan of him stretched out on the recliner with a Starbucks mug of Ethiopian dark blend, his favorite. At least she had that on hand. Or maybe not. Maybe he brought it with him.

"Well, that's better," he says neutrally.

Or maybe not neutrally? Maybe approvingly? Maybe it's her hangover that's neutralizing him; Hannah can't tell. After all, why is he here in the first place?

"Seriously," she says, "I'm glad you're here."

"This is how you get to sleep now?" he says. "Pinot noir and pretzels?"

"And popcorn?" she says impishly. She stares at his beautiful square-jawed face, his eyes—gorgeous nuggets of milk chocolate framed by those thick eyebrows raised in familiar disapproval.

"I had a houseful over last night," she says casually. "It was fun! You should have come."

He regards her with interest. "And what did they eat, all those hungry people? There's no sign of food anywhere and the only garbage is in the refrigerator. You should clean it out."

This would piss Hannah off if she weren't so desperate for his company. "Think what you want," she says.

He sips his coffee thoughtfully. "The payments stop this week, Hannah. I just don't want any grief from you about that. I can see you have bills." He points his chin in the direction of the dining room. "Lots of them."

She lifts her mug from the floor and drinks.

"What happened to the end tables?" he says. "And the coffee table?"

"What?" She frowns, trying to think this through carefully, but the taste of her foot is already choking her. "I thought..." She shakes her head. "Didn't you...? Never mind."

"You thought what?"

"Nothing."

"So you don't know where the tables are, is that it? Good God, Hannah, are you blacking out!"

"No. No, I'm not." She flashes a grin, which takes quantum energy. Keep it light—*believable*. "I gave them to Brice. The painter? Remember him? I just thought...I don't know. That the new ones would be here by now."

Jonah sighs. "You have to get your act together, kid," he says. "You've alienated half the town. You're impossible to live with..."

"What?" she says. "I'm impossible...?"

He nods sadly, his arms sweeping to include the universe of all purchased items. "All the excess. The new furniture, the Audi, the clothes, the vintage alcohol. Come on, Hannah, you can't not know."

She turns away. She wants him here, but she doesn't. Same ole same ole. He can be such a bitchy old matron.

"No one else will be this honest with you," he says, but she still won't look. "And I'm actually worried about you. You have no direction in your life and nothing at all that interests you except shopping, wine, and who knows what other substances. And I got a notice..." he pulls an envelope from the front pocket of his denim shirt. "From the bank."

"What? What notice? For me? Why you?"

"I'm still on the mortgage, remember? They wouldn't give you one on your own."

Hannah purses her lips in a full-on pout. "That's impossible," she says weakly. "How can they send you a notice without sending one to me? I'm primary. I'm the one who inherited this farm, damn it. I was *born* here, remember?!"

He pushes the recliner upright and leans forward. "You did get a notice," he says. "Three of them." He nods toward the dining room with defeat. "Look," he says, "I want to help out."

"You do?" she says pleadingly.

He nods. "I do. I want to buy the farm from you."

What?! "What?" she says stunned.

"Let's face it, you can't do this," he says matter-of-factly. "You can't live here. It costs too bloody much, and instead of living on old goat cheese, you could be eating 4-course meals in D.C. Let me buy you out. I'll be generous. You can go get a co-op or condo and live well. You just have to...I don't know, go to rehab or something, so you don't do it all over again."

When she doesn't respond, he shakes his head, sighing. "Think about it."

She breathes deeply, willing herself up from the ashes. "I can afford this place," she says. "My parents left me a lot of money."

"You've spent it all."

So calm. How does he stay so calm? His righteous aloof calmness has always pissed her off. "It might surprise you to know that I'm writing a book. A memoir, in fact. So it would behoove you to show some consideration since you'll probably be at least a chapter."

"A lot of people write books, and..."

"And nothing!"

"Exactly," he says. "And nothing. A lot of incredibly

talented people write books that amount to nothing. It's a lotto."

"Well, I'm not one of them." She points emphatically to her chest. "I...will be writing an award-winning book. I've won awards before, and I'll win them again." She marinates in rage which, reflected in his silence, looks a lot like asinine stupidity. She is an ass.

"I've known you a long time," he says quietly. "And there's no growing up for you. No maturing. Face it, you're not going to finish a book and you're not going to pay these bills. I love you, but..."

Her heart jumps. "You do?" See? *The hexagram works!*

He nods. "I do, but there's no living with you."

"Fuck you!" she says, fighting tears.

"See there you go, Hannah. You can't listen to anything. The truth is you're a narcissist who can't put anybody else first in your life. A narcissist with no direction at all." He walks to the hall, his giant frame filling the doorjamb. "I gotta go."

"I'm not a narcissist," she says, sniveling. "In fact, if you must know, I'm going to Connecticut to take care of Sydney for a month while Mitsy gets treatment for whatever. She wouldn't tell me, but it's something deadly." She narrows her eyes. "Would a narcissist up and leave to nurse her sick sister and niece for a month? No. She would not. A narcissist would not go near all that godawful sickness."

"That's good," he says, slipping deftly into his leather bomber jacket. "Let me know how it goes. If you want, I'll check on the place while you're away."

"That would be great," she says quietly.

As he's leaving, she says, "People change, Jonah. They do."

He turns. "We'll see," he says. "Just make sure you take care of Sydney and Mitsy and not the other way around."

Sydney

ADJUSTING HER EYES TO the dimming light, Sydney reclines on the surgical bed in the sparse clinic procedure room waiting her turn. She likes being alone in here without her mother to freak her out. Just Syd in the dark with her thoughts. She draws the thin blanket to her chin and gazes blankly at the ABC wall trim and childish cartoon art designed to cheer up the little kids. If it cheers them up or not, Syd wouldn't know, but it has the opposite effect on her. The fact that she's stuck staring at Dora the Explorer and the Powerpuff Girls when she should be hanging with her best friend, Zelda Rodriguez, not to mention Z's new tattooed neighbor, Dane, makes her feel like a loser. Not that Dane knows who she is; he doesn't. But he should.

How it came to this—spending half her life in a clinic—no one seems to know. A fail of the cosmic variety is all she can conclude. A fail so epic it bypassed not only her overly vigilant parents, but also apparently, God himself. Or at least the God she used to believe in. Not that it matters, because God in the slacker department leaves Syd with only herself to rely on, which is scary, but in a way, a relief. After all, she's not likely to let herself down. She's going to be there for herself; it's un-avoidable. So as she watches the winter sun set between the massive mirrored buildings of the hospital extension casting geometric copper glow-lights on the ceiling, the walls, and on top of Dora the Explorer's head like a halo, she concentrates on a game of her own invention—The Anesthesia Game. The game that keeps her alive.

In spite of its name, the trick is not in the forgetting; it's in the remembering. It's in the asking and the telling, or more accurately, the retelling. To play the game properly you need a decent team of nurses and anesthesiologists, no downers or overly efficient professional types, especially if you play the game as often as Syd does. To be swept into the anesthesia abyss as routinely as that, is to lose too much of a short life. She's only fifteen. She shouldn't have to play anesthesia games at all, never mind this often, but whatever. She tries not to waste time feeling sorry for herself. She already knows life isn't fair. Get over it. If you're going to survive, you have to turn it into a game you have a chance of winning, a game that makes up for lost time. A game that teaches you how to be awake even when you're not.

The rules are simple. Just before the anesthesia is adminis-tered, the nurse or doctor asks you about a place anywhere on earth, and you answer it. If you don't know the answer, they can tell you, no problem. It's not cheating. But not knowing the answer right off can make it harder. Your job is to lock it in the airtight safe of your brain and remember it when you wake up. For Syd this involves taking the slim thread of that answer and spinning it into a giant quilt of a tale while she's unconscious. Not a dream exactly, because it has more form than that, more weight. But more like a movie you can walk through and everything you touch turns real.

The first time Syd played the game, it was spontaneous— no planning. The whole idea just exploded like pop rocks out of her head. "Wait!" she'd said to whatever anesthesiologist. "Ask me something, anything. Quick!"

"What?" said the doctor, frowning. "Why?"

Syd doesn't remember which doctor it was, because he wasn't crush-worthy. He was one of the old ones who all look more or less alike when you're lying on a surgical table with your eyes half-closed. She remembers the young ones, or the ones with the goofy personalities like Dr. Sawyers. This was no Dr. Sawyers.

"Just ask?" she'd begged. "Any question at all. About a place, though. A place worth visiting."

"Okay then..." he'd said. "Where were you born?"

Not very creative, but whatever. "Hartford," Syd said, then squeezed her eyes shut preparing to lock the answer away but not so far away that she couldn't remember the question. "Okay I'm ready." She tugged the nurse, Nicole's, sleeve and said, "Ask me for the answer as soon as I wake up. Without the question," Syd emphasized. "Don't give me any clues. Just ask me for the answer. It's important."

Nicole just said, "Fine," without even asking why. That's why Syd loves nurses. Nurses *know*.

That time—the first time 18 months ago, she didn't re-member the question or the answer when she woke up. She'd been confused, headachy, nauseous, disoriented, and horribly disappointed in herself. She'd lost control, and she was not about to let that happen again. But in the 15 procedures since, she's improved the odds. She's learned to take the thread with her when she goes under and not let go. She's learned to build a story.

All in all, she's beaten the game ten times, the last six consecutively, but who's counting? *She is!* So she's gaining. She's taking the light back from The Taker, which is the point. When you consistently take back your light, nothing can kill you, because you're strong enough to tell your own story, to keep your own light. Light is what keeps you alive. When you can keep your light, you win. She's surprised more people don't know that.

Syd's decided that when she's all done and completely cured, she'll write a book about how to beat the odds. About how to keep living no matter what. How to turn on the master switch that someone or *something* felt entitled to switch off on your behalf, but without your awareness. Who wouldn't buy a book like that? An idiot, maybe. Or people who like to give up when the going gets tough. But most people are not idiots. If her book is a best seller maybe she can even open a clinic of her own.

There's activity in the hall just now that distracts Syd from her thoughts. She turns to see her favorite nurse, Rozlyn, stroll casually into the procedure room. Roz is chill and at the same time, hot. Chill because she is super cool, and hot because, well, anybody can see that. You don't have to be a twenty-year-old male. Just watch the heads turn when she floats like a hovercraft down any corridor. She's a Hollywood Barbie with black hair, sky blue eyes and crazy long legs. Roz would beat ordinary old blonde Barbie in a beauty contest any day. Plus blonde Barbie never looked all that smart. Roz is a genius, and her tortoiseshell glasses aren't the only clue.

Roz adjusts the overhead lights from dim to bright, and Syd squints. "Ugh," she says, covering her eyes.

"Gotta see what I'm doing," Rozlyn says smiling. She goes

about her business, efficiently assembling the usual assortment of needles, tubes and bags of fluids like she's arranging the candy display at a convenience store. Totally chill. She takes Syd's hand and rubs the vein on her inner arm with a pad of antiseptic and grabs her weapon. "A little pinch," she says as she inserts the IV.

Syd flinches. Rozlyn's good at this, but Syd's veins have flattened from overuse and are not always so accessible. Sometimes it takes awhile.

"Done!" Rozlyn declares triumphantly. "First attempt!"

She does a little victory shuffle, all Gangnam style, which cracks Syd up. She wishes she could get up and do it with Roz. Syd can't help grinning, not just at Rozlyn's exuberance, but also because small victories matter in a war this big. Syd wants to win them all, every battle. She wants to show up The Taker in an embarrassing win, battle after battle, until he concedes. Until he is *crushed*. The asshole! Oh my God, *what* an asshole.

"That one went well, but you might wish you had that port back one of these days," says Roz. "No more pinches."

"No way," says Syd. "That thing was constantly clogged."

The port-a-cath was a little rubber thingy inserted in Syd's chest when she was first diagnosed 18 months ago. She won't say what she was diagnosed with, not *ever*, because just the word alone gives The Taker too much power. In Syd's mind, it's a temporary issue anyway; a temporary issue that's all but fixed. So fuck The Taker. He can take his disease and shove it up his corroded "arse" as the Irish nurse, Deirdre, loves to say. Syd loves Deirdre's musical accent, not to mention the crazy orange hair and personality to match. So many people Syd would rather be right now than herself.

Syd's vocabulary has admittedly gotten a lot worse since she's been going to the clinic, not because of the clinic—it's pediatric after all, but just the freedom of no one daring to correct her. The look of horror on her mother's face alone is worth it, and hard not to keep pushing right over the edge. *Plunk!*

"That's vulgar," her mother said to Syd once early on for some minor infraction.

"You know what's vulgar?" Syd said. "This bag of radio-active shit going into my blood. That's vulgar." And it was.

Syd's goal is to degenerate her mother's language as much as she has her own. Wear her mother down with vulgarity. Hear her mother actually say, "Fuck!" Just force it out of her. What a goal. At some point maybe she'll rethink this challenge, but for now it meets all the requirements of achieving the impossible. And surviving. *Surviving!*

Anyway, the port was connected directly to a vein in Syd's chest, and the purpose was to give doctors easier access for blood draws and meds. It worked for a while. Not that Syd likes needles, but she wasn't sad to see the port go. It was freakish. And anyway, by her calculation she doesn't have too many more of these procedures. Maybe eight tops. She can deal with it.

Rozlyn's shiny black hair is long and straight today, falling past her shoulders in wisps. It looks like silk against her ivory skin. Syd wouldn't mind looking like Roz when she gets to that age—28 or 30 probably. Old enough to know what to do, but younger than most of the nurses at the clinic. A good age to freeze yourself at, if that were possible. Roz understands things the others don't, like the fact that Syd doesn't want her mother present at every procedure. Not that her mother doesn't mean well, but just… whatever. It bugs her. Her mother bugs her. Just the over-importance she puts on everything to do with this condition. As if it's permanent. As if it has anything to do with Syd at all.

Syd reaches out and touches Rozlyn's hair. "You have so much," she says, mesmerized. "It's like wild black silk or something."

"Yours will grow back," Rozlyn says, shrugging. "You'll see."

The doctors tap on the door and enter. There's tiny Dr. Lee, who does her spinals, and also Dr. Anton, the anesthesiologist, with his cool gray eyes—grinning insanely like a mad scientist with his vial of alien goop. "How's my girl?" he says, winking.

The drama at the clinic among the doctors and nurses is a great distraction for Syd. She sometimes fantasizes about being a doctor herself some day, walking around with a starched white coat and a stethoscope telling people what diseases they have and curing them. But not children—she never fantasizes about treating children. Children shouldn't have to come to a clinic like this in the first place. But then again, why should anybody? It's a bad plan in general if you ask Syd, but God hasn't exactly included her in the grand design.

Dr. Anton checks the IV. "Mom's not around?" he says.

"She's in the infusion room," Syd says. "I want to do this myself."

He looks meaningfully at Dr. Lee, who nods. "Papers signed," she says. "Mom's aware."

"Okay then," says Dr. Anton. "Ready to go to dreamland, Syd?"

"Sure," she says, squirming to straighten herself on the table. "No, wait!" She grips Roz's hand. "Ask me now. Hurry!"

Dr. Anton's gray eyes crinkle at the edges. He frowns and poofs out his lips. "Oh, right, the game," he says. "Go ahead. I can wait a second for something this important."

"Okay then," says Rozlyn. "Yikes—such pressure! Okay… got it. What's the capitol of Thailand?"

Syd grimaces. "That's too hard. I'll never remember. Ask me the capitol of New Jersey."

"You want to change your own rules?" Roz says. "You've answered harder questions than that."

"Fine. But I don't know the answer. What's the capitol of Thailand?"

"Bangkok," says Dr. Lee.

Syd says, "Bangkok, oh yeah! Okay, Bangkok." She nods at Dr. Anton.

"Ready?" he says.

"Ready," Syd says. "Bangkok, Bangkok, Bangkok, *Bangkok...*" she mumbles until her eyes close and she's a bright light adrift in the darkness. On a plane. A vibrating streak of bright light on a plane with no sides. She's greedy with her light; won't let it leak. Holds it in. Her plane departs for Bangkok where she is instantly greeted by smiling people in pointy straw hats who escort her on a long boat in a black river into a city where she is on guard for The Taker. *Where are you? I know you're here!*

There is music in this dream, shrill and foreign with plenty of sharp notes that echo like rubber bands pinging and twanging. She rises up from the river boat into the gray sky and flies high over marshes and rice paddies into a city that pulses with deep vibrating color and rapid movement. She flies down, hovering low over a web of street vendors hawking gutted fish, bowls of spicy food, and rolls of vibrant silk fabric. Moving on, she flies over temples, giant marble Buddhas, and gilded palaces made of gold and porcelain with spires that reach high into the sky, now silver with moonlight. This is *her* Thailand—*her* Bangkok—all hers. It is pure magic; there's no way she can forget this place. "*Bangkok,*" she says. "*Bangkok. Bang-kok. Bangkok.*"

Hovering just above the city, she feels a jolt in her spine and stiffens. *Ouch!* But she forgets just as quickly, because she's learned not to dwell on any distraction. She can't afford to. If she does, she'll lose her way. Fall right back into the clinic and forget where she was. It's happened.

In a second, the sky transforms into a lake of black ink

studded with sparkly crystal jewels. Just as quickly, the moon begins its descent, and the sky brightens slowly from below. Syd races the approaching dawn at the scarlet horizon to fill herself with first light. To drink the dawn's first light until she is drunk with it. Gorged. She's almost there, somewhere between the moon and the rising sun, when she sees The Taker's beady purple eyes staring down, spotting her, recognizing her. She curses him then quickly looks away. Best not to give him any attention at all. None. *Zero.* And anyway, she already drank the light. It's hers—*all hers*—and he can't take that away from her unless she forgets the answer.

She feels a tug on her big toe and tumbles back across the barrier into the material world, opening her eyes in the dim light of the recovery room.

"Hey there, hon."

Syd can't see clearly, but knows it's her mom—a suffocating presence. *Darth Vader.* As much as her mother pretends to be light and airy, she's not. She's weighed down with bitterness, disappointment, and grief that she covers up with a fake smile like drugstore perfume. But Syd knows what's what. She smells it. It stinks.

"All done," says her mom.

Syd's head throbs from the spinal. This was not a great one, she can already tell. Sometimes they're not. Sometimes a little fluid drips out, causing havoc. "Where's Roz," says Syd weakly.

"What's that?" says her mom, a blur in her usual gray sweatshirt, gray hair cut severely short in solidarity with Syd's bald head, not that Syd asked her to or wanted her to. She didn't. *Grow your hair!*

"Get Roz?" Syd whispers. Her mouth is a desert.

Her mom says, "Drink some water first. It'll help the head-ache." She sticks a straw in Syd's mouth. Syd drinks.

Roz taps on the door and enters. Just her energy alone changes everything. "Got another customer," she says softly, and wheels in one of the little kids conked out on another cot. "How you feeling?" she whispers to Syd.

Syd smiles triumphantly. "Bangkok," she whispers. "So... fine."

Roz performs an abbreviated version of her victory shuffle and gently high-fives Syd.

"Bangkok?" says her mother.

"It's the answer," says Syd. "Never mind."

She can see that her mother is hurt from this dismissal, and Syd doesn't want to deal with the long face, so she says, "Bangkok is the capitol of Thailand."

"The game?" says Roz kindly. "We ask her a question..."

Mom smiles. "Oh, right. The game. Well good then, you've won."

Syd vows not to be so hard on her mother, but it's hard not to. And anyway, she's a teenager, so what does she expect of herself exactly? A teenager in a clinic, for God's sake. *Taxi!*

Hours later when Syd and her mom pull up the long, snowy driveway in their Volvo wagon, Syd says, "Dad's home!"

The black Land Rover truck sits in its place in front of the third bay of the garage. A flash of warmth runs through Syd. As crazy as everything is, she feels less crazy when her father is around. Unfortunately, because of his traveling, it isn't often enough.

"Hmmm," says Mom. "He's early." She parks the car and walks around to Syd's door to help her.

"I'm fine, Mom," she says. "Seriously, I can walk."

Her mother holds onto her though, and Syd lets her, whatever.

It's slippery. Maybe her mother's the one who needs the help. As they're treading carefully up the icy slate path to the front step, her mother stops suddenly, issues a slight gasp, and throws her hand to her chest.

"What?" says Syd. "What's wrong?"

Her mother inhales deeply. "Nothing," she says tentatively. "I don't know. A little charley horse in my leg I think."

Whether she's fine or not, Syd wouldn't know, but pardon her if she has a hard time sympathizing with a leg cramp. And besides, when doesn't her mother have something going on? Never. As long as Syd can remember, her mother has complained of one physical symptom or another. There were the migraines and the arthritis and all the crap that preceded the hysterectomy and the infections after. Not to mention the supposed appendicitis and the kidney stones that never panned out. Syd grew up practically expecting to be sick, although when she was actually diagnosed, it blew her mind. But unlike her mother, she won't let it beat her down. She won't. She won't just survive, she'll thrive. She won't let The Taker win.

They get to the top step without another cramp incident. Through the front door, past the hall, Syd sails gingerly into the arms of her dad who says, "Hey sweetness. How's my sugar?" He hugs her mightily as she inhales the crisp yet wooly smell of him.

"I'm okay," she whispers.

"Swear?" he says.

"Swear," she grins, scratching her hairless head under the itchy wool cap. She slinks out of her jacket and throws it on the chair. Another in the endless string of infractions she gets away with when her dad's around.

Her dad has some kind of marching band music turned up uncharacteristically loud on the TV, and her mom marches to the beat straight across the room and turns it down. "Sydney's got a headache," she says curtly. "She just had a spinal for God's sake."

Dad ignores this and smiles impishly at Syd. "I have a surprise for you," he says. "I need you to shake out that headache and hold steady. Can you do that?"

"A surprise?" Syd says. "You do?"

"You do?" repeats her mother as she shrugs her puffy parka loose. Her short gray hair stands at attention from the static. "What is it, Aaron?" She leans in. "What surprise exactly?"

Now Syd is really excited, because this surprise is all hers. Her mother didn't even know about it, which means it's uncompromisingly Dad—100% guaranteed grand slam. "What is it?!" she says, clapping.

"Well, I hope it meets the expectation," says her mom drearily. "I haven't seen her smile in a week."

This pisses Syd off, because what exactly does she have to smile about?

"Oh, it will," says Dad. He beckons with his right hand. "Follow me."

Syd follows him down the long center hall through the great room and into the kitchen. Around the corner, a round ball of cocoa fur charges at her, skidding and tripping, squealing.

"Oh my God!" says Syd. "Oh my God, it's mine? He's mine?"

Dad nods while Mom stands there all Plaster of Paris in her gray sweat suit, hands over her open mouth.

"Can I keep him, Dad?" Syd squeals. "I can keep him, right?"

"Aaron," says her mom sternly.

"Aaron, nothing," he says. "It's a gift from me to my daughter. I should be able to give her a goddamn gift." He folds his arms and turns to Syd. "Yes, you can keep *her*," he says, winking. "It's a she."

"A girl?" beams Syd. This is the best surprise ever. The *god-damn* part of her dad's language doesn't really surprise her since her parents have been a little stressed lately. Lots of tense, quiet conversations behind doors like the low hum of a deadly buzz saw. But Syd knows when her dad is tough like this he's going to fight for her. He's going to make sure she can keep the dog.

She pulls the puppy's tail and says, "Who are you, little girl?" as she tries to contain the creature's frenetic movement. Her splitting headache feels better already, just watching all this life. "Ha ha she's everywhere!" says Syd. "Where did you find her? I looove her!!!"

Her dad lowers himself on his knees beside her; his slick black hair and handsome James Bond ala Clive Cussler face just inches from hers. "A friend of mine," he says. "A guy in the office. She's a rescue. Half chocolate lab, half samoyed."

"Aaron," says her mom icily. "Can we talk? Now."

Looking at Syd, her dad says, "Watcha gonna name her?"

The puppy runs in circles on the marble kitchen floor and then slips, collapsing. Syd could just explode with joy. Just disintegrate into a thousand smiles. "Chocolate lab?" she says.

"Mmhmm," says her dad, "and samoyed."

"Samoyeds shed like crazy," says the spoiler. "And they can be aggressive. Not to mention the germs, Aaron. Honestly." Her arms are all tight and folded. "Honest to God."

Syd's head is dizzy with names that involve chocolate. *Hershey, Nestle, Milky Way, Snickers...* "Godiva!" she shouts. "Godiva! Godiva! How's that? The most sumptuous chocolate."

"Aaron," warns Mom.

Dad leans back up on his knees and rises, straightening his pant legs. "Godiva it is," he says. "Now why don't you watch her for a few minutes while I talk to Mom?"

At the threshold, Mom says, "Don't roll around with that dog, Sydney. Keep your distance. We have no idea what germs and diseases it's got. I bet it hasn't even seen a vet. It could have worms for all we know."

"I don't care what germs it has," mutters Syd after her mother leaves. "This dog is mine." She snuggles the little fur ball in her lap, picks it up and kisses her nose, lets the pup lick her entire face. Hahahaha! *I'm in love finally!* This is the first good thing that's happened in a hundred years, she thinks. If anyone takes this puppy away, she's taking the next train to Virginia to live with Aunt Hannah. Hannah has a farm. Hannah will let her live there with Godiva for sure.

The low hum of the buzz saw revs up and penetrates the wall.

From Mom—"Don't you think I have enough to do?"

From Dad—"We all do our part, Mitsy. All of us, not just you. We have to take this chance. She needs companionship, for God's sake."

From Mom—"I'll have to consult my..."

From Dad—"Your what? Who? What about your husband, for God's sake? You put more stock in that ...what's her name? Pandora? You put more stock in that psychic than any of the people you live with." A pause, then, "I've had it."

All very predictable, actually, and not that disturbing, until Syd hears a door slam, footsteps pound up the back staircase, and her mother break into bawling tears interrupted by whiney little gaspy shrieks. So melodramatic.

She feels bad for her mother; she does. Her mother is no match at all for the Dad/Syd team, and never was. And she does try hard, it's true. But she's just such a drag, which is probably not even her fault, when you think about it. After all, it was bad enough when she was sick all on her own, but now that she has a sick daughter, well. Who can handle that much sickness?

Nobody, especially her. Syd's mom is one person who just cannot learn to relax and pull up a chair in the middle of hell, like Syd and her dad can. Even hell has its heavenly moments if you let them in. But you have to be open to it. You have to let go. You have to remember how to say yes to life even when it pushes you off a twenty-story ledge into a pile of broken glass.

"Right, Godiva?" she says, nuzzling the puppy's hilariously out-of-control fur.

"Right," Syd says back to herself in a high puppy voice.

Finally she has somebody who agrees with her.

Pandora

PANDORA PLACES THE DOG-EARED book beside her on the gray corduroy couch, reaches forward for the joint and puffs thoughtfully. She holds the smoke to the count of five and releases. An electron can be a particle or a wave, she thinks for about the millionth time. This is huge. This could revolutionize her thinking on what can actually be done out-of-body, or *exo-corpus* as she prefers to call it. It would probably work. Maybe. Maybe not. *But maybe!* Collapse the wave, and boom—it's a particle. All potential ends right there. Future defined.

She leans over her pile of books and empty microwave dinner container for the nail file.

But no, not really. It doesn't *really* end right there, does it? No. Because it can become a wave again if it wants to, just—"*OK, now I think I'll be a wave.*" If it knows how to be a wave, it can be one. *Holy shit!* Are you serious, Einstein?

Dead serious, Pandora Madigan. She files the nail of her left index finger which has a snag of a hang nail right...there. *Dead serious.* She reaches behind her for the clipper and snips.

But the question is...can I go back to the moment *before* the incident ever happened? Before the wave collapsed into a particle? Before it was *observed.* And if she can figure out how to go back, can she return the electron *or the person (!!!)* to its quantum state? That is the question.

She hopes she remembers it in the morning.

She knows she can't figure it out now with her stoned-out prefrontal cortex such as it is. But the calculus will not occur there anyway, she knows. The answer arrives only when she lets go of intellectual control, when she surrenders the question to the outreaches of her frontier mind. That...is what will give her the $E=MC^2$ of her (and for that matter, anyone else's) mystical career. If you can call something you've fought against your entire life...a career. More of a prison, right? The prison of what you were meant to do; what you *must* do; what you *came to this earth* to do or you'll just keep coming back again and again in an endless loop until you do it. How many lifetimes will it take?! *Do it now!* It feels like a thousand lifetimes already.

Pandora pulls her long rope of unruly silver white hair into three strands and starts braiding it on the left side. Her fingernails are a mess. She wishes she were the manicure type, but she's not. She sometimes fantasizes about talons of unbreakable purple gel attached to her long, brown fingers. Piano fingers, as her mother called them, not that she ever played. And as long as she's fantasizing, a pair of spiraling gold suns would look great on her thumbnails. If she only had the patience. But anyway, she doesn't.

So to be clear, she thinks, focusing hard, the real question isn't whether one can travel back to influence an event before it happened. Right? I mean, one *can* travel back. After all, even solid objects possess a wave nature. So theoretically it pans out. The real question is—can Pandora do it? Can *she?* And what are the risks?

The phone rings and in her current trance, she practically springs to the ceiling. *Holy crap!* She was just getting comfortable. And who is calling her at 9PM on a Friday night anyway? She searches for her phone under the mess of cushions, finds it, and turns it over. Oh no. *Not her!* But maybe she can do it—talk, that is. Maybe she can talk coherently. She squeezes her eyes shut, searching for a good reason to ignore this call, but. Okay fine.

"Hello?" she says in a rich, low tone. Her *Pandora* voice. "Can I help you?"

"Pandora, I just…I'm so…thank God you answered. I just need your help. Can you help me?"

"Hold on," Pandora says to her sniveling client. "Let's take a breath break."

"O…okay," says the client.

"Where are you?" says Pandora.

"In the bedroom? I'm so sorry to be calling in the evening, really."

"Okay," says Pandora, "here's what you're going to do. You're going to lean back against the pillows, understand? Relax…fully." She waits. "Are you relaxing?"

There's some rustling. "Okay, yes, I'm relaxing. I…I'm trying." She gasps for breath.

Pandora stomps her foot. "Do not gasp!" she commands. "Do not gasp, okay? Gasping is exactly…*exactly* what I do not want you to do."

Maybe she shouldn't have picked up the phone. She doesn't have the kind of patience she needs right now for this messy, undisciplined spirit of a client. She reaches deep, "I'm going to put some music on, okay? And I want you to listen and inhale to the slow count of five then exhale to the slow count of five. Repeatedly. Can you do this?"

"I...I..."

"Can you do this, Mitsy?"

"Yes," she whimpers.

"Okay then, here goes. I'll get back on the phone in ten minutes. That's ten full minutes of conscious breathing. Do you know why, Mitsy?"

"To control myself?"

"You can't cry and breathe consciously at the same time, that's why. We need to bring you back to center before we continue."

Pandora turns her iPod to an Enya album and places the phone beside it. She just hopes she remembers to check back. Or maybe if she's lucky Mitsy will fall asleep to the music and that's that. An evening to herself, which is what she was counting on to begin with.

She stares at the half-smoked joint on the coffee table. The copper ashtray is the shape of a rugged hand with the joint in its meaty palm. There it sits, all ready for her, and now she has to wait which is ironic. It's ironic because if she smoked the rest of that joint she might be in a better position to deal with Mitsy. Not that Mitsy is the reason Pandora smokes pot. She's not. Neither were any of the thirty clients Pandora just suspended from her roster. She needs a break. *She needs a break!*

But for some reason, she just can't let go of Mitsy. Although she'd very much like to. And it isn't because of the woman herself, who's frankly a lost cause. The woman can't grasp *anything*, any spiritual concept, as hard as she tries. And as difficult and complicated as Pandora's life has gotten, she can't share a word of these difficulties with Mitsy, not that she wants to. It's hard to relate to the woman's homogenous, culturally juvenile upbringing. *Just the name!* Not to mention the constant driving complaints of a hypochondriac when your own mental health is borderline unhinged. No, it isn't because of Mitsy Michaels that Pandora won't let go; it's because of Mitsy's daughter, Sydney. That's why. Of Pandora's obsession with curing Sydney. And Mitsy doesn't know that either.

Pandora nods off for a while, jerked awake by the strident change in music from Enya to Pink. *"Raaaaiiiise that glass! Come on...and come on and...raise that glass!"* She grabs the phone. "Are you there, Mitsy?" she says, switching off the music.

"I'm here."

"And are you centered?"

"Yes, thank you, I'm much better."

"And you realize you could do that all by yourself, right? You could just go up to your room, sit back against the pillows and breathe."

"I guess. But I'm just...I don't know. Frantic."

Pandora leans forward for her cigarettes. Not that she normally smokes, just in extreme situations like this. This exact conversation in the middle of psychic burnout, which is probably the correct diagnosis for Pandora's current mental state. "Hold on," she says to Mitsy. She mutes the phone and lights a cigarette, inhaling deeply, luxuriously. Such a wonderful bad habit is this. Such an exquisitely terrible indulgence. And anyway, her old friend Joy told her it keeps the negatives away. Chokes them in a toxic cloud, probably. And God knows Pandora could use some protection from negative influences.

She releases the mute button. "Okay," she says, "you there?"

"Yes."

"What's that sound I hear in the background, Mitsy?"

"Well, that's why I'm calling. Aaron bought Sydney a puppy.

Just brought it home and gave it right to her. Absolutely no consultation with me."

Pandora smiles; this makes sense. "How lovely," she says.

"What?" whines Mitsy. "You know about my arthritis. How am I going to take care of a puppy when I have all Sydney's challenges on top of rheumatoid arthritis...or MS, whatever they finally diagnose?" She whimpers. "How?"

"What does the puppy look like?" asks Pandora. "Is it hideous?"

"Hideous?" Mitsy says. "No, of course not. It's a puppy."

"Describe it."

"Well, it's fluffy and brown and tiny. It's part lab and part samoyed. But I've heard samoyeds are protective and..."

"Hold on. Hold....on." Pandora exhales deeply, listening, channeling. "Okay," she says, "here's the thing. The dog is going nowhere."

"What? But why should I have to take on a dog when I'm already..."

"Listen to me," Pandora says. "You are not taking on the dog. The dog is taking on *you*. Do you understand? The dog is a healing presence." She pauses, inhale/exhale. "I heard that from my sources, Mitsy. I just heard it."

"You *heard* it?"

"Yes."

"You're sure?"

"Positive. The dog is angelic. It's a healer dog. Not every dog is beneficial, but this one is. Her name begins with a G, I'm told. That's all I'm getting. Have you named her yet? What's her name?"

Mitsy hesitates. "Well, yes it does begin with a G. And how did you know it's a she? Because it is a she. Her name is Godiva."

Pandora chuckles at the same time she chokes on cigarette

smoke, immediately pushing the mute button. The last thing she needs right now is to explain her own human issues. This is not about her; it's about Sydney. And Mitsy, maybe, but not really. She sips water backwards, pauses, and un-mutes. "Listen to me," she says firmly. "Are you listening?"

"Yes."

"I want you to do something for yourself that you've never been able to do before, okay?"

"I'll try."

"I don't want you to try, Mitsy. I want you to actually do it. I want you to go downstairs and hug that puppy and tell your daughter that you're thrilled about it. That you're happy to do whatever it takes to bring life back into your home. It's a dead house."

"A dead house?"

"D-E-A-D," Pandora says.

"Uh huh. Oh."

"There's no air in your house, Mitsy. I can absolutely feel it from here. I'm choking on the dead air in your house just talking to you." She takes this opportunity to cough the rest of the smoke from her lungs.

"Oh dear," says Mitsy. "You really are choking."

Pandora sips water. "We've got to heal that daughter of yours," she says. "We've got to do whatever it takes to bring that house back to life."

"Okay. But should I tell her it's a dead house?"

"No, of course not. Use some discretion. Just tell her you're absolutely thrilled about the dog, okay? Because you don't want to know what it will be like if Sydney doesn't get better, and the dog will make her better. It's making her better already. If you think you've got it bad now, never mind. You do not want to know."

Pandora is shivering, shaking, practically convulsing. She's so angry she could bi-locate right into Mitsy's bedroom and strangle the last breath out of her thick neck. Thank God this is a phone conference. The woman's daughter is still alive, damn it. *Her daughter is alive!!* That woman has *got* to get it together.

"I do realize that on some level," says Mitsy. "I do. But I just feel so unappreciated; I can't help it. I mean why couldn't Aaron have asked me first? Why did he have to go out and buy…"

"You're kidding me, right? Because he knew you'd say no, that's why." After a long pause, Pandora says, "Did you hear me? I don't have all night, Mitsy. You would have said no."

"Are you sure? Maybe I wouldn't have. Maybe I would have called you and you'd have told me that the dog would be a healer and I would have gone merrily along with the whole thing."

"You don't go merrily along with anything, Mitsy. Are you listening? *Nothing.* Furthermore, you might have gotten the wrong dog. You or someone you know might have been attracted to another dog, some kind of lunatic newfie-dachshund with a giant slobbering head and stubby little legs. Or whatever mix, you never know. You can't second guess this. *This* is how it happened. Listen to me, this is the right dog. Do not second guess how the right dog got into your dead house, okay? Do not second guess perfection."

"Okay."

"Because your obsessively linear and logical approach to life is going to be the death of you if you don't learn to overcome it, do you understand?" Pandora knows she has to pull back. *Whoa!* She's galloping across the field at breakneck speed, too far ahead of herself, not to mention how far ahead of Mitsy she is. It's pure burnout that's talking now.

She throttles back. "I'm sorry," she says more gently, "but you just cannot afford to make this about yourself. It's about you in some ways, yes, your spiritual constriction, but it's about your daughter, too. Your daughter needs to know that you can release your own troubles once in a while to care for her." She sighs. "Can you do that?"

After a long pause, Mitsy says, "I think so. I'm better. I'll go down and talk to Sydney now."

"You do that. And you get strong for her. She's a spiritual force, that child, I can feel it. We're going to do something together one day, she and I."

"Ohhh!" says Mitsy. "Really? That's wonderful!"

"Something to do with...I don't know...a place. A place in Tuscany, I think." She pulls on her braid, thinking, digging deep. "What's that? Oh, okay. Florence. An estate outside Florence."

"Florence, Italy?!" says Mitsy. "Well, isn't that interesting? Florence was where we all went two years ago before Sydney got sick in the first place."

"Before Sydney got sick?" says Pandora, focusing—*before her wave collapsed.*

"Yes, and before Aaron had the affair."

"What you *think* was an affair," says Pandora. "You don't know, Mitsy. You don't."

"But you said..."

"I said I don't know. I can't corroborate what you told me. It isn't clear. Everything isn't always illuminated at once, or at all. It's very possible that he developed a meaningful friendship, nothing more."

"But I found..."

Pandora's had it with her. She can't listen anymore, and it's not just the late hour or the doobie smoke performing a tantalizing snake dance in front of her. The woman is plain and meddling and irritatingly sequential. Somehow she married a man who is none of these things and had a daughter who is already a mystic, though undeveloped, certainly. But still. Pandora already regrets telling Mitsy about Florence, even though it's a truth of some kind. Not that Pandora knows what she's going to do in Florence with Sydney, she doesn't. Or really, *if*. After all, Pandora hasn't figured out any of the mechanics. But it will be something, she feels certain. Something earth shattering, it feels like. Something seismic, whatever it is. Not that she's in shape to do anything seismic right now.

"You're forbidden to discuss any of this conversation with anyone at all," she tells Mitsy. "Do you understand?"

"Well, that sounds ominous."

"It must float freely in abeyance in the universe."

"Oh."

"It's a *wave*," says Pandora. "Waves collapse when they're meddled with, and then we have nothing but a stinking, stagnant particle. Do you understand?"

"Not really."

"No of course you don't, but I need your word anyway. I need to know 100% that you will not breathe this to anyone, or even think about it."

"I can't even think about it?"

"No. Thinking is doing."

"Okay."

"Good. Now go down and hug that puppy and let the healing begin. And Mitsy…"

"Yes?"

"Evenings are double rate, you know that, right?"

"That's…okay, sure. It's worth it; you're worth it."

Pandora just can't have that woman calling her night and day without some compensation, especially since she's her only client. And there has to be a penalty for cannabis interruptus.

Not to mention all the interruptus on the quantum level that was in full force when the phone call came in the first place. Now where was she? *Oh yes, the wave...*

The next morning Pandora looks in the mirror at her storm of white hair, uneven dark skin and the lines etched around her still startling topaz blues from that 19th century Dutch ancestor. A 68 year old caricature is what she's become. But what does she expect after decades of dedication to the miseries of others? Three entire decades of trying to lift people up, or prop them up, is more like it. Not that she didn't love her clients, or at least some of them, she did. And does. She hopes she helped them, but she doesn't know. She can't feel it at the moment. She's not 100% in the game, or even 40%. She might not even be on the field.

She quickly dresses her tall, fit body in a flowing Ethiopian caftan and flip-flops, hoping the freedom of this loose colorful outfit with its bold African palette will register with her imagination and help her write today's blog. First she wanders across the wide-planked floor of her converted barn home to the open kitchen for a cup of coffee. The coffee cheers her up, just thinking about how defiant it is. She would never have done this a year ago, or even a month. Thirty-five years of insipid green tea. *Blehhhhh!* Even mystics need caffeine once in a while. After all, who needs to be more awake than an exhausted mystic in the process of sorting out the universe? Not just sorting it out, really, but reshaping it. *Transforming it.*

She carries the warm mug to her desk at the other end of the open kitchen/living room arrangement where she situates herself on the comfy old leather desk chair. This coffee and all her recent indulgences are her reward for thirty plus years of helping the helpless, or really, fifty years if you count all that time without pay. All that time *learning*, really. Learning who she was and who she must become, sometimes at the expense of others. Others she loved. But how else does one learn?

She places her mug on a cork coaster and slides her reading glasses on. The steam from the coffee blurs the right lens, and she removes the glasses to buff. Why just the right lens, she wonders. Why not both? Is there a message in this? After all, the right eye is the seat of the imagination—the *mystical* lens. Has her mystical side become blurred, as she's long suspected? *Or even blocked?* While buffing the right lens, she stares out at the snow-capped mountains that surround the sapphire lake in all its majesty. This only cheers her up in theory, since theoretically she knows Lake Tahoe is the most exalted place a mystic could reside. The foot of heaven. *Theoretically*. At least for her.

She parks herself in front of the computer and accesses the blog she was composing yesterday on the Theory of Everything, which is to say the Theory of Nothing, since that's what she came up with. She sips her coffee thoughtfully and nibbles a half-eaten Snickers bar from yesterday—*sooo good!* As a little distraction, she googles Tuscany as a way of diving back into her work. The websites are so enticing—just look. *Wow!* An embroidered patchwork of rolling vineyards, quaint stone villas, and medieval hamlets complete with fortresses accessible only by high winding, stone staircases. So appealing and yet.

Shit. What is she doing?

She crosses and uncrosses her legs, understanding she has thrown all reason aside. And not just all reason, but nearly all instinct and mystical process, because there is no googling in mysticism. *That is not how one gets information!* She sips her coffee. Even the coffee, *please!* Not to mention the Snickers. Who throws away thirty years of dedication to distilled lemon water and broccoli, not to mention tofu, for a month of caffeine and processed chocolate? That is, a month so far. But she will not stand in judgment of herself, as tempting as it is. A month is a spit in the glacial, bottomless lake of eternity. Maybe she'll do it for a year, why not? It grounds her. Where are her cigarettes?

No one understands how demanding the pure life can be. The only way to cleanse yourself of it is to plunge yourself into the murky pit of veniality. *For a time.* Not forever, obviously. Enough to remember what it was like to be tainted. *To be real.* Just think what she's had to give up to hone her craft—all the potato chips, margaritas, and cheeseburgers, not to mention men. Half the time she's on the phone with these knucklehead clients she wants to shave her magnificent crown of pearl white hair in abject frustration. So now they're gone; the clients are gone. "I'm going on sabbatical," she told them. *From you!* All but Mitsy, that is. Well, not Mitsy, really, but Sydney. Not that she's ever spoken directly to the daughter.

But in all this murky impurity, is the mystical gift gone too? No, it's not. It's marginal, but it's there. A trace element. She distinctly heard the words "Tuscany." Not high def, but still, *Tuscany.* Or was it Florence? What does it matter? Isn't Florence in Tuscany? In either case, she was dead on, because Florence is where Sydney was still free. Unblemished. Un-*taken.* Pandora polishes off the rest of the candy bar and licks her fingers. Her gifts are here somewhere. A little blurry, maybe, but still here. *Still here.* She just hopes she can access them when she needs to.

She opens the third drawer down on the left side, retrieves a pack of Virginia Slims, and taps it against the glass-topped desk. She chooses a cigarette thoughtfully, lights it and inhales.

The lake is a bit choppy today, she thinks, staring out. Choppy is so interesting. Energies of all kinds abound in its patterns. Maybe after she writes her blog she'll hike down to the lake for a chat with the native spirits.

She labors on, typing random and disconnected phrases on Love as the fifth physical force, the unified field, but nothing cogent emerges. She's gets nowhere. Disgusted, she wanders to the opposite wall of windows in her living room to feast on the thick forest and above them, the snowy diamond-crusted mountains to her west. So inspiring! Which thought leads her reluctantly to the old wooden easel in the back of the wide room, the contents of her last visual inspiration unfinished beneath a shroud of yellowed linen. She reaches for the corner, daring herself to peek at the canvas for the first time in how many years? Ten? Fifteen? *Look at it! Understand what happened! Stop hiding!*

She shakes her head and drops the cloth. No. Not yet. What lies beneath this veil is too bold, too real, too glaring. Too much to bear, even now. *Too much life force!* Let the memory fade and fade, and with it, her substantial talent. Let it disappear! Unlike poetry, philosophical theory, and mystical meanderings, painting is too concrete, too permanent. There are other means of expression that don't arrest the artist, lock her in a cell, and force her to capture the tortured wild thing within.

That's it; she's had enough. She throws the box of Virginia Slims in the pocket of her caftan, slips into an old pair of sheepskin boots and a long, quilted parka, and heads down to the village for an enchilada and a beer.

Hannah

IT'S NEARLY DUSK. THE sky is steel blue, shimmering, and laced with high, wispy clouds. The air is frigid. Hannah's nerves flash back and forth between high-anxiety—(*what am I doing here?*)—and the sheer exhilaration of the courage it took to come here in the first place. After all, one financial catastrophe after another does not induce serenity. But neither does this. This is just a case of trading one bloody mess for another. If she's lucky, it's a wash.

After a two hour drive from the Westchester Airport in crippling traffic, she has finally arrived at the chateau, as she calls it. The grand and impressive Michaels estate in Darien. The limo pulls up the long, wide driveway of neat, gray pavers lined with stately Belgian block. No expense spared. The terrace is a blanket of white, and the branches of the old cedars hang low with snow. The driveway and slate walks are as crystal clear as if the snow had been ordered not to fall there and obeyed. Everything in its place.

Hannah takes in the five wooded acres and white-washed brick of the stately mansion set back at least two hundred feet and lined with fragrant junipers. It wasn't Mitsy with all the designer taste, Hannah knows. It was Aaron who provided the class and ingenuity to re-imagine this grand spectacle in the middle of a forest. Not that there aren't other impressive homes in the area, there are. But this one, like Aaron, stands out. How Mitsy got a hold of this man and all his, well... *everything*, Hannah will never know. How Mitsy manages to keep him is the deeper mystery.

"Here we are," barks the squat and otherwise silent driver beside her. He hops out and fetches the two garment bags that consume the back seat and oversized suitcases from the trunk, all of which cost a small fortune in baggage fees. But who really cares since Aaron paid for the trip anyway? Aaron and Mitsy, that is, with their combined fortunes. Let's not forget all the money Mitsy inherited when their parents died. She got all the money, or at least most of it, since Hannah inherited the farm. But how was she expected to keep up the farm, for God's sake? To maintain it ad infinitum? To be fair, there was a maintenance fund, but still. How far could that really go with all the improvements she wanted to make?

As the driver awkwardly navigates the garment bags and one of the rolling suitcases up the walk, Hannah wraps her new mink scarf around her neck and buttons the top of her black cashmere coat. Brrrrrr! Thank God she saw the scarf and coat at the Oatlands fashion show last week! Thank God she happened to be there at all! It could just as easily not have happened, and she would have been woefully unprepared for this trip. What would she have worn—a parka? Such shabby couture for the Northeast, even though the weather warrants it. It must be 10 below. And she thought it was cold in Virginia!

Maybe she should just rethink this whole East Coast weather thing and consider Santa Barbara or LA. Somewhere where real writers live—entire communities of them. *Salons!*

She scoots up the slate path on her stiletto-heeled boots, adrenaline pumping. "Helloooooo!" she calls out. "Hell-looooo! Anybody home?"

Who will greet her first, she wonders, the dashingly gorgeous financier, Aaron, or the unsuspecting Syd? After all, her arrival is supposed to be a surprise for Syd, isn't it? Isn't that why they sent a limo in the first place? It won't be Mitsy, no. Never. Shrinking violets don't answer doors. If Hannah's phone hadn't run out of juice she could have called them, reported her slow progress. But what the hell, she's here. She rings the bell. Hopefully someone's home.

Standing there for a minute, the driver scoots the last two suitcases in front of the massive carved door, tooled in Thailand, probably, or Tibet. "Shall I wait?" he asks.

"I guess so." She shrugs. "I have no idea who's here or how we'll get the bags inside if..."

The door opens and Aaron appears in an impeccably tailored charcoal gray overcoat. "Hannah," he says warmly. "It's been a long time. So grateful you're here."

She hugs him. "Mmmm," she hums. "Happy to do it." She pulls back. "I'm looking very forward to spending time with y'all."

He grins, glancing at the bags. "You must be staying for the weekend at least, eh?" he teases, and pulls out a few bills for the driver as he hauls the bags inside.

"A woman needs choices, Aaron. You don't want to see me in the same outfit day and night, do you?"

He ushers her into the vast marble foyer. "So you're staying for a while, right?" he says, almost anxiously. "We do need an upright citizen here." He winks. "Somebody who can pay the bills."

Hannah shrugs out of her coat and hands it to him, smiling. "Well, I wouldn't say Mitsy isn't upright. Not to mention you. And speaking of upright individuals, where's my spectacular niece?"

"Mother and daughter are at the clinic," he says as he hangs up her coat. "They'll be back in a while. Syd had a tough night, so...just some extra blood tests."

Hannah nods. "But it's ok, right? She's ok?" Hannah's not sure she can stay if things aren't solid with Syd. It would just be too much to ask. Way too much. She shivers just thinking about how much she would suffer in such a situation. *It's her niece!!! Her goddaughter!!!* No, Hannah isn't made of titanium, like Mitsy. She's sensitive. People have to respect that.

Eyes darting left and right, Aaron says, "Yeah, I guess so. I mean, things usually stabilize." He shakes his head. "It's amazing what you can get used to. How low you can go without disintegrating."

Hannah can't imagine this, but what peace can she really offer? "And you?" she says. "Where are you going with that coat on? Running out on me already?"

"Just got in myself—through the garage. You're lucky anyone was here!" He pauses meaningfully. "But don't get used to me; I'm as good as gone."

Hannah cocks her head. "That sounded dire. Where are you going? Afghanistan?"

"Work," he says chuckling, "work, work, work. On the plane to Austin tomorrow. What can you do?" He shakes his head.

"Somebody has to pay for all this!" says Hannah. "Business is good?"

"Business is business," he says, shrugging. "But come along, there's someone I want you to meet." He removes his coat and tosses it on the settee. Underneath the outerwear he's all perfectly fitted dark wash jeans and a snug navy sweater, the slick version of male perfection—Jonah's city doppelganger.

He leads her through the grand living room with its broad-beamed cathedral ceiling, massive stone fireplace and diamond-pane doors; past the wide hall of cleverly hidden pantry and utility closets to the expansive French country kitchen where Hannah hears a "yip yip yip" somewhere in the beyond. "What's that?" she asks.

Aaron rushes into the mud room and returns with a wooly pile of brown fur, a round little snout, one blue eye, one brown. "Yip!" it barks. "Yip yip!" and Aaron holds it nose-to-nose for an Eskimo kiss. Endearing, really. Insanely endearing, in fact.

"Our new dog," he says proudly.

"He's not a dog!" says Hannah. "He's a stuffed animal! The cutest damn thing ever!"

"*She*," he says. "Godiva. Sydney named her Godiva."

"Godiva," Hannah repeats slowly, approvingly. "And how is this little truffle going over with my big sister?"

He snuggles the cub and says, "So so. Better though. At first she was pretty adamant, but then." He looks at Hannah, frowning. "I don't really know what happened, as usual. We had a disagreement and she went into the bedroom and reversed."

"Reversed?"

"Well, she doesn't really like Godiva, but now she pretends to."

Hannah sighs. "I don't know what happened to that woman along the way, do you? Once upon a time she was the consummate animal lover. How I ended up pitching manure and she ended up in, well..." she gestures grandly, "...*this!* I'll never know." She shakes her head. "Makes no sense."

"I can't see you mucking stalls," he says, laughing. "Not in those clothes, anyway."

Hannah raises her chin, happy that she's impressed him with her smart gray Lauren tweeds, classic country back-belted jacket and kick-pleated skirt. Fashion brilliance. "Well, now that I allow the riding school to use the barn, my mucking days are over. A girl can only take so much."

"Fair exchange," he says. He offers Godiva to her at arm's length.

Ordinarily Hannah wouldn't agree to hold anything this untidy, biologic and untrained in her present finery, even something this admittedly scrumptious, but considering it's coming from Aaron, she says, "Come here, baby girl. Come over here right now!" She grabs Godiva, but the little creature squirms out of her hands and falls face forward on the marble floor. "Oh! Oh no! So sorry!"

"It's okay," he says. "They're flexible. See? She's already on her feet."

"You can see why I don't have kids," she says. "Too clumsy."

"You would have done fine." He turns and opens a cabinet. "Almost five o'clock. How about a cocktail?"

"Um...oh, I don't know." She'd promised herself she wouldn't indulge around Syd, but then again, Syd isn't here. "Maybe just a glass of chardonnay?" She leans down to play with Godiva, rolling her over and patting her belly. "Or maybe I should wait for Mits."

"She'll probably be another hour," he says. "Let's get you relaxed and feeling at home."

"In that case, I should start by excusing myself and freshening up."

He opens the wine cooler fridge and examines a bottle of white. "Before you go, approve the vintage?" He turns around, bows formally, and presents the bottle. "Only the best for you, m'lady."

"Ha! Well, the best is good enough for me," she says, chuckling.

"Good. So you know where you're staying, right? Upstairs to the left. Newly renovated. The sister-in-law suite we're calling it."

"That would be me, wouldn't it?" She frowns. "Or rather, 'I'." She winks. "Be right back for that wine."

In the foyer, Hannah grabs her purse and the slouch bag containing her PC and piles of overdue bills, flicks the hall lights, and climbs the winding staircase. Not that she's able to pay most of these bills, or really *any*, but she was not about to leave them at the farm for Jonah to inspect, either. And anyway, maybe Mitsy will pay her enough to erase all this pesky financial karma. Or pay a strategic part of it, anyway. $50,000 might seem like a lot to ask, but so is flying all the way up to Connecticut to do whatever it is she's here to do. One good deed deserves whatever it takes.

Winding up and around, she checks out the floor-to-ceiling picture window on the first landing. Even in the dim shadow light, the view is inspiring. Plop this house on a precipice in Santa Barbara and she'd do almost anything to get it. *Anything*. She sighs. Well, not *anything*. Or maybe she would. The point is Mitsy doesn't know how good she has it, but that's not news.

To the left and through the hall, she kicks open the double doors to the suite and feels for the switch. Well, *whoa!* She practically inhales the alluring decor. This is just too grand and yet...so soft and welcoming at the same time. Just too too *Architectural Digest*. Not that she's complaining. Even Rapunzel could live happily locked-up in this suite, no rescue required.

Just the big featherbed alone with its giant cloud of comforters and pillows feels like a five star B&B in Bavaria, maybe, or a mini-palace in Venice. The afghan rug, the chaise lounge, *the crystal chandelier!* It's not like Hannah doesn't know what money is or how to spend it; of course she does. *But this!* This is grandeur on a scale to which she could easily and happily become accustomed—*she already is!*—especially if it came without a debt collector.

She places her bags on the floor by the fainting couch and draws the billowing white satin drapes. Exquisite! In the spacious bathroom, she brushes her teeth, combs her freshly-colored auburn hair, and reapplies her peachy nude lipstick. She wishes Jonah had come with her. If he were here and saw this place, he would realize how much Hannah sacrifices every day. How much she holds back. What she could be spending, but doesn't. It drives her crazy that he never gives her credit for what she doesn't spend. He can be so small-minded.

She tugs at the bottom of her jacket, breathes in and straightens her posture. Chin up; shoulders back. Carriage belies a well-bred woman, their mother always told them. Not that their mother got anywhere with Mitsy, God knows. Mitsy just didn't understand any of the finer touches, but enough of that. Time to go back downstairs and see what this evening has in-store.

There's a knock at the door. "Presentable?" Aaron calls to her.

"Uh, yes sir," she says, surprised.

He opens the door, wheeling her suitcases, one by one, followed by the garment bags.

"Figured you'd need these at some point."

"True, but I could have helped."

"Came right up the elevator," he says, pointing to the hall. "No trouble at all." He hangs the garment bags in the walk-in and holds up his index finger. "One more thing; be right back."

He returns with a Waterford goblet of wine, hands it to her, and leans against the doorjamb, almost filling the frame. "So how's Jonah?" he says matter-of-factly.

"Jonah?" she says, laughing.

He shrugs. "Just wondering. We're so wrapped up in our difficulties here it's nice to come out and play once in a while. Ask about other people, you know?" He leans forward. "See what kind of a mess the neighbors are in." His eyes widen. "Or not? I don't want to assume." He folds his arms. "But you and Jonah were in a bit of a mess, weren't you? And I don't really know how that panned out."

Hannah sits on the edge of the chaise with her wine, amused. She might as well be comfortable. "I figured Mits would fill you in."

He runs his fingers through his thick, shiny black hair. "Mitsy? No. She's pretty consumed with, I don't know, health issues on every front."

"Well, there's plenty of that to consume her I suppose."

"There is, yes." He rocks his head back and forth. "And Jonah?" he reminds her.

"Well, actually, Jonah's great," she says. "We're back to being good friends, so anything could happen." She sips her wine. "He's checking on the ranch while I'm here, as a matter of fact. Helping out with the horses in between selling off pieces of the Firestone Estate. The real estate business is booming."

He nods. "Good. That's good. So you're friends. You're not enemies."

She narrows her eyes, "Uh, yeah? We're friends; of course we are. Seven years of marriage has to count for something, right?" She looks at him impishly. "Not that it did with Richard, of course, but he's another story."

Aaron smiles. "Indeed. A man-child if I ever saw one."

Her eyes widen in surprise. "Exactly!" She'd just assumed everyone in the Michaels' household blamed her for that first catastrophe, but apparently time has brought perspective. "What about you all?" she says. "Mits wouldn't even tell me what disease she has—what new kind of torture you're all in for."

Aaron rubs his dark stubble thoughtfully. "I'm not sure I even know myself," he says. "Arthritis? Some kind of grizzly inflammatory arthritis, I believe. If you ask me, it's stress, but... you know, she doesn't really handle..." He shrugs. "Anyway, things are tough, what can I say?" He glimpses the ceiling. "And I'm not much help."

All at once there's a clattering in the downstairs hall, low voices, and finally, "Aaron? Are you here? Where are you?"

He looks at Hannah meaningfully. "To be continued," he says, and turns toward the hall.

After a gulp of wine Hannah follows, trailing him by a few yards and keeping to the shadows. As she rounds the stairs to the front hall, she holds back so Syd can't see her. Can't ruin a surprise at the eleventh hour, after all! Surveying her family from a distance, she's shocked at how thin both Mitsy and Sydney have become, like something's gobbling them up. So disconcerting. Or maybe it's the lump of gray sweats swimming around Mitsy that makes her look so thin. Since when is Mitsy at weight, though? Or under? *What?!* She's been twice the size of Hannah since day one, and was certainly that size the last time they saw each other. *Which was when?* She can't remember. At least a year. At the Make-a-Wish dance, probably, which was the single most difficult thing Hannah ever did—placing that tiara on Sydney's bald head. *Good God!*

Aaron hugs Sydney and swings his hand toward the staircase, presentation style. "Ta da!" he says and Hannah sashays down on cue.

Syd's hands fly to her mouth, "Oh my God! Oh my God!" she says, wide-eyed. "I swear to God I was just wishing you were here, and here you are!" She grins. "I'm getting really good at materializing!"

"Materialize a hug then," Hannah says as she rushes toward her niece. They dance around and around. "Let me look at you," Hannah says. "Let me get a good hard look."

Syd pulls off her red wool cap. "Still bald," she says, and buffs her head with her palm. "I grew a little back in November, but then..." She shrugs.

"Maybe we'll go shopping for that wig this time?" says Hannah with forced gaiety. "Or are you still opposed?"

"She won't wear a wig," says Mitsy. "Don't bother."

"Not *any old* wig," says Syd. "Mom likes the Jurassic bubble cuts or Farrah Fawcett mardi gras wigs." She throws her hands around her head to illustrate the bulk. "But if I had one that looked like your new cut, I might." She reaches up and tugs a strand. "I love it, Aunt Hannah. Very sleek."

"Why, thank you, cookie! There is such a thing as style even down on the farm, you know—but you have to know where to look."

"How long are you staying?" says Syd. "Don't tell me you're here for the day or I'll explode."

"Aunt Hannah will be here for a few weeks, Sydney," says her mother.

Syd's wide hazel eyes are emphasized by the dark circles beneath them. "Weeks?!" she says. "Weeks?! Really?" She claps her hands. "Hooray!"

"If I can, that is," says Hannah. "If Jonah doesn't drum up a big catastrophe on the farm. There are a couple of brood-mares in the barn about to foal, so you never know."

"Jonah?" says Mitsy, eyebrows raised. "Really?"

"Yes," says Hannah. "Jonah, *really*. He's helping out."

Mitsy nods, considering whatever—maybe Hannah's overall availability, which is why Hannah said it in the first place. In case she needs an out.

"And as far as the foals are concerned, he would need you...why?"

Hannah ignores this, because after all, what can she say—that she delivers foals? Instead she says, "Where's my hug, sis?" As she embraces her sister, she can feel the bones under the lump of jersey sweats that surround her. "God, Mits," she says, "where the hell are you in this pile of laundry? Time for some new duds, I'd say."

"That would be nice," says Aaron from the corner, and Mitsy glares.

Syd says, "I have a puppy, Aunt Hannah! Have you seen her?"

Hannah is mightily impressed by Syd's diversionary tactics which are almost as polished as hers. "Yes, indeed I have seen the pup, but why don't we go see her again?"

Man, would she like a drink.

In the kitchen, Hannah and Sydney tussle with Godiva while Mitsy disappears upstairs and Aaron throws together some kind of chicken dish. There he is chopping, dicing, slicing, and pounding, and as much as Hannah would like to help, she's just too fried. Just too much for one day. And anyway, since when does Mr. Perfect also cook? *Where's the pizza?* It's as intimidating as it is appealing. No cookbooks in sight!

Syd goes upstairs to call her friend, Zelda, and Hannah helps herself to a new glass of chardonnay, having left her other glass upstairs. "So hey, chef," she says to Aaron, "where does sis go while you take care of supper?" She sips her wine. "I mean, is she napping? Reading? What?"

He lifts the top of the skillet and inhales the fragrant steam. "I just hope you know how to cook," he says. "You'll be doing a lot of it."

"Well, sure I can cook," she lies. "But..."

"But what?" He reaches past her for the dried rosemary and thyme.

"But I don't...doesn't Mitsy ever cook? I mean, what does she do?"

He grabs his tumbler of neat scotch and sips, eyes wide. "She visits doctors, takes Sydney to the clinic, and...what she's doing right now."

Hannah nods, "Which is?"

"Probably her twice daily consultation with Pandora."

"What?!" says Hannah. "You're down here cooking dinner while she's consulting a dime store psychic?"

As Aaron stirs the colorful medley of whatever ingredients twice around the pan, he says, "Dime store quality or not, I couldn't say, but she sure charges concierge prices." He shrugs. "She seems to calm Mitsy down, though. She might be the whole reason Mitsy decided to accept Godiva. So maybe it's a good thing? I don't know."

"But what do they talk about? How much is there to say?"

He shakes his head. "If I'm honest, plenty. This house is a goldmine of emotional coal. This story will probably take the rest of our lives, and maybe two or three more to process. It may never wind up."

Hannah grimaces, sidling closer. "*That* doesn't sound good," she says. "What exactly are you saying?"

His eyes sweep the room for spies, settling back on Hannah. Practically nose-to-nose, he knifes the air at the top of his head and says, "We're all up to here. Mitsy quitting on me is the limit."

"Quitting on you? But doesn't she have a...condition?"

"Whatever she has," he says, "she won't talk about it. She's crawled into her little cave and curled up. Been there for half the year already." He nods with emphasis. "That's why I asked her to bring you up here. With all my traveling and her hibernation, Sydney's got to have someone sane to talk to."

Hannah stares at him in disbelief. "This was your idea?"

"That's right," he says. "Those two are oil and water."

"But I can't *live* here, Aaron. At some point I have to leave."

He chucks her chin. "I'll worry about that when it happens. Just hang in there as long as you can. *Please!*"

Well, how can she say no to that?! Of course she'll stay. If she can. If it doesn't get too tough. If Jonah doesn't need her, *plead for her return!* After all, it's Mitsy's family, not hers. So exhausting. "Be right back," she says.

"Twenty minutes to dinner," he calls after her and then more softly, "Please don't tell Mitsy I said anything? Her life is tough enough."

"Yeah, right," she says, "and yours isn't?" She scoots up the back stairs and across the hall to the threshold of the master bedroom, where she hears her sister talking real low.

"But, I mean...what else could it be?" she says tearfully.

As much as she tries to control herself, a rocket explodes in Hannah's head. She marches into the dim lit den of lush spring green textiles and faux painted walls to the walnut canopied bed and grabs the cell right out of Mitsy's hand. "Stop calling my sister, you fucking fraud," she yells into the phone before triumphantly pressing END.

In a barely audible voice, Mitsy says, "Hannah..."

Hannah sits down next to her sister on the bed and clasps

her pale hands. "You don't need to discuss your life with an alien from Mars," she says. "You have *me* now."

"That was my doctor."

Hannah blinks. "Your doctor?" she says. "Oh."

"My rheumatologist."

Hannah freezes a grin. "LOL, right?"

Mitsy shakes her head. "I've been waiting for that call for three days."

"But I'm sure he has a sense of humor. He can't be that vain."

Mitsy places her head in her hands. "The tests were negative," she says barely audible.

Hannah shifts onto her left hip, bending her leg beneath her butt. "But that's good, right? Nothing godawful then?"

Her sister shrugs. "I don't know. If the tests are negative, then what's going on?"

"I'll tell you what's going on," says Hannah, air-jabbing with her index finger. "You are checking out, and none of us can afford that. I did not travel all the way up here to take care of every single person in Darien, do you hear me?"

Mitsy looks up. "Who are you taking care of right now, Hannah? Isn't Aaron making dinner?"

"Well, yes, as a matter of fact he is," she says. "And that's why I came up here in the first place. The man worked all day, or at least half the day, and now he's making dinner while you relax."

"Relax?" she says, chortling. "I wouldn't call this relaxing. I was at the clinic with Sydney all day. He should bloody well try doing that once or twice and see how much fun it is." She lowers her eyes. "But Pandora says I have to give him a long rope. That's what I'm doing. I'm giving him rope."

Hannah jumps up. "He doesn't need a rope, Mits. He needs a wife! You need to get back in the game or you'll lose him."

"Into the *game*?" says Mitsy. "I can barely get through an

hour without falling asleep. My joints ache and my gut is in a knot. My child has been sick for..." she starts to sob, deep heaving sobs.

As much as Hannah wants to kick her sister in the ass, she knows she can't do it now. She hugs her instead, which seems like the right response, but not forever. She will not be party to aiding and abetting the demise of Mitsy Lancaster Michaels. And besides, there's no way she signed up for this level of horse shit. Everywhere she goes, she's surrounded. She might as well have stayed on the farm.

Sydney

SYD'S DAD IS CALLING her for dinner, but she has to finish her conversation with Zelda first. Zelda hasn't exactly been available lately, which Syd understands since she's in school all day followed by theater rehearsal in the afternoon and the garage band at night. And maybe some homework, who knows? She's not exactly the straight A type.

"Z," she says, "are you there? Where'd you go?" She looks at the phone to see if the call ended, but no. Zelda probably muted so she could yell at her brother, not that Syd minds a good argument. She waits, admiring the iPhone her dad gave her last week against her mother's *better judgment*. Of course, everything's against her mother's better judgment, so you have to draw the line somewhere. If it were up to her mom, Syd and Zelda would probably be talking about Barbie dolls through a pair of soup cans connected by a string.

"I'm back," says Zelda, "sorry. I got a text from Dane."

"Dane?" Syd squeals. "Really!"

"Yeah, he might want to be in the band. We renamed it, you know."

Syd's heart pounds. "What! Without me?"

"I'm sorry," says Zelda, "but some of these things are spontaneous, and ..."

"Forget it," says Syd. "Don't say it."

"You have to *be there*, Syd."

"SYDNEY!!!" calls her dad from the kitchen. "Dinner!"

"Well, excuuuuse me for not being there, Z," Syd says.

"I know why you're not there," says Zelda emphatically. "But I couldn't help it. Dane hated the name."

"Dane hated it?" Syd says in a slightly conciliatory tone. "Well, Pink Flash is a little girly. What did you change it to?"

"Bloodbath."

"Bloodbath?" Syd's heart sinks.

"Isn't it great?"

"Obviously you don't hang around a clinic," says Syd. "But whatever."

"Oh. Well, I could talk to him."

Syd knows Z feels bad, which is the point. You don't leave your best friend out of a decision as big as changing the name of a band you invented together. Not that Syd ever got to sing; she didn't. She hasn't really had the lung power since she got sick. But she could manage the band easily enough—drum up a bunch of business on Facebook and Twitter while she's hanging out at the clinic. It doesn't take a genius.

"Well, why don't you come over on Thursday to meet him?" says Zelda.

Syd catches her breath. "Really?"

"Yeah. I mean, if you can come on Thursday. That's when we're rehearsing."

Syd says yes, even though she has another spinal on Thursday. She's given up enough. She will absolutely not give up a chance to meet Dane. Fuck the spinal. She doesn't have that many left anyway, if she can believe the doctors. She'll be damned if Zelda is the one to get Dane, since he's not even her type. Z's into clean-cut all American blonde boys because it pisses off her Mexican parents. Dane is no clean-cut blonde boy. Syd is the one who spotted him in the first place practically the day he moved next door to Z. Devilishly dark-haired, Arab skinned, and soooo cool, he is definitely Syd's type, and not just because it would shock her mother. Although it might have the added benefit of doing that. Plus he's seventeen, so he drives.

"SYDNEY!" calls her Aunt Hannah. "Come on down, little darlin'!"

"Coming!" she calls. "Gotta go," she says to Zelda, and hangs up. She catches her breath before standing. It's hard to breathe sometimes with all the pills she takes to beat the unnamable shit coursing through her body, not to mention the batch of secondary pills she takes to keep from catching infections caused by the first batch. Confusing. But that's neither here nor there. What matters is she has to get her act together before Thursday.

She walks through the hall, stopping periodically for breathers, then down the stairs for whatever dinner she can hold down. When it's just her and her mom, she begs off dinner and eats a bowl of chocolate chip mint ice cream in her room in front of *Modern Family* reruns. But Dad won't allow that, and anyway, who wouldn't want to be with Dad? And of course, now there's Aunt Hannah. Not to mention Godiva, who Mom won't even allow in Syd's room because of germs that don't exist. But anyway, tonight it's actually worth the drain of going downstairs.

"There she is!" says her aunt. "Come join the party."

Syd slips into her chair and says, "I'm not that hungry, but I'll try."

"That's all we're asking, kiddo," says Dad.

Her mom sits glumly at the foot of the table, staring down. With what seems like a lot of effort, she says, "Where are you meds, Sydney?"

"I don't know," she says.

"You must have an idea," her mother drones.

Syd shrugs, "Maybe upstairs?"

"Where upstairs?" says Hannah. "I'll get them."

"I'll take them later," says Syd. The last thing she wants is for this meal—*or any meal*—to revolve around her meds.

"You need to take them now," says her mom. "You need to take them with food."

Aunt Hannah pushes her chair from the table and darts up the back staircase. So much action surprises Syd, since no one has moved like that in this house in over a year.

"In the bathroom, I think," Syd calls out after her. "They're the size of the bathtub, so you can't miss them."

When her aunt returns with the giant pillbox, Syd opens the Monday Evening compartment, and fishes them out. "Thanks, Aunt Hannah," she says. "Oh, and can we go shopping for that wig tomorrow?"

Her mom drops her fork.

"Oh my God, yes, of course!" says Hannah. "What fun!"

Hannah makes everything fun, anyway. They could be digging a ditch.

"A wig, well," says her dad. "That does sound like fun. What color?"

Syd rocks her head. "Not sure, but Aunt Hannah can help me decide."

Aunt Hannah looks from Syd to Syd's sour-faced mom and

back, but says nothing. Syd doesn't really care how much her mom pouts; she's not taking her wig shopping. She needs a break from the utter gloominess of it all. The utter *sameness*. "Plus, I need to change my clinic appointment from Thursday to Friday this week."

Her mother blinks. "You know that's impossible."

"You haven't even asked them yet!" says Syd. "Come on, Mom, at least ask!"

Her dad looks at her mom. "You can ask, right?" he says.

Mom looks directly at Syd and says, "Can you at least tell me why? We have all your tutors to rearrange. And I have doctors' appointments too, you know. It's not a simple matter."

"I'll take her," says Hannah. "If you can't, Mits. I'll do it."

Syd tips back on her seat. "Zelda's having a get-together, that's all. I just need to see my friends once in a while. Okay? Let me live a little?"

Her mom stares down at her plate and back up in slow motion. "I don't know," she says. "I'll think about it. But I'll have to call Ella Rodriguez to make sure nobody's sick over there. You can't be around..."

Dad taps the table firmly. "Drop it, Mitsy," he warns.

Her mom's eyes widen and her jaw drops. She looks away for a second, and slides her chair back. Syd actually feels bad for her, but this is what you have to do to make her see your side of things—that life can't be about nothing but sickness or it's just another version of death.

Aunt Hannah sips her wine, which in the stone silence sounds weirdly loud. "This dinner is delicious, Aaron," she says.

"Yeah, it is, Dad," says Syd. Might as well move on.

"Excuse me," says her mother. She stands and moves slowly across the room to the back stairs and up, closing the door behind her.

Godiva yips in the back room, "Yip! Yip!"

"Can I bring her in now?" Syd says to her dad. "Mom won't even know. Please?"

Her dad puts his head down and runs his fingers through his hair for a few seconds then nods. "Fine, go get Godiva."

Syd walks to the back utility room and hears her dad plead, "You've got to promise me you won't bail out on us, Hannah. We need you. You can see that."

Syd's big concession to her mother was to delay the wig expedition and spend the next three days with tutors catching up on math and history. This involved reading four chapters of <u>The Great Depression</u>, as if her life wasn't depressing enough. But there wasn't anything Syd wouldn't do to clear the decks for the big Dane reveal on Thursday, not that her mother knows about Dane. Her spinal was moved to Friday, thanks to Dad, who made the phone call himself. "Not that hard if you know how to dial a number," is what he said under his breath. But everything's hard for Mom.

For those three days, company was scarce. Aunt Hannah holed up in her suite on her computer, writing whatever...a novel, she said, which is so cool. It figures Aunt Hannah would write a novel. She should be a celebrity anyway; she looks like one. Dad left for Austin on business, and Mom was either buried under her covers or downstairs making list after tedious list about everything from groceries to medications to errands to tutor schedules. Or crying on the phone to that woman, Pandora, behind closed doors.

Anyway, it's finally Thursday and time to find a wig. Syd just hopes they find something good since she's due at Zelda's at 3:30 sharp. She doesn't want to meet Dane in a nubby red ski cap. He deserves more.

At the Wiggly Wig shop in Stamford, no one's in the reception area, so Syd and Hannah walk back and help themselves to the merchandise. Hannah tries on as many wigs as Syd does, not that she needs one. Her hair is to die for. Syd would give anything to show up at Zelda's with Aunt Hannah's gorgeous silky hair.

"How does this look?" says Hannah, the wig all long, straight and black like Morticia.

Syd giggles. "Awesome!" She rips off her ski cap, pulls the hat pin out of a short little punky blonde do, and pulls it down on her bald head. She stares into the mirror. She kind of digs the style but it's itchy as hell. "How's this?" she says, turning.

"Funky!" says Hannah approvingly, which is why Syd likes Aunt Hannah. She approves of things.

A round little ball of an older woman shuffles to the counter from the back room. "Can I help you?" she says in a screechy little voice. She's wearing an obvious wig, shoe polish black, all curly and poufy circa Halloween during the Gothic Invasion of Mars.

Hannah stares open-mouthed and it's all Syd can do not to laugh. Not to curl up and die laughing, actually. Just the look on her aunt's face is enough to make her split a gut. Hannah catches the crest of Syd's laugh attack, and instantly they turn in opposite directions. But even from where she is, Syd can see Hannah holding her legs together so she won't pee. She has a thing about peeing when she laughs too hard; she's famous for it. Imagining Hannah peeing sends tears down Syd's face and she wipes them, trying like hell to swallow her near hysteria, because the little troll lady is getting upset. Syd hasn't laughed like this in a hundred years. She wants to give the little lady some respect, but get real. She can't even talk.

Hannah turns around, dead serious, and says, "Yes I'd like to try on the wig you're wearing. It's perfect!"

The woman blinks. "This is not a wig," she says. "It's my own hair."

"But…" is all Hannah can say at that point, because whatever the woman has on her head is cock-eyed, long strands of her own gray hair poking out the front and sides.

Hannah marches over to Syd with her last sane breath, removes the punk wig from Syd's head, and returns it to its stand. She does the same with her Cher wig, and says, "Bye now!" as they turn and walk outside.

Exploding!

"Oh my God, oh my God!" says Hannah, her hands clutching her chest to keep her heart from popping out.

Syd flips on her ski cap and leans against the closest tree for support. She's weak from laughing. They stand there for a minute, catching their breath, but it's freezing, so they can't stay.

"Get in the car, my little snow pea," says Aunt Hannah. "We're going to go find ourselves a wig made out of real hair instead of hamsters." They ride out another long giggle, breathless. Just the memory of it. Every three seconds their shoulders shake again.

Good times.

In the car, Aunt Hannah pulls out her iPhone and googles Human Hair Wigs. There's a place right in Ridgefield. They're off.

"I'm a little hungry," says Syd. "Not that I can ever eat that much."

"Well, what are you up for?" says Hannah in her jolly way. Hannah, the jolly anti-Mom.

"I can only handle a milkshake right now, I think. I mean it might be the only thing I can hold down." She grins mischievously. "Plus Mom outlaws them which makes them even more delicious."

Hannah smiles knowingly. "Right!" But then says, "Let's not be too hard on Mom though."

"You don't live with her," Syd protests.

"I used to!" says Hannah as she steers down the entrance ramp to the parkway.

"Yeah? And what was that like? I mean, what kind of a kid was she?"

"She was my big sister, so she was always kind of, I don't know...old."

"Ha! I knew it!"

Hannah raises her eyebrows. "I mean...responsible, how's that?"

"You mean uptight!" Syd checks the google map on her phone. "Next exit," she says. "There's a McD's and it's only a mile from the wig place."

At McDonald's, Syd orders a shake while Hannah orders a kid's meal, which cracks Syd up. A stellar move. They finish lunch and roll down the highway to Classic Wigs.

"I'm so glad you've changed your mind on the wigs," Hannah says. "You should have the option, you know? To wear it if you want to, I mean."

"Can I tell you a secret?" says Syd as they pull into the parking lot.

"Oh yeah," she says, squirming expectantly. "I love secrets!"

"OK," says Syd. "Well, just that..." She pauses. "Pinky swear you won't tell Mom or Dad?"

"Lips are sealed," says Hannah. She loops her pinky around Syd's.

"Well, there's a guy I kind of like a lot? Not that I know him, but I'd like to? And now he's in our band."

Hannah nods. "Name? Social security number?" She leans in close. "Details, girlfriend!"

Syd giggles. They leave the car, lock it and head up the stone path to the salon. "His name is Dane and he's Zelda's neighbor," she says. She's a bit winded, so hangs onto the railing, climbing the three steps slowly. She suppresses a grin. "He has tattoos."

"Oooo! Tattoos! So we have to find a very modern hair-piece. Something spiky!"

"Mom would pass out if she knew he had tattoos," says Syd. At the door, she stops and looks at Hannah slyly. "But she would throw me off the Empire State Building if she knew..."

Hannah plants her fists on her hips. "What?"

"That I have one, too."

"What!!!!" says Hannah, her entire face lighting up. "You have a tattoo? Where?"

Syd pulls her ski jacket and sweater up on the left side and her jeans down, revealing her lower hip.

Hannah stares. "A dagger?" she says. "Is that what that is?"

"More of a sword," says Syd. "Just...I'm not defenseless. I can take down The Taker."

They walk into the parlor and down the hall. "The Taker?" Hannah whispers. "*The Taker?!*"

"Yeah," says Syd. "You know. The fucking Taker."

Aunt Hannah's eyes move rapidly side to side. "Ahhhh. I see."

"I knew you would."

"The fucking *Taker.*"

"Exactly."

Hannah takes Syd's hand. "But he's not going to take you."

"No. I'm armed and dangerous."

"But how did you...who? Don't you need parental permission?"

Syd chuckles. "There are ways around everything," she says. "You just have to know the right people."

"Like...?"

"Can't divulge my sources, sorry. When my mother tortures you in the basement with her boiled chicken and beets, you'll be too vulnerable."

"Ugh. I've had that chicken."

They arrive at the salon showroom which is filled with obvious upgrades to the hairpieces at Wiggly Wig.

"Can I help you?" says a sharp looking thirty-something salesgirl with a pile of blonde hair Syd would love to be looking at in a mirror.

An hour later, Syd leaves the store with a $3,500 wig purchased by Aunt Hannah, of course. Who else would make sure Syd had the exact right kind of upbeat hairstyle for her first date with Dane? Or, encounter really. But first impressions matter.

"Z's gonna die," Syd says in the car, admiring the sleek blonde hair and ear-length spiky cut. "She's just...gonna die."

"You look great as a blonde," says Hannah. "Who knew?" She pulls on the front tendrils. "So why don't we go to Bloomie's and get your makeup done? And maybe a pair of fabulous earrings?"

Syd thinks about it—the pros and cons of the natural look versus the sophisticated ingénue. "What the hell!" she says, checking the time on her phone. "We have an hour to kill before they get out of school anyway."

Sitting on a stool at the Bobbi Brown counter at Bloomie's, Syd looks like a movie star. Jennifer Lawrence or something. She can't even believe it. Z might actually pass out, but hopefully Dane won't. Or maybe it would be ok if he did. Syd is exhausted beyond belief, but she's not quitting now. Plus Aunt Hannah treated her to some fierce new turquoise studs and a silver ear collar to show off her new hair. She could have racked up an entirely new wardrobe, but they didn't have the time. Destiny awaits.

They pull up to the Rodriguez house, a mid-size brownstone that Syd actually prefers to her own mega-mansion because it's homier and so colorfully decorated inside. A happy house. A house you would feel okay about messing up once in a while, since it looks like people actually live there. It never ceases to amaze Syd how meticulously clean her mother insists on keeping their house even though she's lost all sense of personal grooming. Syd can't even remember the last time her mother bothered to dress up or even put on a nice pair of jeans. Just sweatpants. Gray sweatpants. Who wears sweatpants anymore?! Her depression might be because of Syd's condition, but whatever. That just makes Syd feel worse. And anyway, it doesn't help anybody that her mother walks around like a commercial for the hopeless and catastrophic end of everything.

They pull up to the garage and Syd hears the music. "They're in there," says Syd. "Can you hear them?"

"Ha!" says Hannah. "Lucky they don't have close neighbors. Shall I stay and wait?"

"No, I'm fine."

Hannah widens her eyes. "Can I at least say hi to Zelda and meet the boy of your dreams? Pretty please?"

Syd has to think about this. She doesn't want to offend Hannah, but she hasn't even officially met Dane. "Um." She bites her bottom lip and finally says, "Okay, fine, but just for a second, and remember..."

Hannah offers her pinkie, and Syd loops, smiling. They jump out of the car and walk several yards to the door at the side of the garage. Syd sighs deeply then opens it. "Hey," she says as casually as she can.

Zelda's fingers freeze on the strings of her electric guitar and Syd can't even look at Dane to see what he's doing. He's a blur.

"Oh my God," says Z. Her hands fly to her mouth. "Look at you!"

Syd looks down. "No big deal," she says, signaling to Z with her hand to keep her reaction in check. Syd's regretting the makeover already, but Z shuts up, so maybe she gets it.

"Hi Zelda!" says Aunt Hannah, going in for a hug. She whispers something into Z's ear, so Syd feels covered.

"And who's this?" Hannah asks, approaching Dane, sitting royally on his drum throne.

"Oh hey," says the rock star. "Dane," he says, waving.

Syd's belly is a volcano of swirling ash. She just hopes she doesn't pass out.

Pandora

ABOVE THE DENSE SEA of aspens, spruce, and ponderosa pines leading from her back deck across the Tahoe basin to Heavenly Mountain, Pandora spots her messenger in the night sky. A novice might think it was a planet or a star, but Pandora knows better. The halo of violet that surrounds him confirms it, though she suspects the halo is only visible to her. She pulls her scarlet shawl tight across her broad shoulders, her dense cloud of white hair whipping in the maelstrom created by the messenger's proximity. She's been avoiding him for years; encounters are costly. One doesn't meet the uncontained energy of the cosmos with one's spindly spirit often, and when one does, well. One pays.

The messenger beams across the sky like a searchlight, exposing graceful lengths of branch, high wire, wisps of clouds and plumes of white smoke from nearby stacks. Pandora watches neutrally, inhaling the pungent, life-giving fragrance of her beloved Sierra Nevada's at night—the sharp pine, the acrid cinder; the apple bite of mountain air. She wants no interruptions to this banquet. *Don't come, Anjah,* she signals. *I'm not ready for you.*

But will he come anyway? At some point it's inevitable. But tonight? Will he come tonight? Or retreat again as he's been doing, sensing her ambivalence, citing her chronic unpreparedness to address her personal issues first. She thinks of these so-called issues as less character flaws than delay tactics—*she needs time!* She's not ready. But will she get the time? Can she afford it? She stands squarely in her worn turquoise cowgirl boots on the redwood deck, a daring stance—long legs planted, arms folded against her vested chest, hands gripping the fringe of her vintage tribal shawl.

A moment of peace descends. She inhales the eternal moment, drawing it all the way to her toes and back. In with the new; out with the old. *Be here now.* Peace reigns. If she can just keep Anjah at bay a little longer, she'll have time to sort through her own ideas first. Figure out a few things for herself before he bombards her with his usual power surge of unsorted information. Ignoring him is the best tactic; that and an arsenal of cigarette smoke to scramble her signal...and his. Which reminds her, where are the cigarettes? If she wants to keep him away, she better start smoking.

She turns toward the wrought iron table behind her, but a few steps in it's already too late. Out of nowhere he wraps his white hot blanket of heat around her head, her shoulders, her torso. She is ambushed by his searing energy. Clenching her teeth, she wills herself centered and dominant, as equal as she can make herself in the presence of his superior matter. She won't succumb; she is no spiritual novice.

Time doesn't pass. Instead it opens and expands, holding

her in its eternal grip, and she becomes agitated. She has never been bold enough to smoke a cigarette in Anjah's immediate presence, but she wants one now. *Needs one!* If only she could reach the table. She steadies herself; feels her feet rooted to the deck slats, trying to recall the protocol to disarm him. He never did understand how difficult these encounters were for her. He never cared.

"Are you ready yet?" he signals.

She looks down to deflect his glare. "I don't know," she says lamely. The heat binds her like a tourniquet. All around her she feels the information he is ready to convey; *wants* to convey, but withholds. A billion bits of raw data captured in his field ready to spring free. Let him convey it for God's sake, she thinks. As long as he's here.

"Yes," she says. "I'm ready." *What the hell.* She'll need the information eventually, she supposes. *Or not.* If she can figure out how to spin her own thread this time, she may be able to do away with him completely. God, how she would love that! But there are no guarantees.

"To heal the girl you must first be healed," he says. His energy vibrates on both sides of her head. "I can't give you any real information until you heal yourself."

She nods back to her stash of marijuana, cigarettes, and paraphernalia on the table. "You came all this way to tell me that?" she says aloud. "I can quit that stuff any time, if that's what you're talking about." Her words issue vapor into the brisk air. "I'm just killing time with sloppy habits. Blowing off a little well-earned steam."

"Your bad habits limit you," he signals.

She pulls away, extracting herself with difficulty from the draw of his magnetic field. "I'm human," is all she says. Let him figure it out. After twenty years of using her as his lightning rod, he should know how much heat she can handle by now. *100% less than he thinks!*

Anjah mercifully dissipates. "A healer's gifts come from her own healing," he asserts.

Pandora raises her chin. "So heal me," she says with a nonchalance she doesn't feel. "Or give me the damn ruby heels and I'll click them myself."

Anjah moves back and forth like an angelic tsk tsk. "You want to heal the girl," he says. "Do you not?"

"Yes."

"Then face the past. Look it in the eye. Time is short."

"Thank you, Captain Obvious," she says under her breath.

He quivers—a question.

"A human term of endearment," she lies. She backs up to the table, reaches for the pack of cigarettes, presents it to him then tosses it into the woods. "My last pack, I swear."

"It's not just the cigarettes," he signals. "Or any other substance for that matter."

She nods, swallowing.

"You have one month, Pandora. At most."

And then, as quickly as he arrived he retreats into the tips of moon-kissed pine. His violet halo spasms, resounding down the long length of his laser trail. "Don't waste it, waste it, *waste it, waste it,*" it warns in a diminishing echo.

The imminence of this message surprises Pandora since Mitsy hasn't mentioned any acute features of Sydney's condition recently. But then Mitsy is underwater herself.

"I'll do what I can," she says, shivering in the chill that remains. She half-heartedly salutes him as he compresses into a dense, sparkling ball, then further into a pinpoint dot that disappears into a fold of the universe. Couldn't you just tell me what to do, she thinks. *Couldn't you just do it yourself?* But she knows it doesn't work that way. Some people are receptors for the information, that's all. How else can the unlimited dimensions of the divine channel itself into this 3D world? Human surge protectors. Put on earth for that, she supposes. *God help me!*

Pandora treads slowly across the deck to the glass doors, which she slides open. She reaches over the ledge to her right, and grabs the flashlight. As she's about to close the door, her renegade Persian feline, Guru, jumps from the railing and shoots into the house. "Why, you little twit," she says. "Where the hell have you been?" She hasn't seen him in a week. But no time to chastise Guru now; there are more pressing matters. She scurries down the twenty stone steps to the steep snowy incline to retrieve her cigarettes. Kicking aside snow with the square toe of her boot, she spots the pack propped up against the stump of a long gone sugar pine. As she bends down to get it, she spots a portion of silver behind it and reaches reflexively.

"Oh my God," she says, shocked. Dropping to her knees, she digs through the snow and frosty scrub with her fingers, unburying the tarnished knife she'd nearly pierced herself with the night Anjah saved her. Not that she wanted to be saved; she did not. She wanted to die like her daughter. She wanted to join Elysha in the beyond.

Elysha is a lit match against the dry tinder of Pandora's addled brain. In five seconds it's an inferno of grief and regret. She pushes back on her thighs and stands, hurling the knife down the forested slope. That knife can come to nothing but grief in her hand. How will she ever face it? *How?* And yet, in less than a month another child could...this is her second chance. She couldn't save Elysha in time all those years ago, but she could save Sydney now. Or is she kidding herself?

"A healer's gift comes from healing herself first."

Maybe some things are just not meant to be.

Back in the house, Pandora changes into a muslin gown, sheepskin slippers, and her hand-embroidered Peruvian robe. She lights a blaze in the fireplace and a pinch of hashish in her jade pipe. She will think about things in peace and without the pressure of Anjah's demands. He knows a few things, it's true. But not all things. He knows Pandora is claimed, for instance. Claimed by him. But Sydney is her own spirit, bound by no one, including Anjah. No one in the spirit realm has tagged the child yet, and maybe never will. After all, just because you have certain gifts doesn't mean you're obligated to share them with a celestial Svengali. Pandora will have to remember to warn Sydney about such liaisons when this is over. For now, the girl feels anything but gifted.

The hashish relaxes Pandora enough to allow the idea of her own daughter, Elysha, to enter softly, crossing the threshold of tragedy into warm familiarity. Oh yes, she was a magical child! Wide-eyed and playful. She'd inherited the piercing blue eyes of Pandora and her Peruvian grandmother, Leila. It was a spectacular mix, that deep copper skin, those blue eyes—visibly confusing to onlookers. Elysha was worth the heartbreak of Pandora's broken relationship with that bozo, Wilfred, from the Bronx. A handsome bastard, but still, *fuck him!* He never cared about anybody but himself. Pandora tries not to blame herself for misjudging his character. Just because she's a mystic doesn't make her any less human. Mystics screw up too.

Pandora sips merlot from her grandmother's silver chalice. Why use a glass when a chalice will do! Sacred things are meant to be used. Pandora doesn't believe in setting them aside, because really...*everything* is sacred, is it not? Every breath, every thought, every action. Everything! She pops a square of extra sharp mountain cheddar into her mouth. *Mmmmm.* The concrete, sequential world can be so comforting when you assemble the right ingredients. Merlot in the chalice; piles of juniper in the fireplace; hashish in the pipe; and the finest aged artisan cheddar melting on your tongue. These things feed the body and the spirit both.

The fire whistles and spits; Pandora gazes to her left out the wall of glass into the western night sky of dazzling marcasite and out of nowhere, she thinks, *signal.*

Everything has a signal!

"Everything has a signal," she says aloud slowly, deliberately, heart pounding. "And every signal can be scrambled or even...blocked." She smiles, raising her arms in excitement. *Yes!!!* Even disease, she thinks. Even disease has a signal. She breaks into a grin so deep it drops to her throat, chest, and belly where it gurgles back up in a gasp.

"Oh this is rich," she says aloud, raising a glass to her muses. "*So rich.*" She might have just decoded the secret to the universe. Or at least the secret to Sydney's cure.

Everything has a signal, including disease! Discover the signal; cancel the disease.

Who needs Anjah anyway? Well, maybe she does, but not yet. Anjah wants her to confront the past first...to deal with Elysha's death before she heals Sydney. But Pandora knows that, at least in the short term, Elysha will only weaken her. Let her daughter's spirit rest peacefully. No need to disturb the past to conquer the present, at least not yet.

But Sydney is a different matter. Sydney still lays claim to this world.

Hours later with half a notebook of ideas and equations committed to paper, Pandora reclines full length on the faded couch.

She sets her head against the gray corduroy pillow and sinks with the full force of mental and physical gravity into her dense cellular mass. As soon as she falls out of consciousness, her astral body lifts out and up with a lightness that always surprises her. There is simply nothing like abandoning the carapace of the material body like a songbird and just...*rising up*. Pure spirit; pure light. *Oh, the freedom!* Not that Pandora plans these trips, not really. And not that there can't be consequences, there often are. Which is why she's been MIA in the ether of late. But oh my God, it's so good to know she's still adept at take-off.

Her body of light stands beside the fireplace with its whistling embers, watching her sleeping physical mass—the slackened jaw and full bottom lip drooling remnant drops of merlot. One arm hangs off the edge of the couch, her hand resting gracelessly in a bowl of melting Cherry Garcia, M&Ms spread across the table. She's not proud of the scene; who would be? But so what? Forgiveness must manifest from the inside out. *Me first.*

From the low end of a cedar crossbeam that connects to the cathedral ceiling above her, Guru jumps, landing on the back of the couch. He walks the length like a tightrope artist, back arched, and finally drops between her shoulder blades. *Thunk!* From a distance, she watches her body lurch, shudder, and come to rest. She doesn't awaken, thankfully, or she would soon find her spirit awareness back inside. That is—unless she were dead—a thought that sometimes challenges her, because what if one day she goes too far? Well, no sense worrying at this point. She's traveled in this state halfway around the world and back without issue. Why freak herself out now? Or at all.

The silver Persian stares ahead, alert and focused. He sees her astral body standing there; Pandora's sure of it. Guru isn't named Guru for nothing. "*Hissssss,*" she mouths, and he returns the promise. He will guard her body while she's away.

Pandora glides to the deck, knowing the one thing she has to avoid on this outing is Anjah. In spirit form, Pandora is more visible to him than in solid physical form, since the physical form conceals her full radiance. Not to mention that as a spirit, she isn't able to smoke cigarettes to deflect her light. Or is she? She's never tried. It might be worth a shot.

At any rate, she must be careful or Anjah is sure to lead her into the lair of his confusing metadata before she has a chance to develop a coherent thread. *About signal!* The signal of disease. First she has to find Sydney, see where she goes when she's knocked out by anesthesia or exhaustion. She has to find the girl and evaluate her signal. Not that Sydney knows she actually leaves her body; she doesn't. But Pandora knows. Tuscany, perhaps. It makes sense since that's the region Pandora connected with Sydney in the first place. She has to start somewhere, so…

No sooner does Pandora rise up from her cottage than she's perched on a rocky cliff overlooking a dark, roiling sea lit by an amber sliver of February moon. But is this Tuscany? She'd imagined gentle hills, rolling vineyards, tidy villages with cobblestone streets. Siena, maybe, or better yet, Il Duomo in Florence—a place of deep spiritual significance and established power. Wherever she is now, it's on a coast. Fierce waves of iridescent sea foam bash the cliffs repeatedly, and even with her limited astral senses, Pandora can tell the air is frigid. Is Italy this cold? It must be. Unless this isn't Italy at all.

To her far left, the diamond-pane windows of a stone field house are alight with a flickering fire. It's the only edifice in sight. She glides toward a murmur within the house that rises and falls with the wind. She's careful not to move through the stone, though she could if she wanted to. But first she must check to see if the enchanting sound comes from living people or spirits. Living people are mostly clueless; spirits are not. It will affect how she proceeds. She peeks in the window.

Inside there are three druid-like figures in black robes kneeling beside a recumbent child, their hands extended above her, chanting a phrase Pandora can't decipher. From the sparse, crudely-crafted furnishings and the dim but abundant candlelight, she knows she hasn't landed in the twenty-first century. A closer look suggests these figures are female. Were there female druids? A medieval abbey, perhaps, or nunnery.

She speculates that even if these women are clairvoyant they won't be able to see her astral body, arriving from the future as it has. So she allows her spirit to penetrate the walls. She has to investigate why she landed here in the first place. For instance, is Sydney the child on the floor? Or is the girl's spirit floating on the cliffs or somewhere nearby? *Why is Pandora here?!* Maybe it has nothing to do with Sydney—just a random occurrence, fragments of the past. It happens.

The women druids, as it turns out, are not novices to spiritualism. Pandora's energy is detected. "Someone's here," says one. Although their language is foreign and ancient, Pandora understands it in her own tongue. The other two stop chanting, rest their arms at their sides and cock their heads toward the stone window seat where Pandora sits. Do they see her? Or just sense her?

"Over there," says another one. She pushes her hood back, sweeps her long black hair to the side, and points directly at Pandora.

The third follows the direction of the first, but it is she who takes Pandora's breath away. Though unlike Pandora in some ways—*she is pale-skinned*—they are otherwise like twins adorned with the same topaz eyes. It's like looking at herself across lifetimes. An ancestor, perhaps, but no. Closer than that. Their eyes connect and lock.

"It is you," says the druid with certitude.

Pandora steadies her energy, trying to conceal herself, trying to retreat.

"It is you," repeats the blue-eyed cleric, and the others stare, too. "It is you and it is I. We are the same thing."

Pandora stares ahead, stunned. The woman speaks truth.

Her ancestral twin stands, walks forward and reaches for Pandora's hand, but Pandora has lost her ability to move. The druid points back to the child. "Come with me," she says.

With Herculean effort, Pandora manages to follow. It isn't easy. This woman owns a piece of her, which makes it difficult to share space without pouring herself into the past. *Without becoming her! And then what would become of her present? Would she regress? Die? Start over?* When she finally gets to the child, Pandora lowers her head to view what she innately knows will be Sydney in all her pain and suffering. She has to prepare to witness the pain.

Pandora comforts herself that they are all here to heal the girl in spirit form, and from there, in physical form. This is how it must work, she knows—correct the disturbances in the energetic fields first and the physical form can repair itself over time. Or all at once; it's not unheard of. The body is a projection of the spirit, not the reverse, as most people imagine. The spirit holds memory of eons of suffering it can neither abide nor release. So they will help her release it. Whether Pandora found this place on her own or was lead here by someone *or something* doesn't matter. Now that she's here, she will do her job.

The two remaining nuns, or druids, whatever they are—*is this ancient Ireland?*—block her view of the child. When she moves closer, they step aside, and the child turns toward Pandora. Pandora gasps, *"Uhhh!"* Her hands fly to her mouth.

The child's skin is a deliciously rich crème du cocoa hue.

Her eyelids flicker in the blinking light, but they are unmistakably familiar. This is no Sydney who lies near death on the stone floor of a medieval abbey surrounded by nuns. This is Elysha. This is Elysha, and one of the women is Pandora. She is looking at herself and her daughter. Their history is long and it appears, tragically repetitive. This is not the first time her daughter has died on her watch. Pandora is sickened by this knowledge. Who brought her here? *Who?*

Raising her head at the level of the diamond pane window on the opposite wall, she glimpses the unmistakable violet of Anjah's halo alight in the distant night sky. She raises her fist at him, *You!* she signals. *You!* And he disappears.

The next thing Pandora knows, she is deep within the moist carapace of her restless flesh and blood, squirming awake in her Tahoe cottage, stretching her long limbs against the length of the couch, fighting awareness. The dawn bleeds blood orange through the dip in the eastern peaks, and Guru's scratchy tongue licks cherry ice cream from the sticky fingers of her right hand. "Yuck," she whispers, retracting her fingers. "Scat!"

Slowly, she pushes herself to a sitting position, trying to recall the night. Was she hallucinating? She's going to have to pull back on the ganja, not that she wants to. She cocks her head, staring into the embers, reaching for the vision, so faded. *But what was it? Or who?* Was it Sydney? Was Pandora too late? Her head pounds. She can't remember it exactly. It's a blur. But whatever it was, wasn't good. Her entire body registers the residue of shock and pain, blocking the details.

Eventually, she rises and treads softly across the wide-paneled pine, staring down at her feet, thinking hard. *Recalling.* Or trying to recall. On her way to the kitchen to make coffee, she stops, pivots in the other direction, hesitates, and heads for the easel. Perhaps...*to solve the puzzle*...but no. *Why now?* Why now after twenty years? Must she start painting again to end this mystery? She stands before the covered canvas, hands on hips. Studies it with her muddled brain, reaches for the stained linen, feeling its viscous fabric, dusty and deteriorating. In a single motion she whips it from the canvas.

Oh God, she thinks. *Oh no!* What's happened here? Her strength crumbles. She drops to her knees.

Hannah

YAWNING, HANNAH KICKS OFF her puffball of a comforter and slides back against the stack of pillows, staring through the windows into the frozen Connecticut dawn. She feels as if she's been away from the farm for months, even though it's only been three weeks. It's still February; how is that possible? Based on her restlessness, it could easily be summer or at least spring. On top of that, her head is pounding and she tries like hell to shake off the remnants of the weirdest dream ever. *Get out of my head!* Although when you think about it, a weird dream might be good for her novel. The weirder the better, actually.

She reaches across the bed for her laptop and furiously types what little she can remember. *The child is sick, but they are trying to heal her.* She cocks her head. *The child is sick?* Maybe not so weird then, since Syd actually is sick. Dreams famously reconstitute psycho-grizzlies into bite-size gummy bears (or the reverse), so there you go. But the child in the dream wasn't Syd, she's pretty sure. Or was it? *Huh*. She can't remember. Anyway, the surroundings were old and decrepit and nothing at all like the chateau or really, anywhere in Connecticut at all. Maybe somewhere on the New England coast, though. It did smell pretty salty. Strange that she remembers the distinct smell of salt water in her dream, but so little else. Can you really smell in a dream? Oh, for God's sake, who cares? She drops her laptop on the mattress and yawns again. She doesn't want to get lost in a weird dream right now. It's not as if the life unfolding all around her isn't weird enough. It is.

In spite of all the household distractions, Hannah has moments when her head swims with nothing but story structure and lyrical language. Nothing polished, but still...*something*. Not *nothing*. Even though nothing is exactly what you would expect with all the nihilistic drudgery surrounding her. No other way to say it, really. The ten ton emptiness of it all. She hasn't even had a drink since Aaron left, just because. Well not *just* because. She promised herself she'd stay clear-headed for Syd, that's why. And by God, she has. Now she can let Jonah know she's completely in control. Made of iron! But all that iron just makes things heavier.

The only way for Hannah to stave off the dead weight of Mitsy's doom and gloom is to indulge her own imagination, not that it's easy. This house is a brain drain. Well, not the house really, but the atmosphere. The house is anybody's dream. *Oprah's!* It's certainly Hannah's. But in spite of the brain drain, she's managed to produce a few focused notes on character quirks and potential plots. Not writing exactly, but composing. Composing in her head, not the computer. And of course a few sticky notes around the house, per usual. She has little time to indulge in the mechanics of committing words to screen in this insane asylum, exquisite as it is.

Her main character is a middle-aged woman terrified of dying, even though she's not even the sick one in her house. Kind of like Mitsy, but not Mitsy. Mitsy is just a muse, if you can call lying around uselessly all day muse-worthy. But writers have to take advantage of their circumstances. *Write what you know!* And anyway, Mitsy is too pedestrian to be heroine material, though Hannah can at least cull from her sister's increasingly strange habits. All the herbs, seaweed and pine cone enemas, or whatever. Ugh. *Ouch.* Pine cones might be a stretch. But unlike Mitsy, the fears of Hannah's character will be original, not obvious and mundane. Hannah is beginning to understand this character so well she thinks the way her character thinks.

She indulges in a good upper body stretch then drags her lazy ass out of bed and heads for the bathroom. Such a fantasy life; she could lie around all day like everybody else. Reaching into the medicine cabinet for aspirin, she imagines her paranoid protagonist—let's call her *Annoya*—projecting herself onto her future deathbed saying, *"If only she hadn't taken that aspirin."* Or... *"If only she had washed her hands of the brain-consuming bacteria before she took that aspirin,"* for instance. Or whatever—*the tainted meat, the month-old milk, the cookies spiked with chips of bubonic plague.*

If only, if only, if only. Maybe that will be the title of her book. IF ONLY –blockbuster recipient of every award ever conceived. And lots of royalties! Royalties to pay for the piles of merchandise she's collected in the last three weeks out of sheer anxiety. Although Aaron will no doubt happily pay for all that stuff since she's here to do his dirty work. Why not? He can afford it. He'll probably wonder why she didn't buy twice as much. Maybe she will. She pops the aspirin in her mouth and washes it down with a cupful of water.

"If only she hadn't washed down the perfectly good aspirin with that cup of contaminated water…"

Now that she has a title, she can focus a little more on the content—that is, the characters and plot. Not too much though, she doesn't want to rush it. Characters have to percolate and plots have to…*age*. Like wine or cheese. It doesn't happen at gunpoint, people. And anyway, she's accumulated more obligations and responsibilities in this madhouse than she bargained for. That's because Mitsy is completely AWOL in her own life. AWOL without admitting it even to herself. No wonder Aaron extended his business trip in Austin for two more weeks.

And Syd is such a warrior, such a powerful creature in spite of her dwindling weight. Her color isn't that great, either, but the doctors never really say anything about general health, as if it doesn't matter. They just smile and check her various chemos and procedures off their lists. *"She's had everything in her protocol this month!"* they say exuberantly, almost giddily. *"We're right on schedule!"*

Hannah, who of course is the one taking Syd to all these appointments lately, wants to say, *"Really? Have you looked at her? Maybe she shouldn't be right on schedule."* Because… maybe she shouldn't. Just a suggestion from the amateur on the bench. *How did she get this job?* But seriously, have they noticed the yellow tone of her skin? The underwater blurriness of her eyes? That shit is poison. How can a person be healed with poison? *"If only she hadn't taken that chemo…"* But Hannah can't go there. Not when it comes to Syd.

Anyway, so far nobody's asked Hannah what she thinks of the whole mess. Aaron doesn't want particulars unless someone needs a check or an insurance number, something specific and expeditious. He can't get off the phone fast enough with anyone but Syd, unless she troubles him with medical details, which isn't often. Mostly it's *"Godiva this, or Godiva that."* Not that he doesn't care; he does. Or at least Hannah thinks he does. *Right?* He must. As for Mitsy, well, she's too busy meditating and zoning out on Zen voodoo to understand how uninvolved she really is. Not to mention the hours of rosary recitation just to make sure she covers all spiritual bases.

Hannah pulls on a pair of worn jeans and a nubby green sweater that she's already worn twice, but not for whole days, so the hell with it. If she learns how to use the Star-Trek washer/dryer down the hall, she knows she'll be given that job for the entire household. Better to play dumb. Every new skill becomes her responsibility. She's already doing the short order cooking. Well, sandwiches and take-out, but still, nobody's thinking about *her* dinner! Nobody's saying, "Hey Hannah, what would you like for dinner tonight?" Not even close. A house this size and the cleaning crew only shows up twice a week! Is Mitsy insane? If not, she's a damn good actress.

Hannah slides her feet into a pair of Ugg slippers and heads downstairs without even combing her hair. She's beginning to understand why Mitsy has allowed her personal appearance to deteriorate to the street level, one corroded curb above the sewer grate. After two weeks without a male anywhere in sight, Hannah has even stopped wearing heels. She's two weeks short of clipping her nails to the cuticle. *No more manicures!* Not to mention that she hasn't changed a purse since she got here, even after purchasing three new ones at Neiman's last week.

Of course she smuggles everything directly to her room in deference to the utterly depressing nature of everything. Shoves it all in the closet. *Have fun in there!* God forbid anyone should be exposed to something shiny and colorful. Even her snuggle-bunny niece has taken to her room when she's not at the clinic or being tutored. Hannah wonders what she does in there. Texting, she supposes, or talking to Zelda, or that boy. Half the time Hannah wonders what the hell she's doing here at all—besides taking full responsibility for the upcoming apocalypse. *Oh that!* What a chump! That and walking the pooch, Godiva. Walking the pooch and periodically bending down to pretend she's picking up poop in a plastic newspaper bag so the neighbors won't arrest her. As if on top of everything else she's going to pick up poop and carry it around. *Good God!*

She grabs a pencil and one of the sticky notepads she's planted around the house. *"If only she hadn't picked up the poop and contracted a deadly parasite, she would be alive to receive her Pulitzer Prize,"* she writes. She abandons the note in her bathroom to go brew some coffee. Caffeine helps a headache, she's heard. Just to add to the utter inertness of it all, she takes the elevator instead of the stairs.

On the first floor, she crosses the grand hall through the great room and into the kitchen, not a soul in sight. It's already nine o'clock. But then again she did hear Mitsy playing some eerie tune on the piano around 2 AM. A song straight out of *Night of the Living Dead—the Musical* if there is such a thing. There should be. They could stage it right here. That's probably where Hannah's weird dream came from in the first place.

From the kitchen, she can see Godiva, her oversized chocolate paws leaning against the top of the doggy gate in the utility room. She follows Hannah's every move, waiting for a walk, no doubt. Or food, probably. A dog's loyalty is limited, she thinks. But then again, so is Hannah's.

Because she figures zombo-Mitsy probably let Godiva out in the wee hours, Hannah takes her time. Give the dog a chance to expand her bladder, for God's sake. This isn't a farm. A dog has to learn some control. She prepares the coffee machine, inhaling the earthy aroma of yesterday's grounds in the process, and thanking the universe in general for the scraps it provides. Not that she's getting religious. Mitsy's antics alone would turn anyone away from God and his employees, *or volunteers*, whatever. Mitsy uses it to cop out on every feeling and obligation she has. And don't think Hannah doesn't plan to lecture that crystal freak, Pandora, when she gets the chance. But things have been a little hectic.

She opens the fridge in the event an alien stocked it with food while they were all sleeping. But no such luck. Fucking aliens. She's going to have to haul off and buy groceries, which is beyond irritating since she barely shops for food in her own house. Not to mention the long list of restrictions placed on the shopper by Command-Mitsy. *From her bed!* Maybe Hannah can find an online delivery service. The idea excites her—another way to conserve energy. And Mitsy can certainly afford the extra expense, if there even is any.

"If only she hadn't ordered her food from the alien delivery service...she would not have grown that forked tongue."

So much genius rolling around in her head these days, she can afford to let that one go.

Hannah releases the doggy gate and pats Godiva on the head. A good dog, all in all, and not a big barker so far. If she didn't poop she'd be a winner. Well, at least she doesn't poop in the house. In the utility room, she opens the pantry closet and pulls out a jar of peanut butter that she brings back to the kitchen. She dips a tablespoon into the jar, pulls out a big gloppy chunk, and licks. Peanut butter & coffee. OMG!!! What a combo! She'll sell the idea to Starbucks and make a million. She pours herself a cup of dark blend and says, "Come on, Godiva, out you go."

While Hannah sips her coffee and licks the peanut butter spoon, she watches Godiva absently through the window above the kitchen sink. The pup slides on the slick surface of last night's snow and ice storm, sniffing as much of the back yard as she can reach before finally peeing. She's on her back legs now, and Hannah refuses to watch her poop. It reminds her too much of her current life. She sips her coffee and cocks her head toward a distant noise. Is that a voice she hears? Signs of life? She moves to the back stairs for evidence.

The murmuring waxes and wanes, but Hannah's curious. She carries the mug upstairs, tiptoeing. Following the low sound up and to her left, soon she's in the neighborhood of Mitsy's suite. Thin curls of pungent smoke emerge from the doorway like beckoning fingers. The hallway smells like a head shop. Hannah can't believe this. What next—a Ouiji board? The fragrance is myrrh, if Hannah remembers correctly from her stoner days. Or maybe frankincense. It's been a while.

"Ommmmm," chants Mitsy deep in the cavity of her dark room. And seconds later, "Is that right, Pandora? Did I do it right? Just *Ommmmm*? Like that?"

A second later she says, "Oh, okay. I thought it was pronounced *mahn-tra* not *maan-tra*."

This is all the rocket fuel Hannah needs to launch straight into orbit. How much can she really take? She's just...had it. She marches into the room; flips open the drapes, and yanks the comforter from Mitsy's lap.

"Hannah," says Mitsy frowning. Not even yelling.

Hannah leans over and snatches the cell phone. "I know it isn't a doctor this time," she says to Mitsy, eyes widening. "Is it? Nooooooo!" She shakes her head back and forth in an exaggerated fashion. "This time it's the charlatan herself, isn't it?" She talks into the phone. "Did you hear that, charlatan?"

"Hannah," Mitsy repeats helplessly. "Please."

"This is Pandora," says the charlatan. "To whom am I speaking?"

Hannah's eyes bug out at Mitsy. "You hear that?" she says. "The so-called psychic doesn't even know who she's talking to! Ha!" She screams into the phone, "Gotcha!"

Silence.

"It doesn't really matter who I am!" Hannah says as she turns and storms out of the room with the phone. "My name is completely beside the point. I'm protecting my sister, is who I am. Protectress-of-the-Naïve-and-Innocent is my name. Call me that!"

She marches down the long hallway and locks herself in one of the chateau's ten extraneous bathrooms for privacy. "A sister who is completely dropping out of life because of Y-O-U!" She sits on the closed toilet and sets her coffee mug on the window sill. *Fucking madhouse.*

"I see," says the lunatic.

"You...*see?!*" says Hannah, opening the blind slats. "What exactly do you *see* in your crackpot crystal, oh fraudulent one?"

"So your sister is dropping out, but not you? You're not... *dropping out?*" says the nutcase. "Is that it?"

"What the hell makes you think I'm dropping out?" says Hannah so far beyond indignation she can't even remember where she saw it last. "I'm right here front and center. Doing everybody's job. And the only one still getting dressed in the morning, I might add."

"Barely."

"Barely?! What's that supposed to mean? Barely what?" She sips her coffee.

"You're not exactly haute couture at the moment, are you?" says the charlatan. "I'm getting rather a sloppy image of you in dirty jeans and a rumpled sweater. Not even clean. Green. I'm getting green with a slight odor. An unfortunate olivey green sweater. Rumpled. I'm seeing rumpled."

Hannah looks down, aghast. Who told this to the fraud? She couldn't *know* that!

"Good guess," she says, "but I'm wearing an orange cashmere sweater with black silk pants. Furstenberg."

Long pause.

"Hello?" says Hannah.

"I doubt that," says the freak. "But you're welcome to snap a picture and send it on over. Will you do that?"

"I will not."

"Considering the outrageous amount of bills you ring up on clothing, you ought to be winning fashion awards in your sleep," says the fraud. "You're an addict, Hannah. A shopping addict."

Hannah's eyes practically pop out, glutinous emerald cat's eyes rolling around on the tile floor in front of her.

"If only she hadn't taken that phone call, her eye sockets wouldn't be vacant..."

"Shopping addict, my ass!" she says. "Is that what my sister told you?" *The gall.* "After all I've done for her!"

"Your sister didn't tell me anything, Hannah. She just told me what a big help you've been. Look..."

"If my sister didn't tell you anything, how do you know my name? Eh? Gotcha! And to be clear, all you're doing is enabling Mitsy to self-destruct instead of taking care of her child."

"I could help you," says the fraud in a maddeningly calm voice. *So this is where Mitsy gets it.* "If you would allow me to do so."

There's a rap on the bathroom door, and as impressed as Hannah is that the invalid actually got out of bed during the day, she's damned if she's going to give her the phone back now.

No. She's taking this roller coaster right through the haunted house and out the other side. She stands up, turns on the exhaust fan, sink faucets, and shower to block out the knocking.

"Help me do what exactly?" she says to Pandora. "As if I need your help."

"Not that I want to, you understand," says the phony baloney. "I'm taking a break from my entire clientele with the exception of your sister who desperately needs me."

"What she desperately needs is to get rid of you."

Mitsy's phone vibrates to announce another caller and Hannah holds it in front of her to see who it is. Maybe it's Aaron. Maybe she can give him a good piece of her rotting mind. But no. *What?* Not only is it not Aaron. It's Jonah!

"But I can't abandon her now," Pandora continues. *Blah blah blah.* "And since you're there, well. I could help you with your addictive nature." She pauses. "As well as your ex-husband."

What?! Hannah's heart stops. "Hold on," she says, and clicks on Jonah's call, but it's too late. She'll have to call him back on her own phone, or maybe he's leaving a message. She won't return Mitsy's phone until she's got his message. *Why is he calling Mitsy!* "I have to go," she says to Pandora. "And just to be clear, I don't need your help with my so-called ex-husband. In fact he's on the other line. We're tight."

"You're going to have a newborn," says the whack job. "Very soon. I'm seeing something new."

Ha! This takes the upside down cake and every other crumb in the psycho bakery. "What the hell?" says Hannah. "I'm not even pregnant. I'm suing you for reckless absurdity, not to mention every dime my sister ever paid you!" She presses END with a flourish.

Even though the knocking starts up again, Hannah doesn't want to leave the bathroom without talking to Jonah. He's only called her once the entire time she's been up here; every other call was initiated by her. She clicks call-back.

"Hello?" he says. "Mitsy?"

"Not Mitsy," says Hannah, though she did think for a second of pretending. *What would he say to Mitsy that he wouldn't say to her?*

"Oh, Hannah, hi," he says. "Why didn't you answer your phone? I've been calling and calling."

"You have?" She grins girlishly and sits back down sipping coffee. "What's up, stranger?"

"One of the mares—Jolie, is in a bit of a fix. Seems she's ready to foal early. I've called the vet."

Hannah isn't that worried about the broodmare. Jolie is tough. Plus she's delivered early before. But Hannah knows an exit opportunity when she sees one. "I'll get the next flight out," she says.

"No," he says, "really. Don't. I'll take care of it. It's in the vet's hands now, anyway. Just keeping you informed is all. Doc just arrived—I'll call you as soon as I know anything." End of call; not even goodbye. What the hell ever happened to courtesy?

Hannah secures her mug with her left hand, and shuts off the shower, sink faucets and fan switch with her right. Time to get out of this mental hospital and back to the other one.

"Aunt Hannah, are you in there?" calls Syd from the hall.

Oh no! *Syd.* It was Syd knocking! "Sorry, sweet pea," Hannah calls, fiddling with the door lock with her free hand. "I didn't hear you, hon."

She opens the door and Syd's slightly yellow pallor is now the palest white. "What's wrong, Syd?" she says. "What's up?"

"It's Godiva," says Syd. "I can't find her. She's gone."

Hannah's eyes slowly widen. "Oh! Oh no!" She slips past Syd, charging down the back stairs, skidding halfway and landing on her rump with the remains of her coffee sprinkled on her sweater and jeans. "I'm so sorry," she keeps saying. "So damn sorry. I forgot about the pup! I left her outside!"

She opens the back door and runs into the frozen tundra behind the house, slipping and sliding in her Uggs on the icy crust, calling, "Godiva! Come here, girl! Godiva!"

Syd follows, shuffling back and forth to keep her balance. "Godiva!" she screams, crying now. "Godiva! Oh no, where are you?"

Hannah's hands cover her mouth. She's paralyzed. *Shit. Shit. Shit!* "I'll get in the car and look," she says. "Be right back." Her ass is killing her from all the acrobatics.

"I'm coming with you!" says Syd.

Hannah has to crawl, hands and knees, to reach the back stairs then up and inside, hanging onto the railing for dear life. She grabs the first two parkas she can find and tosses one to Syd, who's right behind her, breathless. Hannah's parka is huge—obviously Aaron's, but it covers her coffee spill nicely. Not that she cares, and she still hasn't combed her hair. She yanks her purse off the bench and grabs the keys. In less than a minute they've driven out of the circle and onto the road, screaming, "Godiva! Godiva!" into the frigid air. Hannah's heart literally pounds in her throat and Syd's face leaks tears like a soaker hose.

Twenty minutes later after covering the entire neighborhood twice, they see the fugitive perched all *la-de-da* in someone's yard just looking around wide-eyed and duh. Hannah screeches the car to a halt, jumps out and runs to her on the shoveled driveway, but the dog leaps around gleefully in circles and takes off into the wooded glen. Slipping and sliding all over again, but this time using trees for ballast, Hannah closes in on her in a clearing. She falls to her knees, begging, "Puh-leaaaaase, come to me. Good girl! Come on!" She crawls slowly toward the pup who alternately crouches and leaps, daring Hannah to come closer so she can run away again.

Just then Syd appears behind Godiva, tiptoeing between the trees. Very slowly and quietly she leans in, reaches, and finally, snatches the collar.

"Oh my God," says Hannah breathlessly. "Oh my God, oh my God!"

"We have her," says Syd, grinning. "So it doesn't matter."

Hannah pulls herself up on a tree limb, the knees of her jeans ripped to shreds from the ice and sticks and pointy whatnot. Her knees are bloody gizzards. *"If only she hadn't crawled through the nuclear waste after the ungrateful bitch..."* "We're getting a frigging fence around your back yard as soon as I can get a hold of your dad," she says.

In the car, Hannah's heart is still beating a mile a minute, and she knows she can't take anymore. She bides her time; lets Syd cuddle Godiva for a few minutes before breaking the news. "Listen, cookie, I gotta fly down to Virginia today. Jonah called and Jolie's in trouble."

Syd, whose torso is curled protectively around Godiva, straightens up fast. "What? No! You can't leave me here with her!"

"Just use a leash, like I should have. She'll be fine."

"Not Godiva," Syd whines. "Mom!"

"Ah. Ohhhh." Hannah scratches her head. "Well. That."

"You can't go now, Aunt Hannah, you just can't!"

"I have to, cookie. But I'll be back as soon as I can, don't worry. A few days maybe. A week at most."

"A week! No! Plus I have my procedure in a few days."

"Your mom can take you, no worries. She'll be fine." They arrive at a red light and Hannah turns to Syd. "I absolutely have to leave, darlin'. Until I sell my book, those foals are my only income."

Syd stares blankly out the window. A minute later she says, "Take me with you. Please? Me and Godiva? You'll barely notice us, I promise."

"But what about your procedure?"

"Fuck it. Fuck the procedure. I've already had twenty and it's not like they're doing me any good. What I really need is a break."

Hannah scowls. "The procedures most certainly are doing you some good," she says, though she doesn't really believe it. "You're here, right? And you're getting better."

Syd shakes her head. "There's nothing for me here, Aunt Hannah. Nothing at all. Pleeeease take me! You have to! Pretty please!"

"Nothing for you here? Well, that's not true. What about Zelda? What about..." and she winks.

A lopsided grin slips reluctantly onto Syd's pale face, followed by a brief blush. "Well, but." She shrugs. "And anyway, he's..."

Hannah slows the car before making the turn onto their street. "Yes? What? What? He's...*what?*"

"He's pretty great," says Syd.

"Aha! So you've been talking to him!"

Syd nods shyly, dipping her chin. "Yeah, and texting a bunch. But anyway, he's leaving for Pennsylvania tonight. For the entire winter break. His cousins are there." She bats her lashes. "You have to take me with you, Aunt Hannah. You have to!"

Hannah's head is a tornado of swirling debris, so she has no idea what makes her say, "Fine." When you've been living in an asylum this long, everything is part of the same hallucination. Impossible to discriminate.

"Why not?" she says. "We'll take your dad's car."

Syd jumps up in her seat. "Really?" She claps Godiva's paws twice. "Hooray!" she yells, and then, "Let's not tell Mom, okay? She probably won't even notice we're gone. She can just sleep for a week."

Hannah shakes her head; this much is true. And frankly, just seeing Syd exhibit this much enthusiasm is inducement enough to risk everything. Still, there's no way she can just leave with Syd. *Right?* "We have to tell her, Syd. She'll freak out."

"She'll only freak out if we tell her," says Syd. "She won't let me go. She'll forbid it! Saying you'll tell Mom is as good as saying I can't go."

They pull to a stop at the garage and Hannah lays her head in her arms over the steering wheel, defeated. "Just go upstairs and get packed," she says wearily. "Three days—that's all I can promise. I'll call the clinic to reschedule, and if they say yes, we'll check-in with your mom." She lifts her head. "We'll just have to be persuasive. I can't kidnap you as much as I'd like to."

Syd nods reluctantly and hurries inside with Godiva.

In her suite, Hannah phones the clinic, *done!* No argument there, just a list of do's and don'ts. She's right on chemo schedule, so. But won't this little junket throw her off? *What is their plan, anyway?* Best to just go along with everything. *Best not to know.*

Hannah showers the frosty grime from her filthy body and patches up her mangled knees with iodine and band aids. Everything is sore. She blows out her hair for all it's worth because today she's seeing a man. *Jonah!* She can't believe how much she's looking forward to ditching this estrogen palace for the farm. Well, not the palace so much, but the gothic energy inside it. *Mitsy's energy!* She extends her hair with the round-brush, applies the heat of the dryer, and curls it ever so slightly. She's good at this. She's good at looking good when she wants to. This is what she's meant for—this and composing brilliant stories. She just hasn't wanted to look good in a while, is all. The insanity factor.

"If only they hadn't all gone insane..."

Gorgeous silky auburn hair, smoky make-up and clean clothes later—dark wash straight legs tucked into brand new leather knee-high boots topped with a designer tunic in oatmeal knit and a chunky belt—Hannah's ready for anything. She switches to her butter-soft gazillion dollar Ferragamo purse, throws whatever she can fit into her weekender, and rolls it across the hall to Syd's room. "You ready?" she says.

Syd's coloring still isn't the greatest, but she's all dressed, including the spiky blonde wig, which is the first time in over a week Hannah's seen her in it. So this little trip is already putting some oomph back into her niece, oomph that's been missing for a while. How can she say no to that? She strokes Syd's cheek. "You look awesome," she says.

Another blush races across Syd's cheek only to disappear into her pale flesh. The lack of color is disconcerting, but Hannah's the only one who seems bothered, so. "Here goes nothing," she says, pointing to Mitsy's suite. "Wish me luck."

"So the clinic is rescheduled?" says Syd.

"Next Friday at 9 AM."

Syd raises her fist, "Yesssss!" she hisses, and then, "I'm going in with you. Mom can't say no to both of us."

Hannah abandons her suitcase in the hall and treads carefully into the dungeon in search of the dragon. Not that Mitsy breathes fire often; she doesn't. Hannah can count the number of times she's seen her sister explode, which, if you ask Hannah, is a big part of the problem. *Explode!* You might get somewhere.

She walks to the window, pulls the drapes open, and slowly turns the blinds. She approaches her sister's bed and sits at the foot, sinking into the expensive memory foam. After a minute, she jiggles Mitsy's foot. "Hey sleepyhead," she says like the hypocrite she is. "Gotta talk, sis."

Sydney hovers anxiously in the shadows. Hannah can feel Syd's nerves ten feet away.

"Huh? What?" mutters Mitsy, rolling over.

Hannah gently shakes Mitsy's right leg back and forth, but if she doesn't wake up soon she might throw a glass of ice water on her. Or light her hair on fire. She's running out of what little patience she cobbled together in the first place. "Come on Mitsy, wake up! I have to tell you something."

Mitsy opens her eyes. "What?" she says. "What time is it?"

"Eleven-thirty."

"Oh." Ever so slowly, she lifts herself up on her elbows. "Ouch," she mutters. "My joints are killing me."

"Well, just stay in bed and rest," says Hannah. "No worries. Syd and I are just taking Godiva to Virginia for a few days, so no rush at all waking up."

"Okay," says Mitsy, sinking back down, and then, "Wait. What?" Somehow she manages to jolt up, aching joints and all. The covers roll down, and she's wearing the same gray sweatshirt and pants she's had on for three days. Or is it three weeks?

"Jonah called," says Hannah evenly. She explains the situation matter-of-factly, why she has to go and why Syd is better off accompanying her. "We'll be back before you know it. Meantime, you can catch up on your sleep."

"No," says Mitsy, rubbing her eyes. "She can't go with you."

Syd steps out of the shadows. "But I am going, Mom. I have to get the fuck out of this fucking house."

"Syd," warns Hannah. "Be nice."

"I want to be nice," says Syd. "I do. But the thing is—I can't. I want a real mother who has real emotions and doesn't sleep in a fucking cave all day."

"I haven't been feeling well," says Mitsy. "I wish you'd be fair."

"Wow, so sorry you haven't been feeling well, Mom," says Syd. "'Cause I've been feeling fucking AWESOME, as you know."

"You're not going to Virginia, Sydney," she says.

"Yes, I am."

Mitsy shakes her head. "Give me a minute, please, both of you. I need to make a phone call."

Hannah jumps to her feet. "You are not asking that psycho-gypsy whether or not your own daughter should or should not go to Virginia with me for a few days. You. Are. Not. Doing. That!!!" She stomps her foot. "She's a fraud, Mitsy Michaels. Do you hear me? Do you know what she said to me this morning when I lambasted her earlier on the phone? She said she could help me, too. Can you believe that? She said she could help me with my ex-husband, and by the way—I was going to have a baby soon! A baby! I'm not even pregnant."

"Syd has a spinal coming up," says Mitsy.

How Mitsy even remembers these things is a mystery to Hannah. There's not even a calendar in her room.

"I changed the appointment," Hannah says.

"You can't change it; only I can change it. She needs my permission for all medical issues until she's 18. She won't be 18 for three years."

"I'll be 16 in two months," says Syd. "Or maybe you forgot."

"Maybe you also forgot that you put me on the authority list," says Hannah. "Since I'm the one with her at the clinic twice a week, sometimes more."

"Yes, well that's just for emergencies," says Mitsy.

"It must be an emergency then," says Hannah, "because I changed the appointment. It's done."

Syd says, "Get mad, Mom. Go ahead and get angry. Let's see what happens when you actually show how you really feel instead of roaming around all night and sleeping all day." She gets up in Mitsy's face and screams. "You're the worst fucking mother in the whole fucking world!"

Even Hannah feels bad about this, but she doesn't know how to stop it. Maybe this is the only way out for all of them. Still, she takes Syd's elbow gently and tries to back her off.

All at once Mitsy rises like a snake, coiled, erect, and ready to pounce. "What is it you want from me, Sydney? What? You want me to say the F word? Will that make you feel better? Is that what you want?"

"Say it," demands Syd.

Hannah says, "I don't think we really have to force..."

"FUCK!" says Mitsy. "FUCK FUCK FUCK!"

Hannah and Syd stand there agape.

"Are you satisfied?" says Mitsy. Her face is a giant bing cherry. "Are you? Both of you? Are you fucking happy now?"

Syd breaks into a nervous giggle, and Hannah's not sure how to handle it...which way it will turn from here. *"If only they hadn't told the mother..."* She feels kind of slap happy herself. This seems like a one-way road to hell, but then again, isn't that where they've been headed all along?

She grabs Syd by the shoulders and prods her through the room before they break into the same kind of hysteria that drove them from the wig shop. Laughter is the last reaction Mitsy is prepared to deal with—an emotion without purpose. So frivolous. She probably doesn't even remember what laughter is.

Sydney

SYD CURLS UP IN the soft black leather passenger seat of her dad's Land Rover stroking the inside of Godiva's silky ears. "I feel a little guilty," she says.

Her aunt just nods, flicking the left turn signal on their way out of the neighborhood. "Yep," she says.

"Maybe we should have asked her to come with us?" says Syd. She flips down the visor and checks out the wig in the mirror to make sure it's on straight. She got dressed so fast she forgot the little cap thingy underneath, so it itches and slides, which is okay since she only needs it for a minute. That is if she can get her aunt to take her to Z's house in the first place. She's been pushing pretty hard for everything. Maybe there's a limit.

"She wouldn't have come," says her aunt.

"I don't know why," says Syd. "She's been stuck in that house every day since you got here. First she was all controlling of every bite I ate or didn't eat and now she hardly knows where

I am. She's become a cave dweller. She needs to get out." She scratches under the wig. "Not that we invited her."

"She's too afraid," says her aunt.

"Of what?"

"Of everything." Hannah slows to a stop at the traffic light.

"Of me," says Syd. "I did this to her."

Hannah sighs. "No, sweet pea. You certainly did *not* do this to her. She's doing it to herself."

"Well, at least I got her good and mad just now," says Syd. "That's something."

"She said the F word," her aunt says, chortling. "I've never heard her do that before. I'm not sure what it means, though, in the big picture."

"It was a goal," says Syd.

"Getting her to say the F word? Was a goal?!"

Syd grins. "To get her to lose control. To acknowledge how fucked-up things really are instead of pretending everything's all chill when it's not. When, you know…"

Aunt Hannah stops her. "I know."

Syd shrugs. The sky outside is dark and scattered with the kind of charcoal clouds that deliver dangerous things, like rocks and sharp metal objects. Nothing would surprise her. Snow and ice seem too ordinary for what's going on around here. Not threatening enough. She's guessing no one bothered to listen to the weather report before they packed up the car. She sure didn't. Anyway, who cares if they have to drive through a blizzard? There are worse things, like staying.

"Well, anyway, we'll be back before she knows it," says Syd.

Aunt Hannah turns to her and smiles weakly. "I'm not sure what she knows anymore."

"You think she's cracked up?"

Hannah smirks. "I think we all are. But we made our decision, so let's get on with it, shall we? No more doom and gloom."

"You know what would really cheer me up?" says Syd.

"What's that?"

Syd rocks her wiggy head back and forth. Should she ask? She doesn't want to push too far. Or does she?

"Come on, cookie. Out with it," says her aunt.

"Um, well...it would just be so awesome if we could stop at Z's house for a few minutes before we leave?" Syd exaggerates a grin. "Pretty please?"

Hannah frowns, considering it, then bobs her head up and down. *Getting it.* She gets it!

"I see." She poofs her lips. "Dane in the picture."

Syd glances out the side window. "Maybe." But she can't keep a straight face, so she goes for it full bore, grinning. "Can we?" she says. "It's Saturday, so they should be practicing. And anyway, he leaves tonight."

"Welllll...okay, but just for a few minutes. Can you promise me that?"

"Pinky swear," says Syd, offering her pinky, linking it with her aunt's. She squirms in her seat, adjusting her position with Godiva. "Plus they haven't even seen Godiva yet. Think how deprived that is!"

Hannah makes two lefts to get them back on track for Zelda's house. Syd just wants to hug her, but considering she's driving, it'll have to wait.

"So the plot thickens, eh?" says Hannah. "With drummer boy?"

Syd shrugs. "Uh...yeah?"

"What's the main topic? Music?"

Syd pets Godiva anxiously. This conversation's got her

nerves all switched up and churning, mainly in her stomach. "He's different," says Syd quietly. "He's chill. Philosophical."

"Philo-*sophical!*" says Hannah. "Who knew you wanted a philosophical boyfriend! Wow!"

"Well, you know. He's had a kind of a rough deal growing up, too. His mother left them, and his brother was really sick once, so he understands."

Hannah smiles. "So he knows."

"Yeah," says Syd. "But he also knows it's temporary. With me, that is. With my...whatever. My stupid condition. He says it doesn't matter. That I'm a winner and winners win."

"I like him already," says her aunt as they pull up Zelda's driveway. "Winners win. Yes they do! And you're definitely a winner." She parks the car in front of the garage. The doors are closed, and there's no obvious music coming out. "You sure they're here?" she says.

"Pretty sure," says Syd. "I'll go check though. I didn't text cuz I wanted to surprise them." She releases the seatbelt, opens the door, and lugs Godiva with her.

"I'll wait here," says Hannah. "Be as quick as you can, cookie. We've got a long ride ahead of us."

Syd nods and walks to the side door with Godiva who's getting heavier by the minute. Won't be able to carry her much longer. Or maybe Syd's joints are having hissy fits from all the stupid corticosteroids they've been giving her, which is more likely. It happens. She puts Godiva down gently and grabs her leash.

Inside, she looks around. Nothing obvious. So maybe they're not here? Mrs. Rodriguez' car is gone, so maybe they all went out, hard to tell. She should've texted. She walks past the flimsy platform stage that holds the microphone and speakers and says, "Anybody here?" Her nerves are break dancing in her throat.

Seconds later she hears a kind of hushed, "What's that?"

from somewhere in the back. But maybe she's making it up. She walks around the platform behind the drum set and random old stuffed chairs to the storage room in back. Everything's all piled up; there are stacks of crap everywhere. It's like the old *Highlights* magazine puzzles—trying to find the image of a shoe in the face of a giraffe. Something's going on, but what? What is it? She focuses on movement in the right corner under the window below the tool table.

What? "Oh my God!" leaks out of her mouth, and Godiva barks, yip yip yip.

"Oh my God," she says again and darts out of the room, aching joints and all, then tripping on the corner of the drum set and catching herself against the back of a chair before falling on her ass.

Godiva's leash wraps around a speaker and Syd pushes herself forward, rushing like hell to unravel it. "Get me out of here," she whispers desperately under her breath. Hot tears cloud her vision and it takes *f-o-r-e-v-e-r.* Everything is slow-mo. Did she really see that? Zelda and Dane in the corner, all over each other?! *What the hell!*

Moments later she hears, "Syd?" which is Dane's gravelly voice calling out from the back room. "Syd, wait!"

Syd unhooks the leash and grabs Godiva under her arm, only to trip again on the edge of the platform, falling forward and losing her wig in a box of gardening tools. She can't think. She has to get out of here.

"Syd, wait!" he says.

She pushes to her knees then up, collects Godiva and high-tails out of the garage to the car and opens the door.

Her aunt says, "Hey, Syd, where's your…"

Somehow Syd manages to throw Godiva and herself inside before Dane and the worst best friend ever show up at the garage door. "Get me out of here," says Syd, all crouched under the dash. "Reverse. Fast! *Please!* As fast as you can."

Her aunt doesn't ask questions, which is good because Syd can't talk. Tears course down her cheeks onto Godiva's head. Out the driveway, she struggles back up to the seat with Godiva, leans forward and pulls the red wool cap out of her backpack onto her freezing cold head. The seat belt alarm goes *bing bing bing*, and she manages to strap it across her chest, jamming it into the slot like she's murdering it.

This is just too much. But she doesn't want to freak out Hannah in case her aunt decides it's officially too much and drops her back at the house. She wants to go to Virginia. So she boxes the shit in her heart and locks it up with the other huge pile of unnamable crap that's crammed into her tight little footlocker of a life.

Ten minutes later they're on the highway and Hannah says, "Wanna talk?"

Syd swipes her cheek, her dripping nose, and shakes her head no.

Her aunt nods. "Okay then."

Syd could just hug her again. Hannah's the only one who gets her. The *only* one.

Syd's phone starts beeping, buzzing and ringing like a carnival, so she shuts it completely down, nearly throws it out the window, but instead tosses it into the back seat. She won't give them the satisfaction. *Fucking traitors.*

Syd falls deeply asleep, drifting to far-away places like she's under anesthesia again. Anyway it feels like that; like empty space. She stands on the edge of the cliff in the dark, waves of salty sea banging repeatedly against the lower jetty. Moonlight skims the waves as they crash. It's cold. She's wearing a black cloak with a hood, her arms spread akimbo like bat wings. She has the feeling that she could fly right over the ocean if she wanted to. She waits, watching, admiring the wildness of it all.

And then she leaps.

No sooner does she take off into the midnight air but she hears Godiva barking underneath her in the car, all scrunched up under Syd's boots. She must have been sleeping a lot longer than she thought because they're driving across a really long bridge, and Syd has no clue where they are. "Where are we?" she says in her sleep fog.

"Almost New Jersey," says Hannah, whose phone buzzes in her groovy new purse. "Pull that out for me, sugar?" she says. "With the earbuds?"

Syd checks the read-out. "Uh oh," she says. "It's Dad."

"Uh oh, nothing," says Hannah. She reaches for the ear-buds and plugs them in one at a time while Syd presses 'accept'. "Hello, Aaron," Hannah says pleasantly, like he's calling to see what's for dinner. Maybe he is.

"Uh huh," she says as she moves into the right lane. "That's right."

Syd shifts restlessly. She leans down and pulls Godiva back up on her lap.

"Well, no," says Hannah. "That isn't at all what happened. Jolie's foaling, and I have to be in Virginia; it's that simple. Syd's got full endorsement from the docs to come with me, and frankly, Mitsy is in no shape to be looking after her anyway."

Hannah's face screws up, and Syd is so tempted to press speaker she almost forgets how depressed she is about Dane and her so-called friend. But then again, her aunt's got the earbuds in, so the speaker wouldn't work anyway.

"I understand that, Aaron, I do," says Hannah. "Don't think I don't." She rolls her eyes.

A minute later, she says, "I've got a better idea, Aaron. Why don't you go home and take care of your wife? Eh? What a concept! *You* taking care of your wife!"

Her eyes bug out, and Syd feels a little bad because her dad doesn't usually piss Hannah off like this. Usually they're on the same team. So now everything's up in the air.

"I'm not turning this car around," Hannah tells him. "Not doing it. Uh uh."

She's steaming mad. Now that they're on the other side of the bridge, Syd wishes they'd pull over. It all seems kind of perilous.

"So arrest me," Hannah says real low. "We've already crossed the Hudson River. By the time I turn around and drive all the way back, you could practically be there yourself." And then more softly, she says, "She needs you, Aaron. Face your problems, for God's sake. Go home." She hands the phone to Syd. "You talk to him," she says.

But Syd just ends the call.

"What?!" says Hannah, wide-eyed. "Why'd you do that? Don't you want to talk..."

"Let them arrest us," says Syd, smirking.

Hannah nods. "Thelma and Louise," she says.

"Ha!" says Syd, adding, *"If only they hadn't run away..."*

At this, Hannah's jaw practically drops to her feet. "What? What did you just say?"

Syd shrugs. "Just...you know. I don't know. Like we're in some kind of movie and someone says..."

"No, I know," says Hannah, shaking her head in disbelief. "You took those words right out of my head. Out of my *throat!* Oh my God! Well, not even *my* head, really, but the head of my main character, Annoya. That's what she says...*if only*. That's the name of my book!"

Syd grins. "I'm a thief!"

"A psychic thief!" says Hannah, overly impressed.

"And we're bandit fugitives," says Syd.

"If only they hadn't robbed that gas station," says Hannah.

"Ha ha, yeah," says Syd, pointing to the gauge. "But we might have to."

"Whoa," says Hannah, "I'll say. And I'll bet that poop machine could use a walk."

While her aunt gets gas, Syd trots Godiva around the perimeter of the station. It still hasn't actually snowed yet, but the sky is threatening. From the corner of the property she can see the wild river churning underneath the bridge. Big chunks of ice float on the dark surface, and a giant red boat jams through it, back and forth, trying to break it all up, maybe. Who knows? She's glad she's not on it.

Hannah closes the gas tank door and yells, "I'll get that, cookie! Leave it for me!"

She's talking about the poop, which is crazy, since Syd knows even a molecule of dog poop is enough to make Hannah gag. She has no idea how her aunt took care of horses for so long. But she must've had help. Just batted her eyelashes probably. She's the prettiest woman Syd has ever seen. *"If only...I looked like Hannah!"*

"I mean it," Hannah says. She hops in the car, drives over, parks it, and jumps out with a yellow newspaper bag. "Get in the car."

Syd hops on board, watching her aunt lean down with the yellow bag, her elegant cashmere back to the car. She's too dressed up to be picking up poop, anyway, which makes it funnier. After she stands, Aunt Hannah makes a big show of tossing the bag into the dumpster. Syd's chuckling since the poop is still right there in front of them, but that's the least of anybody's problems. Hannah must think she's blind.

When her aunt gets back in, she says, "The doctors don't want you handling poop. Too many germs. You leave the dirty work to me."

"Ha ha, sure," says Syd.

Hannah frowns, but doesn't pursue it. Instead she says, "Let's do lunch on the river, shall we?"

They find a funky river joint that serves burgers, BLT's, and soup. Everything's so different here in New York or New Jersey or wherever they are—New Yorksey—looking out at the water from the restaurant on the cliffs. Syd's just glad to be out of town. She makes an attempt to eat, even though she's not that hungry.

"This is good," she says about the chicken soup. "Nice and hot."

"I'm glad to see you eating," Hannah says. She bites into a cheeseburger. "Mmmm," she moans, catching drips of ketchup with her napkin. After she swallows, she says, "You haven't seen Uncle Jonah in a while, have you, cookie?"

Syd never thinks of Jonah as her uncle since she's really only met him twice. Aunt Hannah always visits by herself. Syd says, "Nope. I barely remember what he looks like."

Hannah's eyes grow real big and she says, "Well, get ready to feast your eyes on one hunk of a man." She widens her eyes for emphasis.

Syd says, "I never think of you as part of a couple. You don't need a man. You're enough on your own."

"Is that a compliment?" Hannah says, raising her chin.

"Hell, yeah," says Syd. "And I'm gonna be just like you."

"Oh?" says her aunt, lifting a french fry. Then she says, "Ready to talk?"

"Not really."

"But can you at least tell me what happened to our expensive little hair piece?" She pops another fry in her mouth. "Your dad might ask about it at some point since it was practically a capital investment."

"I lost it," says Syd. "But I know where it is. Sort of."

Hannah puckers her mouth. "That's all I'm gonna get out of you today?"

Syd looks out the window at the turbulent river, thinking. "They're traitors is all," she says. "I'm not in the mood to put their names in a sentence right now."

Hannah nods. "You don't have to. Just as long as you're ok."

"I'm ok," Syd says, even though she isn't. She bites into her BLT and stares out the window wondering if she'll ever get over any of this.

"Anything can happen, you know," says her aunt. "Jonah and I, for instance. We're getting back together."

Syd doesn't want to say how much this disappoints her, since she thinks of Hannah as being hers. "What about my parents?" she says. "Do you think they'll break up?"

Hannah looks shocked. "What?!"

"Well, you know. He's never home. They barely talk." She shakes her head. "It just seems like everything's falling apart."

"I'm sorry you had to hear that conversation in the car," says Hannah. "I really am. But your dad needed a swift kick in the ass, so I gave it to him. That's all it was. Your parents are fine."

"I know you don't think I did this to them, but I did," says Syd. "They were ok before I got sick."

Hannah reaches for Syd's hands and holds them tight. "It's not over yet. You'll see. He'll head home and they'll work it out. Best thing ever is that you're with me and we're taking a break from them. And they'll have time alone."

"Promise?" says Syd.

"Promise." Hannah winks.

They finish up, pay, and climb back into the truck with a few fries for Godiva. She gobbles them up and before long they're an escape party heading south on the Palisades Parkway blasting *"Moves like Jagger"* on the radio and singing along. And then just like that the sky opens up like a monster pinata, emptying every frozen thing it can think of at the car and the road. They can barely hear the radio for the ice and snow and balls of hail, *ping ping ping!* Syd puts her hands over her ears and says, "If only they hadn't gone to Virginia…" but she doubts Hannah even heard her. It's all she can do to drive.

Eight hours later, including four pee stops and twenty minutes of parking under a highway bridge waiting out the storm, they arrive at the farm. It's dark. Syd climbs in the back to retrieve her phone. Not that she's curious, but she might as well check out any pathetic messages the guilty might have left on VM or text. Not that she cares.

There's a message from Mom, but she'll check it out later. About a million texts from Zelda saying she's sorry and she really wanted to tell me, but whatever, blah blah blah. Only one text from Dane saying he'll call her tonight, as if she'll answer. Who cares, anyway, he's only the one dude she ever completely fell for. The one dude she completely connected with. *Fuck him!* And fuck this fucking condition that makes him think of her 'not in that way', or whatever. Whatever excuse he comes up with; we'll see.

Godiva's all yip yip yip at the horses down in the paddock, which is comical since she has no idea what they even are.

Dinosaurs for all she knows. Life through the eyes of a puppy is real life. No one interpreting things for you; just pure *seeing*. She squeezes Godiva like crazy, getting all grooved out on puppy love, which might be the only real love there is. Puppies are reliable. They're there for you when they're not running away.

Hannah's out of the truck and all giddy, jumping and waving to someone barely visible in the barn lights down the hill, Jonah maybe. "Hey!" she says, jumping. "How's everybody?!"

And even with her high-heeled boots on, she tears off for the barn. The paddock is lit, and Syd can make out a little horsie head between the four-board fence—little ears straight up, pointy. The legs are bent and wobbly as she tries them out, even galloping a little. Syd wants to go down there, but she's a little weak and really tired from the trip. She doesn't want her aunt to know exactly how tired she is, though, in case Hannah regrets bringing her down in the first place. Plus her stomach's upset.

She roots through her backpack for her anti-nausea pills. *Zofran, where are you?* Her limbs go cold when all at once she remembers that she forgot them. And not only them but everything. *Oh my God.* What now? She can't go four complete days without her oral meds, can she? Not to mention all the supplements? She grits her teeth. Well, screw it. Yes she can. She can go more than four days. She can go a month. A year. Whatever. She'll probably feel better than she's ever felt taking a little break from that shit. Who says it even works?

"Syd!" calls Hannah from the barn. "Come on down, cookie! Jonah's here! And look..."

Hannah points with both arms to the foal. Syd hobbles down with Godiva on the leash, trying her best not to make a big production of it. Trying to look chill, like she's any normal kid. A kid with a full head of hair. A kid without body aches and joints that work. She tries to act like the meds don't matter, either—whether she has them or she doesn't.

When she gets down to the barn, Hannah's dancing a jig. Syd would give anything to have that much energy, but whatever. She'll have it eventually.

"Syd! Look!" says Hannah, practically singing. "A filly! A beautiful new filly!"

Syd loops Godiva's leash on the fence post, grinning; she can't help it. No matter how bad you feel, you feel good in front of a baby anything. "So I guess she was right," Syd says.

"What?" says Hannah. "Who?"

"You know, Mom's friend? Pandora?"

"Huh?"

"Your newborn baby," says Syd pointing.

Hannah frowns as she drinks this in. But before she can talk, a super handsome dude with curly black hair struts out of the barn without even a jacket on. Just a leather vest over careless denim, like a cool woodsman. Hannah nearly jumps him. "I'm so happy to be home!" she says, hugging him.

Jonah gives her aunt a sort of hug, but not like he's totally into her, which makes Syd sad for Hannah. She obviously still digs him. But this way maybe he'll leave tonight and Syd can have Hannah to herself.

Jonah comes over and gives Syd a gentle hug. "Hey kiddo," he says. "Haven't seen you in a few years, eh? Look at you all grown up. How you been?"

Syd shrugs, leaning against the gate. "Better now that I'm here," she says.

Jonah's face lights up. "And who's this?" he says, headed for Godiva. This makes Syd like him more.

"Godiva," she says.

"Godiva," he repeats, and leans down to pick her up. "Aren't you cute!" Godiva licks his chin, and they all laugh.

"What'll you name the filly?" Syd asks him.

"That's up to Hannah," he says. "It's all hers."

Syd walks over and offers the back of her hand to the filly's mouth, or muzzle as Hannah informs her. She strokes the white blaze that runs all the way from her nose to her black ears. She's so awkward and yet, so beautiful.

"I'm good at names," Syd says.

"Then name her," says Hannah. "Go ahead."

Syd grins. "Yeah?" she says. "Really?"

"Really," says Hannah, nodding. "Whatever you want."

Syd considers this, arms crossed. "Okay. Ireland," she says, not sure why. She turns around. "Is that okay?"

"Well, isn't that a slick name," Jonah says.

"Interesting," says Hannah approvingly. "Why Ireland?"

Syd shrugs. "No reason. Just came to me. I've never been there, but…" She tilts her head up. "I had a dream about it once, I think."

"Ireland it is," says her aunt. "We have to register it, so the name will be a mile long by the time we finish. "But that's what we'll call her—Ireland."

They wander back up the hill to the car. Jonah unloads their suitcases, and when they get inside, Hannah invites him to dinner.

He shakes his head. "No can do, Han. Abandoned everything today for that little Irish filly down there. Have to get back to it." He grins. "But she was worth it. Jimmy's gonna check on her later and I'll be back in the morning. Got some real estate to sell tonight."

Hannah walks him out and Syd can hear her begging. "Come on, Jonah; let me treat you to dinner after all you've done. Please?"

Syd just chuckles because Hannah can't really cook, but Jonah must know that. And even though Syd picked up a million cooking tips from her dad, she's too nauseous and exhausted to eat dinner anyway. She'll take a nap, maybe. Just for a few minutes and be better after that. She sits on the edge of the beautiful bright yellow couch by the window. This must be new. Just the color of it alone cheers her up. Leave it to Aunt Hannah to buy a daffodil yellow couch. She pulls off her sheepskin boots and cuddles into the corner. The next thing she knows, she's back on the cliffs, walking on the long path into a cottage with a big fireplace, and in front of it—a bunch of ladies in robes. It's weird, but in a way, familiar. They catch her when she falls.

Mitsy

MITSY STARES BLANKLY INTO the darkened room. Everyone has abandoned her—her husband, her sister, her own daughter. Even Pandora doesn't answer the phone. She's completely and utterly alone in a vortex of disaster. She sits with this for a moment the way Pandora has taught her. "Sit with your discomfort, Mitsy. *Feel it!* Be okay with it. Learn what it has to teach you." But a thought interrupts this reverie and she cocks her head upward. Did everyone abandon her, she thinks suddenly. Or was it she who abandoned them?

The truth descends like an anvil. Where did it come from? The truth says, "Mitsy Michaels is a fraud." It says Mitsy Michaels has been a fraud her entire life. Even her name is fake. Her real name is 'Mildred' after her paternal grandmother. Who would name a child Mildred? *Mil-dread!* And then nickname her Mitsy? The name Mildred conjures images of an old buxom matron; the name Mitsy—a perennial toddler. Her life has been

126

spent magnetically driven to one pole or the other. Matron or child; child or matron. Which is she today? She's been playing these roles so long she doesn't know anymore. She's a shape-shifter, constantly adjusting herself to suit the needs of others. The only true thing she's ever done is give birth to Sydney Grace.

Thoughts of this child, this powerfully strong, desperately sick child, causes Mitsy's lungs to collapse, her chest to heave, her eyes to blur with grief. Sydney was right; she's been a ter-rible mother. She knows this. Sydney deserved more. Somehow this magical child has been gifted anyway. She's been gifted with grit and force beyond anything Mitsy's weak DNA could have ever endowed. Or Aaron's. She came from somewhere else, some far off planet in a distant galaxy. A place of strength and courage. Her very matter is foreign to Mitsy. Any attempt to mother her was an act. And it didn't help that Aaron was hardly around.

Mitsy's not sure exactly when it happened, the unclenching of this fist of a life, the release of all responsibility to others, to anyone but herself. At first she thought it was a good thing—a brief break from her devastating reality—all those day trips to the clinic, night trips to the ER. The constant pretending that everything was fine; that *she* was fine, when she was not fine. When she was a head-on collision with a tractor-trailer expected to get up, dust herself off, and walk away smiling. Just the utter sham of an idea that she could actually assert herself against Sydney's disease; that she could draw a line the disease couldn't cross. The sham that she is now or ever was in control of anything, including herself. She's nothing but a grenade of compressed emotions, a danger to herself and everyone around her.

Mitsy rubs her temples hard. It doesn't help; nothing helps. She drags herself to the edge of the rumpled mess of a bed. The unraveling began with Aaron, she thinks. When he convinced her to let Hannah help out while he traveled, though Mitsy honestly never thought her sister would actually come. And even if she came, Mitsy never thought she would be much help, just benign company. Someone to talk to, even though they weren't especially close.

But Mitsy did need company. Her heart ached with a loneliness she couldn't name, never mind overcome. When Syd got sick, Mitsy abandoned most of the friendships she'd had in Darien, not that there were many, and not that they were deep. All of her friendships were based on Syd—PTO committees, for instance; class mothers; scout leaders. Aaron was always good at making friends, but not Mitsy. At least not since college.

She gazes slowly around the room, details obscured by the blinds and drapes she'd drawn when Syd left with Hannah earlier today. Another great excuse to bury herself in blankets and pillows. Whether it's a good thing or not for Syd to be gone, Mitsy doesn't know. Once she told Pandora that she didn't know how much longer she could hang on—that there appeared to be no end to the pressure. Mitsy only knew how to be in control. Or rather, how to *pretend* to be in control. But there was no control here, real or pretend. That's when she gave herself to God, or at least to her idea of God. Whether he's actually listening or not, she doesn't know. But Pandora listens. Pandora is her gateway to God. That's why she's got Pandora.

Mitsy drags herself across the room, and forces herself to open the blinds. She needs some light in her cave. Of course there isn't much light outside either. The skies are already dark; storms threaten. Hannah and Syd have been gone for hours now, and no one's even bothered to call her back to let her know they're safe. So maybe they didn't arrive; maybe they aren't safe. But so what? It isn't safe here either. Both ends and everything in between are a death trap. They are all dangling off the roof of a skyscraper in gale force winds. And she's the only one who seems to know it. Her newly revived belief in God aside, she is hopeless, despairing. She falls to her knees and weeps.

However much later it is when she comes up for air, she remembers that she called Aaron earlier, but will he come home? Probably not. And anyway, what good would it do? If she knows one thing it's that Aaron isn't in love with her anymore. Whether he had that affair or not doesn't really matter in the end. He's a good enough man, and he loved her once. When people promise to love each other in good times and bad, they have no idea what they're saying. Can you really promise to love someone who is so depressed they can give you nothing in return? Can you promise to live in an emotional desert forever just to keep someone company, someone who barely knows you're there? That's not love; it's duty. Anyway, the truth is she doesn't love Aaron either. She never did.

She raises herself from her knees against the frame of the antique Biedermeier chair and walks to the gilded full-length mirror on the back wall. She flicks the switch that turns on the overheads, shielding her eyes from the glare. What she sees in the mirror startles her. Her dull, steel gray hair is matted. *When did she last shower?* Her washed-out sweat pants hang loosely and she can barely find herself under the baggy sweatshirt. Her eyes are red, the skin on her face blotchy. She must be a newt or a frog squirming out from under a rock. She feels slimy.

She resolves to get something to eat, until she realizes it would involve leaving the bedroom. Since Aaron left and Hannah took over, Mitsy's been walking steadily backwards from the great outdoors, to the yard, to the house, to the piano in the conservatory, to the kitchen and up the back stairs to her room. All in reverse. She's been hiding in this room for days, if not a week, maybe longer. How would she know? She's been surviving on valium. Something about Hannah's reckless cheer made Mitsy retreat into full alienation. Not that it's Hannah's fault. And anyway, it was Mitsy who invited her in the first place, even if it was Aaron's idea.

A sour odor wafts over her, and she realizes it's coming from her skin. And probably her hair. Not to mention her clothes. She'll force herself to shower; she must. Whether her husband or her daughter returns or not, whether one or the other decides to stay with her or not—she will have to shower eventually. Even if she dies from rot, they will clean her up in the morgue. They will clean her up, dress her in nice clothes, arrange her hair and apply makeup to her face. Death would only improve matters. She sheds her clothes and walks into the shower.

In the shower she remembers an exercise Pandora gave her once. She told Mitsy to close her eyes and imagine herself in the penthouse elevator of a skyscraper. This elevator represents Mitsy in her present life, Pandora said. "Go down very slowly, one floor at a time, stopping at each floor. Each floor represents a life you've lived. Each time you press the button for the next floor down, release the persona of the floor you're on. *See yourself.* See who you were. Then release it."

Mitsy finds this helpful now as the hot water rushes over her. *Shed it!* Shed this lifetime altogether and keep going down "until you reach the truth" is what Pandora had said. "Somewhere along the way you lost it. Somewhere along the way you became someone else."

Mitsy knows she was right.

As she showers, she gains strength of some kind, or maybe it's just the scouring off of the life she's been leading. She scrubs hard with the loofah, scrubs her forearms, legs, her shrunken breasts, her bony hips. She barely recognizes herself so thin. She must have lost ten pounds in the last week alone. *She's got to eat!* But eating will take courage. Eating is a sign of life. And if there's one thing Mitsy is terrified of, it's that.

Afterwards, she towels off and applies lotion to her scaling skin. She deodorizes and sprays, going through all the motions of caring for herself. Of caring *about* herself. All the while in her mind, she descends one floor at a time, searching for herself in the elevator. Searching for a seed of truth.

Down ten or so floors she's reminded of a dream she once had of herself on an island in a cold place somewhere north. On the ocean. Maybe Block Island or somewhere off the coast of Maine. She and other women held hands, formed a ring and danced joyfully around, giving praise to something or other. Or someone. No way to know. Witches or sorcerers, perhaps. It didn't matter. Just the sorority of it all, the friendship, is what gripped her. Even in the dream. There was love among them. She hasn't known intimacy like that in this lifetime at least, maybe more.

She slips into her underwear, but they're huge. It won't do, and probably wouldn't even stay up. She wraps the towel around her and walks on the lush green Persian rug to the threshold, staring into the hall. Into the wilderness. Can she leave the room? Can she do it? Maybe she should just slide into a robe, change her sheets, and go back to bed. That would be progress enough, wouldn't it? She's clean now at least. But in her heart she knows getting clean is not courageous enough. It won't bring Sydney back. Bringing Sydney back will require a much greater degree of risk. She must try. *She wants to try.* Muttering a prayer, she steps deliberately over the threshold and forces herself down the hallway almost robotically, to the guest suite to rummage through Hannah's wardrobe for something that fits.

Hannah's room is a catastrophe. This makes Mitsy nearly laugh out loud. Some things are still predictable. And yet her messy sister can manage to pull herself together enough to take care of Sydney...

The doorbell rings, and Mitsy jumps. *Are they home?* Did they turn around? Or maybe it's Aaron? But why wouldn't he have a house key? She freezes. She needs more time. She's not even dressed. The bell rings again, more persistently. She walks to the front window where she can see an old red sedan parked in the driveway. It must be a mistake. She doesn't know anyone in Darien with a car like that. She steps back to wait it out; surely they'll leave. In the meantime she roots through Hannah's drawers for underwear.

She slips into a pair of white lace panties, not a thong, thank God, and they fit. As does the matching bra. In all of their sibling history Mitsy has never come close to fitting into anything of Hannah's. Hannah was the beauty, and God knows, still is. And she loves *things*. She loves fashion. She has a sense of design that Mitsy never had. Every tiny detail of Mitsy's house was selected by Aaron and the stunning young female designer on whom he himself had personal designs. Not that this issue was ever tackled directly by Mitsy or Aaron. How could it be? With all that was going on with Sydney, it was just too threatening.

The doorbell rings again and again. She ignores it, although it's getting under her skin, raising her anxiety. If it keeps up she'll need more valium, but she doesn't want the valium. She doesn't want it ever again, plus it's all the way across the house in her bedroom. While the bell keeps ringing, she finds a pair of jeans, pulls them on, zips and buttons. Oh my God, they fit! Now she hears knocking—*bam bam bam*! Relentless knocking accompanied by a man's voice, though she can't make out what he's shouting. In the closet she finds a sweater—soft, rose-colored cashmere. She slips it on. She ignores the pile of boxes and bags of whatever, everywhere on the floor of the huge walk-in closet—shoes and purses and clothing never worn. More than Mitsy could manage to purchase in a decade.

The knocking doesn't end. She runs a comb mechanically through her short wet hair and walks slowly downstairs. Maybe something's happened. Something terrible. Hasn't she been expecting such a thing for years? Maybe it's here. *Finally!* Once it's here, she can lay her body down and die in peace. The thought grips her and it's all she can do not to crawl back to her room.

"Syd, come on, open up!" says the voice.

Syd? *What?* Mitsy holds her breath. She can do this for Sydney. She hesitates at the door then unlocks it. Ahead of her is a tall attractive young man with wild black hair, black eyes, and brownish skin. A chiseled physique.

"Can I help you?" she says.

"Oh, hey," he says. "I'm um, my name is Dane, and I'm a uh, friend of you know, Zelda. Zelda Rodriguez? And also Syd." He shuffles back and forth on the stone stoop, looking down. "I'm in the band."

"Sydney has a band?" says Mitsy, incredulous.

He scratches the back of his head. "Yeah, kind of. And we had a disagreement sort of, I don't know. But I have to talk to her." He looks up and around. "Is she home?"

Mitsy blinks. "Will you come in?"

He nods nervously and enters.

As Mitsy closes the door, she says, "Unfortunately, Sydney is on her way to Virginia. She's probably there by now."

"Oh. What, with her aunt? With Hannah?"

Mitsy freezes. "You know Hannah?"

"Yeah sure. Met her a few times over at Z's place. Who are you?"

"Who am I?" Mitsy blinks back tears. *Who am I?* "Well, actually, I'm the uh, the mother."

"Syd's mother?" he says.

It feels like a lie, but she says, "Yes."

His eyes widen. "Oh."

"Did she talk about me?"

He shakes his head. "Not really. But you know, I haven't really known her a long time. We just moved here a few months ago." He smiles, "But we talk a lot, you know? On the phone. And we text. She's a great kid. Very wise. And smart, real smart."

Mitsy nods absently.

"I texted her a bunch today, but she's not picking up. I didn't know she was going to Virginia. I'm supposed to be in Pennsylvania myself."

"Supposed to be?"

"Winter break. But I canceled the trip. I um, I just…" He scratches his head again. "I disappointed her, and I feel bad. Terrible, really. I need to…I don't know, talk to her, but she's pissed. She won't pickup."

Mitsy stares at him. "Is that your car?" she asks.

He turns. "Yeah. That's mine."

"You have a license?"

"Uh, yeah, sure. Of course. I wouldn't drive…"

"What did you do to upset her?" Mitsy says.

He shakes his head. "I just…it was all a big mistake is all. I want to tell her; I want to be honest. But she won't pick up. You have to be honest to the people who matter."

"I see."

"It's not a good time in her life to lose friends," he says. "Or mine—in my life. I need her too."

"Are you sick?" she says.

"What? No. No, I'm not."

Mitsy doesn't know what comes over her. "Will you drive me down to see her?"

"To Virginia?" he chirps, wide-eyed.

"Yes," she says. "Right now. We can take my car."

His head juts forward in disbelief. "Seriously?"

"Yes. I just have to get some boots."

"Hell yeah!" he says, excited, then throttles back. "But... why? Right now, I mean. Why now? You know...with me?"

Mitsy looks up at the cathedral ceiling to the skylight where the moon's already risen. "Because," she says, "I disappointed her, too."

He jiggles his keys, hesitating. "I'll go, of course," he says. "But she might not want to see me. Just so you know."

"She might not want to see me either," Mitsy says as she heads toward the kitchen for her boots.

Pandora

SHE PLACES HER RIGHT hand an inch or so above the top of her coarse, braided hair and holds it there for a minute to stabilize her crown chakra which is starting to pickup empath static from one insane source or another. Probably Mitsy's chronic negative vibe, she thinks, which is like putting your tongue in a live socket. She reaches for her cigarette pack with her left hand, taps it down and pulls one out with her teeth.

She'd like to stop smoking, and fully intends to put the brakes on this little joy ride, but not yet. What she found on the easel last night was too upsetting. And not just upsetting to her—but to Guru also, who arched his back and screeched like an owl before running his claws down the back of the couch. He did so much damage to the corduroy fabric she would have chased him outside if she'd had the wherewithal. But after seeing the painting, she was practically asphyxiated with shock. Guru was only expressing what she could not.

136

She'd pulled the linen drape back over the canvas so fast she can barely remember what she saw. But not really. It was Elysha, *but not Elysha*. And the wings—had she painted the wings? She has no memory of it. And so faded; all of it so... faded, nearly devoid of color. Not just devoid as in a mere absence. Devoid in a way that suggested something had sucked the life right out of it from behind the canvas. Every time she thinks she understands the mystical world, something new comes along and kicks her in the ass. To show her how small she is, she supposes, how insignificant. But where does it end? Every mystic has her limits. At least this one does.

She drives the freakish image from her mind like a serpent. *Be gone, illusion!* Or what she hopes was an illusion. Or maybe she never painted what she thought she'd painted in the first place. It's been a long time. *Thirty years.*

Lighting the cigarette finally, she takes a long thoughtful drag, smoothing the crease on her gold, ankle-length, wrap-around Indian print skirt. But then again, she knows what she painted. She painted a portrait of Elysha before she was injured. She abandoned the painting to care for the actual child. But it was a whiplash of a demise, so not much caretaking all in all. *So fast!* Now you see her; now you don't. And no matter what Pandora did, what healing techniques she employed, she got nowhere healing the injury that erased her daughter from view.

Unlike others who have passed over before and since, Pandora has never seen Elysha in her mystical travels. She's been searching for years. You'd think she would have seen her own daughter, seer of the nether regions as she is, but no. Things that weaken us are actually intended to make us stronger, Pandora knows. We have a choice to accept the challenge or not. Or at least that's what she tells her clients. But it hasn't worked for her. Elysha's death weakened her without a doubt, and she's never really recovered. The truth is she's not interested in getting stronger, now or ever. Anyway, in the mystical world, your opponent grows with you. The bigger you are, the bigger the obstacles. Pandora has had enough opposition for a lifetime.

After Elysha died, Pandora abandoned artistic endeavors of every kind—her beloved oils, watercolors, pastels, textiles, pottery, even the wall frescoes she'd been creating for local merchants. And she hasn't returned to any of it since. Neighbors and villagers sometimes ask her about it; even try to commission work, which is why she doesn't socialize. Not that she's the type. What in the world would she talk about? *Particles and waves? Ha!* She throws her head back in a hearty laugh. Ahh, now that feels good!

God, she is so removed.

If she has the psychic strength, she'll revisit the painting later on to confirm what she hopes was a hallucination. After all, she was more than a little out of it last night, as evidenced by her residual shaky crown chakra this afternoon, for one thing. Whether the misalignment was caused by her own bad habits, astral travel, someone or other's negative energy, or the new world order, doesn't really matter. The effect is the same. Her balance is off; her chakras distorted. No hashish for her tonight, or even wine.

Well, maybe wine; she'll see. One or the other has to go. Or should go. She needs to be sane and in control since everything around her appears to be unraveling in unprecedented ways. Ways ordinary people would not ever be able to process or even ascertain. *Wake up, people!* She takes another long drag then squashes the cigarette in the ashtray while she exhales through her nose like the fire dragon she is. That is, if you go by Chinese astrology. She's tempted to go back to the easel, but she won't, not yet. She has a blog to write, and it's long overdue. Not that she's in the best frame of mind to write a blog, but if she cops another look under that drape her frame of mind will be as disjointed as everything else in her life. She might as well write.

Snuggled into her favorite thick, hand-knit red woolen socks, she shuffles across the house to her office, looking casually for her phone along the way. It's nowhere so far. She lost track of it last night, so it's no doubt out of juice and undetectable. So be it. She could use some time without the distraction, anyway. At her desk, she dumps a pile of Raisinets into a small bowl of hammered copper handed down to her from one Peruvian ancestor or another. This gives her the idea to write about ancestral energy, or what she likes to call *Energetic DNA,* since it sounds more erudite. She types frantically between exquisite bites of chewy chocolate raisins, elaborating on the kind of energetic code that likes to circle the body template like a swarm of bees—ours to accept or refuse. But just the idea of anyone contracting a diseased condition out of sheer ignorance when they could easily have refused the energy, galls her. It galls her because in many cases ignorance is passively deliberate. It's a choice. She's had it with ignorant people.

"This code is handed down ancestrally to those too stupid to know what they're taking on," she types madly. *"Dad's tendency to injure his head, for example, or Mom's nervous tics. Even complex diseases. Some conditions and behaviors are caused by physical DNA, of course, but some are not. Some are caused by energy left behind by imbecilic or ill-intentioned ancestors. To be clear, the energy is NOT the ancestor, just energy that was attached to that ancestor's spirit in its lifetime. Energy cannot be destroyed, so it continues on this plane seeking to attach itself symbiotically to a new host. This host is usually a relative with*

compatible weaknesses—(i.e., equal stupidity). If the host wakes up to this reality, understands and believes it, s/he can drive the symbiotic energy away. Crisis averted."

She finishes the first draft and re-reads it, placing the cursor tentatively over the words '*stupid*' and '*imbecilic*' and all derivatives, briefly reconsidering. The tone is a tad harsh, she has to admit. But right now she can't think of equivalent words with less bite, so she lets it go. And anyway, at this stage of the game, why shouldn't she tell it like it is? Time is tight. Don't people understand that? *No, they don't.* Human destiny is jerked between the so-called experts who rely exclusively on the linear material plane for information and those who give it up to God without taking any responsibility whatsoever for their own endowed power. *Power endowed by God!* Pandora has had it with all of them. *She is so burned-out!* If no one sets this straight, humanity is screwed. She digs through her desk drawer for a miniature Snicker's but only finds a Milky Way. She unwraps it and pops it in her mouth, finding the lack of caramel and nuts insufferable.

By the time she finishes the blog, it's nearly four o'clock and she hasn't even been outside yet. Hasn't eaten anything but chocolate, either, not that she has any regrets. The powder blue sky has dimmed to dove gray. She wanders into the kitchen and gazes through the sliding glass doors to the patio. A late winter flurry settles like Spanish lace on the pine boughs outside. She never tires of this. Nature is all she needs. Nature and the occasional Snicker's bar.

A few more logs on the fire and she's set. A few more logs and a glass of chardonnay, and her planet is back on its axis. Simple pleasures. Staring out at the lake, she sucks its glacial refreshment in like a mental margarita. Bliss! But then. Her eyes narrow...*what?!* She grabs her glasses from the counter because...*what is that?* Her attention is drawn upward. She steps closer to the door, focusing intently on the distant sky over Heavenly Peak.

The sky surrounding the peak looks...wired. Magnetic. A swirling lava lamp of colors and hues she's never seen or imagined. Brand new, unnamed colors. Where did they come from? *Why are they here?* Keeping her eyes on the spectacle, she pulls her tribal shawl down from the door hook and slips into the fleece slippers next to Guru's feeding station. When she steps out onto the deck, Guru jumps from somewhere in the forest abyss onto the railing which he traverses full length before turning and retracing his steps. And then repeats.

Wrapping the shawl around her, she blurts, "Scarlet Rave!" naming the magnetic red. Then "Zeon Blue!" The names just come to her.

Guru shoots down onto the table, stiffening. She can see how affected he is by the atmospheric change that hovers over the mountain like a storm of liquid light, spreading outward. Dripping, swirling electric yellows and greens, and then this color she's never seen before...a new primary, perhaps. Not red or blue or anything familiar, really, just...what is it? Where did it come from?

"*Eldra,*" she hears in her head. "*The color is Eldra.*" She's never seen anything like it, and wonders if Guru sees it too. Color is her specialty; she's an artist. Or at least she was. *But this!* She knows the eye needs cone cells to interpret color, to decipher one color from the next. But is this a new color? Or have her eyes grown new cones? Have everyone's?

She steadies her hands against her sides. They sting with vibration. The particles around her are charged, the nap of her energetic field pulled taut by the storm. She is in full, almost painful, focus. Are her poles in danger of being reversed? It feels that way. Is everyone in danger? *The Earth itself?* She wants to ask Anjah, not because she wants to see him; she doesn't. But he might be the only entity in the entire multiverse who knows a damn thing about this phenomenon. Sometimes things turn so bizarre you're happy to see anyone at all with half an answer or a random guess. It's not as if she has colleagues. Hers is a lonely profession.

As soon as she thinks of Anjah, she wishes she hadn't. She turns and hustles inside for cigarette ammo to chase the possibility of him away. Just the brief mention of his name can bring him down, she knows. He doesn't require much encouragement. Hands shaking, she lights a smoke before she returns to the deck, just in case. But it doesn't matter. By the time she returns to the patio he's already materialized in the southern sky. She spots him in the distance from the corner of her right eye. He was practically here before she thought of him, anticipating it. He rides a flume of the deepest violet light she's ever seen. *Colors are changing! Transforming!* He stops shy of the patio, a hovercraft. Guru swipes the purple air.

"You're wasting time," Anjah pulses.

She holds tight, defiantly inhaling the cigarette to neutralize his effect.

"You have less than a month," he says.

She exhales right at him, interrupting his rhythm. He skips a beat.

"The colors are for you," he signals. "But that's all I can do without your cooperation."

She scowls, thinking, *the colors are for me? Why me?*

But in this world, thinking is speaking. In response to her interior thought, he spins an aurora so vivid it makes the Northern Lights look like a 40 watt bulb.

"Sooner or later you'll understand," he says.

She points her cigarette directly at the magnetic storm and shakes her head, her body still agitated from the charge. "You're trying to kill me, Anjah, aren't you? You're trying to electrocute me for smoking a few cigarettes."

"I'm giving you what you need to do your job," he says, "in spite of the cigarettes." He spins the new primary—*eldra*—over his field like a top.

"Show-off," she says. "I don't need your fancy new crayons. I don't even need plain old blue and red. Take it back, all of it! I haven't painted in twenty years. The last thing I need is a new color."

She turns toward the door. It's cold out here and she's uncomfortable. And anyway, who needs this shit? But as she lays her hand against the sliding glass door, all at once—she gets it. Oh my God, she gets it! *Signal!* Her jaw drops; her eyes widen, and she turns her head back toward Anjah. But he's gone. The vivid colors spin in his wake as he jettisons upward and out.

Pandora remains on the deck for awhile, stunned. Her back turned against the glass doors now, she looks through the trees in the direction of Heavenly Peak. The cigarette between her fingers is burned to the filter. She holds it up to the falling snow until the ash sizzles, thinking—*color has signal*—specific and powerful. It has frequency. Frequency that can heal. But how does she apprehend it? How does she snatch a slice of high-fidelity megawatt signal from another realm and pin it to the material plane until it sticks—*to make it actually work?*

This is her job. Whether she does it or not, whether she even wants to do it, is entirely up to her, she knows. What she may never know is who might be depending on this exact information. An obscure but faith-filled creature, perhaps, hoping beyond reason for a miracle—*this* miracle.

Sydney.

She shivers at the thought. Yes, maybe Sydney. *Probably* Sydney. Not that Pandora knows exactly which color to use, what it would do, or how to retrieve it. Or if she even has the psychic strength to try.

Well, she's not doing anything this minute. The aurora isn't even visible anymore; it disappeared with Anjah. For all she knows, it was just another in a long line of hallucinations. *But not really.* Right now she has to return to the canvas. She needs to settle one issue at a time, once and for all. Should she keep the canvas and try to understand the optics—both on the painting and in the sky? *Are they connected?* Or should she just throw the damn thing in the fire and watch it burn? She's stuck. She doesn't know.

She just doesn't know.

Back in the kitchen, she pours a glass of chardonnay to the rim and sips it down so it won't spill in transit. She carries it through the open kitchen past her office into the back, then to the right toward the living room. At the easel, she touches the edge of the deteriorating linen cover with her free hand, lifting it just barely then dropping it. And again. *And again.*

Damn it, she just cannot look, at least not now. Witnessing it again is a commitment to understand it. *To do something about it.* Witnessing it means she has to use her spiritual aspects to harness its meaning. Witnessing it means she has to harness the meaning and transform it. The only thing she's in the mood to transform this very minute is her utterly irritating sobriety.

She hears Anjah's warning in her head. *"You have less than a month. You're wasting time."* She doesn't particularly care about her own time, but she cares about Sydney's. Why exactly, she couldn't say. But maybe this canvas will give her a clue that will help the one child who needs her. The one who still lives.

Then again maybe it won't.

She places her glass on the window ledge of the western wall and instead of uncovering the canvas, opens the palette of colors she'd blended all those years ago. The lovely creams, chocolates, and roses. The joyful hibiscus and commanding cobalt blue. The paints have dried from exposure, of course, but they're recognizable. She doesn't have to guess what they are. The tangy fragrance of linseed oil still permeates the palette. How she loves that smell! How she misses it. Reluctantly, she slides the palette back into the easel shelf and walks away.

At the fireplace she bends low, carefully stacking wood and kindling which she lights with a long match. The fire animates the hearth, and her eyes search the flames for answers. She returns to the couch, settling deep into the corner and staring ahead. She sees the aurora in the flames—a storm of violet and magenta which, though exquisite, pales in comparison to the palette Anjah teased her with this afternoon. He knows color is her master, even now. Color has frequency; color has signal. *New colors have new frequency!* New signal.

She tucks her legs underneath her and allows the flames to carry her thoughts. The colors in Anjah's aurora were brilliant, she thinks. Dense and malleable, nearly liquid. The particles were charged. Her roaming thoughts seek connection anywhere in the field. Color is light with different wavelengths, she thinks. Colors are waves. She sips her wine.

It all gets back to waves.

Mitsy

"NO OFFENSE, MRS. MICHAELS, but if you keep screaming like that I won't be able to drive. It's late, and my nerves are a little fried."

Mitsy burrows into her seat, her right foot poised to hit her virtual brake if she needs to. Every time Dane passes a car, never mind a semi-trailer, she has a panic attack. "I'm sorry," she says. "I haven't been out of the house in awhile."

"That's cool."

"And I don't even know the last time anyone drove me anywhere."

He glances at her sympathetically.

"Don't do that," she says.

"Don't...?"

"Don't look at me!" she snaps. "You're supposed to be looking at the road!"

"No one's on the road right now," he says evenly. "Just us."

"Well, maybe now. But at any moment..."

A sedan whizzes by on the right.

"See!" she screeches. "See what I mean?" She checks her seatbelt, pulling it taut.

The index finger of his right hand taps the wheel. "Maybe we should turn around," he says.

"No!" Mitsy switches to her deeper, more commanding voice. If they turn around she's pretty sure she'll never leave the house again. They've been gone almost two hours. She can't afford to squander that kind of progress. She hesitates, gathering her humility like sharp little tacks. "I'm sorry," she says quietly. "I can be a pain. Just ask Sydney."

"Yeah," he says, chuckling. "I know."

"What?" she says. "What's that supposed to mean? I thought she hadn't mentioned me to you. Isn't that what you said?" She folds her arms tightly.

"Oh," he says. "Right."

"Well, did she or didn't she?"

He tips his head to the left, stroking his scruffy chin. "She um...she mentioned you once or twice," he says, shrugging. "But nothing significant. Just the usual mother stuff."

"The usual mother stuff?" she says. "Like 'she never comes out of her room all day'? That kind of stuff?" Mitsy doesn't know what's gotten into her; all this confrontation isn't like her. She feels completely out of control in a new way. Like a wild hibernating bear must feel waking up in a zoo.

"Sure," he says, "I mean, look...Syd and I didn't really talk about other people. We talked about...life. And not even talk so much as email and text. But I'd feel pretty shitty if I betrayed her confidence." He shifts positions. "I'm in enough trouble with her already."

He has a nice profile, Mitsy thinks. His pile of dark curly

148 REA NOLAN MARTIN

hair practically reaches the top of the car, and he has a strong jaw. His black eyes are a little disturbing in the dark, though— hard to see. She understands why Sydney is attracted to him, even though he has no pedigree whatsoever. Not to mention a foreign look that can't be trusted. He's nobody she would pick for her daughter.

"It's not that you're a pain," he says, glancing at her again. "It's just that I'm not sure this is a good idea in the first place. Not you, but me. Chasing her down, I mean. She left for a reason. She's, you know...pissed." He turns toward her, shrugging.

"The road?" she says, pointing. She's trying to tone it down, but it's not easy. After all, what is she doing? No one even knows where she is. Or cares, she thinks. No one even cares.

"She's *really* pissed," he repeats with emphasis.

Mitsy leans forward and turns the heat up to 75. She should have worn her heavy jacket. She's lost too much weight too quickly, and she has a terrible chill. "You weren't the reason Sydney left," she says, "unless you had your little disagreement yesterday."

"No," he says, "it was today. Just before she took off, I guess."

Mitsy raises her chin nobly. "She was angry at me first then. I'm the one who's ruining her life."

He frowns. "Nah," he says. "She's pissed at the disease."

"The..."

"The *disease*," he interrupts. "Don't tell me what it is. She doesn't want me to know. She doesn't want to give it any power. I agree with her."

"You do?" says Mitsy, surprised. "I do too! My psychic told me not to ever *ever* even *think* the name." She moves her hands in wide circles. "Just visualize light all around her. I do it every day. A hundred times a day!"

"That's awesome," he says. "You're a good mom."

She gasps. If only it were true! But it would be impolite to correct him, so she lets it go. An SUV filled with college-aged girls slowly passes on the right, grabbing her focus. All of them healthy, laughing, glowing. Big heads of thick, long hair.

"The power of words," he says.

This surprises her also. Just that he knows the power of words without a mystic mentor even telling him. Mitsy wouldn't have known that at his age. Or really, any age. Not without being told.

"She's an indigo babe," he says, grinning. "I knew it right away."

Mitsy's eyes widen. "An indigo babe?"

"Yeah, you know, an advanced creature of the fourth way."

"The fourth way?"

"Well, just…Gurdjieff? The philosopher? Inner freedom and all that?"

Mitsy's had enough of people talking gibberish to her. Even though she could certainly use some inner freedom herself, she has no intention of learning anything tonight. She needs to settle down, is what she needs. Get comfortable. "Do you mind if I turn the radio on?" she says, clicking the button to her oldies station.

"Sure. Whatever you like."

A few minutes later he raises his voice over Aretha Franklin's 'R-E-S-P-E-C-T!' saying, "Not a big Gurdjieff fan, eh Mrs. M?"

She heaves an exasperated sigh. He looked like the strong silent type. If she thought he was a talker she would never have asked him to drive her all the way to Virginia.

"What about Nietzsche?" he says. "A very cool dude. Now there was a thinker."

If she doesn't engage, maybe he'll stop.

Snowflakes have been hitting the windshield sporadically, then steadily, and now all at once. "Turn on the wipers," she says.

He futzes around trying to find them.

"Over here; right there!" she says in a shrill voice.

"Got it," he says. "Hey now, relax. I swear I won't kill us."

"How do I know you won't kill us?" she shrieks. "I barely know you!"

He turns, scowling. "I'm not going to kill us," he says tightly.

"For God's sake!" she says, "Pay attention to the road!" She flicks off the music. "Concentrate. It's dangerous out there!"

A few minutes later he says, "I don't see us getting too far like this."

"Sorry," she mutters. "I've lost my manners again."

"No, I mean...yes...*that*. But also..." he waves his hand at the windshield, "...*this!*" The snow is picking up speed; all at once sleet pounds the hood.

"We're not stopping," she says. "I have to see Sydney. If you want to get out, go ahead. I'll drive there myself."

He just keeps driving silently, so...mission accomplished. Clearly her earlier complaints had the intended impact, since he's now driving under the speed limit with both hands on the wheel in what is an increasingly steady snow with intermittent sleet. As far as she's concerned, the silence makes it bearable. At least the boy can focus, and she can concentrate on her meditations to decrease her nearly insurmountable anxiety. She chants OM as quietly as she can from the back of her throat. She's afraid to go into full meditation mode, since she doesn't want to fall asleep, or even into a trance. She doesn't trust his driving without her constant vigilance.

Hours later, somewhere in south Jersey, the snow turns into a full-on blizzard. Skid marks surround them and several sedans are sidelined from spin-outs. Huge trucks barrel onward, scaring the hell out of anyone with a nervous system. Mitsy clenches the sides of the seat, unsure of her next move. She wants to get to

Virginia to reclaim the daughter that won't answer her phone. Pandora is also a phone defector, but Mitsy knows Pandora will surface again. After all, Mitsy is a paying client, and Pandora seems to care a great deal about her. Or Sydney, maybe, but either way. Thank God there's no emergency though, because no one who can help her is on deck.

Lights blink ahead of them, and a giant spotlight shows a pattern of orange cones directing them to the exit.

"What's this?" she says.

Police lights flash on top of the state trooper vehicles, warning them to slow down. As they get closer, they're channeled into a single lane.

"What in the world is going on!" Mitsy says.

"Looks like they're closing the highway," says Dane.

Sure enough, down the line all vehicles are being directed to the exit by troopers in fluorescent jackets waving giant flashlights.

"What do we do now!" Mitsy screeches.

He shrugs. "We get some gas, I guess. I could use a food break, too. I'll check my phone and figure another way down there."

Mitsy glances at her watch. It's nearly midnight. "We have to stop," she says. "Overnight."

He scowls.

"I'm sorry," she says, "but it will take us forever at this rate. Plus it's super dangerous." She stares at him, as if just noticing he's in his teens. "Does your mother even know you're here?"

"I don't have a mom," he says. "And my dad is dropping my kid sister off in Pennsylvania to visit our cousins for the break. So, no worries."

"Phew!" she says aloud. "I mean, I wouldn't want you to get in trouble on my account."

He shakes his head. "We're pretty independent in my house, Mrs. M. As in unsupervised," he says with a sardonic laugh.

Since his independence suits her at the moment, she doesn't comment, just files it away for future reference. However, just for the record, she does not want Sydney hanging out with an unsupervised male. "I'll get you a nice room and you can rest up," she says, reaching under the dash for her purse. She fishes around in the dark, under the seat and behind it before she realizes she didn't bring one. *She left without it!* She left without her purse, her license, her *money* and her clothes. That's how long it's been since she'd held herself responsible for...really, anything. Thank God she remembered her phone!

"Uh..."

"What?" he says as he merges the car into the single exit lane. "Something the matter?"

"Did you bring a wallet?" she asks.

"Yeah. Of course. I have a wallet." He frowns at her. "I'll be happy to pay my own way, Mrs. M, if that's what you're getting at."

She shimmies uncomfortably. "No, it's just that I, uh. Well, I forgot my purse, Dane." She swallows hard. "I have no money. I brought no money."

He exits the turnpike, his eyes wide. "That so," he says. "Well, then the room won't be so great, but I can probably swing one."

"One?" she says. "Don't you have a credit card?"

"It has a $500 limit," he says, "and this baby's gonna take a lot of gas to get us to Virginia."

"Oh dear," says Mitsy. "I just didn't think this through, did I?" She wrings her hands. "What will we do? We have at least another four hours on this drive, and that's if the weather cooperates."

"Hey!" he says, pointing. "Look there! A Super 8!"

"What? Oh. Well." She steadies her trembling chin. "I've never stayed in anything like that," she says as evenly as she can.

"We'll be lucky to get any room at this point," says Dane, drawing closer. "Lots of cars already pulling in."

Mitsy debates calling Hannah or Aaron to phone in a reservation with their credit cards. But she doesn't want to give anyone the heads-up on their decision to visit Sydney. And anyway, like Dane said earlier, Sydney may reject them both if she knows they're coming. No, she doesn't feel like informing anyone. It's an adventure. A hideous, terrifying adventure. And it's too late to turn back.

Dane drives into the Super 8 parking lot and pulls over to the side. "Stay here," he says. "I have to jump ahead of the rest of these guys if we want a room."

"Well, not one room," she says. "Right? Two?"

"We'll see, Mrs. M. Depends on what they have and how much they cost."

While Dane's in the reception office, Mitsy tries Pandora again to no avail. *What has she done with her phone?* Or maybe she's ignoring Mitsy on purpose. Not that Pandora would offer much practical help in a situation like this, but you never know. She might be wealthy, or at least able to lend Mitsy her credit card for an emergency. But anyway, no luck.

She starts a rosary, using her fingers, which are cold at the tips since the car's turned off to conserve gas. She wishes she'd brought gloves. At this point, though, she's just lucky she's dressed. And not just dressed, but dressed in Hannah's expensive clothes. She was really a mess this afternoon. Not just this afternoon, but for weeks, if she's honest. She recites a couple of *Hail Mary's* praying for financial intervention when Dane knocks on her window nearly giving her a heart attack. "Aaaaaaa!" she screams.

He jumps back. "Hey, sorry. Just want you to know we got a room, and it's the last one they have. We can keep looking if you want."

"One room?" she says, lowering the window. "Just one?"

"Yeah," he says, dancing from one foot to the other in the frigid air. "But the guy says the other motels around here are also full-up. They're sending folks to him."

"Well, then how is it they have a room left for us?" she asks.

He shrugs. "Dumb luck, I guess."

"We better take it," she says.

"Good! Because I gave the guy my card." He climbs back in and drives them around the L-shaped building to the back entrance and parks. "M'lady," he says gallantly opening her car door.

Mitsy is a wreck. She can't believe she has to share a room in a Super 8 Motel with a foreign teenage boy. A complete stranger! But what choice does she have?

Dane leads her up the stairs to the top floor of the two story building. He slips the key in the door of # 210 and holds it open for her. "Oh, I forgot to tell you, the guy says there's a bit of a leak in the roof. But he said it's not a big deal, and anyway he gave us a 20% break, so we can probably afford to split a bagel in the morning."

Mitsy enters suspiciously, looking upward. Nothing apparent, but the room has a damp, musty odor, and there are brown spots on a few of the ceiling tiles. "We'll make do," she says tentatively.

"That a girl," says Dane. His hand sweeps the garish blue room presentation style. "Which bed would you like?"

"Have I said I can't believe this?" she asks. "Because I can't believe this." She gives him a worried look, and sees that he can't even look her in the eye.

"No offense, Mrs. M, but I can't believe it more than you can't believe it."

After a minute, she points to the twin bed nearest the stripped down bathroom. "Okay, I'll take that one," she says. She doesn't want to have to pass his bed every time she has to urinate, which is generally quite a lot at night.

They take turns in the bathroom and then lie down on their respective beds. Mitsy's skin is crawling with just the idea of fleas and bedbugs, not to mention lice. No sooner does he flick the overhead light switch next to his bed then the ceiling tile begins to drip, steadily spilling water on the floor between their beds.

"Hey, Mrs. M," he says.

She wants to pretend she's asleep, but no one could sleep through this. "What?"

"You gotta laugh, right?" He starts cracking-up, nearly convulsing, which gets her laughing for the first time in so many years she can't count.

Ten minutes later she says, "Okay, Dane, that's enough. This isn't a fraternity house." She rolls over, covers her head with the pillow, and shuts down. Tomorrow is another day as Scarlet O'Hara aptly put it in the middle of a war. And if this isn't a war, she doesn't know what is.

Hannah

HANNAH IS HAPPY TO be home, but she'd be a lot happier if Jonah were more welcoming. Not that he's unwelcoming, per se, but he's welcoming in a stand-offish way that brings out the needy Hannah instead of the impish, fun Hannah capable of winning him back. He probably knows that. That's probably why he's doing it. He probably secretly loves the needy Hannah. Needy Hannah needs him. Or maybe he doesn't love the needy Hannah. Maybe he loves the independent Hannah who can take care of herself. *Who's that?* She's been gone so long she can't remember which Hannah she is when she's with him and which one she's not.

She sips the tall Dunkin' deep roast she picked up this morning along with a box of crullers and Boston cream donuts which are on the kitchen counter. At some point, depending on how long she stays, she might have to find the time to actually shop for food, but not today. On the other hand, if Jonah agrees to stay for dinner, she'll find the time. But what would she cook? Just the idea of it freaks her out. But why should it? She certainly picked up plenty of pointers from her efforts in Darien. She's not a complete nincompoop. So maybe a tuna casserole? Meatloaf? Tacos? Oh my God, she's so indecisive. Just thinking about all that cooking exhausts her. And anyway, who says he's even staying.

On the bright side, the sky is all big, open, and cornflower blue. There's not a flake of snow on the ground. In their stead, tiny white snowdrop flowers are sprouting everywhere. Compared to Connecticut, spring comes a month or so earlier here, though it doesn't always stay. Sometimes it reverts, so you have to savor the day, which is exactly what Hannah's doing. She absorbs the heat of the full sun as it enters the picture window, spreading in a wide arc past her yellow couch to the center of the room and back out to the rolling fields. It's so inspiring. Inspiring but not perfectly *perfect*.

It would be perfectly perfect if she could plop the Michaels' Darien chateau, complete with all its delicious architectural and interior flourishes, right on top of this exact hill. Dream house on dream property. Why can't she have both? Who says she can't? If she publishes...*when* she publishes...her book, or *when* she gets back with Jonah (or both!)—her dream mansion on her dream plot will be spare change.

"Hey," says Syd behind her.

Hannah jumps. "Whoa, you startled me! Those quiet little cat feet of yours!" She's just glad her coffee's half gone so it didn't spill all over her new heather-blue angora tunic and sleek black leggings.

Syd, on the other hand, isn't wearing anything sleek. She's drowning in gray jersey pants with a purple tee-shirt, lost in their slouchiness. Mitsy's had too much subliminal fashion influence on this child. Godiva darts out playfully from behind Syd, but Syd's not playing. She moves slowly.

Hannah says, "I'll let her out."

"Thanks," says Syd, yawning. "I'd still be asleep if she hadn't jumped all over me."

"Ooo," says Hannah. "Better not let momzy know she slept on your bed."

Syd nods unenthusiastically.

"You okay, cookie?" Hannah asks.

Syd nods, yawning again. "Just tired. Weird dreams. Somewhere, I don't know, on a big vineyard."

"A vineyard, wow! Sign me up for that dream. Mine was on some crazy cliff in a smoky house in the smelly middle ages."

"What?" says Syd.

"My dream. The middle ..."

"No, no, just...I've been there, too."

"That's funny," says Hannah grinning. "I didn't see you."

"Yeah. I don't know," says Syd. "Just...weirdly familiar."

"If only they hadn't met on the Irish Sea..." says Hannah for no reason. She's never even been to the Irish Sea, and couldn't point to it on a map if you offered to pay her entire debt in exchange for the right answer. Although obviously it's near Ireland. If an Irish Sea even exists.

"That's it," says Syd, wide-eyed. "The Irish Sea."

Hannah sips her coffee, thinking. "Is that why you named the filly Ireland?"

Syd shakes her head groggily, wanders over to the couch and drops. "I don't know why I named her that," she mutters. She curls into the corner of the couch, knees to chest. "You need more furniture in here," she says.

"Working on that," says Hannah. She lays her cardboard coffee cup on the jelly cabinet sideboard and cinches the belt of her tunic. "Go treat yourself to a Boston cream donut," she says. "That'll wake you up." She herds Godiva through the kitchen to the mudroom. The pup is confused by the new floor plan, so Hannah keeps leaning down, nudging her forward. "Be right back," she calls back to Syd.

Hannah is not so secretly hoping to see Jonah pass by on his way into the village. He's showing the old Johnston estate this morning, she thinks...or wants to think, since that would take him right past the farm. Best to be visible from the road, ready and waving. She got up at 6AM so she'd be presentable whenever he passed by, or better yet, stopped by. She wants to prove she's a reformed woman, an early riser liberated from her previous lazy habits. Not that she ever thought of herself as lazy, but he does.

And then of course she'll have to initiate that awkward conversation with Aaron today, when she delivers the oral bill for all her hard work and dedication. Fair is fair. Of course if she had her own money she'd have taken care of Syd for free, but she doesn't. She needs the money. Facts are facts. And Jonah won't believe a word Hannah says if she hasn't paid all her bills, or at least made a dent in them. He doesn't get the fact that her plunge into irresponsibility was a result of her depression over his departure. Or maybe her plunge came first, she can't remember. There were too many plunges. At any rate, Jonah's departure certainly didn't improve things.

At the door, Godiva jumps into the matted winter grass and pees a downhill river. Her nose points to the paddock, where the filly throws her magnificent sable head back and neighs. Godiva's whole body tenses, her ears piqued. Just in case she tries anything funny, Hannah reaches back into the mudroom for boots. The dewy hill would be a sliding board in these slippers, and with her luck Jonah would drive by at the exact moment she landed on her ass. Although, in that case maybe he'd come running? But no, she reminds herself, the idea is to prove she's responsible. Falling on her ass on purpose would have suited the old Hannah, but not the new one. No more helpless maiden. Maybe.

She keeps her eyes on the pup as she pulls a piece of rope from a hook on the outside wall. The last thing she needs is another big chase. She slips the rope around Godiva's head like a noose. "Gotcha," she says.

Godiva squirms uncomfortably, keeping her eyes on the horses. She delivers a deep throaty bark, "Rrrrruffff!"

"Whoa, not very ladylike," Hannah says, chuckling. "But okay, let's take a stroll to the barn, shall we?"

On her way down the slope, Hannah thinks maybe she'll set her novel in fourteenth century Ireland, not that she knows anything about it, but she can always Google. And after all, she has had the odd dream about it, if it even was Ireland. How would she know? As she walks, she feeds story threads through her mental spinning wheel. She imagines the whole scene wherever it is...*wait*. She stops mid-hill. What was that noise? She turns back toward the house. Huh.

She's probably hearing things. But what if it was Jonah? What if he parked in the driving circle on the other side of the house and walked through the front door? She waits, listening for his voice, but hears nothing. But would she hear from this distance through closed windows? Probably not, which just proves she's hearing things in the first place. Her phone rings, and she pulls it out of her pocket. Shit, it's Aaron. She hesitates, gathering enough moxy to confront him.

"Hello, Aaron," she says, continuing down to the paddock.

"Hey, Hannah. Just checking on things down there."

"Oh, I thought you were calling to yell at me again."

He sighs. "Come on, I didn't yell. You did."

An old green truck chugs up the dirt road, and she cranes her neck to see if it's Jonah. Not that he owns an old green truck, and not that he'd be coming from that direction.

"Maybe I did," she says. "But you deserved it."

"So are things okay?" he says. "Syd doesn't answer. Everybody safe and sound?"

"We're great," she says. "Couldn't be better. Woke up to a smoky sunrise and a perfect spring day. And oh yeah, give a hearty welcome to our latest family member, Ireland. A filly."

"Ireland, eh? Great name."

"Syd named her. Of course her registered name will be a mile long, but that's what we'll call her."

"Love it! So all's well?"

"Perfect."

"Good, because not only does Syd not answer her phone, but Mitsy doesn't either. Two strikes."

"What?" says Hannah, confused. "You didn't fly home last night?" Godiva pulls hard, yanking, and Hannah slides on the wet grass, her arms akimbo. "Oh my God!" she says, and the phone jumps out of her hand. She gathers her balance by leaning forward, planting her feet firmly on the ground. She's not going to fall. But it was close. She pulls Godiva in the direction of the phone, reaching for it in the grass. "Hello?" she says. "Sorry, Godiva dragged me down the hill. She's getting quite large. Did you have any idea how large she would be when you got her?"

"I didn't fly home last night," he says. "Airports were closed."

"Oh. But you tried?"

"Uh huh. I'll get out of here sometime today, hopefully. Departures are really backed-up, so I don't know when. But to repeat…Mitsy doesn't answer her phone."

Hannah shrugs. "What else is new? Look, I need to discuss money, as unpleasant as that may be for both of us."

"So you're not worried about Mitsy?"

"Not as worried as I am about getting paid."

There's a long pause followed by, "Okay."

Hannah hears shrill laughter in the background. "Are you on a sales call?" she says. "Or with somebody?"

"Yeah, sorry. In the hotel lobby, but go ahead. You need money. How much?"

Down at the paddock now, she leans against the four-board fence admiring the newly baptized Ireland—her long awkward legs and the flirty white forelock between her ears. This filly is going to pay her way, Hannah thinks—*knows*. She's gorgeous!

"Hannah? How much?" he repeats.

"Well, what do you think is fair?" she says coyly.

"Whatever you think is fair," he says. "You've been fantastic. A Godsend. I wish you would move in with us."

"By which I assume you mean Mitsy and Syd," she says. "Since you're never there."

No response.

"Anyway, I'm in a bit of a temporary pinch," she says casually. "So I could use, oh I don't know, $10,000 to start?" She grits her teeth.

He coughs, which turns into a coughing jag, which doesn't give her any confidence. Maybe she should have started with $5,000 and worked up.

"To start?" he says with a rasp.

"Things have been tough," she says. "But it's temporary. I'm writing a book. A prize-winner."

"Hannah, are you in trouble? Confess. What's the real number?"

"Jonah's probably moving back in, so it isn't what it sounds like. It's just been difficult to manage…"

"What's the number?"

She turns, resting her back against the fence. Godiva busily digs a hole in front of her. "Fifty grand off the top, but then there are all the repairs..."

"Holy crap."

"I only asked for ten thousand, Aaron. And...I earned it."

"That would be $2,500 a week, not that I'm going to argue."

She grins into the wind. "You're not?" She dances a little two-step.

"No, but that's a pretty steep stipend going forward. Is that what you discussed with Mitsy when you signed on?"

"No. When I signed on I didn't have time to think straight. You all seemed so desperate I was only concerned with helping out." She pauses. "I would appreciate it if you would not share this with your wife, Aaron. She can be a bit critical if you haven't noticed."

She turns toward the barn, placing her right boot on the bottom fence board, leaning in. He doesn't respond, so she says, "Aaron? Are you there?"

"I'm here," he says. Moments later, he says, "I'll give you whatever you need, including the repairs, if you move in with Mitsy and Syd for a year."

"What? *A year?* Are you insane? That's an eternity."

"I know, but...Hannah, listen. You've lived with her for the last month; you know how it is. I can't stay. I just...I can't take anymore."

"What?! What are you saying?!" she says, nearly choking. "And don't forget I have Jonah to think about."

"I'm saying...I don't know. The decision is killing me. Don't think it's been easy. It's been hell." He hesitates. "And don't tell Syd."

"Don't tell Syd what?" she says. "That you're...divorcing

her mother! Is that what you're saying? And don't you think she'll notice!"

"No...yes, of course, but I just need some time to sort out the details. And I'm not saying the D word yet. I have to...I just...I need time. And space. When it's time, I'll tell Syd myself. I don't know. I'm just...so confused."

"I'm not moving in for an entire year, Aaron. You can't abandon your own child."

"I'm not abandoning her, Hannah. I adore her, for God's sake. This..."

"Don't name it."

"Fine, this *thing* is killing me. Us. It's killing all of us. I don't even recognize Mitsy anymore..."

Hannah lowers her voice to a growl. "Sydney comes first, Aaron. I'll do what I can, but you're her father. All I can promise for now is to continue on with the same arrangement until I'm needed back home permanently." Although, she thinks, a couple hundred grand, which is what it really amounts to with all the repairs, is a pretty damn good salary for a year's work. *And no more debt!* "I'm not giving you a blanket no, though," she says. "I'll consider it."

"Thanks," he says quietly.

She turns back toward the house, distracted by a noise. *Oh my God, there's...Jonah!* All six feet two of him waving enthusiastically. "Gotta go," she says, waving back while making haste up the hill with Godiva.

"Promise you won't say anything to Syd," Aaron says. "Swear?"

"Whatever," she says, ending the call. Anyway, she can't have a dead serious conversation like this with her...well, *employer* practically, when she can barely think straight. Jonah's here! She slows herself down to a casual walk, leaning down to casually pat the dog's head, not wanting to seem overly eager. Just...wandering up to say hello. This is going to be a great day, she already knows. She practically has to dig a hole and bury herself to keep from floating.

"Hurry!" hollers Jonah.

"Hey, did you drive in the front?" she yells up, smiling. That sound she heard must have been his car door slamming. "I didn't see you driving up the hill."

"Yes. But hurry!" he yells.

All at once sirens blast behind her. She barely turns to look when an ambulance passes to her left in a dirt cloud, followed by a police car. Probably their crazy stoned-out neighbor, Dirk, shot himself in the foot again, she thinks.

But no. The ambulance wheels into her driveway, and Jonah rushes to meet it. *What?* There must be some mistake. *Wrong driveway!* Hannah freezes. Then reality strikes and she breaks into a run pulling Godiva, who howls along with the siren.

Jonah disappears into the house with one of the medics. The other two follow with a stretcher.

"Oh my God," Hannah says under her breath. "Oh my God!" It can't be Syd, she thinks. *Don't tell me it's Syd.* Though she didn't look well this morning; it's true. But still, she was walking, talking. *Oh my God!* She stumbles up the two cement steps into the mudroom, where she releases Godiva. Her heart pounding, she follows the commotion through the kitchen into the living room. Syd is stretched out on the couch, ashen. The medic takes her vitals.

"Pulse is extremely elevated," he reports. "Blood pressure too."

Hannah steps around Jonah and sits on the foot of the couch, rubbing Syd's leg. "Are you okay, cookie?" she whispers. "What happened?"

Syd opens her eyes slowly. "I'm...okay," she mutters.

Jonah steps closer. "I found her on the kitchen floor, passed out."

"I was just getting a donut," Syd practically whispers.

"They have to know her history, Hannah," says Jonah.

Hannah reaches into her back pocket for her phone. "I'll get Mitsy," she says. "Or Aaron. Aaron says Mitsy isn't answering." She looks at him frantically and he lays his heavy hands on her shoulders, grounding her. "No, wait...the clinic," she says. "I'll call the clinic and let them speak directly to the doctors. That way..." She pulls her phone out of her pocket and fumbles with the contact button. That way, she thinks, she won't break her promise to Syd never to speak or even think the name.

"Don't leave, Aunt Hannah," Syd mumbles.

Tears pool in Hannah's eyes, blurring her focus. She hands the phone to Jonah. "Here's the number," she says, shaking. "Can you make the call? I'll um...I'll stay with Syd."

Jonah nods reassuringly and walks into the kitchen to make the call. Hannah is overwhelmed with gratitude. She knows she has to call Aaron and at least try to get Mitsy, but she can't do it yet. She has to collect herself. Or maybe Jonah will call them, too. Maybe he'll fill in where she can't.

"I have to get her to the hospital," the medic says abruptly.

Hannah watches in wide-eyed disbelief as they lift Syd onto the stretcher. Hannah's hands cover her open mouth and her heart beats so fast she's surprised she's not on a stretcher herself. Suddenly nothing else matters. If anything happens to this child, she thinks, I won't survive. This child is as much mine as anybody's. The realization strikes her like lightning. She's electrocuted.

Somehow she makes it to the driveway, where she climbs into the back of the ambulance. She holds onto Syd's leg, kissing it repeatedly through the thin blanket. "I'm here, cookie," she says. "I'm here. Hang on, sweet pea. Hang on."

Syd mumbles something, and Hannah leans closer. "What, sweet pea? Did you say something?"

"Name a place," she says. "Ask me about a place."

"Oh!" Hannah whispers. "The game. But you're not...this is not...anesthesia."

Syd struggles. "Name..."

"Italy," says Hannah quickly. Tears spill down her cheeks. She leans forward and strokes Syd's bald head. "Italy," she repeats. "Anywhere in Italy, how's that?"

Syd smiles; her head turns limply.

"Is she okay?" Hannah asks the medic, swallowing the words. She pulls his sleeve. "Is she okay?"

He nods. "I'm working on it."

Outside, Jonah hands her phone to the driver. "This is her doctor at the clinic," he says. "He'll fill you in." He turns to Hannah. "I'll meet you down there," he says as they slam the doors behind her.

"Oxygen!" commands the paramedic. "We're losing her."

Sirens wail.

Sydney

SHE STANDS ALONE IN a stone grotto, shielded from the spring rain. Tiny, evenly-spaced shoots dot the expansive hills like splashes of green paint against tall brown stakes as far as the eye can see. A brisk wind blows the skirt of her gray muslin tunic and she crosses her arms for warmth. When will they allow her back? She wants to tell them "Tuscany" when they ask, or more specifically, "Gaiole", not that they would recognize that name, or that she would even remember it. But that's the word carved into the stone block at the vineyard entrance—*Gaiole*. She doesn't want to place too much stress on herself to remember though. This is all stressful enough.

Usually when she plays the game she's an observer, a visitor from Connecticut. She hasn't really had a body on any previous trips, or at least not one as heavy as this. On the other trips, she was all energy and light. She touches her face, pokes her cheeks. Yes, this body feels different, more permanent, but

168

she can't be sure. Her senses are definitely more alert. Her vision is vivid. The rain smells like fresh linen. The grotto smells earthy like the root cellar under the carriage house on the back of Hannah's farm.

Sydney thinks her other body is in Connecticut right now. Or is it Virginia? Yes, that's it, though she barely remembers how she got all the way down there from her home. She hasn't been there long, she knows that. She was there, and now she's here. She narrows her eyes, thinking hard. They put her out. Or she passed out, whichever. When she wakes up she has to tell them where she went. She sighs deeply. How will she remember all of this?

She runs her fingers over her flaxen hair, woven in a thick braid that runs half the length of her back. It has heft. This pleases her. She hasn't had hair in a long time. She wants to unbraid it and shake it out and *feel* it. But she isn't sure how long she'll be here or if other people will think her loose hair is odd and inappropriate. The hair on the few female passers-by is bound and hidden under cowls, scarves and hoods. Best not to draw too much attention to herself.

Her hair pleases her as does the fresh scent of jasmine, which is surprising, since she has no memory of encountering this scent before. There's no jasmine in Connecticut that she knows of, at least not wild. Yet this place seems familiar in an inexplicable, ancient kind of way. The rain abates, and she steps out of the grotto in her rope sandals, spreading her arms like wings. *She knows things.* She knows things about Tuscany that she shouldn't know. When she came to Tuscany with her parents before she got sick, they went to Florence, but not this village. Not Gaiole. Yet this part of Tuscany is more familiar to her than Florence was in every way—recorded in her body, almost. Cellular.

The countryside is breathtaking, invigorating. She whirls around, feeling life force within her. *Feeling strong.* The strength is so empowering she doesn't want it to end. She hasn't felt this strong in a long time. If she goes back, will she feel this strong? *Does she have to go back?*

In the distance, a small stone house is built into the hill. A woman, also in a gray robe, walks briskly up the dirt path in the other direction, carrying a water bucket. Two other women bow their heads in conversation at the doorway. Everything is slow and peaceful. Falcons sweep the lower fields. Close to the house, a rooster pecks the grass, raises his head and crows. Buttercups and wild mustard peek from crannies along the length of the stone wall. Syd doesn't really know why, but she might want to stay. She's somehow connected here. The only thing that's missing is her family.

The shower ends and the sun blazes through a passing cloud. A burst of violet light flashes in the corner of her left eye, drawing her sight up to the now azure blue sky. On the horizon, the violet light pulsates anxiously, demanding her attention. She has to think, but then it comes to her. Oh no, she thinks, *The Taker.*

She reevaluates her situation. The Taker is here to take her, she remembers. But she can't remember where he wants her to go. Or why. She might be losing her memory or her resolve. She's supposed to fly away, but she's too solid. She can't lift off. So she should fight him, she knows, but she doesn't feel like fighting anyone. Will he take her from here? Or has he already taken her and left her here? She squints into the brilliant sun, her right hand a visor against the radiant glare. His purple halo is denser than she remembers. The Taker has all the light. She's a heavy mass, no match for him right now. Even though this body feels stronger than her real body, her light is nearly gone.

From her standing position, Syd tries to inhale the light that surrounds her, but it isn't working. The warmth doesn't penetrate. She can't breathe it in. She's too solid. Behind The Taker she sees a rainbow made of an explosion of colors she's never seen. The colors arrest her. She can't look anywhere else. Exquisite colors she can't even name are emblazoned on the sky in an arc. She looks down at her drab cassock then back up to the electric aurora. She wants the color. *She needs the color.* Something tells her that if she doesn't get the color, she'll disappear. She reaches up, but nothing happens. She tries to spring off a nearby stone—to launch herself into the sky—but she's a hunk of steel. Gravity clings to her like a magnet.

A gong sounds, and she turns to her right. In the doorway, a woman strikes the metal slab with a rod, calling a name she doesn't know. Is it Italian? It sounds like Alicia. The way she says it, "A-lis-i-a," like a song, is so musical. Syd likes the name, but it isn't hers. She studies the scene to see when Alicia will appear. She doesn't. Syd's kind of hungry, actually. If it didn't mean explaining herself, she wouldn't mind sharing a meal with the women. Hunger is one more thing she never experienced in her other lucid dreams. She steps toward the house, then remembers the rainbow and turns back.

The colors are gone.

Pandora

PANDORA'S HEAD JERKS AND she awakens with a start. Her rheumy eyes widen, staring ahead, and she pulls herself slowly upward on the couch. Oh my God, she thinks, not the couch again. Well, she can't blame her vagabond sleeping entirely on the hashish or cabernet. Or was it vodka last night? She rubs her head. It's not the anesthetics, really, that keep her there; it's the mesmerizing fire. Unless fire is an anesthetic. She leans forward, sighing deeply. It probably is.

The truth is she seeks answers, not anesthesia. She seeks insight through twists of consciousness illuminating answers from new directions. The dancing flames speak to her. She seeks truth from the alluring reds and oranges, the piercing white and the penetrating blue of the burning wood. Why blue, she's always wondered. Blue is cool, not warm. How does a red hot fire produce a cool blue flame at its center? It seems unnatural, and yet like so many secrets of the universe, it isn't. Yin and yang are often contained in the same object, but we don't see it until it's in a state of separation. Until it's broken.

She rubs her sticky eyes and draws Guru onto her lap. "I need your help," she tells him, scratching his neck. He purrs. "We need to clean up our act, little buddha. We need to clean it up fast."

Pandora stretches her long brown arms and elegant piano fingers into the air, articulating them like a dancer. She rises slowly. It's true she needs to clean up her act, she thinks, but how? How will she do it? How will she end all this lovely non-sense—all the wallowing, the luxurious casting about in a vast sea of unknowing? *It's over.* There can be no more unknowing, only knowing. *Quantum knowing.* There's not a crack of room for doubt. Just thinking about it generates anxiety in her belly, and she's...afraid. The great and powerful Pandora is afraid! Her spirit is surrounded with the very information she needs. She reaches out with both hands, grabbing the air. *It's right there!* But she's too burned-out to retrieve it.

The information hangs on her spirit like fishing weights—*sinkers.* She is sinking. She can only ignore it so long, but she's not ready to examine it yet. Or process it. Or feel its significance. Something about this time, this process, *this* information, is radically different from anything previous. Nevertheless the download has initiated, and she knows it.

"Damn you, Anjah," she says aloud. "You think it's easy to draw the infinite into the material? To give it form? *To define it!* Well, it isn't. It's hell!" She picks a burgundy-stained wine glass from the glass-top side table as she passes by, and pitches it across the room. It smashes against the white tiled kitchen wall into shards. "*You* do it, Anjah, damn it!" she whimpers. "You bloody well try to do what I do."

Spent, she shuffles into the kitchen to clean up the broken

glass before Guru treads through it. It's a chore; life is a chore. Fuck it all. She swallows two aspirin with a cup of standing water and begins the coffee prep. She should be drinking green tea, she knows, but deep down she feels as if the time to rebuild may have passed. She may actually have blown it. A sickening feeling courses through her. *I may actually have blown it.* Something tells her she's blown it before, that this is not the first time, though the details aren't clear. She fills the carafe with tap water and pours it into the reservoir. Just to get to the point where she can think straight, she needs the caffeine. She can stop it later, maybe, when she has a plan. *She needs a plan.* To get to the plan, she needs caffeine.

While the coffee brews, she picks Guru's hair from her black leotard top; tries to brush it off her wrinkled skirt, but it sticks. It's everywhere. She needs to clean up. She needs to shower and clean up the house. What am I still doing in yesterday's clothes? she thinks. I'm disgusting.

She pours coffee into her earthen mug, shakes cinnamon over it and scans the room for her phone. Not here. She must have left it on the couch. She realizes she hasn't seen it in a while, and wonders if it's even charged. To think that she once made her living by phone is a staggering thought. If it weren't for Sydney Michaels she would happily never use that contraption again.

In the living room, she lays her coffee on one of the end tables and digs under the oversized corduroy cushions where she finds too many things—a purple wide-toothed comb, a crushed cigarette, a crumbled cracker. She pulls the cushions entirely off the couch to reveal all the archeological artifacts at once.

Ah! The phone! She pulls it out of the crease and brings it across the room to the sideboard where she plugs it into the charger. Checking her voicemail—oh my God, Mitsy has called her five, six, seven, eight…fifteen times! She checks the text messages, only one. *Sydney has gone to Virginia with Hannah,* it says. Huh, thinks Pandora. Well, that's hardly worth four alarms. Good for Sydney! Good for Hannah, too, for taking her. So maybe that's it. Maybe the thrall of anxiety Pandora's feeling isn't hers after all. Maybe it's Mitsy's. Mitsy all alone and missing her daughter. Well, screw it, Pandora thinks. Mitsy needs to be alone. She needs to be alone to figure out who she is underneath all that sediment. Pandora will give her a call later on.

She replaces the cushions and stares down at the pile of paraphernalia on the varnished burl coffee table. The sour stench of creosote chokes the air. She opens a window, allowing a burst of fresh pine into the room. The air invigorates her, emboldens her. She takes her coffee and walks to the easel, staring. Breathing deeply, she stares at the stained linen cover. She sips her coffee, thinking, I can do this. I can figure this out. She snaps the cloth from the canvas and forces herself to look, to stand there and look for as long as it takes.

The paint is faded. *She will not leave!* The paint has faded significantly since the other night when she first viewed the painting. So it's happening. Elysha's spirit is fading by the day, so much so that it no longer resembles Elysha. Or does it? It no longer resembles the Elysha of Pandora's memory. That Elysha was strong, elegant, and as blue-eyed as a Siamese cat. That Elysha had sheets of silk black hair draped over her shoulders and down her back. That Elysha did not have a tattoo. That Elysha was not bald. *Bald!*

Pandora's stomach churns. Is Elysha trying to tell her something? Pandora hasn't seen her child anywhere in any realm since the day she died. *What are you telling me, baby?* She strokes the canvas with her index finger. *Are you in there? Are you leaving me a message?* Or just leaving me?

The phone rings, startling her. Coffee jumps out of the mug. She steadies herself and walks to the sideboard to see who it is. It's Mitsy, of course. She doesn't want to deal with Mitsy yet, but she probably should. She knows the painting and Mitsy and Hannah and all of them are inextricably connected somehow. She knows she's known this for some time, but has no idea what to do with the information. But now she has to face it. She looks frantically around for cigarettes. She can't talk to Mitsy without one. Look what I've done, she thinks. I've gone and got myself addicted. She's allowed herself to become weak, and now what? What will happen now? She turns back to the painting. Is it an illusion, or is it fading before her eyes?

It's fading before her eyes.

She accepts the call while rooting through the drawer for a smoke. "Hello, Mitsy" she says. "Hold on a second." She grabs one, lights it, and inhales the smoke, freezing the last moment of unknowing. Capturing it.

"How can I help you?"

Mitsy

"PANDORA?" SAYS MITSY. "IS it you? Where have you been? It isn't you, is it? You sound exactly like your voicemail. It's your voicemail isn't it?"

"It's me," says Pandora. "Flesh and blood. I lost my phone, but as you can tell, it's been located."

"Well, I'm in Virginia," Mitsy says frantically. She points to a fork in the country road. "Turn there," she whispers to Dane. "To the right."

"What?" says Pandora. "You're breaking up."

"I SAID I'M IN VIR-GIN-IA," Mitsy pronounces loudly and with exaggerated articulation. "VIR-GIN..."

"Got it," says Pandora. "How did you get there?"

"I drove."

After a pause, Pandora says, "Well, that's amazing, Mitsy Michaels. Kudos to you. I'm impressed—you driving all the way down to Virginia? Huh."

"I came to see Sydney," says Mitsy. "To surprise her. She came down here with Hannah for a few days against my better judgment, not that I gave them permission. I emphatically did not. But I, um..." she chokes up, "after they left, I...I realized I haven't...I don't know, Pandora. I just haven't been the best mother."

After a lengthy pause, Pandora says, "Wow, Mitsy, this really is progress."

"Oh my God you nearly killed that pig!" Mitsy shrieks.

"Excuse me?" says Pandora.

"Oh, not you," says Mitsy. "Dane. Uh, rather me...I. I almost killed a pig. Driving."

"What the hell is a pig doing in the road?" says Dane. "A fucking pig!" He smacks the steering wheel and belly laughs. "Pigs are awesome! Look at that porker!"

"What's going on?" says Pandora.

"Nothing," says Mitsy. "Just...a pig."

"I'm not seeing you behind the steering wheel," Pandora says. "I'm not getting that image."

"Oh," says Mitsy. "Well...we're switching. We just switched."

"Have you seen Sydney?" Pandora asks.

Mitsy detects anxiety in her mentor's voice, which helps her forget the blatant lie she just told. "Why?" she asks Pandora. "Are you sensing a problem? Are your sources telling you there's a problem? Do you *see* a problem?"

"Don't play games with me, Mitsy. I see whatever I see from here, but you're right there. Are you saying nothing's up, or that you just haven't seen your daughter yet?"

"You're making me nervous," Mitsy says.

"Answer my question."

"Okay, well, no, nothing's up that I know of, and no, I haven't seen her yet. Two no's."

After an uncomfortable pause, Pandora says, "Then why did you call?"

"You can't pass a tractor on a narrow dirt road!" Mitsy screeches. "Do you know how dangerous that is?!"

"I have to, Mrs. M," says Dane. "The dude is moving an inch an hour."

"Country courtesy," Mitsy hisses. "Farmer's etiquette, Dane. Have some goddamn patience!"

"Mitsy?" says Pandora. "Hello? Why did you call me?"

"I don't know," Mitsy says. "I just...I hadn't talked to you in a while, and if I'm truthful, yes, I suppose I have some separation anxiety."

"Mitsy?" Pandora says. "Are you there? Hello? Mitsy?"

The phone goes dead.

"Damn!" says Mitsy. "The signal is terrible here!" She slams her phone on the center console behind the tissues. "What the hell!"

"Well, it is the country," Dane says. "Fucking pigs and whatever. E-I-E-I-O."

"You should watch your language, young man. Show some respect."

He turns, narrowing his eyes, "But..."

Mitsy says, "We're right up this hill, Dane... Hey, what's your last name anyway?"

"Lazur," he says. "It's Czech. We're Czech, Armenian and Sicilian. A real smorgasbord."

"Smorgasbords are Swedish," says Mitsy. "Oh my God, we're here!" Her hand flies to her chest as she points up a steep dirt road. "Right there about half a mile up." She shakes her head in disbelief. "It's been so long since I've been home—a decade, maybe more. I can't believe I'm here!"

"Home?" Dane says.

"This is where Hannah and I were born," she says. "Where I learned to ride..." The words catch in her throat.

"Ride what?"

"Horses," she says.

"Whoa. Can't picture that, Mrs. M."

He drives a few more yards, pulls the car over, shifts into park, and gets out.

"What are you doing?" says Mitsy. "We're almost home. Get back in the car!"

"I'm not going. I'll walk to town and get a bus or something."

Mitsy casts about wildly, outraged. "What are you talking about? You drove all the way here! Less than a mile and we're there!"

He nods. "Yeah, well. I've done some crazy shit in my life, believe me, but this takes the cake."

She freezes; he means it. "I can't go there without you, Dane," she says.

"No offense, Mrs. M, but you have to. If I go I might freak Syd out for good. Small chance she'll forgive me eventually, but not if I force it."

"But how will I get to the top of the hill?"

"Drive?" he says, shrugging. "It's your car. You must've driven it before."

"Well, yes, but."

"Sorry, Mrs. M. You were good enough company, I guess, not that I want to share another motel room with you or anything. But I have to find a way home."

"If you just drop me at the farm, I can let you have the car," she pleads. "Can't you just drive me the last mile?" Even after coming all this way, she knows she can't drive. Not yet. Maybe not ever. She looks down at her lap, at Hannah's designer dark wash jeans. Everything else is a mess—she didn't even get a shower this morning—no water!—but the jeans are still crisp and fitted. She's ridiculously grateful for this pittance.

He turns, staring into the brown scrub that borders the dirt road. There's a fluttering inside and a quail emerges, teetering across the road like a cartoon.

"Hey look at that!" he says, delighted. He furrows his thick eyebrows. "What the hell is it?"

"It's a quail," says Mitsy as pleasantly as she can. "There are quite a few of them around here." Maybe he'll relent, she thinks. If he likes quails. *Oh please, relent!*

A car pulls up behind them.

Mitsy leans over the console so she doesn't raise her voice. "Get in," she says with authority. "That car needs to pass." *Get in and drive me one more frigging mile!*

Behind them, a man sticks his head out the car window. "Got some trouble?" he asks in a deep, familiar voice.

Mitsy puts her head down. Oh my God, she thinks, it's Jonah. At least it sounds like Jonah. *Oh my God, oh my God.* What has she done, exposing herself like this?

Jonah gets out of the car. Or maybe it's not Jonah. She turns quickly. No, it's Jonah.

"Do you need a hand?" he says, leaning down. He studies her through the window. "Mitsy?" he says, perplexed. "Mitsy, is that you?"

She stares down at her quilted black boots, the long legs of her jeans stuffed haphazardly in the shafts. Even in these trendy pants she is one big fashion don't.

He knocks on the window. "Can you open this?" he says, and waits until she's lowered the window. He places his hands on the window frame. "I can't believe you got here so fast. How did you know? Hannah said you weren't answering the phone." He checks his watch, frowning quizzically. "But how could you make it down here in three hours? Did you fly? Is this a rental?"

Mitsy finally turns toward him. "Know what?" she says.

"You mean...you don't know? You didn't talk to Hannah?"

She shakes her head, slowly but surely seizing with fear. *What is he talking about?!* She doesn't want to know.

Jonah steps to his right, peering over the hood of the car at Dane. "You drove her here?" he says.

Dane nods.

"Well, is the um...is the car okay? Why are you standing in the middle of the road?"

"I just...I'm leaving from here," he says. "Hitching a ride to whatever wheels will get me back to Connecticut." He nods at Jonah. "Not to be rude, sir, but who are you?"

"Sorry," Jonah says. He steps to the right, leans over the hood and extends a hand. "I'm Syd's uncle. Sort of."

Dane accepts the gesture graciously. "Dane," he says. "Friend of Syd's." He shrugs. "Sort of."

Jonah looks back toward Mitsy. "Why don't we all just go up to the house and talk?" He raises his chin at Dane. "You, too," he says.

Dane shakes his head vehemently. "No, not me, sir. Syd's not ready to see me yet. She hasn't answered a single text. I'm heading home."

Jonah shifts his weight from side to side. "Syd's, uh...she's not at the house right now."

"Where is she?" demands Mitsy.

He waves toward the hill in the direction of the house. "How about I fill you in up there?" He nods at Dane. "You, too, buddy. Don't worry; we'll get you a ride home one way or the other."

Jonah's expression brokers no compromise. So imposing,

Mitsy thinks. She never noticed this quality in him before. And it works because Dane obeys and slides reluctantly back into the car. *Thank God!* Her attachment to this adolescent is inexplicable.

"She better not be there," Dane says. "I'm not kidding. She means a bunch to me and..."

"She's not there," Mitsy snaps. "Something's wrong; can't you tell? You seemed like such a smart young man at first."

Dane shifts the gear into drive and accelerates, kicking up some dirt. Neither one speaks as they follow the winding dirt road uphill past acres of undulating pasture and white four-board fencing. "Where is she?" he finally says. "What do you think..."

"I don't know," she says, quivering. "I honestly don't know."

Still driving, he reaches over and grabs her hand, holds it on top of the tissue box on the center console, his eyes looking ahead at the road. "It's ok, Mrs. M," he says. "Whatever it is, it'll be ok. Don't give up. You gotta believe."

Mitsy's eyes well up. It's been so long since anyone's considered her feelings that she barely knows how to respond. Everyone's just so damn busy telling her to buck up and get over herself. *But how?!!* How does one do that when one's daughter is...

Dane leaves his hand right there, gripping hers. It gives her strength. "There's the house," she says, pointing to the right.

"Wow," he says. "This place is just...holy shit! Some kind of Shangri-La!"

"It is, isn't it?" Misty says. She looks at him pleadingly. "Please stay?" All at once tears stream down her face. "Please, Dane?" Her chest is racked with grief. "I beg you."

Hannah

HANNAH PACES BACK AND forth in the sterile black and white hall as they transfuse her niece in a nearby hospital room. Bulging bags of burgundy-red blood are emptied into the fragile veins of the magnificent but fragile Sydney Michaels. Hannah wants to know whose blood it is. Whose blood is worthy of those veins? For instance, did it come from a drunken slob who needed the cash? Or did it come from a church lady? How many infections was it tested for? There are probably plenty of infections they don't even know about. Hideous new infections from sexually deviant perverts who tripped past the blood bank on their way to the liquor store. *Where does it all end!* What inventive new torture is God hiding up his omnipotent sleeve to spring on them next? If s/he's even watching at all.

It's all Hannah can do not to lose her mind. Is she crazy, or is it slowly leaking out, thought by crazy thought? That's what it feels like. She places her hands on either side of her head to hold it in. But then again, why would she want to hold onto the toxic swill swimming around in her head right now? She paces. And paces! Pacing helps her collect her thoughts, to sort them out. *To choose the worst ones possible to dwell on!* The physical act of pacing somehow helps to remind her that she has to *keep-it-together.* That if she doesn't, Syd will have no one at all. Hannah is *it.* Hannah is all that's left.

A bespeckled, white-coated female oncologist from this morning's team walks purposefully down the hall toward Hannah. A fresh-faced, twenty-something dark-haired man with a clipboard accompanies her. Hannah gets a bad vibe from just...you name it, their general attitude. She turns her head. She doesn't want to talk to anyone. *This is not her job!* She's here to give Syd a break from the dreary medical stuff. *Where the hell are the child's parents!* She turns her back to the duo. Maybe they're headed for another room.

"Mrs. Michaels?" says the doctor.

Hannah flips around. "No," she says. "Not Mrs. Michaels. I'm Hannah Chandler, as I said earlier."

The doctor checks her notes. "Sorry," she says, then raises her chin, smiling efficiently. "Mrs. Chandler." Her curly brown hair is clipped back in a sloppy chignon. She looks about fifty—either that or she's been up all night. "I'm Dr. Blanca."

Hannah nods noncommittally. *I don't care who you are! Don't talk to me!*

"I see that your name is on the list here," says the doctor. She looks up. "I'm allowed to inform you of Sydney's condition."

"I'm her aunt," Hannah says. She runs her thumbs back and forth against her index fingers. "I'm just here...to...to..."

"I understand this is difficult," says the doctor. "But we have information, and the parents aren't here. And you already signed for the transfusion, after all."

"But that was an emergency," says Hannah. "Right? So are you telling me there's another emergency?"

"I'd rather not have this conversation in the hallway, Mrs. Chandler. I've called her parents and they haven't returned my calls yet. It would be most useful for Sydney to have an informed advocate at her side."

Hannah strokes her chin, her cheeks, her neck. She nods almost uncontrollably. "I see. I, uh...I...okay then..."

To Hannah's left, a nurse sticks her head out the door of Syd's room. "She's awake now," she says.

"She's awake!" says Hannah. "Can I see her?"

"Of course," says the nurse. She looks at the doctor. "Unless..."

The doctor nods. Her phone rings. She pulls it out of the hip pocket of her white coat and checks the number. "It's a 203 area code," she says.

"That's Connecticut," Hannah says almost jubilantly. "That's probably her mother. Hooray! You can talk to her mother, and I can go inside to talk to my Goddaughter undisturbed."

The doctor holds up her index finger, mouthing 'hold on' to Hannah, then says "Hello?" into the phone. Hannah keeps going. She's halfway into Syd's room when she hears the doctor say, "Oh, yes, Mr. Michaels, thank you for returning my call. This is Dr. Blanca."

So, Aaron must be home, Hannah thinks. *Finally!* Thank God. How did she become mother and father to this child, anyway? She never signed up to become another parent to Syd. She signed up to give Syd a trap door, a way out. She takes a second to recover her composure before parting the curtain.

"Hey cookie," she says. "How are you feeling?"

Syd has more color. Or, Hannah should say, she has *some* color. Only now that her cheeks are pink does Hannah realize how pasty white she'd become. But why me? she thinks. Why not the doctors at the clinic? Couldn't they tell she was anemic?

Syd's lids pop open. She reaches out with her left hand. "Aunt Hannah," she says groggily. "Thank God you're here."

Hannah slides into the seat next to the bed and clutches Syd's hand. "Of course I'm here, cookie. Where else would I be?" She kisses Syd's white-knuckled fist.

"What happened?" Syd says. She points to the intravenous in her left arm. "Why was my blood count so low?"

"Well, that's something we'll have to discuss with the doctors. We have plenty of time for that."

Syd frowns. "They're not going to make me go back home, are they?" She shakes her head. "I don't want to, Aunt Hannah. I want to stay on the farm. I can't get well at home." She stares pleadingly. "I can't."

Hannah pats her hand. "We'll see."

Syd grimaces, cocking her head to the left as if searching for something. "What was the question?" she says. "What did you ask me?"

"What?" says Hannah.

"The Anesthesia Game." Syd turns her head toward Hannah pensively. "Did you ask me something?" Her eyes widen with panic. "I don't remember it," she says. "I'm trying, but I can't remember."

Hannah leans in. "No, cookie, I didn't," she lies. "I didn't ask you anything; there wasn't time. You just blacked-out and that was it."

"Are you sure? Because if you did and I don't remember, that's a terrible sign. That means The Taker..."

Hannah leans up, bringing her face right over Syd's and whispers, "Fuck. The. Fucking. Taker."

Syd's chest inflates with concern. "I know, but..."

"But *nothing*," Hannah says firmly. "There wasn't time to ask you anything. The Taker is lost somewhere in space, spinning in eternal orbit. You are not his concern."

"I'm not?" She gathers a slight smile.

"No. You are emphatically *not*. Where's my warrior girl, huh? Where did she go? Aren't you the one with the dagger tattoo?"

"Yeah," says Syd shyly.

"Right?" says Hannah. "And anyway, why would he waste his time on a vampire like you?" She points to the IV pole. "Look at all that bloody red blood!" Her eyes widen evilly. "You can't kill a vampire no matter how hard you try. Everybody knows that. Even The Taker."

Syd breaks into a grin. "It's true," she says. "I never thought of it that way."

"Vampires live forever," says Hannah confidently. She sits back in her chair and folds her arms. "And anyway, if I see The Taker I'll personally ring his slimy neck."

"Ha ha," says Syd. "Good."

Behind her, Hannah hears, "Mrs. Chandler? May I speak to you outside, please?"

Hannah squeezes Syd's hand reassuringly, leans over and kisses her forehead gently. "Be right back, cookie."

When she gets into the hall, Dr. Blanca corrals her into a side conference room with the young man and his clipboard. She closes the door and asks Hannah to take a seat on the couch. The young man has a nametag that reads "Ronald". He extends his hand.

"I'm Ronald," he says searchingly.

Hannah nods. "I can see that."

Dr. Blanca and Ronald take seats on the orange chairs facing Hannah's orange couch. Right now orange is the most alarming color she can think of. She's never felt so trapped in her life. Orange is a dangerous color.

"I thought you talked to the father," Hannah says. "Didn't you just talk to Aaron Michaels?"

"I did," says Dr. Blanca. "And he authorized me to share the information with you."

Hannah wrings her hands and wrists and quivers right up to her neck. "What information? Isn't he coming? Where is he? He can't delegate every damn..."

Ronald swings off the chair, around the glass coffee table, and sits eagerly beside Hannah on the couch. He reaches reassuringly for her hand and she swats the air, nearly smacking him in the face. "Don't touch me," she says, shaking.

He shrinks back. "Sorry," he says soothingly as if he's played this act a thousand times. "Can I get you some water?"

She looks at him, leaning in eye-to-eye, their faces inches apart. "You can get me a martini, how's that?" Her eyebrows rise while her mouth straightens into a thin determined line. "Straight up, three olives. Just keep them coming, and we'll get along fine."

"Mrs.....er...Chandler," says the doctor, "we do understand your reluctance, however we must continue. Someone on premises has to be informed of this child's situation."

"I don't even know what illness she has," says Hannah wildly in a voice she barely recognizes. "And I don't want to know! Okay? How's that? Syd and I have a pact that we'll never utter *the word*." She raises her trembling chin. "Her parents know; that's enough."

The doctor pulls on her right ear, considering her next move. "Very well, I won't tell you the diagnosis, but I must tell you that we, in consultation with her doctors in Connecticut, have determined that she will most likely require a bone marrow transplant in the very near future."

Hannah's eyes fill with spontaneous tears; it's hopeless. Ronald touches her shoulder and she's too freaked out to remove his hand.

"I'm sorry," he says gently.

Hannah chokes back a hurricane force cry. "She didn't remember the question," she mutters through tears. "She didn't remember that I asked her to tell me 'somewhere in Italy'." She gulps air, gasping. "Anywhere at all!" she says incredulously. "It could have been Rome or Capri; it didn't matter as long as it was somewhere in Italy."

The doctor stares ahead. "Italy?" she says. "I'm sorry; I don't know what you're talking about." She pauses. "Should I?"

"It doesn't matter," says Hannah. "It's just...the game. The Anesthesia Game that Syd plays to keep things under control. She asks a question and then remembers it when she wakes up. But this time...she didn't remember." Hannah puts her head in her hands and wails. "This time I told her I never asked her the question, but...I lied!" She looks back up at the doctor. "I lied to my niece," she whispers.

Ronald nearly curls up in her lap. "There, there," he says, handing her a new wad of tissues. "Let me get you some water." He jumps up.

Hannah blots her face. "I just want to know if that'll do it," she says to Dr. Blanca.

"I'm sorry," says the doctor sympathetically. "If what will do what?"

"The transplant," says Hannah. "Will that do it? Heal her?"

The doctor nods tentatively. "It might," she says. Then more reassuringly, "It has a good shot."

"Okay then," says Hannah into her lap. "Thank God."

"Even though it's unlikely you'll be a match, the entire family should get tested," says the doctor. "The easiest matches are generally found with siblings, but we know Sydney doesn't have any."

"No," says Hannah, "she doesn't." Her hands are trembling.

"Does she have any cousins?"

Hannah's chin drops to her chest. She shakes her head. "No," she says. "But I'll get pregnant right now if you think she could wait that long."

"I'm afraid we can't," says Dr. Blanca. "And I can't give you a clearer prognosis until we find a match."

Hannah nods. "What, um...what's... involved?"

"It's a simple mouth swab," she says. "No pain I promise."

"And, um..."

Ronald hands her small cup of water and she sips while he rubs her back in irritating circles. Even though she would like him to stop, she allows this small gesture of misplaced kindness to continue unattacked. She's just glad she doesn't have access to a pair of scissors or a knife. She feels capable of anything right now. "What do we tell Syd?" she asks. "And...when?"

Dr. Blanca brushes a wayward curl off her pale forehead as she glimpses her notes. "Her father wants us to wait," she says. "He expects to be down here early this afternoon, depending on flights."

Hannah reaches out to Ronald for more tissues. "So she'll be going back to Connecticut tomorrow? For treatment?"

"I can't say for sure," says the doctor. "This facility has an excellent transplant program if she chooses to stay. That will be up to her parents. But in truth, our program is much more leading edge than the one she's in. I don't think she can do better, as long as you all have accommodations."

Hannah's head is a bowl of spaghetti, her thoughts all starchy, tangled up and impossible to separate. If Syd stays, will Mitsy stay too? Will Aaron? It's a carnival of possibilities.

On the other hand, if Syd returns to Connecticut, what then? Will Hannah go with her? If so, for how long? *And what about Jonah?* She dishes this idea around in her head until she realizes it doesn't matter. If Syd and Jonah are placed on the scale of justice, Syd's little body outweighs Jonah's ten to one. A thousand to one. Syd wins hands-down every time. So somehow Hannah has to figure out how to deal with this terrifying reality without running away. She can't play the crazy aunt this time. She has to take charge. God knows the parents are useless.

Whoever thought Hannah would be the only one standing?

She returns to Syd's room to tell her she's going out for coffee, another lie, since she's on her way to the ground floor to get her mouth swabbed. But anyway, Syd's asleep, so she leaves with her conscience slightly less eroded.

After the swab, which, as the doctor promised, was not an issue, Hannah grabs a coffee from the nearby cafeteria along with a couple of blueberry muffins, hoping Syd will indulge with her. On her way down the sixth floor hall to Syd's room, she stops cold, incredulous at the sight in front of her. Is that Mitsy? Mitsy Michaels dressed in...*are they Hannah's jeans?* They sure as hell aren't Mitsy's waist-high dungarees! Hannah barely recognizes her sister out of the usual sweats. But it definitely is Mitsy, not just based on the fact that she's walking with Jonah, but also on the outgrowth of her gnarly gray haircut, which was nearly shaved when Hannah first arrived at the mansion. Now her hair hangs haphazardly to her ears, sticking out at all angles like a hedgehog. She looks damn good in those jeans, though.

In spite of all the questions Hannah has regarding Mitsy's instantaneous appearance, or really, appearance at all considering she's an agoraphobic hermit, Hannah is in no hurry for the answers. She takes a seat on a nearby bench down the hall.

She wants to let Mitsy and Syd have their say without anyone picking Hannah's brain for the real reason Syd's been hospitalized. After all, only Hannah and Aaron know about the transplant. Let the rest of them revel in their ignorance. Hannah only wishes she could revel with them. Once Aaron appears and they go into conference, it's all over. But Hannah will be damned if she's going into conference with the doctor and Ronald again just to update Mitsy. Even Hannah's first rate imagination can't conjure up a freak show freaky enough to animate that scene. And anyway, Mitsy is Aaron's job, not hers.

Pandora

EVERY TIME PANDORA TOUCHES the painting with the tip of her finger, the color fades from the canvas. "What are you trying to tell me, Elysha?" she whispers, mesmerized. She has to figure this out now.

No answer is whispered to her from the ether; no one guides her from the next realm. Her breath becomes rapid and she stomps her foot. *So frustrating! My God!!!* All that's left of her daughter is an image that's vanishing before her eyes, and yet she can't stop touching the picture as if touching it will inspire the information she seeks. Yet it doesn't. *But it must!* After all she's seen and all she's done in every corner of the mystical world, the situation before her right now is unprecedented. It's a phenomenon she's compelled to investigate at any risk. Even if it means the destruction of the painting.

Her fingers at her lips, her eyes searching, she digs deep into the pool of consciousness available to her. The painting is the past, she knows, and she, Pandora, is the present. But where's the future? *Where?* One thing she cannot afford to do right now is to search for the future through the tedious, plodding sequence of time. *There's no time for it!* Somehow she must figure out how to surpass time, to rise above it, without bypassing it entirely. Her temples pound. *There is a way!*

She raises her neck to realign her posture and breathes deeply to recover composure. She looks to her left across the pine-planked room to the kitchen and from there through the plate glass windows over the tall pines to her mystic lake. Even from across the room she can see mist rising from its chilled surface, guiding her sight upward toward Heavenly Mountain.

She sees it then.

Oh my God, she thinks breathlessly, it's back! A plasma cloud of brilliant color circles the peak, igniting it. The hot reds and wildly energetic oranges and other tantalizing colors dance seductively around the center. The center is illuminated by...*that blue.* The cool pool of electric blue in the molten center of all that perilous heat draws her in like a desert mirage. The power is there, she knows. *Right there.* The power she seeks is unequivocally zeon.

She shakes her head thoughtfully. But how do I get to it? *How?* She knows it won't be easy, and may even be impossible, but somehow she has to try. Something tells her now... *has been trying to tell her all along*...that wave function can regenerate in the middle of that storm. Or out of that storm. Or around it. Her vision penetrates the color...right there, she thinks, pointing. *Right there!* As if to confirm her understanding, the blue light blinks repeatedly, spitting splashes of zeon in every direction like a paint gun. Does anyone else see this, she wonders. Or is it only me?

In her mind's eye, she scans the data she's been collecting

about color and waves and particles and the frequencies of health and disease, and suddenly all doubt is released. *She knows!* She knows that this is it, the answer, the sum of the parts. What she cannot figure out is the equation—the quantity and combination of A plus B (or C? D? E?) that will render the result she needs. She can't figure out how to get the zeon blue in the first place or how to apply it therapeutically. How to secure the right calculus to derive the answer she already knows—that in some way or in some combination, zeon holds the signal of the cure. But she'll get it, by God. She'll get it. She will not give up.

It's right there!

Instinctively she closes her eyes and reaches out with her left hand, pointing toward the aurora. She breathes deeply, drawing the magnetic current to her core. Eyes opened, she touches the painting with her other hand at the space directly between Elysha's eyebrows. Seconds later a signal jolts through her system and she is thrown against the back of the couch where she lies stunned for some time. She has no idea how long. So this is how it works, she thinks. *Like this.* A human conduit. Or maybe that's just one way.

Fragile from the jolt, she pulls herself up slowly against the back of the couch. She stares at the ceiling as she approaches the painting, afraid to look. After all, Elysha's image may be gone completely now, a hole burned through all that was left of her. It's possible. More than that, it's probable, given the force of the surge. Gathering emotional strength, Pandora lowers her chin then her eyes, forcing herself to look.

Before her is the painting, the one she abandoned twenty years ago, fully restored in fresh, lifelike color. She sees the unmistakable penetrating ice blue eyes, the ringlets of sun-kissed mahogany hair, the tawny skin, the full lips, the sharp, irrepressible *knowing*. She sees Elysha, yet...not Elysha. Not exactly. Pandora can't take her eyes off the image. It's as if she just put down the brush, as if Elysha were coming through the canvas about to speak. But the picture is not the child Elysha. It's a holographic amalgamation of every age and lifetime Elysha has ever lived. *It's her spirit.* Her vibrant spirit. In this painting at least, her child lives.

But what does it mean? Pandora is so close to the absolute center of a seismic truth she can't quite process. Does it mean she'll get Elysha back if she accomplishes this impossible task? If she draws the future into the past to ignite the present? Will it bring her daughter back to life? And what will happen to Pandora if she succeeds? It's not without risk.

Her chest vibrates with too much excitement, too much hope, too much life. She doesn't know whether she's rejoicing or grieving. A little of each perhaps, or a lot of both. Every emotion she's ever experienced burns at the altar of this moment. She has never felt so much of anything at one time. Her mind and body respond greedily. She wants a drink. She wants a smoke. She wants to walk naked through a harem of powerful men who lay prostrate at her gold-sandaled feet. She wants to part seas and burn bushes with the touch of a finger. She wants to ascend the ladder of desire until the only desire left is consummation with the Infinite. She wants to burn there—in the eternal flame.

But for now, she'll settle for a cigarette. She scrambles through the drawer of the hutch for a smoke and grabs one; lights it. The flame ignites her weakness. *Forgive me,* she thinks. *I'm so weak!* But to lay down all her lovely crutches at this age at this time is even more overwhelming than the task at hand. And the one thing she can't afford to do at the apex of this much unraveling is become overwhelmed. Whatever she's being called to do, cigarettes, at least, are part of the deal.

The phone rings, startling her. She glances down; it's Mitsy again. Of course it is. Mitsy is part of the circuit. Mitsy and Hannah and Sydney are a circuit, but only Pandora can access the energy. Once the energy is conveyed, it has to travel through the entire circuit to heal the child. *Hopefully* to heal the child.

"Hello?" she says.

"Pandora?" says Mitsy, nearly intelligibly. "Uh uh, uhhhh…"

"Calm down!" Pandora commands. "I can't understand you." She inhales her cigarette.

"She…she…she needs a…a transplant," Mitsy sputters.

Pandora's heart stops. *Is it too late?* Exhaling, she turns back for a look at Heavenly Peak. The aurora has disappeared. *Where did it go?* Has she waited too long? *Again?* How many lifetimes will it take? She walks robotically to the couch and sits, listening to bits and pieces of truncated information punctuated by Mitsy's long and irritating wails.

"I'm sorry," she tells Mitsy. "I really am."

"But can't you hhhhhheeeeeelllllp?" Misty wails. "Can't you… can't you get tested too?"

Pandora frowns, cocks her head, and listens for inspiration. *Can I?* But how could she be a compatible match? What chance would there be that she is? Her DNA is Peruvian, Ethiopian, Caribbean, Scandinavian and Dutch. She's anything but British, Irish or Scotch, which, as far as she knows, is Sydney's entire heritage. And even though Pandora knows there's more to every story than meets the eye, she doesn't see her place in this story as a donor of anything physical. That's not what she's here for.

"Please?" Mitsy begs.

Before she answers, Pandora inhales a long, thoughtful drag. Exhales. "Well…I can certainly take the test. Why not?"

"Oh my God, would you?" Mitsy says. "Oh my God, thank you!"

"But I'm not a match," Pandora warns. "Please don't count on me for that. You know nothing about my ancestry. Most of my tribes are pretty far south of yours."

"Oh."

"But I'll do it anyway, just because every effort is an energetic vote for the child's survival. The more votes the more chances there are. Energetically, that is. Which in the end is what counts."

"I didn't know that," says Mitsy.

"And I'll publish a blog, too. I'll try to get others to register for her specific marrow. There's got to be a match out there somewhere, right?"

"It might be me," says Mitsy, "I don't know. Or Aaron or Hannah, although it's unlikely. But that's it. That's our entire family."

Even though Pandora has a sinking feeling, she says, "See her in the light, Mitsy. See your daughter filled with light. Always! Do not let your thoughts deteriorate into fear and anxiety. If you do, your daughter will absorb *that*. She needs light, not fear."

Mitsy calms down. "I'll try."

"You do your daughter a disservice when you fall apart."

"Ok," she whimpers.

"And take care of the dog. Dogs tend to empath the sickness of those they love. You cannot afford to lose that dog."

"Oh. Well, Godiva seems fine. I just saw her."

"You can't afford to stumble around in the dark," Pandora says. "Do you hear me? Don't drop your guard for a second. Think and act with a confidence you don't feel."

Pretend, Pandora thinks. Like me. I'm pretending, too.

"Okay," Mitsy snivels.

"Try it out on me," Pandora says. "Right now. Speak to me with confidence."

After a moment of silence, Mitsy says, "Stop telling me what to do, damn it!"

This takes the air right out of Pandora's lungs. She's never heard Mitsy exercise any authority whatsoever in any form. At least not to her.

"How was that?" Mitsy says tentatively.

"That was...breathtaking," says Pandora. "All right then. Proceed. But use your authority for purpose, Mitsy. To guide people. Not to bully them."

"Don't tell me what to do!" Mitsy commands.

"Enough."

"Sorry," Mitsy says.

Pandora rolls her eyes and ends the call. Hoping her efforts aren't hopeless is the best she can do at this point. After all, she didn't climb on board this sinking vessel for Mitsy's sake; she did it for Sydney's. As long as the girl's alive, there's hope.

She crushes her cigarette in the ashtray slowly. So much to think about. She turns to her left to see if the plasma cloud has returned, but it hasn't. She glances back at the painting which has faded again, so she knows the life force was temporary, not fully received or sustainable. Of course it wasn't. It was a message.

Message received.

She folds her arms. But if the geomagnetic storm comes and goes randomly, how can she rely on it to heal anybody? And if it only comes and goes on Heavenly Peak, how will she conduct it all the way to Virginia? Can she do it remotely? *Is her astral body strong enough?* Probably not, she thinks. How could it be? She's been taking such terrible care of herself. In truth, she doesn't know what will happen to her own life force if she even tries to transfer the zeon charge all the way to Virginia.

A lump forms in her throat and she can barely swallow. It's a risky plan filled with literal astronomical variables. For instance, if the aurora comes and goes, is there a way to harvest and store the zeon? And if so, how much should she harvest? Is it possible to take too much? Too little? And what about isolating it from the other colors in the first place? And conducting it all the way across the country to Sydney? Her head spins.

She walks purposefully to her computer, sits down, and searches "auroras". Reads madly about the massive magnetics in the solar superstorms and how coronal mass ejections (CME's) can send pulses of magnetized plasma barreling into space and from there, right into Earth's orbit. How the magnetized plasma wreaks havoc on the electrical grid. How these storms are capable of disabling satellites and GPS's with ejections that have the potential to travel over 1,800 miles per second. This set of facts stops her cold. Is she capable of surviving such an experience? *Is she insane?*

She reads further that geomagnetic storms are not exclusive to Alaska, Scandinavia, and northern regions, as she had thought. They have in fact been spotted as far south as Hawaii, Mexico and Cuba. *What?!* And these events have been associated with the sunspot cycle, it says, so they are becoming easier to predict. That they are even slightly predictable by scientific measures gives her hope. Though science is not the likely means by which she will know.

She will just know.

She sits back on her desk chair, thinking about how far south Cuba is from Virginia. Pretty far. So an aurora of this magnitude is scientifically possible in Virginia. It's not unprecedented. But would she have to go there? She hates flying. Well, not astral flying, but plane travel. And could there be a geomagnetic storm approaching that area now? Is that what this is all about? Is Anjah behind this with all his pushing and prodding? She doesn't know. To be truthful, she's never fully trusted him. Just something about him that's so…manipulative. He's a high intelligence without doubt, but their relationship is so combative. *He thinks he owns her!* She will not be owned.

She realizes that she's probably been given all the information she needs—from Anjah or elsewhere. She realizes that it resides somewhere accessible to her, though she has not yet attempted to retrieve it or process it. But processing everything with her physical brain isn't really the point. After all, most of the data derives from mystical channels. She gets exactly what she needs when she needs it, and only then. Which is not to say what she does is easy; it isn't. Getting exactly what she needs when she needs it requires quantum faith on the deepest spiritual level.

And right now, that's exactly what she lacks.

Sydney

SYD SHAKES OUT A powerful dream-like experience that returned her to Bangkok, a place where she was once strong. She tries to remember how long ago that was. Probably months if she remembers correctly. It was even before Aunt Hannah came to Connecticut, so—early winter. But this time The Taker came closer, his pulsating purple halo brighter and more threatening. At least it seemed that way. This time when she tried to dart at the horizon to take back the dawn's first light, *the living light,* he completely blocked her path. This was unprecedented.

Maybe he was more aggressive because the light was different this time. It really was. Not just the quality of light, but the colors themselves. Colors on fire. Colors on steroids. Colors on crack. Colors she craved like love or drugs or life itself. She was pushed to risk her life to suck the colors into her bloodstream, as if they possessed the cure for everything. Not just the cure for disease but the cure for evil and hate and mortality itself.

204 REA NOLAN MARTIN

But anyway, she failed. Not because she didn't try, but because she couldn't get to the light without going through The Taker. He wasn't saying she couldn't have it exactly; just that she had to pass through him to get it. At least that was her understanding. Even now she thinks *no fucking way*. She will not negotiate with a terrorist. Something inside her just *knows* not to sell her soul, which is exactly what The Taker wants. Her soul. At least she thinks he does.

But there are consequences for refusing him. In rejecting The Taker's demands, she lost her light. Or more clearly, she was unable to take back the light she'd already lost. She can't live without it; no one can. It's her vitality, her life force. How can she compromise that? Compromising that would be like negotiating for her breath or her heartbeat. She's not giving up exactly. But she does feel as if her power is breaking down. And that's an unsustainable condition.

Oh my God.

A single tear drains down the left side of her face, and she feels someone wipe it. The physical contact startles her, and she opens her eyes. There stands...Mom? *What?!*

"Mom," she says groggily. "Why are you here? Aren't I in Virginia?"

"Yes, Sydney, you are," says her mother with forced brightness. "We're all here now."

Syd frowns. "What! Why?"

"Well," she says uncertainly, "to support you, of course."

Just by the way her mother says this Syd knows the panic switch in her mother's brain is on full tilt. She squints, focusing more closely on her mother and says, "You look awful. Are you okay?"

Her mother's eyes widen freakishly, her face frozen with incapacitation. Syd knows what she's done. Timing is everything.

Her mother has looked like shit for years. It's probably the reason her father's gone half the time. Someone's got to get through to this woman. *Wake up and get over yourself, Mom! You're not the one who's sick!* It might as well be Syd who delivers the news.

"Well, I haven't gotten much sleep lately," her mother snaps.

"Yeah, but..." Syd's head feels heavy, like it's filled with water. "Still. You look...old. Sorry."

"Oh."

"I'm not trying to be mean, Mom. Just, you know...your overall dreariness has an effect on people."

"I see. Like..."

"Like me," Syd says. "The way you don't take care of yourself makes me feel responsible. Like I might be too much trouble. Like I might be...I don't know...dying."

Her mother gasps.

"Am I?" This is a real question as far as Syd is concerned. She's not putting anybody on. *Why is her mother here?!*

Before her mother can answer, a rush of new energy enters the room. Before Syd can see who it is, she hears, "How's my girl?" in an unmistakable, deep-throated voice.

"Dad?!" she says, smiling. She tries to raise her head.

He squeezes her toe. "Yes, indeed," he says then hands a cup of something or other to her mother. "You feeling okay, Syd?" He walks around front and kisses her on the forehead.

Syd lays her head back on the pillow. "Much better since I got all those bags of blood and FFP."

"What's FFP?" says another male voice, also familiar.

Syd looks around, trying to focus. Out of the shadows and behind the curtain enters *Oh my God! Dane? No!* Maybe she's not dying. Maybe she's already dead. *What are these people doing in the same room?* All at once she feels a crush of despair. "Why are you here?" she groans.

"See, everybody?" says Dane. "I told you this wasn't the most ingenious idea. I should've gone home."

"Right about that," says Syd weakly. "What the hell?"

At that, her mother stands and prods her father by the elbow. "Let's leave the young ones alone for a few minutes," she says.

"Let's not and say we did," says Syd. "Where's Aunt Hannah anyway? Leave me with her."

"Hannah and Jonah will be by later," says her father. "Your mother and I will be in the parents' lounge if you need us."

When they're gone, Syd says, "Why are you here, Dane? Haven't you done enough damage?" She turns her head away from him. "Not that I care," she adds.

He pulls a folding chair from under the window ledge and sets it up closer to her bed. "Your mom needed someone to drive her down," he says. "I came to the house to see you and she begged. I couldn't refuse."

"I thought you were going to Pennsylvania."

"I decided not to. I decided to try to mend things with you instead."

She struggles to sit, and he jumps up to help, holding her back forward while he rearranges pillows for support.

"You can adjust the bed from under there," she says, pointing down. "Just pull the lever. Duh."

He looks down, puzzled, then jerks the lever so hard she's thrust forward like a slingshot. Stunned, he stands with one hand over his mouth saying, "Oh my God, Syd, are you okay?"

"Yes, asshole, I'm okay," she says, though a part of her gets off on the slapstick. She accidentally releases a giggle.

"Ha ha, good," he says, his handsome chiseled, dark-eyed face all lit-up, grinning.

Syd wants to die laughing at the comedy of it, her in a hospital bed with an IV stuck in her arm catapulted forward by an apologetic traitor. But she'll be damned if she lets him know how hilarious she thinks it is in theory. She's still in the mode of wanting him to jump out a window, and since they're on the sixth floor, this window would be as good as any. "I wouldn't be patting myself on the back if I were you," she says.

"I know we're not in the best place right now," he says, "but I hope you let me explain."

"You came down with my mother?" she says, reaching for the cup of water on the tray table. "You drove seven hours down here with my *mother!*" She takes a sip. "Are you insane?"

"I am now," he says, his eyebrows raised hopefully.

Syd bites her bottom lip to stop from chuckling. After all, she hasn't spent seven hours with her own mother in the last seven weeks. He might be a traitor, but he's a little bit of a hero for accomplishing that feat. "Who drove?" she says.

"I did. And for the record, it took more like ten hours."

"You'd get more points if you put up with her driving," she says. "Her foot hovers over the brake the entire time. We stop/start the whole way until one of us hurls. Usually it's me, with the chemo and all."

All of a sudden she realizes her cap isn't on, and he's never seen her bald. She throws her left hand over her head, blushing. "Get me that cap," she demands, pointing with her chin to the window sill.

He retrieves it. "Allow me," he says, sliding the red knit cap gently over her head. He sits down again. "You're beautiful without it, though, Syd." He nods reassuringly. "Seriously."

"Oh really," she says. "Is that why you were screwing around with Zelda? Because I'm so beautiful?"

He lowers his chin, staring down. He places his heavy hand

on her left leg which is tucked under the thin hospital blanket. She feels his warmth, but shivers from the unexpected touch.

"I wasn't screwing around with her, Syd," he says.

"What would you call it? Not that I care."

"We were crawling around looking for the guitar pick I dropped. It was my last one."

"Oh really? You lost your guitar pick in the storage room?" She rolls her eyes. "I don't even know why you're bothering to lie. I couldn't care less."

"I'm not lying," he says. "I was playing in the back since that's the only room with a window. I was composing a new song and I wanted to look out at the woods with those frilly trees, you know?" He moves his fingers all around, dancing. "With all the fresh snow weighing the branches down like heavy karma, right? Karma so frozen you don't even know it's there, never mind get rid of it. But how great you feel when it's lifted." He smiles. "You know?"

Syd sighs. "Did you tell this to Z? Is that why she got all romantic? And anyway, who cares? I wasn't like, I don't know. Forget it."

"I don't talk to Zelda like that because she doesn't get it."

"You got that right," says Syd.

"Look," he says, "we were crawling around and she kissed me kind of spontaneously. It was just the moment, that's all." He shrugs, "I kissed her back because, why not? I don't have a girl-friend, and honestly, I didn't really know you were available."

She lifts her left arm, IV tubes and all. "Yeah, right. I'm not available."

"No, not that. I mean, I know you're ahead of your age, but you're a couple years younger. I don't know. It seems like a lot. Like whatever might happen isn't going to happen yet." He flashes a grin.

She turns her head. This guy knows how to climb out of a ditch. "Z's only a year older." After a long silence, she says, "I don't care if you go out with Z as long as you didn't pick her because you think I'm a slug." She blinks back a threatening tear. "A slug with a...whatever."

"You're not a slug," he says. "And anyway, I'm not sure I'm going out with Z. She feels as lousy as I do about you walking in on that. She wouldn't hurt you for the world."

Syd frowns. "Is she here, too?"

"No. Just me and your mom and dad and aunt and uncle. Like I said, I drove your mom down here." He leans forward, widening his eyes. "In a fucking apocalyptic snow storm!"

"Ha ha ha!" She can't help herself. It's quite the image.

"And that's not all," he says. "She forgot her wallet, so I had to put us both up in one room of a sleazebag motel when the sleet got so bad they closed down the highway!"

"Oh my God! No!"

"And there was a fucking leak in the ceiling between our beds! *Drip drip drip* all night long!" His fingers trickle down like raindrops.

Syd is laughing so hard now, her stomach aches. "You're killing me!" she squeals.

"Oh yeah!" he blurts, tears of hilarity coursing down his cheeks. He raises his arm. "So help me God!"

She can barely get it out—"You...stayed...in a motel room with my...mother?!" She slaps the side of the bed so hard the IV pops out and the whole pile of attached wires start going *'beep beep beep'*.

A nurse walks in briskly. "What's going on?" she says as smoothly as she can. "Something going on in here?"

The nurse is followed by her mother who's followed by her father. "What's happening?" says her mother frantically. "Are you okay, Sydney? Is everything okay? Why are you crying? What's all this beeping? Did something happen?"

Dane stands and holds the chair out for her mother.

"Dane?" she says anxiously. "What's going on here?"

"Just...I don't know..." he's still laughing too hard to answer. "Sor...ry," he manages, but he can barely come up for air, which is contagious to Syd, who's now got the hiccups.

"Well, it looks as if you two have made up, anyway," says her father.

"I don't know about that," says Syd. Just the idea of Dane in a motel room with her mother makes her burst out laughing again punctuated with a long stream of hiccups which does Dane completely in. He laughs long and high like a girl, which kills Syd all over again, so this might never end.

Luckily there's a rap on the door frame and Hannah strides in like a runway model in all her high-fashion auburn-haired glory. Jonah is in tow, the perfect masculine complement to all her girliness. The focus thankfully shifts.

"Hey cookie!" Hannah says brightly then nods to Dane. "How nice of you to drive my sister down here! Wow!" She raises her eyebrows. "Yikes!"

"What's that supposed to mean, Hannah?" snaps her mother. "Yikes? Really?"

Her father places his hands on her mom's shoulders to calm her down, but she shrugs them off.

Dane tries hard to force a lid on all the uncontained residual comedy. He doesn't dare look at Syd and vice versa.

The nurse finishes the IV and assists Syd as she tries to sit back up. "Don't overdo it," says the nurse firmly.

Syd looks from guest to guest and says, "Don't take this the wrong way, but are you sure I'm not dying?"

Her father frowns. She tries to read his expression to figure out if she has half a chance at survival.

"Absolutely not," he says. "No. Not at all. We just came to support you."

"And get tested," says her mother with obvious effort.

"Tested?" says Syd. "For what?"

Her mother looks hysterically at her father, who clears his throat. "You'll be getting a bone marrow transplant, Syd," he says evenly.

Syd freezes. "I will?"

"Dr. Blanca will be by shortly to explain the technicalities, but the transplant is the best treatment...the best cure for you." He glances down. "A transplant will cut the whole process short, if I understand her correctly. Cut out years of chemo."

"Chemo that doesn't work, you mean," says Syd.

Dane moves toward her and picks up her hand.

At the base of her bed, her father clutches her blanketed toes. "It could take a bit of time, though. She said that uh, well...at least so far... none of us is a match."

"Aaron," her mother says, "is it really necessary to divulge every little step along..."

"Yes," he says, staring her down. "She deserves the truth." He looks at Syd. "But the doctors are hopeful they'll find a match soon. No one's giving up. Not even close."

Silence descends on the room with a black cape and a scythe. Syd is breathless. *Giving up?* Since when was that even a suggestion? Nobody talks until finally Syd says, "How long do I have? You know, before...you know." Each word weighs a metric ton.

Her mother gasps again and darts out of the room. When no one attends to her histrionics, Dane excuses himself and follows her.

"Oh, they have time to find a donor, don't you worry," says her father on a fake high note. His voice cracks.

There's a rap on the wall and Dr. Blanca peeks around the curtain, sort of smiling. Syd has a sinking feeling.

"How are you doing?" she asks Syd. "Your color has definitely improved."

Dr. Blanca glimpses her chart. She pushes her glasses on her nose a couple times, stalling. Or maybe that's just Syd's psychic antennae picking up static. She hopes she's wrong. In her experience people never stall for good reasons.

"So...let me explain what's next," she says, and dives headfirst into an explanation of the whole transplant procedure—or BMT as she calls it—the crippling chemo prep beforehand and the long quarantine after. "We have every reason to believe you'll do well with this, Sydney."

Syd shrugs. What can she say? *Nothing.*

Dr. Blanca checks the chart. "We've done as much as we can in-patient until we get a match. At that point, there'll be some serious preparation, as I said. But for now, I think it would be an excellent idea for you to take a break from the hospital, what do you think?" She smiles. "For a few days anyway."

Syd nods. "Yeah, get me out of here. But where?"

Her father says, "Wherever you want, honey. Wherever you feel most comfortable. Here or back home."

"Here," she says.

Her father rubs his chin stubble. "No need to be hasty, Syd. Don't you want to think about it?" He nods side to side. "Take the evening and let us ..."

"I've thought about it a million times already," she says. "Every time I see myself whole I see myself at the farm."

He rubs his hands together nervously. "Ok. Very well then. We'll all settle in and wait for the donor."

"All?" says Syd. *Seriously? All of you?!*

"Where else would we go?" he says in a raspy exhausted voice.

Syd shrugs. "Work? Remember that?" She's testing him, but he doesn't know it. If Dad doesn't go to work then Syd's in worse shape than anyone's letting on.

"Well, I'll eventually go." He smiles. "But not…just yet."

"Okay then," says Dr. Blanca. "We'll release you to-morrow as long as your numbers are reasonable. Sometime late morning, I'd say. We've got some new meds which may make you tired and mildly nauseous."

Syd shrugs. "What else is new?"

Dr. Blanca and her father file out; Jonah stands at a distance; Hannah sits on the folding chair on the side without the IV.

"It'll be okay," Hannah says softly. "I promise." She takes Syd's limp hand tenderly, lifts it to her lips and kisses it.

Syd watches Jonah watching Hannah, thinking Hannah doesn't even know he's there. Is he in or is he out? Syd wonders. She just hopes he leaves Hannah alone while Syd's at the house. She wants the independent Hannah all to herself, not the one all worried about where she stands with Jonah. As if sensing this, he turns and leaves.

With all the comings and goings, Syd is suddenly over-whelmed with exhaustion. She can't absorb it all. First The Taker, and now all this…medical mystery and human drama. How much more can she take?

Hannah strokes Syd's cheek as she falls asleep. "You okay, cookie?" she asks.

Syd barely opens her heavy eyelids.

"You're gonna be okay," Hannah says, nodding repeatedly. "You believe me, right? I wouldn't lie to you, sugar."

With great effort, Syd says, *"If only they hadn't gone to*

Virginia…" She looks searchingly at Hannah, "Right? *She wouldn't have…*"

Hannah gulps. "She wouldn't have had as much fun," she interrupts. "If they hadn't gone to Virginia, life would have dragged endlessly on."

With that, Syd retreats into her other world like an ocean wave returning to its source. She stands in the cave like a shadow, watching the ivy-covered cottage at a distance, illuminated by a full moon. The Taker's purple halo hovers ominously, pulsing, waiting. Wild boar chase each other playfully in the lush vineyards.

Without warning the cottage is engulfed in flames. Someone drags one of the women out by her feet. Another woman remains. Syd wants to help, but she can't move. She watches as the walls of the cottage crumble, revealing the injured woman inside, her clothes and skin charred. The woman's right arm reaches up in desperation towards a pair of eagles flying awkwardly into the night sky. A squirming creature of some kind is clutched between them in their claws.

Everyone is screaming.

Mitsy

NO SOONER DOES DANE park the car on the side lot than Mitsy bolts out the passenger door, heading straight downhill for the paddock. "Don't follow me," she calls out behind her. "I need space."

And she does. Nothing she's said or even thought has ever been truer. Right now her brain is a torture chamber of hideous thoughts and desperate fears. There's no sorting through them; they're radioactive. No matter how much Dane tries to comfort her—*why Dane? Why not Aaron!*—she can't calm down. If Pandora were here, she'd order Mitsy to march directly upstairs and meditate. *Just breathe deeply!* But Mitsy doesn't feel like breathing deeply. What she feels like doing is visiting the horses. It's been so long. *Why has it been so long!* The truth is Mitsy was meditating with horses long before she even knew what meditation was.

Head down, arms swinging, half-sliding down the gravel

culvert in her haste, she arrives at the fence where she reaches out for the filly, Ireland. "Come to me," she begs. *Show me the way out of this hell!* The filly neighs and bucks playfully under the careful watch of her mother, Jolie.

In spite of the usual ravages of recent motherhood, Jolie is a splendid beast—a handsome chestnut racer with a white star on her forehead and chrome on all four legs. As much as Hannah complains to Mitsy about the extravagant expense and tedious labor of maintaining the ancestral estate, she knows what she's doing with horses. At least she can pick a good one, Mitsy thinks, and whoever thought that would happen? Unlike Mitsy, Hannah never even rode as a child. She never wanted to. She barely rides now.

The other broodmare, Daizee, peeks out plaintively from the opposite side of the barn as if to say, *What about me?* Mitsy wanders down to pet her. Hannah keeps them separated because the new foal is too rambunctious, Jolie too protective. Like Mitsy, Daizee needs space. Judging from her full belly, she'll be foaling any day now. This gives Mitsy a thrill she hasn't felt in some time. She hasn't been present for a foaling in decades. How she loved it once! All that new life just standing up and walking around—practically born upright and mobile. Miraculous. *Life!*

She strokes Daizee's pale gray muzzle. "Good girl," she says soothingly. "Good mama."

The words sound so foreign. When was the last time anyone spoke them to her? *"Good girl, Mitsy. Good mama. Difficult job well done!"* The answer is never. No one has ever told her that. If someone had, maybe she could have gone the distance instead of giving up and falling completely apart.

She wanders back to the paddock and leans against the fence, staring out at the familiar, inspiring scenery. Soon it will be a riot of honeysuckle, magnolia, forsythia, wisteria and wild dogwood. Standing here in the dirt and muck like this, she admits to a measure of peace even in the midst of the emergency that has become her life. She wonders how she ever got so separated from the earth. *From the dirt!* She reaches down and feels it beneath her fingers. Was it Aaron? Can she blame him and his sanitized, urban ways? His corporate mentality? Still, she could have had horses in Connecticut if she'd wanted them. He would not have denied her that. Why didn't she want them?

Conversely, she wonders how Hannah ever got stuck with the farm. Not that her sister loathes it; she doesn't. In some ways it grounds her. Still, Hannah was much more suited for the refined, extravagant life Mitsy pretends to lead than she was ever suited for mucky barn stalls, laborious hay fields, and lactating mares. Are they leading each other's lives?

Mitsy remembers meeting Aaron when the Loudoun Hunt chased through their farm, as they did every Sunday in autumn. Mitsy's and Hannah's dad, Jock, had been the Hunt Master years before, and he'd granted permission for the Hunt to pass through their property in perpetuity. It was always a thrill to see them in their crisp scarlet coats, black helmets, tan breeches, and high black leather boots as they galloped through the fields. Jock installed jumping coupes down the hill to advance the challenge. Aaron was an experienced equestrian who was equal to the task. Aaron's father, a famous trial lawyer from D.C., was grooming him to join the prestigious hunt, though it never actually happened. Instead, an impossibly lucrative job offer seduced him to Wall Street. Life took over and he never really rode again.

On that particular Sunday nearly thirty years ago, Mitsy was brushing the stallion, Infidel, who'd been reserved for Aaron. She was fit and athletic then, a golden-tanned, long-legged country girl with her own mane of sandy, sun-drenched hair and impressive riding skills. She belonged on a horse farm. Why did she allow herself to turn her life over to Aaron, anyway? *What was she thinking!* It was not what she'd imagined for herself. No matter how hard she tried, she never got the hang of corporate life. She sees now that she lost her power when she stopped doing the thing she loved. When she lost her power, her self-respect spiraled, as often happens to frauds.

"Hey," she hears behind her.

She jumps. *Shit!* She told Dane not to follow her down. But when she turns, she sees Aaron instead. She didn't even recognize his voice. "Speak of the devil," she says.

He sidles up against the fence a few feet to her right. "Is that what I am now?" he says. "The devil?"

Mitsy purses her mouth. "Just reminiscing," she says.

He places his foot firmly against the bottom board of the fence and stares out at the rolling hills. Sighing deeply, he says, "Things are tough."

She nods.

"We don't know what's going to happen here," he says.

She turns away. "Don't say it."

"Not saying it won't make it not happen."

She doesn't speak. She won't be consumed by the vortex of Aaron. Aaron in possession of all her power. *Give me my power back!*

"I'm proud of you for driving down," he says. "I know it wasn't easy." He waits for her to reply, but she doesn't, so he says, "Great jeans. I haven't seen you..."

"They're Hannah's," she says curtly then turns to face him. He's still indecently handsome, she thinks. She's not equal to his physical presence or really anything about him. Was she ever? But back here on the farm, she at least sees who she was when they met and why he fell for her. Here on the farm, she understands the natural habitat of her authority, where it dwells, as it always has, awaiting her return. Reflected in the deep, liquid eyes of the horses and the rich, fertile soil underfoot, she has hope that she may one day recover herself. This prospect makes her bolder.

"What's happened to us?" she asks. "Where did 'we' go?"

He blinks. "I don't know. We're disappearing."

"Not you," she says. "You're fine. I'm the one who's melting away."

"Well, we can't afford that, can we?" he says. "Right now neither one of us can melt away. Our daughter needs us both."

"Easier said than done." After a pause, she shocks herself by saying, "Where will you stay while you're here?"

He closes his eyes; opens them slowly. "At the Inn," he nearly whispers.

She nods. He's staying at the Inn. Probably already registered. Of course she knew it was over before she asked, or she wouldn't have asked. Aaron isn't staying with her at the farm because, let's face it, they've been a cardboard couple for years. At least now they're acknowledging it. This must be progress of some bizarre sort. She feels oddly calm, like she's locked herself in a vault to open at a safer time.

"Syd will know," she says. "She'll wonder. Do we really want to make this point in front of her right now? And everybody else?"

"Just tell her it's a hen party," he says. "Let all you women bond. Jonah won't be there either, not sure about Dane, but I can put him up in the Inn if he doesn't go home. So in a way…"

"Please," she says. "Do me the favor of not manipulating this into something good and worthy."

He nods, pausing. "At least now we can move forward," he finally says, and gives her a friendly pat on the shoulder.

"There's someone else," she says, "isn't there? Don't insult me by denying it."

He grimaces, considering whatever. "It's not about that," he says. "It's about…"

"I knew it."

He points his finger threateningly. "Intimacy is not about sex," he says. "It's about sharing and understanding. The only one you've ever shared anything with is that…whatever you call her…psychic."

"Who else was there to talk to?" she snaps. "Not you! Unless I was lucky enough to catch you on your way out the door."

"You leave it all up to me," he says angrily. "All of it. Every single gruesome medical detail! Because of that woman you won't let the doctors tell you anything significant. You don't even know the full diagnosis, never mind prognosis! You call that a partner?" He leans in hard on the fence rail. "How is one person supposed to handle all that?"

Mitsy would spit fire if she could. "One person? And who might that be? I was the one caring for her day in and day out. Cleaning up after …" Her whole body shakes. "Before Hannah came along, it was only me. Me! In the clinic…and the hospital. Excuse me if you had to hear a few medical terms from the doctors. Somebody had to hold onto…"

"Onto what?" he says.

"Onto hope," she says. "Hope."

"Oh really? Because it felt a lot more like fear and anxiety mixed in with a good dose of despair."

A dog barks behind them and Ireland neighs. They both turn, only to see Hannah standing there with a slobbering, velvety brown Godiva on a rope.

"Oh hey," Aaron mutters.

All Mitsy can think is—*so now Hannah knows.* She was

certainly close enough to hear. But maybe she already knew, Mitsy thinks. Maybe that's why she came up to Connecticut in the first place. Or maybe that's why she left.

"Hey y'all," Hannah drawls, waving her hand coquettishly.

Mitsy never acquired the coquette gene. It would have made life so much easier, she thinks. One flirty wink dissolves everything toxic right into thin air, or at least delays its impact. All the coquette genes went to Hannah. Hannah's got more than she can use.

"I can just..." Hannah points uphill at the house. "If you all are..."

"No, that's okay," says Aaron. "We're done." He half-smiles at Hannah, ruffs up the top of Godiva's head, and walks away with his hands in the pockets of his perfectly fitted navy cashmere pea-coat.

After a moment, Mitsy says, "So. You heard?"

"Yeah, sorry. Terrible timing."

"It's over," says Mitsy.

"Over? No." Hannah shakes her head. "It's nothing we can't fix," she says brightly, her flirty auburn hair swinging forward as she bends.

"I don't even care," says Mitsy. "Honestly. Fix what? It's been over for a long time."

"But look at you!" says Hannah. She waves her hand up and down, "You're a different girl down here. Hell, you look the part more than I do."

"So what? I don't live here anymore."

Index finger to chin, Hannah analyzes the situation. "Let's go take care of a few things," she says.

"Such as?"

"Oh, I don't know. Your hair? Your nails? Your face? Your..."

"Are you kidding me, Hannah Chandler?" Mitsy shrieks.

"*My hair?!* My nails?! My damn *face?* Maybe you're unaware that my entire life...my daughter is..."

"All the more reason to pull yourself together, Mits. Don't you think it would tickle Syd to see you looking chic for once? Don't you think it would help with Aaron too? And now that you've lost weight..."

"So you're the reason Sydney said that," Mitsy says with disgust.

"Said what?"

"That I look 'awful'! That I look...'old'."

Hannah grimaces. "Oh, wow. Sorry. But no, I'm not the reason for that. Syd's on her own there. Definitely not a collaboration." She pulls her pearl white cashmere sweater coat tightly around her waist and cinches the belt. "However it does prove my point."

Mitsy narrows her eyes. "Is that all you can think of in the midst of this crisis?"

"What?"

"Appearances!" Mitsy juts her chin forward for emphasis. "All you can think about is how I...*look?* Not how I *feel?* Is that how empty you are?"

Hannah postures, hands on hips. "And your life is so full, right?" she says. "Sign me up for your very full and satisfying life led curled up in the dark cave of your total waste of a designer bedroom. Come on, sis. Looks may not be everything, but they do reflect self-image. And yours sucks."

Mitsy punches the air. "And I suppose your self-image is excellent? That's why Jonah left you? That's why half the inventory of Saks and Neiman Marcus is piled in the guest closet in Darien? Clothes you'll probably never even wear? Clothes you probably can't even pay for!"

Hannah huffs. "Wow! Look who's been spying on her guest!

And not just her guest, but her *sister!* And not just her sister, but her medical proxy! Her sister who dropped everything to assume all *her* responsibilities!" She glares at Mitsy. "But let's not get sidetracked by your lack of ethics. This is about you, not me. It's about how much better you'll feel when you're dressed like a woman instead of a wrestling coach."

"Fuck you!"

"Good, Mitsy, get it out! Scream it out! Curse it out! *Finally!* Go ahead and blame me for this disaster. Or Aaron. Or Syd. Or God! But get your act together so we know who you are!"

One of their phones rings, startling them both. Their reactions excite Godiva, who jumps and spins at the end of the rope, barking. Their rings are identical; they can't figure out whose phone it is. Since the caller could be Syd...or a doctor... they fumble earnestly until Mitsy finally locates hers in the rear pocket of her jeans. Checking the read-out, she tells Hannah, "As much as I'd love to continue this engaging conversation, I have to go."

"Probably that nutcase psycho babble gypsy," Hannah spits. "The only one you ever listened to. Aaron's dead right about that."

Mitsy turns her back on Hannah and walks briskly around the paddock and down the hill in the opposite direction. Hannah is correct; it's Pandora. The last thing Mitsy wants is to be overheard. "Hello?" she says in a low voice.

"Just returning your call," says Pandora. "And checking up on the situation."

"Checking up?" Mitsy doesn't like the sound of Pandora's voice. "Is something wrong?"

"No, just...stay in the light is all. Don't go dark. Promise me."

Mitsy's heart rate accelerates. "I can't believe you called right now—that you just said that." She gasps for breath. "Aaron's leaving me."

Pandora pauses. "This was a hell of a time for him to tell you that."

"To be honest, I pushed him. I already knew it was over, and I pushed him."

"All right then. You asked for it. You're not a victim."

"I thought I was ready to hear it, but I was wrong. He's leaving me," Mitsy whimpers. "He's really doing it."

"Listen to me, Mitsy. I don't care if he's jumping off the Sears tower into a barrel of porcupines. YOU stay in the light. Syd is the only one who matters right now. We have no idea how this will all play out, understand?"

"Why is everyone saying that? Why are *you*?! Are you getting...? Are your sources telling you...?"

"Never mind my sources. This is me telling you that your ability to stay clear and upbeat is critical to your daughter's recovery. That's it. Can you do that? Can you stay positive?"

"But you're the light, Pandora. You're the one."

"We're all light, Mitsy. We're children of light. That's who we are. But most of the time we choose darkness. Darkness is a choice, do you hear me? *It's a choice!* And it's a choice you've made most of your life."

Mitsy is struck with a torrent of pain and grief that she damns up behind a familiar wall of anxiety. "Ok."

"Ok then. Now tell me why you called."

She collects herself. "I was just wondering if...you, um... if you...got tested?"

"I told you not to count on that."

"I know. I won't, but...it wouldn't surprise me if ..."

"I got tested this morning, Mitsy. Just looking at me the director said it was highly unlikely, which I already knew.

More importantly I wrote a blog last night, which as of an hour ago received over a hundred responses. People are getting tested. We'll find someone; I know it. But stem cells and DNA are not the real issue."

"They're not?"

"No."

Mitsy is perplexed. As far as she knows, stem cells are the only issue.

"It seems like they would be," Pandora continues, "but they're not. The real issue here is light, plain and simple. Getting enough light. Drinking in the light. Absorbing the light. *Becoming the light.*" She pauses. "Understand?"

Mitsy can't focus. It's all too abstract. "But... how?"

"By not contributing to the darkness, Mitsy. By staying clear. By magnifying what little light you have. By drawing it in and storing it up for the dark days."

All at once Pandora's vague words gather, form, and crystallize. All at once Mitsy understands. Sort of. If light is our true currency, she thinks, we are all in trouble. Every one of us, especially Syd. We have all been squandering light. The problem is Mitsy has no idea how to get it back. If she ever had any to begin with.

Hannah

IT'S LATE THE FOLLOWING morning by the time Jonah, Hannah, and Mitsy get Syd back from the hospital in the truck. Jonah carries her into the house and lays her on the bed in the first floor guest room. "There you go, kiddo," he says.

"Thanks," says Syd. "This is a million times better than the hospital."

"I'll say," says Jonah as he moves around the foot of the bed to the other side. "Let's get some light in here, huh?" He raises the blinds on the small window to her right, revealing the panoramic view of the back pasture and frog pond. "Keep an eye out for a pair of eagles," he says. "Not sure where the nest is, probably back toward Round Hill. If you spot them, note the time for me, will you?"

"Sure," she says. "Eagles are good luck."

"We could all use a little of that," he says, winking.

He pulls the quilt from the foot of the bed up and over Syd's bone thin body. Standing on the threshold with Godiva, Hannah's heart is filled with gratitude for him and the fact that Syd is able to recuperate here with her in the old family home. As magnificent as Darien is, it lacks something. What? Something warm and fuzzy she can't put her finger on. Oh yeah, Jonah!

Godiva lurches forward, her large paws aiming for the mattress where she gets a good lick of Syd's face. Syd grins broadly, reaching out. Thank God Mitsy isn't here to reprimand them all, Hannah thinks. Too many germs! Although she does seem to have calmed down a bit since their blow-up yesterday. Or maybe she's just given up.

As if reading her mind, Jonah says, "Okay if I take the pooch with me today, Syd? I'll give her a little exercise and let her hang out in the truck with me. She's a great truck dog. And anyway, she's getting a little big to be jumping on beds."

Syd nods. "Be a good girl, G," she says then leans over slightly for another lick.

Jonah scoots Godiva out the door, and Hannah follows him past Mitsy, through the living room into the kitchen. Before he leaves, he hesitates, then turns around and spontaneously envelopes her in a gentle hug. Her cheek is pressed against his gray corduroy jacket. The musky smell of him intoxicates her. *It's been so long!* She wraps her arms around his waist, and it's all she can do not to moan, not so much with pleasure as relief. She thought she might never feel his arms around her again.

He pulls back, arm's length, his huge hands on her shoulders. "I didn't know you had it in you, Han," he says. "I really didn't. You've been so strong."

Hannah gazes into his heavy-lidded cocoa brown eyes, black curls falling boyishly across his forehead. She won't let herself cry. Can't let him know how much this means. Doesn't want to scare him off! This is the new, improved Hannah. The

Hannah that can stand on her own and survive. Can she really do it? Her chin trembles slightly. The jury is out.

"Okay then," he says, "time to go. I've got an appointment at the Thompson estate."

"*The* Thompsons?" she says.

He nods.

"Wow! That's quite a coup!" The Thompsons are the social elite of Loudoun County. They own the largest estate around—over 500 acres with three mansions and a slew of barns and outbuildings. Their family has been in Loudoun for two centuries.

"The main thing is to keep it away from developers," he says. "But...no guarantees, I suppose. More importantly, I hope Syd is settling in. But if you need me again, call."

Hannah swallows hard. The lump in her throat feels like a jagged rock. "I don't know what's going to happen," she says. "But I'll do my best to keep her happy."

"Good luck with..." He cocks his head back toward the living room where Mitsy is staring into space.

"Yeah, right." As she escorts him out the mudroom door, she says, "Will you be seeing Aaron later?"

He nods. "Aaron and that kid, Dane. They're coming over tonight. Aaron might look pulled together, but he's actually a mess."

"Yeah, well. He kind of gave Mitsy the boot yesterday."

"I heard. The manure piles up."

"And Dane decided to stay?"

Jonah shrugs. "Yeah, I mean, he seems to really care. Says he has the week off for winter break anyway. Not sure how he's going to get home if Mitsy stays here."

"Everything's a question mark," Hannah says. Maybe it's just the intensity of the roiling in her belly, but she actually wants him to leave. Everything's floating on the surface, it seems, flotsam for the inevitable undertow. What will the world look like in a week? She can't imagine. Who will be left standing?

"See you tomorrow," he says. "I'm bringing all the guys to see Syd around eleven, unless…"

"We'll be fine until then," she says firmly. "Don't worry. Plus Syd could use a little space."

"Okay. I'll check on Daizee on my way out. She's no more than days away, you know. Just a heads-up. Her milk is coming in."

Hannah nods. "Maybe that's a good thing—a birth."

"Yeah," he says. "It's always a good thing, right? Anyway, Doc will be up here later on to examine her, but call me if you see anything unusual before that. You can watch from the PC if you want. I put cameras in the barn."

She wants to say 'I love you', but she doesn't dare. "Wow, thanks!"

He waves behind him.

Hannah's phone buzzes; it's Syd. "Cookie?" she says, walking directly back in.

"I need a bucket," says Syd. "I feel like…" she gags, "…like I…"

"Be right there."

Hannah pulls a bucket from the mudroom shelf as she passes through, marveling at the fact that Syd called her instead of Mitsy. Not that Hannah trusts Mitsy, either, especially after their last exchange. Having a sister—*or a mother*—whose first line of defense in any emergency is a gypsy freak in California does not engender trust. Not to mention everything else about Mitsy. Hannah hightails through the living room past her sister.

"What's the hurry?" Mitsy says.

"Syd's nauseous." Hannah swings the bucket behind her.

Mitsy follows Hannah out of the living room and down the narrow hall. She barely places the bucket on Syd's lap before the poor child turns inside out vomiting. Mitsy rushes in to rub her daughter's back, but Syd elbows her mother away as she gags and heaves. Mitsy retracts her hand as if she'd been smacked, and leaves the room.

When Syd's done, Hannah hands her a washcloth from the bedside table and takes the bucket into the bathroom across the hall. She cleans it out and returns it to Syd. "Any better?" she says.

Syd shrugs. "I don't know."

Hannah checks the giant pill box for today's selection. "Take all your anti-nausea meds?"

"Yeah. Not supposed to take anymore until late tonight." She lurches forward and Hannah pushes the bucket under her chin to catch it.

After this bout, Hannah cleans up again and returns the bucket. "Is that it?" she asks.

Syd nods. "I think so, but..."

"But what?"

"I just..." She looks up at Hannah. "I wish I had some pot."

Hannah screws her finger into her ear to clear the metaphorical wax. "What?"

"Yeah, don't tell Mom, okay? Just that sometimes Z and I would smoke a tiny bit when I was nauseous and it really helped."

"They have medical marijuana for that."

"They gave me that once at the clinic. In a capsule? But I couldn't tolerate the capsule. I threw it right back up. I need the kind you can smoke. Right now I can't even keep water down."

"I'll call the doctor..."

"No!" says Syd. "They'll give me the kind I have to swallow. Or none at all. Or they'll re-admit me. I won't be able to keep anything inside me unless I smoke it. Plus I just...I don't want to deal with them. Please don't make me deal with them right now? I just got home."

"I'll think about it," Hannah says. She turns toward the door and hesitates. "Where did Z get it from, Syd? The pot? From Dane?"

Syd shakes her head. "No. He won't even smoke it. Something about his brother, the one who died."

Hannah nods. "Okay. Just wondered what kind of influence he was—being older and all. But I guess you and Zelda are your own bad influences."

"Don't tell Mom?" she pleads. "Please? I just can't stand feeling this way. I want to feel good. I want to eat. I want to *live!*"

"Oh cookie," Hannah says. She rushes over and kisses the top of Syd's bald head. "Be back in a few. Try to relax for now. Breathe from the belly. I'll fix this; don't worry."

"Aunt Hannah?"

"Yes, darlin'?"

"I love you."

Hannah's heart is a marshmallow at the end of a red hot stick. "Me too, sugar," she says. "I love you, too."

Back in the living room, Hannah sits on the chair adjacent to the yellow couch where Mitsy is spread out, her back against the armrest, her long legs still covered in Hannah's jeans. It's only eleven o'clock, but the charcoal clouds darken the sky and the diffused light is eerie and threatening. It feels more like dusk in the middle ages.

"It can't be like this, Mits," Hannah says.

Mitsy raises her chin. "Like what?"

"You all offended. Me fighting battles on two fronts." She

folds her arms. "We have to be one thing on one side." She points back, indicating Syd's room down the hall. "Her side," she whispers.

Mitsy stares back out the picture window at the darkening sky. "Of course I'm on her side. She just doesn't believe it."

"Can you blame her?"

Mitsy's eyes shrink into little slits. "How dare you!" she says in a low, mean whisper. "I've been dealing with this nightmare for…"

Hannah holds up her hand. "This is exactly what I'm talking about. This is exactly what we can't do."

Mitsy huffs. "Fine."

Hannah pulls off her boots and curls up in the chair. "We could be here a long time. We have no idea when they'll find a match, or…"

Mitsy leans forward. "That's where you're wrong," she says. "They'll find a match all right."

"Well, that sounded confident."

"It's about the light, Hannah. About believing in the light."

"Huh?"

"You heard me."

Hannah shifts positions. "Every time you talk to that gypsy you come out sounding like a lunatic."

"I thought you said I sounded confident."

"A confident lunatic."

"Or just maybe she gives me good advice. Have you thought of that? Maybe you're dead wrong about her." She points her finger at Hannah. "Maybe she knows what she's talking about, and you're just too un-evolved to hear it."

Hannah waves her fingers on either side of her head. "She's all…out there, Mits. Can you deny that?"

Mitsy waves her fingers back in imitation. "Well, maybe

we're all out there with her." She folds her arms. "Maybe we just don't know it."

Hannah shakes her head. "Name one solid thing about her."

"She got tested."

"For what? Rabies?"

"Very funny, Hannah. No. She got tested for Syd. To be a donor." Mitsy sits back with disgust. "And she wrote a blog last night that recruited hundreds of new donors already."

"You can't believe everything she says."

"Oh she'll find our donor, all right. She'll attract one right to our door. That's how she works. She's a *healer*."

"Then why hasn't she healed Syd? Or you for that matter?"

Mitsy stares out the window ignoring her.

After a minute, Hannah says, "Sorry, Mits. I don't mean to jump on you about her. It's just that this is a concrete job, this healing. We're dealing with a real..."

"Don't say it," Mitsy snaps.

"Don't worry," says Hannah. "I don't even know what it is." She closes her eyes and inhales deeply. "Though I have a few ideas."

"Don't..."

"Look..."

Mitsy's chin quivers. "I'm just trying to stay in one piece; can't you see that! "You're not her mother. You think you are, but you're not. You don't know what it feels like to see your own flesh and blood suffer like this. It's like..." She gasps for breath. "It's like I...failed her." Her chest heaves up and down. "A mother is supposed to protect her child."

"You didn't fail her," Hannah says. "You didn't cause..."

"I'm just afraid if something goes wrong..." Mitsy hangs her head, slowly dissolving into a whimper that escalates into deep, growling sobs.

"It won't go wrong," says Hannah gently. *Though it might.* She wants to comfort Mitsy at the same time she wants to punish her for being so derelict. She approaches her, places her hand on the back of her head and says, "I'm sorry, Mits. Seriously. I won't badmouth that woman again. I swear. If she's your way of coping, so be it."

Even over Mitsy's deep, gripping sobs, Hannah hears Syd heaving in the other room. She can't help them both at once. "I'll be back," she tells Mitsy. "Just making sure Syd is comfortable."

In the guest room, Syd says, "My stomach won't settle down." She burps, which turns into a medley of hiccups. The hiccups make her gag. And so on.

After a few rounds of this, Syd looks up at Hannah and using air quotes, says, "*If only she hadn't left the hospital...*"

"No way!" says Hannah. "You belong right here."

"But I'm such a pain in the ass..."

"You're anything but that." Hannah sits beside Syd, holding her hand as she drifts in and out of focus. Ten minutes later Hannah gets an idea and says, "I'll be right back."

In the hallway, she peeks into the living room to be sure Mitsy is still out of pocket, or maybe even asleep, only to see through the picture window that her sister is halfway down the hill heading toward the paddock. Good. Now Hannah can take care of Syd's nausea without interference. She runs up the front stairs to her office on the left and rummages through the desk drawers for the old cigar box with her bag of pot. Is it still there? She hasn't had any in so long she isn't sure, but there it is—drawer 3 in the back under the sticky pads. She rolls a quick joint, checking out the window to confirm Mitsy's location. She's leaning against the paddock fence feeding carrots to Daizee. Perfect.

She grabs some matches and runs back down the stairs into Syd's room. She opens the window a nudge and lights up then walks briskly back across the room and kicks the door shut.

Syd's eyes open wide. "Is that what I think it is?" she says.

Hannah slides the bar on the lock. "Yep. I just hope it's not too old to work on that nausea. It's been up there a long time." She lights it up, inhales just to get it going, and holds it out to Syd. "Sit up," she says. "Do you need help?"

Syd shimmies up. "I'm good." She takes the joint, sucks in the smoke, holds it, and releases with a big cough.

Hannah waits nervously for her to stop coughing. She doesn't want the cough to bring on more retching. "Maybe just inhale a little less," she tells Syd while she checks on Mitsy out the window.

"Mom's gonna kill us," says Syd, chuckling. She hands the joint out to Hannah. "Your turn," she says.

"Oh no, sugar. I got it started, but that's it for me. If something goes broke here, I'm the only one who can fix it. Your mother won't even drive."

After the next toke, Syd visibly relaxes into the pillows. "Heavenly," she says.

"Yeah?" says Hannah. "For real?"

Syd nods in slow motion. "For real."

A few minutes later, Hannah says, "Tummy?"

"Nothing coming up," Syd says. She draws a horizontal line in the air with her hand. "Just...all...chill."

"That quick, huh?" Hannah settles in at the bottom of the bed and massages Syd's left foot. Nothing seems more important right now than this—Syd's feet. When she finishes the left foot, she moves to the right. "Working out all the stress," she says. "Maybe we should get a reflexologist out here for you."

"A what?"

"A reflexologist. The feet are mapped out according to internal organs. I think the toes are the brain, but I can't swear to it, tee hee."

"Toe brain," says Syd real slowly. "I know a few of those." Her eyes move left to right. "Dane might be one."

"Ha! I thought you two made up."

Syd shrugs. "We'll see."

Twenty minutes later, Syd says, "Can I have some yogurt? I think I could eat some yogurt." She stares ahead. "Or a milk shake? Something creamy and yummy." She smacks her lips. "Or maybe a fajita."

Hannah chuckles. "Jonah stocked the fridge this morning, so let me take a look." She stands and slides the lock open. Her hand on the knob, she says, "Be right back with culinary delights."

Syd says, "Hannah Banana."

"Oh my God, remember when you used to call me that?" Hannah says, turning back to Syd. "You were so adorable with those chubby little dimpled legs and crazy curly brown hair..."

"If only she hadn't lost her hair..." says Syd mischievously.

"If only she hadn't lost her wig!" says Hannah, and they both explode laughing.

"It's not really funny, but..." laughs Syd. "Ha ha ha!" Her eyes are tearing in a good way. "But I can't stop!"

"Laugher is the best medicine!" says Hannah. "Not to be trite, but it's true!" She points to the door. "As I said, be right back!"

Syd throws the blankets off and says, "I'm coming with you. I want to see that refrigerator for myself."

"Really?" says Hannah. She moves back to help Syd up, holding her at the waist.

She opens the door to the hall at the same time Syd says, "I wish you were my mother," in a dreamy voice.

There's a gasp in the hall and they both lean out to see Mitsy a few feet down the hall staring blankly back at them.

"She didn't mean that," says Hannah. "Did you, cookie?"

"Mean what?" says Syd, giggling. "Look at me! I'm standing!" She takes a few steps down the hall. "The girl can walk!" she says.

Hannah looks at Mitsy piercingly, placing her index finger on her lips. *Drop it!* is the message.

Mitsy stands back as Syd passes her. Hannah can see her sister trying to pull it all in, every resource she has. "Feeling better?" she asks Syd stiffly.

"Hell, yeah!" says Syd.

"What's that smell?" says Mitsy, sniffing. She eyes Hannah suspiciously. "What is that? What's going on?"

"Just some nausea medication," Hannah says, grinning, and Syd throws her head back laughing.

Mitsy follows them down the hall and through the living room to the kitchen. "Nausea..." Mitsy says, her eyes registering the download. "Not...? You didn't...? Is that a marijuana cigarette I smell?"

Syd laughs out loud. "You should totally have some, Mom."

"I most certainly..."

"Hell, I could've gotten a prescription if I had the time to drive an hour to the dispensary," says Hannah. "This is a totally legit med."

"This could have negative consequences..." Mitsy says. "On her lungs...and taken in combination with other drugs... you have no idea..."

Hannah whispers into her sister's ear. "Lighten up. Okay? We're laughing. Have you noticed? Your daughter is *happy*. And she wants to e-a-t."

In the kitchen, Syd opens the refrigerator door and considers the contents. First she pulls out a bottle of milk, then opens the freezer and grabs a quart of vanilla fudge ice cream. "Jonah has great taste in food," she says.

"Jonah has great taste in everything," says Hannah.

Mitsy shakes her head at Hannah. "You're a teenager," she says. "When the hell are you going to grow up?"

Hannah pulls a couple of spoons out of the cutlery drawer and digs into the ice cream. "If growing up means paralyzing myself with misery like you, then never, I hope."

"You got my daughter *high?!*" Mitsy says, shaking her head. "And you're high too!"

"No, I'm actually not, but right about now I wish I were."

Syd pours a pint of milk into the blender and reaches behind her for the ice cream, which Hannah hands her. She dumps a few tablespoons of ice cream into the blender. "Don't be so stuck-up, Mom," she says. "Life is short. Very short, as a matter of fact."

Mitsy's expression freezes. Even Hannah can't find the words.

The whirring blender fills the void. Syd reaches up into the cabinet for some chocolate chips.

"Better check the expiration date on those," Hannah says. "I didn't even know they were up there."

Syd backs up, leans against the counter. "I'm a little weak still," she says.

Mitsy places her arm around her daughter and walks her to the table, sits her in a chair. "You okay?" she says.

Syd nods. "Mom?"

"Yes?"

"I just want you to have fun. Why can't you ever have fun?"

Mitsy sighs deeply and sits on the chair next to Syd.

"You're not living," Syd says. "You're half dead."

"But..."

"She's right and you know it," says Hannah as she pours the milkshakes into three glasses, squirting chocolate syrup on top and stirring.

Mitsy bites her lip. "I'm just...conservative. Square."

Syd laughs. "*Square!* Really? Hahahaha!" She smacks the table.

"What do you want me to do, Sydney?" Mitsy asks in earnest. "Whatever it is, I'll do it. I just want my daughter back."

Hannah places the milkshakes in front of them and sits across from Syd. They're surrounded on two sides by windows featuring views of the front yard and carriage house. Hannah can't believe how comforted she is, even under the circumstances, having company again in this empty house. *Especially* under the circumstances, she should say. The house is useful. *She's useful!*

"I just want you to take one tiny little toke of the joint," Syd says, pinching her fingers. "Please?" She grits her teeth in expectation.

Hannah raises her eyebrows. *Will she?* The suspense is killing her.

"Oh, Syd, I don't know. No, I'm sorry. I just can't. Somebody has to be responsible in this bunch."

"That would be me," says Hannah.

"I," says Mitsy. "That would be 'I'."

"See, that's exactly why you have to smoke dope, Mom," says Syd. "You treat everybody like they're inferior."

Mitsy's eyes bulge in genuine surprise. "I do?"

Hannah nods. "The child speaks truth."

"And anyway, Aunt Hannah's the writer, not you. She can twist language around anyway she wants to. She's the boss of it."

Hannah chuckles. "If only she hadn't smo..."

"No!" Syd holds her hand up in protest. "Don't say it!"

"What?" says Mitsy. "Say what?"

Syd starts on a giggle spree that infects every living thing in her radius, including her reluctant mother. Hannah's heart might pop, not just because Syd is enjoying herself like this, but because Hannah hasn't seen her sister smile in about ten years. Just this one unexpected joy in the middle of dead-on heartbreak makes life worth living. A crystal clear waterfall in the middle of hell, just exactly when you think you won't survive another minute.

When Syd comes up for air, she says, "Smoke the joint, Mom. It will relax you. Seriously." She nods like a charming wide-eyed bobble doll. "I swear. Okay?"

Mitsy stares down at the milkshake then out the window at the fruit trees she and Hannah planted so many years ago. *When they were carefree!* "Will it make you happy, Sydney?"

"Yes, Mommy, it will!"

Hannah sees what this does to Mitsy. *"Mommy."* How it corrals every memory of childbirth, motherhood, innocence and the wide open world that was once available to her and Syd individually and as a pair. She nods slowly, hypnotized.

"Okay then," she finally says, choking-up. "I'll do it."

Sydney

"HA HA, MOM, WHAT a stoner! I can't believe you smoked a joint."

"Neither can I," says her mom. Leaning forward, elbows on the table, she rubs her temples. "To be honest, I don't understand why people do this to themselves."

"They do it to relax," says Hannah. "Think of it as a glass of wine without the calories."

"It makes you stop thinking about unimportant things," says Syd.

"It makes you stop thinking about important things, too," her mom says woozily. "I couldn't even order a pizza right now."

"Hooray!" says Hannah. "Just open up that moldy brain cave and air it out a little. It's about time."

"Hey I know!" says Syd. "Let's dye Mom's hair!"

"No way!" says Mitsy, guarding her head. "Leave my hair alone."

"Please, Mom? I want to see you look your age again, please?"

Syd watches transfixed as her mom runs her fingers through her dull gray hair, which has grown a bit in the last couple of months since she's been living in her bedroom. You'd think hair wouldn't grow in the dark, but it does. It's not a plant. It sits about ear-length right now, and if you ask Syd, that's worse than shaved. It looks like she's wearing a shitty bathing cap, or just a cut-out box. No style at all. If Syd had hair, it would have pizzazz. People aren't grateful enough for their hair, she thinks. It's a terrible thing to waste.

"Come on!" says Syd. "I can't color my own hair. I wanna color yours!"

Hannah hangs back. She won't weigh-in for some reason. Syd's obviously on her own with this coercion, which is fine. She's not dropping it. "You must have some hair color upstairs, right Aunt Hannah?"

"I do," Hannah says in a fake bored voice, as if she could care less. She slurps the bottom of her milkshake nonchalantly.

Mom frowns suspiciously. "This sounds like a set-up. Is this a set-up?"

"Not at all," says Hannah. "I've always got heaps of hair dye and makeup lying around. It's my hobby, if you haven't noticed."

"In any case, the answer is no," Mom says. She taps the table. "Isn't it good enough that you got your mother high, Sydney? On an illegal drug?"

Syd rolls into helpless laughter. "The best, Mom, seriously," she says, catching her breath. "I never thought you'd loosen up enough..."

At this, her mother raises her eyebrows and Syd doesn't know what's coming. They wait. Finally her mother says, "Fine. Do whatever you want with me."

Hannah grimaces. "Nobody meant any harm, Mits."

Her mom shakes her head. "No, I mean it. Turn me into something happy-go-lucky. Just do it. Loosen me up."

"Really?" say Hannah and Syd at the same time.

Hannah jumps up. "I was trying out a few colors before I flew up to Connecticut. Pretty sure I have a box of Garnet, Rosewood, and Amethyst Brown."

"What color is your hair now?" Syd asks Hannah.

"Rosewood," Hannah says.

"Okay then Amethyst Brown," says Syd. "Mom shouldn't have the exact same color as you."

Mom frowns. "As long as...it's not purple. Is it purple? Amethyst...sounds. Purple." Her words are all slow and drawn out.

Hannah shakes her head. "Not purple," she says. "Softer auburn with subdued highlights. Sophisticated, but not stuffy. *Modern.*"

Mom rolls her eyeballs as Hannah disappears like a magic trick. While she's gone, Sydney says, "You're the best, Mom. I mean it."

Her mother places her hand over Syd's hand and nods. "No, you are," she says. "You're the best. This is the least I can do."

Syd beams contentment. It's a day she'll never forget—the day her mom quit her job as manager of the universe. The day her mother climbed into the hellhole with her, settled in, and surrendered to whatever fun could be had in a pit of pythons. *You'd be surprised!* Today, her mother became a member of her team, and this alone might cure them both.

Hannah returns with the box of hair color and gets her mother on a bar stool by the sink. She works with hot pink rubber gloves like a pro. Syd is so happy all of a sudden she hardly knows herself. *Who is she?* She could be anywhere doing anything. Floating on a sailboat in Tahiti—Dane feeding her peeled grapes while Z swabs the deck. She can't think of a single thing she'd rather be doing than watching her stoned mother get her hair dyed, ha ha! She breaks into a helpless fit of giggles that gets everyone else going with her. Her mother tries hard to suppress it, which makes it even funnier.

"I'm glad this is all so amusing, Sydney," she says, even though she looks equally amused, or bemused, whatever. *Mused!*

Syd's phone buzzes and she pulls it out of her pocket. "Thinking of u," is the text from Z. She returns the phone to her pocket. What's she gonna say, "Thinking of you on your hands and knees scrubbing the deck of a schooner in Tahiti while Dane and I spit grape seeds at the fish?" No, she won't do it. All she wants is to watch her mother's transformation. That's it. She's never occupied a moment so completely in her entire life.

After dyeing Mom's hair, Hannah rinses it via the sink hose and wraps it in a towel. From where Syd sits, the wet hair does have a little bit of a purplish highlight to it, which tickles her silly. Just one more volcanic guffaw to rein-in. She doesn't know how she'll stop laughing if after all this hoopla her mother ends up looking like Barney. But Hannah looks satisfied with the results, so maybe it'll be okay. Hannah's an obvious genius at fashion and style. She plugs in the hairdryer and pulls out a round brush to blow out the victim's hair.

"You should've been a Hollywood makeup artist," Syd says dreamily.

"Let's wait and see," says Hannah. "You haven't seen the final reveal."

"Can you get me a mirror, Hannah?" says her mother.

"Oh no, not yet. No way!" Hannah says. "Not until your hair is all brushed out and we've got you made up."

"And dressed in a designer outfit," adds Syd.

"Wait a minute," says her mom. "I said okay to the hair, not the rest of it."

"Just do it, Mom," says Syd. "You're already this far in." She releases a big yawn.

"Hey, cookie," says Hannah. "You getting tired? Let's get you installed in the living room and we'll finish up in there. You'll be more comfortable."

Syd can't argue with that. Her body wants to go horizontal. On their way in, she loses her balance slightly and grabs the doorjamb. Her tee-shirt rises and her loose fitting pajama pants swing low on her hips.

"What's that, Sydney?" says her mother in a high voice.

"What?" says Syd. "Sorry, I gotta go lay down."

On their way into the living room, her mom says, "Is that a tattoo, Sydney? I thought I saw a tattoo on your buttock."

Syd sits down on the yellow couch, curls up in the corner and gathers the soft aqua lap blanket to her chin. "I don't know," she says. "What did it look like?"

"Are you feeling okay, Syd?" Hannah asks.

Syd nods. "Just...tired."

"Seriously? That's all?" Hannah says.

Syd nods again. "Seriously."

"Sydney?" says her mom, looking kind of comical with a towel wrapped around her head like a turban, spikes of amethyst poking out. "Is that a tattoo?"

"Um. Maybe."

"When did you get it?"

Syd rolls on her side to reveal it fully—might as well get this over with. "It's a knife," she says. "A dagger, actually. I got it a year ago."

Her mother breathes heavily. "A year ago? What possessed you? Who did it?" She screws up her face. "A *dagger?*"

"I got it from a cousin of Z's who specializes in these things. He's an artist, no biggy. He knew what he was doing."

"You could have gotten hepatitis, Sydney. Or AIDS! This is not a laughing matter."

"She got a dagger as a symbol of fighting back," says Hannah. "So she can defend herself."

"So. You. Knew. About. It?" says her mom in controlled little syllables.

"Aunt Hannah happened to see it one day at the wig shop," Syd says as casually as she can. "When I was climbing up on the stool. She had nothing to do with it. She wasn't even around when it happened."

Syd can see Hannah eyeballing Mom again with one of those sister-*drop it!*-signals. It takes a second, but it works, thank God. Mom settles into the bar chair Hannah dragged out from the kitchen. "I see," is all she says.

Hannah starts combing through her sister's new reddish-purply brown hair, and Mom says, "I'm glad you're fighting, Sydney, honestly. But please don't get any other tattoos. Will you promise me that?"

Syd sighs. "Yeah, I guess." She blows air through her lips like a horse. "Although…"

"Although nothing," says Mom.

Syd flaps her arms. "I did want some wings."

Now Hannah, standing behind Mom, sends the hairy eyeball straight to Syd to end the conversation. Her expression is so extreme it nearly sends Syd back to comedy purgatory where you can't stop laughing even though a red hot creature with a pitchfork is warning you to stop. She has to turn toward the window to get a grip. If she returns Hannah's screwy look, her mother will get even madder. She stares out the window to ground herself, but her focus is completely changed. She can't believe what she's looking at. "Oh my God," she says! "Look! Eagles!" She climbs up on her knees and points.

Perched in the pin oak, left of the barn at the level of the cupola, are two massive birds. "Are they eagles, Aunt Hannah? They are eagles, right?"

Hannah rushes forward. "Where?"

"Right there!" says Syd, pointing. "What time is it? Jonah wanted me to note the time."

"Two o'clock exactly," says her mother. She slips off the bar stool and hurries to the window.

"Eagles right on our property," Hannah says, awestruck. "Jonah said he's seen them, but I didn't really believe him. I thought they were probably vultures."

"They're really eagles though, right?" says Syd. Her eyes are a little blurry and she doesn't want to mislead anyone. Plus her joints are starting to ache like crazy.

"Without a doubt," Hannah says. "Look at their white heads and tails. Those are bald eagles all right." She looks at Syd meaningfully.

"Eagles are protectors," says Syd. "This is really good news."

"Doubly good," says Hannah. "Right? You wanted wings... here they are!"

Syd visualizes The Taker in her mind's eye. She looks right at him while her super-loud inner voice screams, "Take *that*, sucker!" She screams it so loud in her head, she's surprised Hannah and her mother don't ask her who she's screaming at.

They all stare for a while, kneeling against the back of the couch, shoulder to shoulder, all in a row. On the left is Hannah, Mom in the middle, then Syd. All at once the eagles take flight across the field, their wings spread out in a straight line. It's something to see. When they're gone, her mom turns to Syd, and kisses her forehead. Syd doesn't remember when her mother kissed her last. She doesn't kiss her back; she's too stunned.

She settles back into the couch as they all resume positions.

Things are changing, she thinks. Definitely changing. *She feels it.* If only her body didn't feel like a pile of molten lead—like she's being pulled straight down into the earth's core—everything would be perfect. But Syd is used to feeling like shit. *Soldier on!* She can deal.

Back at her station, Hannah strategically clips the sides and back of Mitsy's hair, applies a marshmallow-sized dollop of fluffy white mousse, and starts the dryer. Syd hasn't had hair in so long, she's riveted. *So this is how you comb it!*

Next Hannah blows Mom's hair out with a small round brush, giving it some lift. As the hair dries, it looks more auburn than purple, which is good and bad. Good because her mother actually looks great; bad because it kills the hilarious comedy featuring her mother's punk hair.

"Wow, Mom, you look…a-ma-zing!" she says.

Hannah steps back, evaluating. "Okay, good. Now for the makeup." She runs upstairs and returns quick before Mom has a chance to locate a mirror.

"I haven't really agreed to the makeup, Hannah," Mom says.

"Yes you have," lies Hannah.

"You have, Mom," Syd swears. "You're so stoned you don't even remember," she adds with a giggle.

Her mother doesn't protest, so Hannah just continues. Syd lays her head against the back of the couch for a minute and must've dropped off to sleep, because when she wakes up, the vision of her anti-mother stands right in front of her. There is no way this is her mother. *No way!*

"How do you like it, Sydney?" her mother asks, hands on hips. "Are you satisfied?"

Her hair is short, edgy with a light to medium auburn color. Purplish highlights, but nothing you'd be tempted to mock, even on a woman that old. The shape and color of the clipped boyish hairdo suit her angular face, emphasizing her wide-set, blue-gray eyes. Or maybe that's the awesome makeup Aunt Hannah used—still natural, but like someone took an airbrush to her spotty skin and dull features.

"You look like a model," says Syd, awestruck. She sits up and rubs her eyes. *Is this for real?* For the first time in Syd's life she sees the resemblance between her mother and Godmother.

"Oh for heaven's sake," says her mother, flicking her hand.

It's not just the hair and face. She's wearing a pair of Hannah's slim, black leather pants, a fitted gray sweater, and a silver chain necklace that falls almost to her waist. She dropped ten years at least. "No seriously, have you seen yourself, Mom?"

Enter Hannah through the hallway rolling a full-length oak swivel mirror that she slides in front of Mitsy. "Ta da!" she says.

Syd can see that her mother is completely overwhelmed by her image. It takes her a minute. Her jaw hangs low while she stares, speechless.

"Good job, right?" says Hannah, polishing her pretend medal of honor.

"Mom, seriously, Dad would faint."

"This is not about your father," says her mom, all tight-lipped.

"Still," says Hannah. "Syd's right. When was the last time you dressed up?"

"I don't like where this conversation is going," says her mom.

Hannah holds up her hands in surrender. "Okay. You're right. This is about you."

"It's about me," says Mom, still stunned. "Not Aaron." She looks at Hannah. "Isn't it?"

Hannah nods. "It's about you taking back your life, Mits."

Her mom looks back in the mirror and then to Hannah and Syd. "That's exactly what I'm going to do. I'm going to take back my life."

After she catches her breath, Syd says, "I was the one who took your life away, right Mom? I did that."

Her mother's freshly painted pink lips form a shiny O. Her hands rush to cover her mouth as if it might betray her. Finally she says, "Of course not."

Syd nestles her brittle bones into the corner. "Are you sure? Because I know I'm a lot of work."

"It was me, Sydney," she says. "Not you."

"I," says Hannah.

Her mother shoots Hannah a dirty look. "Touché," she says then turns back to Syd. "I lost my life all by myself without any help from you, Sydney. Long before you came on the scene, I tried to live a life I had no business living." She walks to the couch and embraces Syd. "I'm going to take better care of you, I promise."

"Just take better care of yourself, Mom. Okay?" Syd has to suck back a whimper. Some days are just too much. She doesn't want to ask where her mother thinks she belongs. She's afraid of the answer.

Her mom claps her hands and faces Hannah. "Where can I get a good horse around here?" she says.

Hannah cocks her head in disbelief. "You mean...to ride?"

Mitsy nods slowly, smiling.

"Mits, you've been lying around in bed for months. You're completely out of shape."

"Plus you might still be stoned," says Syd.

"You refuse to drive a car!" Hannah says. "How will you possibly manage..."

"I'm fine," interrupts her mother. "I'll take it slow. I just need to...ride." She rubs her hands together anxiously. "I really, really need to ride. I need to... feel the wind."

Hannah considers this. "Okay, but I can't hook you up

until I talk to Jonah tomorrow. He'll probably join you just to make sure you're all right."

"You never forget how to ride a horse, Hannah. My muscles still hold the memory. It's instinctual."

"Only if you have muscles to begin with," says Hannah. "And you don't."

Mom ignores her. "Where are the quarter horses," she says, "and the thoroughbreds? Are they in the other barn?"

Hannah nods, pointing out the window and waving down the hill. "Way down by Junior's riding school," she says. "He works them for me."

Mom just stands there pining for horses, of all things. Pining to ride horses in her leather pants and fitted sweater complete with designer hair and makeup, not to mention high-heel boots. This is like rubbing a bottle and having a genie produce a celebrity mother for you. *Who is this?* Syd's never even heard her mother mention horses before. She can't imagine her mother riding a bicycle, never mind a living, breathing animal. *A fucking horse!* Her mother hates animals! She didn't even want Godiva! Plus she's no athlete. The mother Syd knows is the opposite of everything she's looking at right now.

Arms folded, legs in a confident stance at the window, the woman pretending to be Syd's mom surveys the fields. Her eyes shrink into slits like she's trying to see something very small. She pokes her neck forward and asks Hannah for the binoculars.

"Why?" says Hannah. "What do you see?"

"It's what I don't see," she says. "Daizee. She left the window."

They look at each other with expectation.

"I'll go down," says Mom.

"I want to go, too," says Syd. But she's not sure she could make it to the kitchen, never mind the paddock. Her body's caving.

Hannah must've noticed, because she tells Mom, "Let me get the laptop. Jonah hooked it up to a camera in the barn. You can go down while Syd and I watch from up here." She checks her watch. "Doc's due here shortly anyway."

Her mother points her hands in a prayer steeple. "Thank you, Hannah," she says. "Thank you so much! Sydney, is that okay with you?"

Syd smiles vaguely. She doesn't want her mother to know she's practically narcoleptic. She just nods.

While Hannah's getting the laptop, Mitsy spots the vet driving up in his truck. "The vet's here!" she hollers up to Hannah. "I'm going down." She looks at Syd. "Are you sure? Do you want me to stay?"

Syd shakes her head. "Go lead your life, Mom. Seriously. I've never seen you so excited."

Her mom runs into the kitchen, through the mudroom, grabs whatever bulky jacket—probably Jonah's, and charges down the hill like a high-heeled colt. "See you later, whoever you are," Syd mutters to the window.

Hannah returns with the laptop and sets it up on a tray table in front of her and Syd.

"The vet is here," Syd says woozily. Wow is she tired. Not just tired, but headachy and dizzy. "Did you hear Mom say... about the vet?"

Hannah brings her head down to eye level with Syd. "Are you okay, cookie?"

Leave it to Aunt Hannah to notice what her mother doesn't. She shrugs. "Just really tired."

Hannah feels her forehead. "You're hot," she says.

She runs into the kitchen and comes back with a thermometer, which she puts in Syd's ear. When it beeps, she reads it and declares, "101."

"I just want to sleep," says Syd.

"They told us to bring you in if it got over 101," says Hannah nervously.

Syd slides down behind Hannah and rests her head on the cushion. "I have a headache," she says.

"I'm going to get you some water, Syd, and you have to drink it right down, okay? You might just be dehydrated. They told me that can raise your temp."

Syd nods in her half-sleep.

The next thing she knows Hannah's lifting her up to sip the water. She forces herself to drink it, which takes awhile. One thing she does not want to do is go back to the stupid hospital today or ever. She tries to pretend she has energy, but she doesn't have the energy to pretend.

Fifteen minutes later, when she's finally finished the water, her mother reappears. "False alarm," she says, then tunes into Syd and Hannah. "What's going on here?"

"She's got a bit of a fever," says Hannah. "101. I'll take it again in fifteen minutes."

Mom eyeballs Hannah in some kind of evil code, and they disappear into the kitchen. To Syd it sounds like things might be getting a little testy; she's not sure exactly why. Not that she can make out what they're saying; she can't. They're talking in loud whispers. She just hopes the one who wins is the one who wants her to stay right where she is.

In the middle of it, someone's cell rings, and eventually her mother moves into the dining room with her phone. Syd can see her mother from the couch through the archway, but her mother's not tuned in to Syd. "Hello," she says.

Next Hannah steps into the dining room, saying, "Mitsy, come on! You don't need that gypsy anymore! Look at you! You're a different woman for God's sake. You have me now! And horses!"

Her mother turns her back on Hannah and says into the phone something like, "What?! Are you sure? Oh my God! Oh my God!"

To which Hannah remarks, "Oh my God, *what?!* Don't believe a word of her bullshit, Mitsy, damn it!"

Syd's belly is a stew of anxiety just listening to all this tension crack like a giant rotten dinosaur egg over their perfect day. But she's too tired to get overly involved, so she lies in wait.

Her mother drops the phone and stares at Hannah, her features all exaggerated and bugged-out like she just reentered the atmosphere. *What's next? The Animal Uprising?* Syd can't take the pressure. Can't they see she's not feeling well?

"What?" says Hannah. "Out with it. Not that's it true. It isn't." She jabs the air with her finger right at her mother's face. "Whatever that woman told you is a lie."

"I thought you were going to leave me alone about her," says Mom.

Hannah's hip juts out. "I am...I was. I'm trying."

"She's a..." says Mom, but Syd can't make out the words.

Then Hannah says something like, "blah blah blah.... Dracula?"

"No..." says her mother, but now she's really whispering.

Hannah leans in. "A...that's impossible."

Things are blurry now, but Syd makes out her mom wandering into the living room like some kind of supermodel zombie, based on her wired expression. "Sydney," she says, "you'll never guess..."

Syd tries to raise herself on the couch to hear the earth-shattering news, whatever it is, but before she can get all the way up, she collapses. The next thing she knows, she's hovering over what looks like an ancient crime scene revealed by the light of a full harvest moon, staring down at a bloody child draped in a gray muslin robe in the center of a burning cottage. Behind her, vineyards roll for miles. In front of her, The Taker's purple light vibrates in the shadows. All at once, two eagles dive down at a blinding speed, lifting the child. Clutching her between them with their talons and burdened by her weight, they fly low and unsteadily across the moonlit fields.

Pandora

PANDORA'S HEAD IS A spinning globe. She's trying to stop the rotation at an angle that gives her maximum visibility into the slip of the universe that contains the resources she needs to heal Sydney. At the same time she heals Sydney, she must somehow manage to hold the parallels open so she can slip back through them unharmed. So she can stay alive. To do this, she has to pry open time itself to create a portal into Sydney's past—the lives she's lived with Pandora and the lives she's lived without her. She's never done anything like this before; it's a vexing task. But this is what she has to do to investigate the source of Syd's disease—the moment it happened and why. The moment her energy crystallized into this exact disease at that exact time. If only her head were clear, but it isn't, and it's too late now. She has to work with what she's got. What she's got is a muddled brain, very little time, and the attention span of a gnat.

The only thing Pandora knows for sure is that in spite of

all the focus on stem cells and bone marrow, her physical DNA is not the real answer. It's her energetic DNA that aligns with Syd's in substance and sequence. No one has to tell her this; she knows it in the same way she knows the Earth spins on more than one axis. The way she knows the Earth, like the humans it hosts, is a living thing with subtle energetic bodies that live simultaneously on other planes in other dimensions. Wherever we go, the Earth in one of its forms is our home.

Not that the doctors would know about Pandora's energetic DNA—or Syd's. They wouldn't. It's too esoteric. Their brains aren't trained to reach that far for answers. The evidence they seek is physical, concrete, and directly in front of them. They don't know that the physical plane is only the crystallization of all the energetic planes combined. Or for that matter, that we, too, in physical form are the crystallization of our energy on other planes. The information they use is in front of them, but much of the information they need is beyond their reach.

Pandora's energetic DNA matches Syd's at the intersection of at least one lifetime, probably more. That DNA—the energetic DNA they share—is apparently so powerful that it has downloaded into the physical plane in spite of incalculable hereditary odds. Pandora didn't even know it was possible. Sometimes what we think are miracles are really just facts of another nature, she thinks. Facts from another timeline. New information and virgin energy flows into the universe moment by moment, day by day. Nothing is fixed. The mistake we make is thinking it is.

What Pandora has been able to discern so far is that Syd's energetic DNA was damaged by the embedded memory of a distant trauma. Damaged and recorded, its toxic expression was inescapable without intervention. Not just physical intervention, but the intervention of gifted mystics or healers—practitioners who understand the prismatic composition of energy and its infinite and layered manifestations from multiple lifetimes.

Pandora has every reason to believe healing of a spiritual nature was attempted in the distant past, but failed. She herself could have been part of the attempt. Physical intervention is a last ditch effort effective only after a trauma has manifested. It didn't have to get that far, Pandora knows. She should have trusted her gut. She should have passed Mitsy over and worked directly on Syd. *But how?* The mother and aunt are an integral part of both the pathology and the healing. And somehow, whether she likes it or not, so is she.

She spreads the ankle length, raw silk of her finest Peruvian skirt and kneels on the bare floor in front of the window that features Heavenly Peak. *Tahoe, you are my shaman!* She draws the view into her memory, ballast for the journey, closes her eyes, brings her hands together, and moves into it. Immediately before her, as real as the sparkling indigo jewel at the base of the mountains, is the karmic wheel in all its power and complexity. *The actual karmic wheel!* She has only seen it once before and not in its entirety. She is mesmerized, awestruck, humbled. Her task is to spin it through centuries and incarnations on planes both physical and etheric then enter it in the exact place that will prevent the whip of destiny from breaking their necks. She has to enter it in the place where their memories overlap—hers, Mitsy's, Hannah's and Syd's. Enter it; transform the moment; and move on. It's their only hope.

The wheel spins and they all spin with it. They spin in colorful Mongolian costumes and rich, velvet Saxon robes. They spin in Egyptian tunics and the alabaster robes of the Delphi oracles. They are worldly aristocrats and rebellious clerics. Plainclothes villagers and eccentric theatrical performers. Grecian sandals, stacked heels, and army boots caked with mud. They spin as men and women, primitive and sophisticated, laughing and plotting, innocent and manipulative. They are all things human and yet so particular in their various features, wardrobes, occupations and stations of life. Their personalities, biases and belief systems vary with each incarnation. How will it end? How will she know when to press the button that slows the wheel down long enough for her to re-enter from another lifetime? *This lifetime!* Maybe she won't. Maybe it's just a terrifying game of roulette.

Pandora comes in and out of her trance, seeking knowledge and skill for the future, but understanding that the wheel can only be slowed down in the moment when her DNA is transferred to Syd. If she does it before that, there could be hell to pay. What condition she'll be in when the time comes, she can't know. For instance, will she be awake or under sedation? She's not sure what method the hospital prefers or what method is best for her. In the meantime, all she can do is investigate and prepare. And the stem cell transplant is not the only thing she has to worry about. *Were it only that simple!*

In order to make the physical DNA stick, Pandora knows she must capture the glue that will hold it in place. The glue is *zeon*. Zeon alone holds the signal. Without it, Syd's weak body will most likely reject Pandora's cells. The connective tissue between their lifetimes can be catalyzed only by the powerful frequency of that precise color; she knows that now. It's what Anjah's been trying to show her all along—or what she's known in spite of him—with Anjah and her it's sometimes hard to tell the difference.

But how will she do it?

Last night, after hours of astral travel in every known corner of the multi-verse, she saw what looked like the possibility of a geomagnetic storm developing close to Earth. It appeared to be gathering in the stratosphere at a point threatening the northwest quadrasphere, somewhere around latitude 36.30N and longitude 77.5W. This is more or less in the vicinity of Virginia, West Virginia and Maryland. Whether or not the storm will materialize, or whether Pandora will be able to access the zeon from that particular storm (or at all), remain huge questions. And even if the storm materializes, will it come close enough for harvest? *Will it come so close that it destroys them?*

Timing is another factor. Must she harvest the zeon in perfect synchrony with the transplant? Or can she do it in advance and bring it into this dimension for storage? If she stores it, can she stabilize it? *Or will it blow them all up?* She doesn't really know its full potential. And how in hell will she manage to activate the zeon at the same time she slows down the wheel in the exact moment her DNA enters Syd's bloodstream? *She is only one person!* How much is expected of her? Too much, but what else is new. She is a grossly undervalued employee of the universe.

She rises from the bare floor, her knees and head throbbing. She's in it now—the center of creation itself—right where she always wanted to be. Not that she knew what it would feel like. The energy inside this bubble is chaotic and combustible; the pressure nearly unbearable. Whether she's equal to it or not she'll soon find out. All she knows is that this time, she has no choice.

She lights a cigarette and stares out at her inspiration, bidding farewell to her mystic lake. The slow, punishing burn of the smoke in her throat feels sooo good. *Burn away!* She doesn't regret not stopping sooner. She can't stop now, either. Whatever's holding her together today, good or bad, is the lubrication that will squeeze her through the eye of this needle. There's no time to rip out the seam and sew it back the right way. *This* is the right way. In any case, it's the only way.

She finishes her smoke and approaches the covered easel twenty feet away. Should she lift it one more time? *Good luck or bad?* She fingers the edge of the worn linen, considering the consequences. If the image of Elysha has disappeared, Pandora may lose faith. If it has returned fully, her confidence will soar. She combs the fingers of both hands through her long, loose white hair several times, brushing it back and tying it in a simple knot at the nape of her neck. She won't look at the painting; she can't. It might mess with her already unsteady head.

The stakes are too high.

Before she can change her mind, she pushes a screeching Guru into a traveling crate and carries him out to the front where her two suitcases are lined up on the slate walkway. She can't do it without Guru. She hopes the taxi arrives before she loses what little courage remains.

Hannah

WHILE THE NURSE PREPARES Syd for her bedside transfusion, Mitsy sits just outside the room on a bench in the hall, head in hands. In front of her, Hannah wears a groove in the tile floor, twenty feet up and back, one corridor to the next, and again. Her tenth trip in she stops in front of Mitsy, arms extended. "It's going to be okay," she says, as much to herself as to her sister. "The doctors agreed that if Syd holds this transfusion, they can begin the chemo prep for the transplant. It'll all work out."

Mitsy looks up. "The treatment is extremely aggressive," she says. "I just don't know if she can..." She chokes up. "...if she can..."

Hannah slides down beside her sister and envelopes her. "She'll survive!" she tells her. "Hell, knowing Syd, she'll thrive!"

Hannah has to force herself to believe her own words. The fear that grips them both is palpable, although neither caves into it, at least not verbally. Their thinly veiled expressions say it all. *"Don't scratch this scab!"* They're both dangling by a thread a thousand feet over crazy town. Either one of them could drop at any moment. They have to be careful what they say and do. *And think!*

Mitsy sits up straight and gazes absently ahead. The corners of her blue-gray eyes are misty, but her eyes are bright, accentuated by the natural brown and beige tones Hannah used to soften her sharp features. Seeing Mitsy like this, through a softer lens, melts Hannah's heart. The recent past dissolves like a cube of sugar in hot tea. All she sees now is the beloved sister who allowed Hannah and Syd to pull her out of the shadows. Shadows she'd been hiding in for years. The glare of the light must have smarted, Hannah knows. But she did it. Mitsy did it. It's one brave choice that will open her to another and another. A choice that allows infinite possibility where there was none.

"We're on the cusp of everything," Hannah says urgently. "I feel it. The cusp of all of us becoming who we really are. We just have to unravel this knot. This one knot."

Mitsy's chin quivers. "It's a big one," she says. "Really big. And twisted."

They're distracted by a shuffling noise down the hall. Around the corner in a fast moving pack are Jonah, Aaron and Dane.

"What's happened?" says Aaron, walking briskly toward them. "How is she?"

Hannah jumps up and heads toward the posse to spare her sister the retelling of Syd's collapse, but Aaron seems almost unaware of her. He looks up and over, distracted.

"So she's okay?" he says, his eyes searching somewhere behind Hannah.

"Uh, yeah, so far," says Hannah. "She's getting transfused. But I wouldn't say..." She turns, follows his eyes, and sees that he's staring, open-mouthed, at the wondrous new version of his wife. If he looks any harder, his eyes might erupt.

"What..." he says, "Mitsy, what...? Is that...? What did you do?"

Mitsy just sits there completely disinterested in his or anyone's reaction to her appearance. She doesn't even answer.

Aaron walks toward Mitsy, while Hannah moves in for a sympathy hug from Jonah. His embrace is disappointing, half-hearted. Is he staring at Mitsy, too? Well, who could blame him, Hannah thinks. She looks pretty terrific. "Meet the new Mitsy Michaels," she says.

Dane, whose view is blocked by Jonah, steps around to see what's going on. He claps his hands. "Holy shit, Mrs. M, I didn't even know that was you!"

"Down, boy," says Hannah with a chuckle.

"Wow," he says, "you look friggin' hot!"

At this, even Mitsy suppresses an amused grin immediately covering her face with her hands.

Misunderstanding the silence, Dane turns to Aaron. "No offense, Mr. M," he says.

"No offense taken, Dane," says Aaron evenly. He considers the situation for a few seconds then says, "Mitsy, you really do look..."

Mitsy doesn't wait for him to finish. She rises from the bench and says, "I'm going to get some coffee, anybody else want some?"

"I'll take a cup," says Hannah. "Unless you need company?"

Mitsy shakes her head and walks briskly down the hall in the opposite direction, her posture tall and erect. Still rocking those black leather pants stuffed into four inch heel boots. Hannah can't remember when she last saw her sister walk with that much confidence. She's surprised Mitsy even knows how to walk in heels. In spite of the convergence of so much hell, Hannah's relieved that she and Syd were able to pull that off. That they were able to squeeze a thing of beauty out of so many layers of shit. Leave it to Syd to make that happen, Hannah thinks ruefully. It never would have happened without her.

A memory flashes before Hannah. She's twelve years old and Mitsy is sixteen. Hannah watches Mitsy perform dressage with her chestnut stallion, High Noon. There they are in the ring under a perfect cornflower blue sky, dazzling spectators and judges at the Oatlands Plantation on a crisp September morning. How proud Hannah was to be Mitsy's little sister then! Hannah, who would rather be on a runway than a horse, nevertheless understood the nobility of a horse and its rider. The fusion of communication moved from the brain of the rider through the body of the horse, as if they were one magnificent creature. And that day, they were. Hannah had forgotten all about that aspect of Mitsy—the nobility—until now.

When Mitsy disappears behind the double doors, Aaron says, "So...what did you do to her? How did she...I can't picture her allowing..."

"That's not the same woman I drove down here," says Dane, wide-eyed.

Jonah clutches Dane's shoulder and shakes him affectionately. "Simmer down, bucko," he says with a smile. "She's taken."

"You can thank Syd for the makeover," Hannah tells Aaron. "She was the force behind it. Mine was the easy part—a little of this, a little of that."

Aaron's eyes fix on a point somewhere in the distance. "How, uh...when can I see Syd?" he says.

"Right now," says Hannah. "Last I saw, she was groggy, but awake."

Aaron nods absently, raps on the door, and enters. Jonah stands in the hall, fidgeting, hands in pockets, mouth pursed.

"What's up?" Hannah says, concerned. *Something's up.*

He shrugs distantly.

"Oh by the way, we saw the eagles," she says. "Two of them! Syd made us note the time for you. It was exactly two o'clock."

"Oh yeah?" he says, but he's not tuned in.

Hannah reaches for his arm, and he withdraws it. "What...?" she says perplexed. "Did I do something?"

He raises his chin and scratches the emerging scruff on his neck and jaw line. "This is not the time," he says.

Hannah's heart sinks. "Is it Syd?" she persists. "Or maybe the Thompson deal? Didn't it go through?"

"No," he says. "It went through. Look, I gotta go check on the mare. Doc says she was restless. After you all left with the ambulance, she laid down, so. It's imminent."

Hannah nods. "Is there any way we can watch from here? On the laptop or iPad? I think it would really help Syd. And also Mitsy..."

"Yeah, you're so concerned about Syd, aren't you?" he says with disgust. "It's all about Syd."

She backs up. "Well, of course it is."

He turns and storms down the hall, shoulders hunched. She starts to follow him, but he waves his hand in a back-off gesture that feels exactly like a slap in the face. An invisible but nearly impenetrable barrier goes down between them. *She's been here before!* But this time she has no idea what she's done.

This long, punishing day wears interminably into the evening, and not just because Jonah doesn't reappear. Syd sleeps mercifully through much of it. No one's confirming her ability to endure the bone marrow prep yet, or ever. In fact the doctors' appearances are so few and far between they're like mirages when they finally show up. This gives Hannah more compassion for the years Mitsy spent doing this on her own, Aaron traveling as he did. *Did he really have to?* Maybe he didn't. She gave him the credit all these years, but maybe he was the real coward after all. Not that either one of them would appreciate Hannah's judgment. Neither of them really deserves it. She's clear on that. These situations are worse from the inside than anyone on the outside could ever guess.

Aaron and Dane sit with Syd on and off beyond the three hour transfusion and into the dinner hour. Syd doesn't eat. Periodically Aaron steps out of the room, disappears down the hall, and reappears with a bottle of water or coffee. Every time Aaron steps out, Mitsy goes into the room. She won't give him the satisfaction of answering a single question, though he tries. At six o'clock, he grabs a sandwich from the cafeteria and brings back a few for the rest of them. Mitsy holds up her hand in refusal. Hannah dives in. Dane eats everything that's left.

An hour later, Aaron steps out of the room. Dane lingers. Aaron looks directly at Mitsy and says, "I'm going to take Dane back to Jonah's townhouse. Is there anything..."

Mitsy turns in the other direction, arms folded, staring out the window at the distant hills.

"Come on, Mitsy," he says. "For God's sake..."

She turns around. "How dare you."

He steps toward her and she retreats. "We've got a sick child," he says. "Can't we have a conversation about her?" He drops his arms in exasperation. "Whatever's going on between us can wait!"

"You're right about that," she says. "It can wait forever as far as I'm concerned."

Aaron pokes his head into Syd's room and gestures to Dane, "We're leaving," he says. "Gotta go now."

When he appears in the hall, Hannah sees for the first time that Dane's eyes are rimmed in red. Another casualty of this disaster. "Anyone have some Advil or something?" Dane asks. "I have a splitting headache." He rubs his temples. "I never get headaches."

"Well, this'll do it," says Hannah.

Mitsy pulls a pill box out of her purse and hands him whatever. Right about now Hannah realizes that her head is splitting, too. *Where does it all end?* Ugh. She doesn't want to know.

An hour later, Syd's sleeping, Mitsy's brooding, and Hannah excuses herself to call Jonah about Daizee. After all, it's doubtful in his foul mood that he would even call her if Daizee foaled. Although it's not like Jonah at all to indulge a foul mood in the first place. Something terrible must be wrong, but what could be worse than Syd's current situation? But there you have it—everything and everyone is under its spell, not just Syd. She punches Jonah's number on her keypad and waits. Maybe things have improved. Six rings in, he answers.

"Hello?" he says curtly.

"Hey," says Hannah. "Sorry to burst into your evening, but I'm just wondering about Daizee."

"Yah, well, she's laying down, but nothing's happening. I'm with her now, but about to head up to the house and watch it online."

She repeats her earlier request. "Can we watch it here?" she says. "Online? It might pick up some spirits…"

"Signal's not so great over there," he says flatly. Silence.

Even though Hannah knows the signal's not that bad—*she's on the phone now, isn't she?*—she doesn't push it. Instead, she trots down the hall and ducks into one of the small conference rooms, the ones where they deliver all their rotten news, and shuts the door. This is a conversation she doesn't want overheard.

"Can you just please tell me what's wrong?" she says. "I've got a lot on my plate right now, if you haven't noticed.

"Oh, do you?" he says. "And what would that be?"

She curls her features up like a fist. "Excuse me?! It's not like you to be such an asshole, Jonah. Seriously. You know exactly what I'm dealing with here...Syd..."

"Oh really?" he says. "Syd?"

Hannah's just...speechless.

"No clue at all what's pissing me off?" he says.

"No," she says. "But I'm all ears."

"You're all worried about Syd, is that right?" he says.

"Of course that's right." She leans back on the stiff couch cushions, exhausted. Her head aches something awful, and with this lovely new twist, she just wishes she had a nice refreshing bucket of sulfuric acid to pour over her head.

"Look, I'm sure you care about Sydney, Hannah. But the game's over as far as the Florence Nightingale routine is concerned."

"What the hell is that supposed to mean?"

"It means Aaron told me what you're charging him for helping out in Darien. He must've thought I knew. How very mercenary of you."

Her body goes limp.

"You did it for the money."

"No. No, Jonah. I didn't. I love that child with all my..."

"Your designer heart?" he says. "Is that what you love her with?" His breath is heavy. "Honest to God, I thought..."

"What?" she says. "You thought what?"

"Nothing."

"You thought I changed?" she says. "I have. You thought we might have a chance? We do!" She gathers steam. "I told Aaron what I needed to get out of hock," she says. "I'm not technically charging him for taking care of Syd. But I helped him out of a hellhole and he seemed completely fine with helping me out of mine."

"There's something wrong with the logic here," he says. "Something very wrong with you trading the care of your niece for that much money."

She swallows a lump the size of a gold coin, and clears her throat. She stands and walks to the water cooler. "Then I won't accept it," she says. "That's all there is to it. I'll forfeit all of it." Tears brew, bubble up, and spill over. "Don't you think I'd sell the farm to get her back?" *Oh my God, she's Vesuvius.* She can't manage anymore; he's done her in. She leans over the counter and turns inside out.

"Hannah," she hears him say softly.

"Fuck you!" she screams and pitches the phone against the far wall. "Fuck you and all your fucking principles."

Life's a mess, really. Principles pile up and press you into a corner of your own making. Right now, Hannah doesn't care if she has a place to live or not, if she's interred in debtor's prison, or not. If she ever sees Jonah again, or not. *The hell with him!* She and Mitsy and Syd have each other, and that's all they need. It's all they ever needed.

Who knew?

Mitsy

AT TWO AM HANNAH falls asleep on the recliner in the cramped hospital room, as Mitsy curls up on top of the thin white blanket at the end of Sydney's bed. Her right hand rests on her daughter's ankle; she feels the warmth. Her child is alive.

She barely closes her eyes before she tumbles like Alice into the rabbit hole of her dream. And just like Wonderland, it's insane. At first she knows it's insane—it *feels* insane—but soon she becomes so much a part of the activity that it makes sense. It's as if someone plucked her out of Virginia and dropped her in an ancient burning cottage in the middle of nowhere, surrounded by vineyards and spirits and powerful attachments to complete strangers that couldn't feel more real or familiar.

She feels her awareness sink into the broken body of a young woman with the gravity of a lead weight. She and this woman are one. Instantly, she experiences confusion and a storm of physical and emotional pain. Where the emotional pain is coming from she doesn't know until she looks up. There against a blood orange moon she watches two eagles fly away with her youngest sister, Alicia, clutched precariously in their talons. Her heart wrenches and she cries out, "Nooooo!"

On her knees, she reaches forward, but there's something wrong with her legs and she can't get up. Someone calls out "Marguerite, where are you?" Is she Marguerite? She must be. Though what she's doing there, she has no idea.

She tries to protect her gray robe from the fire that smolders around her. Columns and walls crumble. Another sister, Helaina, is being dragged out of the cottage at a distance by someone Marguerite can't see. Marguerite fears she may be left to die. She wonders why no one sees her or Alicia. Do they even know Alicia's been rescued—*or was she kidnapped?*—by eagles? Her head spins with terror. Where are the eagles taking her beloved sister? Do they mean her harm? Will she ever see Alicia again? *Who lit the fire?!*

Just as the smoke overcomes her and she is about to expire from the fumes, one of the reviled gypsies from a camp in the lower village scoops her up and lifts her into her muscular arms. This woman has the strength of a man. Someone calls out to the gypsy, "Dorenia," he says, "hurry!"

Carrying Marguerite, Dorenia charges out of the fire with a steady, confident gait. Marguerite inhales a sharp fragrance from a tiny metal container on a string around Dorenia's neck. The spicy orange elixir keeps Marguerite alert for a brief period. Her senses are piqued. She hears the gypsy's jangling bracelets, earrings, and the charms clinking on her belt and shoes. The brilliant red and green dyes in the raw silky fabric of her dress and kerchief stick to the walls of Marguerite's imagination. This is what a savior looks like, she thinks. *Sounds like. Smells like*. Even as she feels her spirit diminish, the memory burns an indelible image in her mind. The orange elixir helps her collect her thoughts, but the spicy scent diminishes in the charred air. It's all she can do to whisper her final words in Dorenia's ears, "Find...her," she says, choking on the smoke. "Save...her."

"I will," the gypsy says. "I promise."

Hours later, Mitsy awakens in the hospital room, her eyes feasting on the red hot dawn through the window as it burns like a wildfire, striated, across the hills on the horizon. Her tongue is paste. Her head aches with a nearly unbearable pressure she can't remember experiencing since she was last in Darien. She can't go back to that; she won't. She'll never be that weak again. She loathes that helpless woman. Whatever pain she has to bear from whatever condition or stress she might have, she will bear it in silence and with dignity. She will push through it. The farm has restored her self-respect. She won't misplace it again.

"Hey," whispers Hannah from the recliner in the corner. She's covered to the neck in a white blanket. "Weird night."

Mitsy pushes herself up and off the bed slowly and gently, trying not to awaken Sydney. She beckons Hannah out to the hall. They drag themselves like zombies to the ladies room, where individually-wrapped toothpaste and brushes sit in a basket. Other baskets with mini-deodorants, combs and lotions are scattered about. They do what they can with what's there.

When they're finished, Hannah grumbles, "Want me to get you some coffee?"

"Let's both go," Mitsy says. "I need a walk." She checks her watch. It's only five AM, but three hours of sleep is better than none, she supposes. Not that she feels like it did any good.

They lumber along the smooth tile floor in stocking feet, first notifying the nurse's station that they'll be downstairs if needed. They walk like they slept in contorted positions in tight spots, because they did. Their limbs move stiffly. Their skin smells as antiseptic as their surroundings. They're not so young anymore. Stress shows up everywhere—etched on the soft flesh of their cheeks, inscribed on the grainy corners of their enflamed eyelids. Hannah reaches over to slip an errant lock of Mitsy's freshly dyed hair behind her ear. Mitsy tucks the designer label of Hannah's mohair sweater beneath the collar.

On the way to the elevator, Hannah says, "I had a wicked dream. You, Syd and I were in a burning building. Pure chaos."

Mitsy processes this information, waiting for more as her own dream slowly regurgitates. *Was it the same dream?*

"I don't know what happened to Syd, if it even was Syd," Hannah continues. "It didn't really look like her, but in my mind...it was definitely her. Probably because the girl was in trouble, I don't know."

"Where was it?" says Mitsy as she presses the elevator button.

Hannah shrugs. "I don't know. Middle of nowhere in more ways than one. It was confusing. Someone I didn't trust was carrying you away in her arms. But it wasn't you, really. Or you had a different name. And..." She stops herself.

"And what?" Mitsy says.

"Nothing. Just a dream. I can't remember all of it."

"Or you don't want to," says Mitsy. "Because I died, right? And you're afraid to say it."

The elevator doors open and they enter, Hannah staring at Mitsy. "I wouldn't say..."

"I did," Mitsy says. "I died. It's okay."

"Are you guessing that, or do you *know?*" Hannah says, frowning deeply.

But Mitsy doesn't answer, because she loses her breath, hanging onto the waist-high steel rail in the elevator as it descends. "Is it my imagination, or is the pressure in this elevator a bit much?" she says.

"There's a lot of pressure in general," Hannah says, "physical and otherwise. My sinuses are killing me, for one thing. But I don't think it's the elevator."

"It's like a layer of the atmosphere was injected with plutonium," says Mitsy. She frowns at Hannah. "So it isn't just me? Because I don't want to go back to that creature I was. But my limbs and just...everything feels so heavy."

Hannah shakes her head. "I don't know, maybe it's both of us. Let's see how we feel after a gallon of coffee."

Downstairs at the breakfast station, they place coffee mugs on their tray then select a banana, a croissant, and a couple of bottles of water. After they pay, they find a table flanked by two oversized armchairs in a corner of the café.

"These chairs look comfy," Hannah says sleepily. She climbs into one of them and huddles up, shrinking into the warmth of her coffee. She blows on the steaming liquid, and sips. After a minute, she says, "There's something I have to tell you, Mits."

Mitsy is rooting through her purse for any kind of painkiller. Her head is in serious danger of imploding. "What's that?" she says absently.

"Not that I want to," Hannah says. She sits back in the chair, crosses her legs, and takes a sip. "I definitely don't want to."

Mitsy finds her tin of aspirin and throws two in her mouth. "Well, go on," she says, mildly irritated.

"Jonah is pissed at me," Hannah says. "Because of, uh... something I did that I haven't told you about."

Swallowing a bite of banana, Mitsy grimaces. "For God's sake, Hannah, just say it. Isn't there enough drama in our lives?"

276 REA NOLAN MARTIN

Hannah's hands shake as she clutches the warm cup, burying her nose in the steam. "I, uh...that is, Aaron..."

Mitsy freezes. "Oh no, Hannah, you didn't..."

"What?!"

"You didn't sleep with..."

"What?!" Hannah exclaims, at the same time jumping back and tipping the chair into the wall. "God no!" A stream of coffee splashes her chin, her sweater and pants and general surroundings. "Ouch! Oh my God, this is so fucking hot!" She grabs a pile of napkins from the tray and blots the coffee on her lap, the chair, the table. "Are you kidding me?" she says, still reeling. She runs to the station for a new pile of napkins.

When she returns, Mitsy says, "It's not as if I can't see the attraction. You're more suited to him than I ever was. If you hadn't been so young when Aaron first came to ride..."

"No!" Hannah's jade green eyes are the size of quarters as she continues to mop the coffee from the table, rim, and floor. "Good God, Mitsy." She shakes her head. "But that'll make my confession so much easier." She dumps the napkins in the trash and sits back down. "All I want to do is patch things up with Jonah," she says. "That's it."

"Then what is it?" Mitsy says. "What's the big bad news?"

"I got into a bit of a financial mess," Hannah says. She bites her bottom lip.

"Uh huh," Mitsy says instead of— *what else is new?*

"It all happened after Jonah left," says Hannah. "It wouldn't have happened if he hadn't left."

"Why? Because if Jonah had stayed he would have paid your expenses?"

"No." Hannah sits back, considering that thought. "To be honest, my expenses were part of the reason he left." She leans forward earnestly. "I got into a bit of a spending problem, I think. I don't know."

"You don't know? Come on, Hannah, you certainly do know."

"When you asked me up to Darien, I was just starting to write a book. An awesome book!" Hannah nods confidently. "Award-winning, in fact. The concept is just amazing! It's called..."

"Get to the point," Mitsy says.

"Fine, but you know I can do it, Mits. I can easily write a book. You remember my early beginnings, don't you? I have it in me! The title is...*If Only*...and the concept is..."

"Hannah."

"Okay, fine. So I wanted to write the book, but you needed me, so I was conflicted, but of course I flew up. It was the right thing to do." She shakes her empty cup. "I thought I could write the novel at the same time I helped with Syd, but I ..." She shakes her head. "Anyway, in the end, Aaron agreed to pay my expenses."

Mitsy shrugs. "That's it? Well, of course we'll pay your expenses, Hannah. It's only fair. And anyway, I told him that would be the deal from the get go. End of story. You're absolved."

"Not exactly. I got myself into a big hole, and I knew Jonah wouldn't believe I'd changed unless I came up with a way to pay it all off. So..."

Mitsy raises her eyebrows. "What's the number?"

"A few days ago Aaron told me if I spent the next year with you and Syd, he'd pay the entire amount."

Mitsy smacks the table. "Bastard! So he's been planning his escape!" She closes her eyes, absorbing the deceit. *She knew it.*

Hannah sighs. "Sorry, Mits. But it wasn't premeditated, at least on my part. We didn't even strike the deal until the other day."

"What's the amount?"

Hannah looks around. "I need a refill," she says.

Mitsy places her hand over Hannah's. "It's okay," she says. "Whatever it is, I'll pay it, not Aaron. Neither one of us needs his money."

Hannah's slim torso shakes, her eyes tear, and she chokes up. "I didn't do it for the money, Mits. I did it because I love you both. Syd is like..." She pats her chest. "...my own."

Mitsy nods solemnly. "How could I doubt that?"

"Okay then." Hannah rocks her head back and forth as if to give herself momentum. "Fifty thousand dollars is what I told Aaron. Plus uh...repairs."

"How much for repairs?"

Hannah stares at the floor. "Something like, I don't know... two hundred?"

"Two hundred thousand?!"

Hannah buries her face in her hands.

"Holy shit!" Mitsy says, genuinely floored. "$250,000? What about the farm; is it mortgaged?"

Hannah breathes deeply. "About forty percent." She shuts her eyes. "I had to, Mits."

"The horses?"

"Jonah owns half of them. He wants to buy the farm from me. Send me out to pasture in a townhouse in DC or somewhere he thinks I can't get into trouble. I thought we would get back together." She runs her hands through her hair. "I honest to God thought there was a chance."

Mitsy stares at her. "All those new clothes in the guest room, Hannah, my God."

"I know."

"You have to return every one of them."

"But now we can share them!" Hannah says wide-eyed. "You fit in them too!"

Mitsy glares and Hannah shrinks. "Fine," Hannah says miserably.

"You have a problem," Mitsy says, understanding that Hannah isn't the only one with an escape hatch. She has one too. They all do. "Go get your refill," she says, "and bring one for me."

While Hannah fetches coffee, Mitsy performs a few calculations in her head. Last she remembered she had about two million in her account, based on her portion of the inheritance that Aaron had invested. Obviously living with him, not to mention living in her bedroom, she had no reason to spend it. As much as she'd love to lecture her sister for the next two hours, there's too much going on to waste that kind of time. After all, Hannah supplied a lot of energy just when Mitsy could barely breathe. How can Mitsy deny her now?

When she sits back down, Hannah says, "I've turned over a new leaf, Mits, I have. I swear."

"We might have to tear up your credit cards," Mitsy says.

"Ouch."

"Just so you won't be tempted." Mitsy picks at the croissant. "Anyway, who owns the other horses?"

"Huh?"

"You said Jonah owns half. Who owns the other half?"

"I do," Hannah says. "Well, that is as long as I don't have to sell them, which I probably do." She hunches back up in her chair with her coffee, knees to chin. "But I don't really want to since they include the brood mares, and that's my only real source of income. The foals, I mean." She glances out the window. "I could sell the foals, though. I practically have to even if the rest of the debt is met. I have ongoing costs, too, you know. The farm is outrageously expensive."

"I'm sure it is, but it's not exactly been managed well either."

Hannah stares up and back. "Doc says Ireland is really healthy, a perfect specimen. She'll pull in…"

"We're not selling Ireland," Mitsy says abruptly. "Forget about it."

"*We?*" says Hannah in a high thin voice. Her eyes tear instantly.

Mitsy nods. "Yes, 'we'." She sips her coffee. "How many horses are there altogether not counting the foals? And how many does Jonah own?"

"He owns three stallions altogether. Two thoroughbreds and a quarter horse—ages 3, 4 and 7. Excellent riders."

"So there are three left?

Hannah nods. "Daizee, Jolie, and Dorenia."

Mitsy's heart stops. "What was the last one?"

"Dorenia. The gypsy."

"What do you mean?"

Hannah's face lights up. "Gypsy Vanner—a newer breed, basically. Although it was under our noses all along. Remember the caravan horses? Well, they've finally been refined into a spectacularly beautiful breed with credentials." She leans forward. "I had to have her, Mits. Prettiest show horse ever. The popularity of the breed is supersonic. She's black and white, feathered. Pricey, so…" She shrugs. "Jonah was pissed at that, too. But honestly, when I breed her next year, her foals will be worth the most."

Mitsy mines her brain for information. *Dorenia…where has she heard that name before?* "Her name sounds eerily familiar," she says.

"It's a gypsy name," Hannah says. "Roma. She's a pistol. Smart as hell, with a mind of her own. But Jonah says they're making steady progress with her training."

Mitsy leans forward. "I'll pay you the full $250,000 for Dorenia and Ireland," she says.

Hannah's chin quivers. "You will?"

"Yes, I will. You'll title Dorenia to me and Ireland to Sydney."

"But…"

"That's the deal."

"Can I have Dorenia's foal?"

"Only if you can pay market price." Mitsy raises her chin. "It's a business decision, Hannah. You have to have a reason to save money…or at least to stop spending it." She looks Hannah squarely in the eye. "If I could ride all the way down here with a teenage boy in the condition I was in…"

"And agree to a makeover!" Hannah adds.

"Exactly. If I could force myself out of that hole, you can do the same."

Hannah sips her coffee, gazing out absently into the café. "Fine," she says. "Deal." But before they can shake hands, she frowns, squinting at something across the room. "What the hell is that?" she says.

Mitsy turns as a statuesque woman with bronze skin, wild white hair, a colorful silk skirt, red wool cape, and cowboy boots stands at the entry, looking around. Her eyes search the room and come to rest on their table in the corner. She moves gracefully toward them.

"Are you Mitsy Michaels?" she says in a rich, melodic voice.

Hannah points to Mitsy, stupefied.

The woman steps toward Mitsy, offering her hand. "I'm Pandora Madigan," she says.

Mitsy can't believe what she's looking at. It could be an Egyptian queen, an Amazon empress—the nexus of so many genes—the elegant stature, the topaz eyes, yet nothing at all like Syd. "But you don't…"

"No, I don't," she says. "I look nothing like anyone who could possibly share DNA with your daughter. I already know that." She nods her magnificently exotic head firmly. "But evidently I do."

Mitsy pushes back her chair, jumps up and hugs her. "Oh my God, you're really here," she says, as if just now comprehending how long she's waited for this moment. "You're really here!"

Pandora hugs her loosely. "They won't let Guru inside the hospital," she says. "And I need to find a place for him fast."

"Who's Guru?" says Hannah stiffly.

"Who are *you?*" says Pandora, her deep-set, heavily lidded eyes sweeping Hannah's hunched figure.

"Shouldn't you know my name? Aren't you psychic?"

"Oh, right, the belligerent skeptic," Pandora says, not so much with disdain as a degree of interest.

"Oh right, the heretic fraud," Hannah retorts.

Mitsy steps back and shoots Hannah a warning glance.

Hannah throws up her hands. "Sorry." She looks reluctantly at Pandora, waves her white paper napkin saying, "Truce?"

Pandora raises her chin elegantly. "No need for a truce," she says. "I never engage in war in the first place. Make peace with yourself."

Mitsy gazes at Pandora, stunned into her old dependent self and trying hard to resist the fall. It isn't easy—just the strength of the woman's presence is intoxicating. "Please," she says, "have my seat. I'll pull up another chair."

Pandora lowers herself, straight-backed, into the seat then throws her head back and sighs. "Those red-eye flights throw me completely off balance," she says. "They should be banned."

"You took the red-eye!" Mitsy says. "You must be exhausted!" She drags a wooden café chair from the adjacent table. "Can I get you a cup of green tea?"

Pandora shakes her head. "No, no. This day calls for coffee," she says. "Some days just demand it."

Hannah raises her eyebrows. "Coffee, eh?"

Mitsy glares at her. "How do you take it?" she asks. She has to admit that she's a bit relieved the coffee ban has been lifted. Mitsy doesn't know how she'd fare without any herself, and there was a time Pandora forbade her to have any.

"Black," she says. "In a to-go cup. We have to deal with Guru. He's in some kind of holding tank upstairs by the lobby door." She nods at Hannah. "He's my Persian."

"Oh?" Hannah says. "You keep your Persian in a cage?"

"Doesn't everybody?" Pandora replies drily.

"I should get something for Guru to eat then, too," says Mitsy. She scans the counters. "Some tuna maybe?"

Pandora rocks her head back and forth, considering. "Perhaps."

"Hold the mayo," says Hannah.

To Mitsy's surprise, Pandora purses her lips, amused. "Yes, no tuna salad," she says with a glint in her eye. "You see, Hannah, I do have a sense of humor."

"I suppose you'd have to in your line of work," Hannah says.

Pandora sighs, pulling on a lock of her thick white hair and placing it behind her ear. "I do run into some kooks," she says. "Not naming names."

Mitsy can see that Pandora and Hannah, though deeply engaged in a battle of subtext, are amused by their repartee. Or maybe not. It's hard to tell, the way they eyeball each other suspiciously between punch lines. Even so, for the first time, Mitsy sees that whether or not they like each other doesn't matter. They're well-matched on some insane level, as if they're competing with each other for the same thing. But what would that be? She leaves them to their own devices. Whatever their fight is, it isn't hers. She walks off for the coffee and tuna, wondering what she'll find when she returns.

After some inquiries at the deli bar, Mitsy scores a small bowl of plain tuna and a black coffee to-go. When she gets back to the table, she finds both Pandora and Hannah sitting limply in their chairs, their heads lobbed to the side, asleep, Hannah snoring softly. Mitsy nudges Pandora's shoulder, startling her.

"Wha-wha," she stutters, followed by, "Oh. Oh. Thank you. I forgot where I was."

The outburst wakes up Hannah, who places her head in her hands, deeply rubbing her forehead with her thumbs. "Mitsy, do you have any more of those aspirin? My head is bucket of cement. Oooph."

Mitsy isn't sure whether or not Pandora would approve of the aspirin. But she's having coffee, so maybe. She hands Pandora the coffee cup and tuna bowl and says, "Maybe Pandora can come up with a safer medication?"

Hannah leans in, her eyes half-closed with what Mitsy can see is pressure. She feels it herself as she did in the elevator, even though she's already taken aspirin. It softened the edges, but that's about it.

"What do you suggest for a headache, oh mighty healer?" Hannah says.

Mitsy's face tightens. She gives Hannah the evil eye, but this time, Hannah ignores her.

After a long sip of coffee, Pandora says, "You can try the aspirin, but it probably won't do much good."

"Why?" Hannah says.

"You don't want to know." She takes another sip.

Mitsy doesn't like the sound of that. "Why?" she says quietly. "Does it have something to do with Sydney?"

"All of us," Pandora tells Mitsy gently. "It has to do with all of us." She pats Mitsy's hand comfortingly.

Hannah leans forward. "You people just love innuendo,

don't you? You just love to tease and then withhold. Makes you feel so goddamn important to make everyone else so goddamn dependent."

Mitsy's heart rate quickens.

"You couldn't handle the information I have," Pandora says evenly. Her amazing blue eyes, so startling against her bronze skin and white hair, stare Hannah down.

"Try me," Hannah says. Then after a long pause, "I'll tell you what information you have—nothing. No information whatsoever in your crackpot crystal ball."

Pandora raises herself from the chair, wearily pushing against the arms. "Believe what you want," she says. "This is not about you, anyway. It's about Sydney. That's why I'm here. Now, if you'll excuse me, I have to take care of Guru and see Dr. Blanca." She turns to Mitsy. "Shall we go?"

Hannah points to Mitsy. "Stay," she says. "I want to know what this kook has to say before she donates her whacked-out DNA to a member of our family."

"Hannah," Mitsy warns.

Pandora sighs. "It's okay, Mitsy," she says. "I knew this was coming."

"Of course you did," says Hannah.

Pandora gathers her breath, looks directly at Hannah and says, "If you insist, which you clearly do, the pressure is caused by a mounting geomagnetic storm around the 39th parallel in the stratosphere roughly above Baltimore. Satisfied?"

"Well, what does that mean exactly?" asks Mitsy earnestly. "A magnetic storm? What will happen? When will it end?"

"Soon our bodies will feel heavy," Pandora says wearily, "if they don't already. After that, lights will flicker, electricity will be spotty, and the tech equipment will experience a degree of failure—can't tell how much. It depends on how close it gets."

"Equipment failure?" Mitsy says. "But doesn't Sydney's procedure depend on some of that equipment? At least during the transplant?"

"Sydney depends on *us*," Pandora says. "Equipment was never more than that...equipment. Electronic gadgets are external expressions of the faculties we ourselves possess intrinsically but are too asleep to engage." She shakes her head. "It's just so much easier to stay asleep and pretend to be useless. To let the machines do our job."

Pandora backs up a step to offer Hannah her hand. "Enough?" she says.

Hannah's red-lined, sleep-deprived once bright eyes dart back and forth searching for a way out. Finding none, apparently, she summons up the humility to shake Pandora's hand. Mitsy is relieved at this gesture until she sees Hannah's hand jerk back as if receiving an electrical jolt.

"What the hell?" Hannah says. "Do you have a buzzer in your hand?"

"Oh, so you can't handle the energy, eh?" Pandora says. She shakes her head as she turns toward the door. "You never could." To Mitsy, Pandora says, "If you think your sister will deter me from helping your daughter, fear not. She'll figure it out at some point." She waves her long, elegant hand dismissively. Her fingers are exquisite. "It doesn't matter to me a lick when that happens."

Mitsy hands a baffled Hannah two aspirin as they shuffle behind Pandora. Hannah is silent.

"What will we do about the uh...the magnetic storm?" Mitsy says to Pandora.

"Do?" Pandora says then shrugs. "There's nothing we can do but hope we'll adjust to the frequency and pressure. But I can't promise that. Now, let's get on with things. I need to feed

Guru and consult with Dr. Blanca." She smiles. "Blanca—the white knight. Her name is perfect."

"The white knight?" Mitsy says.

Pandora turns to look at Mitsy behind her. "We're in archetypal times, my friend. In archetypal times, absolutes rise to the top. If her name were Dr. Negra, we might worry a tad. But her name bears light."

As they rise in the elevator, each one of them gasps for breath, including Hannah, who Mitsy knows would rather die than show any further weakness to Pandora. It's not the pressure that bothers Mitsy, or the encroaching headache. It's the fact that there's a storm out there that could bring them all down. But even with the pressure of the many unknowns before them, she is inexplicably comforted by Pandora's presence. The woman inspires as much confidence in Mitsy as she does suspicion in Hannah. She's not sure why. Maybe it's her stature or the velvety richness of her voice. Maybe it's the mystery of all she claims to know that others don't. Or maybe it's the pungent fragrance that emanates from her skin, jasmine with overtones of spicy orange, like a fine tea from a foreign port. Alien, yet somehow familiar.

Sydney

THIS TIME WHEN SYD hears the name "Alicia!" released in a strangled screech, she knows the voice does not call out for someone else; it calls for her. In this place, Syd and Alicia are the same, soaring high above checkered vineyards, deer and wild boar foraging beneath them from a terrifying distance, the size of ants. The eagles clutch her by the back of her robe, but the robe is oversized and she is slipping, shifting, choking, and praying that they land her safely and soon.

Alicia knows the winged pair has saved her from the wreckage, but she doesn't know where they came from, where they're taking her, or why. She can only hope that when they finally deliver her, they return to the cottage for her sisters. Her sisters are herbalists, she remembers. This practice pays their livelihood. They grow the herbs themselves, mix them, and administer them when called upon. When confronted with obscure and stubborn ailments, however, they use Alicia, or rather Alicia's energy, to heal.

The discovery of Alicia's healing energy was an accident. At the age of five, she reached out for the hand of a madman and he instantly came to peace. If anyone were to ask Alicia now, she would say the only miracle that occurred that day was a simple act of kindness. She would say that kindness and compassion heal. But ever since that day, their lives have been interrupted by a continuous stream of pilgrims from Rome, Naples, and Venice. Candles burn interminably in their cottage. So is that what started the fire? Or was it burned in protest over what the arsonists might have perceived to be heretical practice?

The eagles glide low over a camp of disreputable gypsies. She knows of them. Her sisters disapprove of their dark practices and errant lifestyle. Helaina calls them frauds; says she'll pick up the axe and swing at the next one who wanders into their community. Community of what, though, Alicia is momentarily uncertain. She has to better attune her signal from another lifetime to the hills of medieval Tuscany. She's not quite there yet, not to mention the discomfort of the eagles' sharp, scaly talons against her back.

She forces herself to focus, to seek and find. Soon she remembers they are a community of maiden women called *Beguines*. Although they are outwardly dedicated to a holy life, they are not religious clerics. In her household at least, sacred practices tend to be unorthodox and unsupervised, as they would most certainly not be in a convent. None of them wishes to be a sister of the cloth.

Alicia remembers that Helaina is not as committed to the Beguine lifestyle as their older sister, Marguerite, but since their parents were killed, Marguerite is in control of the household. Helaina and Alicia have no choice but to obey Marguerite or she will promise them in betrothal to strangers, separating them for life. In this society maiden women must be married or committed to a chaste community. This is the opposite of the reckless gypsy life, bearing children of any sire, kicking sand in the face of common dignity. Helaina, especially, resents the foreigners' freedom to live as they choose. Alicia knows that if Helaina could, she would happily lead a gypsy life. At heart, she is an undisciplined spirit that eschews discipline and authority. She is a renegade without outlets for her abundant desires. Any issue she has with the gypsies is based on envy.

Hanging just above the camp now, Alicia is released into the long reach of two gypsy girls. They encircle her and place her gently on the ground, covering her singed robe with a brilliant red scarf. The eagles rise up, flap their massive wings, and soar into the night sky.

"Will they return for my sisters?" Alicia asks, terrified.

"Your sisters are not our concern," says the older girl. "You are."

"But my sisters will be wondering where I am!" Alicia cries.

Ignoring her plea, the girls strap her to a cart and pull her across the cluttered camp into the tent of an elderly woman seated atop a crystal-encrusted cypress throne. Her face is a raisin, her steel gray hair pulled tightly back into a long braid. Spangles, fringe, colorful rose and emerald silks adorn her emaciated body. Alicia has seen gypsies before, but none as brash as this.

"Here she is," say the girls in a single voice. They untie the strap and prod Alicia forward toward the ancient queen.

"Child," says the old woman in a deep, craggy raisin voice. "Here you are, and here you will stay."

A wave of nausea sweeps through Alicia. "But my sisters..."

The woman waves her hand dismissively. "It is they who agreed to send you here in the first place."

Alicia is stunned. "That can't be true!" She's certain it's a lie. This woman is wicked.

The queen opens her arms. "Come forward, child," she says more kindly. "You are the magical spirit we've awaited. This is where you will develop your skills. You belong to us now."

Lying on her right side, Syd feels a gentle stroke on her left cheek, and opens her eyes to a bronze-skinned woman with fierce blue eyes and a riot of white hair, dressed in a red cape and a colorful skirt. She wears tourmaline, emerald, and topaz rings on three fingers of her long, worn hand.

Syd's not sure who she is anymore—(Alicia? Syd?)—or where she is. The room is dark. Is she in the gypsy camp? Inside the tent? This woman is younger and more beautiful than the gypsy queen. More vibrant. Still, there's a connection somehow. Perhaps this woman is a younger attendant of the queen's? Or a sister? A daughter? Syd tries to talk, but the result is gibberish. She's not even sure it's English.

"Shhhh," the woman says gently. "There now, Sydney, wake slowly from your other reality."

So now she's Sydney, not Alicia. She feels like both, like they are interchangeable. She searches the room for a familiar object or image to ground her. The spicy orange fragrance that titillates her sinuses doesn't match the other hard, cold references in the room—the red laser lights, the beeping equipment, the pillows and bed. Oh, so she's in a hospital. *Again!* But this time she's somehow managed to drag a living breathing gypsy out of her dream and into the room with her. *OMG!* Does anyone else see the woman? Or maybe Syd's on morphine. Is she on morphine? Is it because she's dying?

"Where's my mother?" she mumbles. "Where's my aunt?"

"Shhhh," says the gypsy. "No need to worry. They went home for a rest. They were here all night, and will return when they can."

Syd rolls slowly onto her back and tries to push up on her elbows, but collapses. Her arms have no strength. *She* has no strength.

"Let me help you," says the woman kindly.

She walks around the foot of the bed to the windows, and opens the blinds. "That's better," she says. "Light is what you need." She regards Syd meaningfully, staring deeply into her being. "Light is what everyone needs."

She returns to the bed and maneuvers the buttons to raise Syd to a seated position. She knows how to maneuver the bed; she doesn't have to ask. Wherever she came from, she's able to adjust to this modern setting. She pours water out of the plastic pitcher into a plastic cup, pulls a glass vial out of her skirt pocket, opens it and taps liquid into the cup. "Drink this," she says, and hands it to Syd.

The woman is surrounded by a haze of yellow light. Maybe it's just where she's standing in the morning sun, but still, she's spectral. Syd can practically see through her. Is she real? Is the drink real? "What did you put in the water?" she asks the woman.

"Just a little potion—an elixir to strengthen your vitality for the road ahead."

Syd glares. "Why? What's going to happen?"

The gypsy shakes her head slowly. "Nothing we can't handle together," she says quietly.

Syd accepts the cup, and smells the water. "It's spicy."

The gypsy nods. "Tell me what's in it," she says expectantly. "I think you'll figure it out, Elysha. It's within your ken."

Syd stares at her, confused. "Why did you just call me Alicia? You called me Sydney earlier, didn't you?"

The woman nods. "I did."

"Then why did you just call me Alicia? That was a dream. In this place I'm called Sydney."

The woman nods knowingly. "I will call you Sydney if you wish, but in my heart, dear child, you will always be Elysha. I named you that once."

Syd tries harder to climb out of the dream, or make the hallucination disappear. "If I drink this, will you leave?" she says.

The woman chuckles. "No, dear, not at all. I'm here to save you. It's a promise I made to Marguerite lifetimes ago."

"You mean Mitsy," Syd says. "Don't you? You mean my mother."

The woman looks away. "Your mother *this* time, yes."

Syd doesn't know why she knows these things. This woman's presence is an avalanche of information hovering over Syd's head and collapsing into her brain in piles too high to sort through or even shovel. Information for which she has no context but a dream. She inhales the woman's pungent orange spice, redolent of a memory she can't name. She's been on morphine before; she knows what it does. It makes you float on ceilings and wander into portals of unseen dimensions. But somewhere in its haze lies a truth that's hard to extract any other way.

"Frankincense," she says, and sniffs again. "And jasmine." She searches her limited memory of spices and fragrance to identify the missing component. The answer comes on a trail of steam from a gypsy's tent. "And lemongrass," she says, though she has never smelled lemongrass in her life.

The woman claps her long, bejeweled hands joyfully. "You remember!" She draws the folding chair to the bed, smoothes her colorful skirt beneath her, and sits down. "You are exquisite," she says. Her spectacular eyes glow. "You are divine. In all these centuries your spirit remains pure and fully aligned." A tear travels down her right cheek.

As Syd sips the liquid, the trail of heavy slumber that followed her from one world to the next dissipates and clears. Her vision sharpens, her eyes focus, but the woman remains. She takes another sip. Still here. A nurse enters the room, efficiently tends to Syd's bedside monitors and IV. She takes Syd's temperature and pulse, and then says, "The doctor will be here shortly to see you both."

Both? Syd grips the sheets to keep from floating up. She has never felt less grounded. How many hallucinations can there be in a single room?

"Thank you," says the gypsy to the nurse.

Syd swallows a lump.

When the nurse is gone, Syd says, "Who are you?"

The woman smiles, squeezes Syd's hand and says, "My name is Pandora Madigan."

This takes Syd a minute. "Oh," she whispers. *Pandora.* Her mother's obsession. *The voice on the phone.*

Before she can question further, Dr. Blanca marches into the room and fixes her gaze on Syd like a period at the end of a sentence. "Well, here we are," she says. "Everything in its place."

Syd looks around. "Where?" she says. "What place? What do you mean?"

Dr. Blanca tilts her head quizzically. "You don't know?"

Syd shakes her head.

"Sydney, this woman..." She points to Pandora. "...is your donor."

Syd looks over at Pandora, wide-eyed. "My...what?"

The doctor nods, smiling. "Your bone marrow donor. She's an exact match."

"But...that's crazy."

"At times DNA crosses ethnic boundaries," says Dr. Blanca. "People are complex creatures from myriad places." She folds her arms. "We are not one thing."

"No, not that..." says Syd, trailing off. *How can this be!*

Pandora moves to the foot of the bed, looking down at Syd and laying her hands on Syd's blanketed feet. "What's mine is yours," she says like a disembodied oracle from another realm.

Or maybe it's the morphine.

Syd struggles for focus again. Her brain is a tangle of opposing thoughts and emotions. This is an insane coincidence. And yet, why not? Her connection to this woman is undeniable. Didn't she just drag her out of a dream? The boundaries of reality and imagination are so stretched and fused she can't determine what's really happening, if anything. Is anything happening? Maybe it's still a dream. Maybe her entire life is a dream. Maybe everyone's is.

"Am I on drugs?" she says.

Dr. Blanca shakes her head, smiling. "IV Methotrexate," she says, "no opiates. The generous woman sitting beside you truly is your match. You're not imagining it."

Syd swallows hard. "When will the transplant..." She can't finish the sentence. Her earlier clarity is wearing off.

"We're not sure," says Dr. Blanca. She shifts positions, pushing her hands deep into the pockets of her white coat. "Your blood counts...and just your core vitality...are not where we'd like just yet. We're hoping a few days of rest and IV nutrition will restore you. As long as your system will tolerate it, we'll continue to prep, but ongoing, that will depend on your condition." She turns to Pandora. "And Ms. Madigan here will of course require some rest as well. She just arrived from an all night plane trip, after all."

"I'm fine," says Pandora.

"And I trust someone is caring for your cat?" inquires Dr. Blanca.

"A cat?" says Syd.

Pandora smiles serenely. "Guru," she says.

"Guru is the best name ever," Syd says with effort. "Guru should meet Godiva."

"Perhaps he has," says Pandora. "He went home with your mother and aunt about an hour ago. They don't take cats at the hotel."

Dr. Blanca points her pen at Pandora. "We'll run some more tests on you now, Ms. Madigan," she says, "if you don't mind. Afterwards we'll send you off to the hotel for some sleep." She extends her hand. "Meet you again around 4?"

Pandora shakes the doctor's hand.

"You're staying at a hotel?" Syd asks wearily. "You should stay at the farm. It's....bet...ter." Her words trail off.

"Your mother offered," says Pandora. "But I'm..."

"No. Stay there," says Syd, yawning. "Please? Stay in my room if you want."

"But your aunt..."

Syd blinks. She remembers Hannah's position on Pandora which seems like ancient history, since less than a week ago Pandora was just a phone psychic to them. But now she's not. Now she's...*a donor?* Syd still can't get this through her head. If Dr. Blanca weren't right here in the same room with them, she'd think it was a scam.

"Aunt Hannah will adjust," says Syd. "She's just protective. She has to get...to... know...you."

"I don't know," Pandora says, shaking her head.

Dr. Blanca says, "Come with me, Ms. Madigan?"

Pandora holds up a finger. "Be there in a minute," she says.

When the doctor leaves, Pandora tells Syd, "Before I go, there's something I must give you." She places her hands on Syd's belly. "I'm going to place it right there, okay? No matter what, don't let it go. Don't give it to anyone, anyone at all. Whenever you close your eyes, you'll see it. When you open them, you'll imagine it. It's imperative that you hold onto it without exception."

Syd's eyes are rolling back in her head. It's impossible to keep them open. "In my dreams, you mean?" she mumbles.

"Anywhere," says Pandora. She turns to the window, raises her hands, closes her eyes, and gathers the streaming light. Syd can see it like she can see the window and the door and the black TV on the wall behind Pandora's wild white hair. It's happening. It's real. Like Merlin, she collects the light and forms it into a dense orb, top to bottom, side to side, and around. She shapes it, condenses it, rotates it, and smoothes the borders between her palms until it's a perfect radiant sphere. When she's satisfied, she places it in Syd's belly. Just like that.

Before she's finished, Syd is asleep, but the orb burns within her, warming her. She is warm...*finally*. Whether it's a dream or not doesn't really matter. What matters is that this crazy woman cared enough to do it. She formed an orb from the streaming light, and gave it to Syd for safekeeping. People have done loving things for her before—her parents, the doctors, the nurses, Zelda and Dane, and especially Aunt Hannah. But no one has created an orb out of streaming light and placed it in her belly, ever. The light is vibrant, nourishing, and deeply familiar. Its presence recharges her, ignites her. *How long will it last?*

Almost without transition, she is Alicia standing in front of the gypsy queen on her cypress throne, commanded to drop the red scarf and open her singed gray robe. Threatened, she complies.

The queen smiles with satisfaction, beckoning. "There it is, the light, just as I thought. Bring it to me, dear. You will be highly rewarded."

Alicia shakes her head. "No," she says.

Affronted, the queen says, "You must!"

"No."

"I can take it if I wish," says the queen. "But it's preferable that you surrender so it won't be damaged. If you force me to seize it, you will suffer unduly, as will your light."

Alicia closes her robe and ties the red silk scarf around her waist to bind it. "The light is mine," she says. "Surely you have your own."

The raisin-faced woman stands and glowers at her. "No one has it but you," she spits. "And you don't even know what to do with it!" She walks unsteadily toward Alicia. "Well, of course there are others, but very few, and none in the western territory, save you. Enlightened beings are rare."

"You cannot have my light," says Alicia. "I've been warned to keep it at all costs."

The woman stomps her foot. "Very well then, your sisters will die."

"No!"

"You give me no choice."

The moment the queen grabs her elbow, Syd separates from Alicia. They are two creatures in parallel spheres. She watches helplessly from afar as the queen summons her guards to restrain the girl. As Alicia squirms with discomfort, the queen waves her hands over the girl's belly teasing out the light, lumen by lumen, with some kind of chant. The light is pulled toward the queen in spite of its substantial resistance. The process is excruciating. Even from afar, Syd feels the burning pain as if it were her own.

"You see that I will have what I want whether you like it or not," the queen tells Alicia. "But this way, the light will be compromised, and that is a travesty you will pay for with your sisters' lives."

Alicia says, "Then take it. Take the light. Spare my sisters!"

"That's better, dear," the queen says.

The gypsy tickles her fingers over Alicia's belly and the light is tendered forth in its fullness. Devoid of it, Alicia collapses. "Bring me to my sisters," she whispers. "You have what you want."

A tall, strong woman, much younger, appears in the tent. She points accusingly at the orb in the queen's possession. "What have you done?" she demands.

"I've accepted a gift," the queen says piously, then hands the orb to her guards.

The younger woman, also dark, approaches. The queen points her twisted wooden scepter threateningly in the woman's direction. "What's mine is mine!" she says. But the younger gypsy overpowers the queen and casts her to the ground. As the queen struggles to rise, the woman lifts Alicia in her arms, and carries her off.

"Bring her back, Dorenia!" the queen commands. "The orb is worthless without the girl!"

From her cosmic perch, Syd gasps. *She weeps!* Whose destiny plays out here? Hers? Her family's?

Sensing the emotional involvement from beyond, the queen turns her head up and to her right in a penetrating stare, her eyes magnifying with each dimension, until they are bulbous, hideously large, and all Syd can see of her.

"You!" she says, waving her fist directly at Syd. "I will get you, yet!" She reaches greedily through the continuum with both arms until every feature of her physical body is distorted with warp.

She certainly has power, Syd thinks. Or anyway, force. *Can she capture Syd as she'd captured Alicia? Can she move through time?* Syd is moving through time; so why not the queen?

Syd closes her eyes to reconfirm the presence of light in her belly—the orb Pandora created earlier. It remains. The queen has something, but she doesn't have this. Relieved, she darts upward and out and as far from the camp as she can get. What the queen has done to her sisters she may never know.

Pandora

PANDORA STANDS IN THE parking lot in the shadow of the oncology wing, smoking. Just in case Mitsy or Hannah or a random tobacco nazi happens by to thwart her efforts, she steps behind the dumpster. She chokes, coughing wildly, not because of the smoke, but because the dumpster reeks of acrid waste.

This might be her last cigarette, or next to last or the one after that. In any case, this is definitely her last pack. She would stop right now, but wants to assuage her dependent nervous system so she doesn't pass anxious DNA along to Sydney. After all, who wants DNA in a state of withdrawal? *First do no harm.* And anyway, even though Pandora knows there are many reasons for her presence here, she stubbornly believes that her physical DNA isn't one of them.

She sighs just thinking about the girl, her child by any name. Her presence reignites everything—joy, love, jealousy, passion, grief, transcendence—every human emotion and more. It's too much. More than Pandora can name; more than she ever knew was there. Lifetime upon lifetime pile upon her, layers of emotional sediment, memories she can barely absorb. It's clear she caused the child harm at least once, perhaps many times, but it was never intentional. *Was it?* She loved the girl. Still loves her! The girl is a placid and noble spirit, a balm. All she's ever been missing is the light the gypsy stole.

She throws the cigarette butt on the ground and squashes it with her boot. That precise light—the girl's original light—can't be duplicated. It must be found and restored. The absence of that light is the reason for the child's sustained vulnerability through lifetimes. *The things people don't know about illness! The things they aren't ready to hear!* Yet in spite of the absence of that light, the child has gone on through so many lifetimes. How has she done it? The strength she must possess to reincarnate again and again in search of that light!

Head bent in reverie, Pandora pushes her way through the revolving door of the lobby and marches to the elevators, enters, and presses the button without looking up.

The child's original light lies somewhere beyond them, she knows. Somewhere beyond them in an ancient realm buried behind a storm of zeon blue. She knows she's here to cancel the signal of the disease one way or another. But it's more than that. If the child is to truly survive she must not only retrieve her light, she must own that power in such a way that it can never be repossessed. When she does—*(and she must—the struggle cannot go on forever!)*—Pandora will bring the child with her to Tahoe. The child will become Pandora's student, her protégé. This is their destiny. Their second chance! This is what Elysha's painting has been trying to tell her all along. *We are the same thing. Heal Sydney; heal Elysha. We are one!*

Half in a trance she wanders down the second floor hallway through the double doors of the lab, where she's directed to a ladder-back chair. She hangs her cape on a hook behind the door and sits.

Pandora knows the child belongs with her. Is there even a question? The other women know little to nothing of the spiritual realms. Mitsy has never been more than an amateur, and in this lifetime at least, Hannah has interest in nothing but material goods. Those women don't deserve her. Pandora isn't perfect, God knows, but at least she tries. She sees the sisters now so clearly in her mind's eye. It must be the physical proximity. There they are, Mitsy and Hannah in Tuscany, all those lifetimes ago, women of magic—herbalists, healers—even their income depended on the child's light. Ever since the light was taken—*five, six, seven lifetimes ago?*—the two of them have led the droning sequential lives of pedestrian sleepwalkers. Nothing more. There is no way the girl's gifts can flourish under the influence of such lightweights. Pandora's mind is made up. She will heal the child at great expense to herself, and she will bring the child home. The child is her reward.

"A little pinch," says the technician.

Pandora looks down at the tube, half-expecting her blood to be a clear stream, entirely absent of color. "I'm so tired," she tells the man. "I wonder if we should do this after I've had some rest."

"We'll draw more blood later, anyway," he says. "You'll be a pincushion by the time you're through; don't worry."

All at once Pandora's head feels as if it's encased in a concrete vault. Her temples pound. "Do you feel the pressure?" she asks the man. "The changes in atmosphere?" It's coming upon them sooner than she expected—the storm. She can see the free-floating plasma particles everywhere! Can't anyone else? Sometimes her gifts make her feel like the only living thing in a dead sea of belly-up fish.

"Excuse me?" the technician says as he releases the tourniquet and deftly removes the needle. He places a ball of cotton gauze on the puncture site. "Hold this," he says. "Apply pressure."

"The atmosphere," Pandora repeats eerily as she presses down on the cotton. She's surprised her blood isn't spurting everywhere from the drop in barometric pressure alone.

"You mean outside?" he asks absently, his back to her, counting the vials of her blood. He turns around. "Hey, are you okay? You seem...I don't know...a bit spacey. You want some juice or water?"

Pandora shakes her head. "No, never mind." The man's an idiot, she thinks. The ionosphere is practically collapsing on their heads and the little people go on. They feel nothing. She covets their ignorance.

A little wobbly, Pandora holds onto the arm of the chair as she stands. "Maybe I will take that juice," she says.

She finishes a cup of cranberry juice and wanders into the lobby of the lab. A rakish young man with curly black hair and a dark complexion approaches her. The resemblance of cultural blend to her own is astounding. But not just that; there's something...else. He could be her son. She connects with him instantly. *Who are you?*

"Ms. Pandora?" he says good-naturedly.

"I am she," she says evenly, in spite of the spinning outer layers of her etheric brain. Her signals are picking up so much friction in the atmosphere, it's a wonder she's not spiraling down the corridor babbling in some indigenous dialect.

"Hey, my name is Dane," he says. "Friend of Syd's? The gang asked me to come get you."

"Nice to meet you, Dane," she says, extending her hand.

She's rewarded with a strong, firm handshake and an engaging smile. She regards him with interest—his dark eyes, long black lashes, dark curly hair and olive skin. "If you don't mind my asking, what is your heritage?" she asks. "You seem familiar to me."

He bobs his head back and forth, shyly. "Oh well, you know, all over the place, really. But my dad's folks are from Sicily and the Czech Replubic, I think. And I don't know, Armenian thrown in." He shrugs. "Your basic rescue dog."

Pandora smiles. He's in this mix for a specific reason, she knows. *But what?* "Well, I'm ready to go," she says, and pulls her red cape from a hook on the wall. "I believe my bags have been taken to the hotel already?"

"Actually, I've got them in the car," he says. "But well, Mrs. M says she'd rather have you stay at the farm." He looks down at his feet. "She really wants you there. My mission is to convince you."

Pandora nods. "I don't think you can convince me, Dane," she says. "Sorry, but I'm the solitary sort."

"Okay, let's see, well..." He smacks his lips. "Here's the hard sell—there's definitely a comfortable room for you with your own bathroom. And the scenic view at the farm is cosmic!" His dark eyes widen in an attempt to tantalize her.

She is tantalized. "Cosmic, eh?" *What's he trying to tell her? What message does this boy bear unaware?*

"Oh yeah, and there's a baby horse about to be born in the barn. They're keeping tabs on it from the laptop at the house; everybody's ready to pounce. So it's much more fun than a hotel. More like a zoo-tel!" He claps his hands. "If I were invited, I'd be at the farm, trust me."

"But you weren't invited?"

"Not really. Not to sleep anyway. The guys are elsewhere."

He frowns, rubbing the back of his neck. "Hey, is it my imagination or is the sky falling?"

She studies him. "What do you mean?" she says cautiously. *The answer is 'Yes'!*

"Just pressure, I don't know. My joints and my head... maybe I'm coming down with something. Just a fair warning."

She shakes her head. "It's not you," she says. "The ionosphere and atmosphere are compressing from a geomagnetic storm. That's all." For some reason, she holds nothing back.

"That's all?!" he says, rubbing his temples. "Are you a scientist or something?"

"Sort of," she says. "The mystical variety."

"Oh wow, well that's my kind of scientist!" he says. "The fourth way and all that, right? We're more than we pretend to be!"

"Yes we are," she says, amused. "At least some of us are."

"Ha! Yeah!" he says, nodding. "Not everyone, that's for sure. At least not yet."

As they fall in step down the corridor, she says, "A baby horse then?" She wants to turn his attention away from the pressure to prevent amplification. One thing she doesn't need is for the solar storm to accelerate its schedule. Right now, there's still time. Barely.

"In the barn," he says as they turn the corner. "Any time now."

"Birth is auspicious," Pandora says more to herself. "Another good sign. *New life!*"

"You got that right," he says. "I'm thinking it's a great omen for Syd. A filly was born just a little while ago, too. So...two babies!"

They arrive at the elevator bank. He presses the down button and they wait.

"They call them foals," he continues. "I've never seen

anything like it. The little tight body and long, spindly legs. Jonah showed me some videos." He waves his arm. "They stand right up and walk!"

Pandora smiles to herself. The boy is genuine, such a rare quality.

"Syd named the last filly 'Ireland'," he says, "which I really dig. It came to her, *Ireland!*—just like that. Had to be."

Ireland, Pandora thinks—her life after Tuscany—another place of great struggle for Sydney. The ocean, the cliffs, the long, dark winter nights. Pandora clearly remembers wandering in astral form to their cottage on the cliffs, the surf pounding beneath them. More ritual healing. Or she should say—attempts at healing. All doomed without that light. This will be the last time, she resolves. This time, the child will be healed.

"Today's foal will be an Aries," Dane continues. He taps his fingers impatiently behind him against the wall. "Like me. I think Aries would be an awesome name for the little guy, don't you? If it's a guy it's called a colt, they told me. Aries creatures are strong. There are scientists who believe Christ was an Aries, did you know that?" He nods. "That he was born in the spring. I read a book about it."

"How did they figure that out?" she asks.

"Supercomputers," he says. "They figured out there was a giant astronomical event, probably a star explosion or something visible from the Far East, big and bright enough to direct the wise men." He shakes his head. "Aries are leaders."

Pandora regards him closely, intrigued. *Who is this boy—a guide?* "Are you Elysh...uh...Sydney's boyfriend?" she asks.

He jockeys his head back and forth bashfully. "Not really, but I wouldn't rule it completely out in a few years. I have a few things to work out first."

"You? Not Sydney?" says Pandora, surprised.

"Yeah, you know, I have to deserve her."

"Oh. I see."

"Syd's deep, you know. You can't bullshit her." He raises his eyebrows. "An indigo babe. There aren't very many of them around. At least she's the first one I've met, and I would know."

The elevator finally arrives; doors slowly open. Doctors, nurses, aides disperse.

"Yes, she is," Pandora says, chuckling. "She's an indigo babe."

Dane smiles, but doesn't look directly at her. "Yeah, well, most people don't know what that is, so I'm glad at least the person donating DNA understands who the hell Syd is. You know?"

"I do."

"I wouldn't want her to get a dummy's DNA or anything. She's no dummy."

Pandora smiles deeply at the way the universe constructs an event or a life. The way the right people show up without anyone even realizing it, even the people themselves. The way it conspires to develop its citizens and move them in the intended direction of their lives. The way it gathers and illuminates then takes a bow and exits, leaving the rest up to us.

The elevator is empty; they enter alone. She is relieved by the silence.

And yet, she thinks, even with the help of God and the created universe, there is still so much to be done. So much to be done without any instruction, or at least without human instruction. So much must be divined. Intuited. Of this event it can be said that everything is in its place. Signs of birth and life and archetypal names surround her. The storm approaches. Coronal Mass Ejections threaten the horizon with their arsenal of healing frequency. And guides, such as this familiar young man, accompany her and Syd. On some primary level, each understands his role.

THE ANESTHESIA GAME   309

"The button's stuck," he says, pressing it this way and that. "But hold on; I can get it going. It's just loose."

While he tinkers, she lays deep in thought. How will the pieces of this massive, moving, cosmic puzzle assemble and join on all connected planes? Will it be peaceful or volatile? The answer rests squarely on Pandora's shoulders, and yet she herself is unsure. The test is Sydney's, but it's also hers, Pandora's. What will she be able to let go of this time that she has been unable to release in the past? That's what will make the difference. That...and how she does it.

How?

"There we are," says Dane, folding his arms proudly. "Down we go. It's a slow boat though."

Pandora is so focused, she barely hears him. Free-floating plasma particles surround her, reminding her again that particles have a determined path. *Can he see them?* To direct real change, the kind of change she's been charged with directing, she must convert to an indeterminate path. *Be a wave,* she thinks. *Be a wave.*

Just as she thinks this, the elevator rocks in a jerky fashion, up, down, and sideways before plunging at a rate so rapid her feet levitate as her head strikes the ceiling hard. She is thrown against the boy, his body cushioning hers, protecting her as they strike the steel wall before falling to the floor like a sack of rocks. Bursts of light circle her head, followed by a confusing blaze of extravagant color. She fights to hang on, to check on Dane. Her eyes won't open.

Darkness.

Hannah

"YOU'RE ALMOST THERE, MITSY! You almost have her! Don't give up," Hannah coaches—or really, begs—from the back wall of the barn stall. What she's thinking is—*better Mitsy than me*. Although Hannah knows she could still be recruited. Better to play cheerleader than get her manicured hands into that biological mess.

As instructed by the vet on the phone, Mitsy pierces the red bag of bloody placenta then moves aside as it empties. This is not a normal foaling, not at all the way it should go, but it isn't hopeless yet. Mitsy kneels back down, breathing heavily, taking stock of the situation. Then slowly, she reaches her gloved hand into the birth canal to locate the foal. Hannah's amazed at her sister's courage. How did she go from an agoraphobic recluse to a competent (or at least willing) equine midwife in less than a week? The power of nature, she supposes. Or at least the power nature has over Mitsy.

"The foal isn't low enough," Mitsy says anxiously. "I can't feel it."

Hannah stares at Jonah's concerned face in her phone screen. "Did you hear that?" she asks him. "She can't feel the foal."

Jonah turns the camera on Doc Benton, beside him, who's driving the truck at breakneck speed.

"Tell her to reach up as far as she can," Doc says. "To her elbows if she has to. Then tell me what she feels."

Mitsy reaches deep. She grimaces, kneeling at an awkward angle, her face against Daizee's hindquarters, her eyebrows deeply knit. So far, Daizee tolerates the intrusion.

"There it is," she finally says. "There it is!"

"She feels the foal!" Hannah tells the men. "But Daizee's not contracting."

"I feel the hooves now!" Mitsy says.

"How many?" asks Jonah.

Mitsy struggles, blindly feeling the form with her hand. "Two," she says. "Definitely two legs."

"That's good; that's good," says Doc, his head bouncing around like a slapstick clown. They're clearly on the bumpy dirt road now, several miles south.

"Mitsy, can you grab hold of the legs and pull them?" he says. "Twenty minutes is too long. The foal has to get oxygen fast."

Mitsy reaches in just as Daizee's contraction pushes the legs downward. She removes her arm as the foal begins to show.

"There's a hoof!" says Hannah. "Right there! I see it! Oh my God, it's right there!" She turns the phone around for the men to see. "Do you see the hoof?"

"We're only a minute away," Jonah says. "Keep trying. If you can grab them both, do so, and pull."

"Firmly but steadily," says Doc. "If it's in the right position it won't hurt the foal. It looks like the right position to me."

"But there's only one hoof," Mitsy says cautiously. "I don't see the other one. It must be caught."

"Shit!" says Hannah. "What should we do?"

In a storm of friction, the men disappear from the screen. Her phone is a coal black void. "Damn phone!" she says, pretending to throw it against the wall. Instead she shoves it in her pocket and rushes to the hall to dial them back on the land line.

The land line is dead.

"What the hell!" she screams. All at once the sky darkens and the lights in the barn dim then completely black-out. This is a bizarre state of affairs for eleven AM, she thinks. Where the hell is the daylight?

"Hannah?" calls Mitsy. "I can't see you."

"I'm here," she says, trying not to sound anxious. After all, anxiety is contagious, and the last thing they need right now is an anxious midwife. Hannah's only interest is in holding Mitsy together until this foal is born. What they need is blessed ordinariness. But so far there is nothing normal or ordinary about this day.

Hannah feels her way slowly around the dark stall, through the hall, and over to the window ledge of the front room. Against the dim window light, she sees the outline of the emergency lantern. She grabs it and flicks the switch. *Light!* At least the lantern works.

When Hannah arrives back at the stall, Daizee is snorting and wheezing. Closer inspection with the lantern reveals foam forming around her muzzle. Her tongue hangs out. Hannah grabs a squirt bottle of water from the ledge and drizzles some on Daizee's tongue. "There, there, girl," she says soothingly.

The mare struggles mightily and then, in an apparent second wind, contracts. The contraction is so strong, Mitsy recoils. Even Hannah feels it. *Was it a contraction or an earthquake?*

Anything seems possible in lighting this compromised. Distress is evident in the mare's bloodshot eyes as she contracts again. But this time, instead of releasing, the foal appears to be pulled back into the canal.

"Noooooo!" says Mitsy. "Noooo! Get back here!" She turns to Hannah, wild. Even in this poor light, Hannah can see Mitsy's eyes—so red from lack of sleep, mascara pooled in dark pouches below them. Her freshly colored amethyst brown hair is slicked to her damp head. "I don't know," she says desperately, nearly weeping. "Hannah! The foal may be gone!"

"No," Hannah says, determined. They will not lose the foal here! Not during Mitsy's maiden attempt, not to mention all the larger issues they're yet to face. Where's the self-proclaimed gypsy healer when you need her, Hannah would like to know. She lays the emergency lantern on the hay and without even thinking, pulls on a pair of long gloves and kneels beside Mitsy, gently nudging her aside. *"If only she hadn't put her hand in that bloody mess…"* crosses her mind, but she control/alt/deletes it. No time for regrets, or even ghosts of regrets. Time for action.

She reaches up the birth canal, feeling around. "There it is," she says. "Right….there." She catches her breath. "One of the legs is caught in the pelvis. They call it an elbow lock. I've never released one, but I've watched Doc do it.

"Come on, Daiz," she says. "Give us one more contraction. Oh my God, Daiz, come on…"

"Come on…" begs Mitsy. "Please! Don't give up, Daizee!"

Just as the mare delivers another weak contraction, the truck bearing Jonah and the vet screeches onto the gravel. Jonah leaps out, followed by Doc, running. The sky has lightened a shade from coal black to steel gray. They leave the engine running, headlights streaming into the barn.

"Damn computer went down!" Jonah says breathlessly.

His long legs carry him there in a few strides. "Damn technical piece of crap blanked out about an hour ago. I thought Daizee was sleeping."

"Same with ours," says Mitsy. "Everything in the house is on the blink."

"Didn't the generator go on?" he asks.

"Off and on," she says. "But I think there's a problem with the generator, too."

"There it is," says Hannah. "I can feel it—a hoof."

"Holy crap, Hannah," he says when he realizes she's the one tending to Daizee.

Secretly pleased, Hannah knows she couldn't have planned it better. Not that she planned it at all; she didn't. Jonah's never seen this side of her—the roll-up-the-sleeves farm girl side. No one has, including Hannah.

Doc Benton pulls on a pair of gloves and gently moves Hannah aside. They watch, riveted, as he tugs gently on the one free leg, then reaches up, grimacing, grunting. "There we go," he says.

Daizee neighs soulfully.

"Sorry, girl," he says. "Come on! Come on! There! Ooooo. Got it!"

"Oh thank God!" says Mitsy, trembling.

Slowly, he brings the left leg down, even with the right then grabs them both firmly in his big hands and tugs. The long spindly legs appear followed by the white muzzle; the forehead; the wet, flattened ears. They hold their breath. The foal opens its eyes and blinks.

Hannah gasps, grabbing Mitsy as they both nearly collapse onto the hay in exhaustion and excitement. "He's okay," says Mitsy, crying. "Oh my God, he's alive, Hannah. He's alive."

"Might be a she," Hannah whimpers, nearly as emotional as Mitsy.

"Normally I would leave Daizee to do the rest," says Doc. "But none of us knows how long she's been at it or how much strength she has left."

Jonah, kneeling at Daizee's head, juts his chin at Hannah in a 'best to leave' gesture, which Hannah instantly decodes. It means they don't know what's next or how bad it will get. It means *leave us alone* so we can concentrate on the horses.

Hannah pulls off Mitsy's gloves then her own and rotates Mitsy in the other direction. "Come on," she says. "Let's let them do their job."

They walk into the alcove and scrub up at the sink in silence. As they enter the paddock, Hannah looks up. She is nearly speechless at what she sees, but manages to whisper, "Damn, look at that!" A pair of eagles circles the barn so close she can almost touch them.

"Oh my God," says Mitsy, mesmerized. "That's got to be a good sign, right? Eagles are auspicious? Aren't they? I remember you saying that."

Hannah nods, but really, what does she know about this day? Its secrets are locked in this vault of steel gray featuring atmospheric pressure so low it feels like an iron boot instead of sky.

They walk out of the paddock and up the hill for a better view. Hands on hips, Mitsy stares at the eagles, the barn and beyond it all into the fields. "The sky is a weird color," she says.

Hannah nods. "If I didn't know any better, I'd say tornado."

Mitsy turns to her. "When was the last time you had one here?"

"Decades at least. These foothills take the steam out of them; they love a flat plane."

Mitsy smiles. "You know more about nature than you admit to."

Hannah shrugs. "More than I want to, maybe."

"I don't remember any tornadoes when we were kids," Mitsy says. "But everything's changing." She shakes her head plaintively. *"Everything."*

Hannah doesn't know what to say. It's true. Everything's up in the air and threatening to knock them out. She doesn't want to bring up more than they can chew in a simple conversation. She finally understands why Mitsy never wanted to talk about her life once Syd got sick. What was there to say that wouldn't explode in her throat?

Suddenly, Mitsy's face lights up. "But look at what we did in there!" she says with more life than Hannah ever remembers seeing in her sister. "And you!" Mitsy wraps her arms around Hannah and hugs tightly. "You stuck your hand up there! You just *did it!* You never even thought about it." She shakes her head. "And I've never heard you talk like that before. Like a pro!"

Hannah places her fingers modestly over her mouth. "Shucks," she says. "Well, that's because I've never done it before. That was a first." She widens her eyes playfully. "And hopefully a last."

As they stand on the hill, hugging, swirls of wind kick up. In the adjacent field Jolie gallops in a tight circle that progressively widens until it includes the entire periphery of the field. Ireland clumsily follows.

"Takes your breath away, doesn't it?" Mitsy says, tears spilling. "All this." She waves her arm right to left just as a brilliant violet light shoots like a comet above the hills on the western horizon.

"Whoa!" says Hannah, rubbing her eyes. "Did you see that or am I hallucinating?"

A strange screech pierces the air behind them and they turn toward the house where the gypsy's Persian cat, his back arched, screeches into the wind. He stares ahead, his strange eyes reflecting the filtered light like diamonds.

"What the hell?" says Hannah.

"Better get him inside," says Mitsy. "How did he get out anyway?"

As they trudge up the slope to retrieve Guru, Godiva races out from the front hedge of juniper. She trips on a rock, is knocked off-kilter, and lands on her oversized head.

"What the...?" says Mitsy.

"Don't know," Hannah says, wide-eyed. She assesses their options. "I'll get Godiva, but let's leave the feline warlock out here for the eagles, shall we?"

Mitsy shakes her head in admonishment as they labor up-hill. "You know we can't do that," she says.

"Unfortunately, eagles don't eat cats, anyway," says Hannah. She stops for a second to catch her breath. "My body feels like dead weight, like I'm dragging a freaking rhinoceros uphill with every step." After a few shallow breaths, she says, "That was a hell of a workout down there."

"I feel the same way," says Mitsy. "Not to mention the hideous headache. Imagine how Daizee feels."

Just then Guru charges downhill, still screeching, but now he's also jumping up on his back feet and clawing the air.

Mitsy puts out her arm to stop Hannah. "He's trying to tell us something," she says. "I'm sure of it. Animals see things we don't."

"He's casting a damn spell on us is what he's doing," says Hannah, though she stops obediently. That cat is as insane as its owner. He might claw their eyes out. Best to stay back.

Mitsy approaches the cat carefully, bends at the knees and circles it for capture. She closes in on him, but not so fast. The thing darts between her legs and out the other side. Hannah chases Godiva with as much luck. It's not that the animals are moving so quickly, as much as the women's reflexes are nonexistent. Hannah's arms and legs feel like cast iron. She's honest-to-God not even sure she can make it up the fifty feet to the house—with or without the dog. She stops at a cedar tree and leans against it for support.

"Hannah," Mitsy says, turning. "Do you think...?

Bent over with hand-to-chest to support her heavy breathing, Hannah says, "What?"

"The magnetic storm...?"

As if in response, the raptors rise from the barn roof, wings flapping, then set off in synchronous flight into the vast abyss. In flight, their impressive wings spread straight out, nearly touching each other at the tips as they disappear into a vanishing point beyond the hills. The wind is so loud it's impossible to hear anything more than ten feet away. Mitsy points down to the barn, where Jonah's half-hanging out the window hollering something that might as well be Arabic for all the sense it makes. Hannah places her hand behind her ear to indicate they can't hear him.

The next thing they know, he's running up the hill, shouting, "It's a boy, ladies! We've got ourselves a colt!"

Before they can even rejoice, the sky blackens. Guru's fur stands practically on end as he continues to screech and claw the air. The lights in the house flicker then die. The generator kicks on like a rumble of thunder, then hiccups and chokes. All the way down the thirty-five miles of rolling hills, barns and homes turn to shadow in the inky sky.

"Oh my God, Hannah," Mitsy says, gasping. "No!"

"What?"

"Sydney! The hospital!"

"I'm sure..."

"And what about Dane!" Mitsy says. "Where is he? He left hours ago to get Pandora!" She pulls her cell phone from her back pocket, fidgeting madly. "It's dead," she says.

Hannah stares at her, frowning.

"They couldn't have called us if they wanted to," Mitsy says. All at once her terror is backlit by bands of brilliant color the likes of which Hannah has never seen. "Is that...?"

"What?" Mitsy says, turning. She freezes. "Oh my God! What is that? It's like...an aurora or something."

Hannah's skin and hair are on fire with static electricity. Anymore and she'll ignite. Even her eyes...

Before she can finish that thought, Jonah appears out of the corner of her right eye, his slumped figure exiting the barn, head down. Hannah sees him, knows what it likely means. *Not Daizee! No!* Realizing that such an outcome would be more than Mitsy could bear right now (or maybe ever), Hannah places her hands on her sister's shoulders and steers her toward the house.

"Come on," she says reassuringly. "Let's take a ride to the hospital. Everything's all right, you'll see."

Not that she believes a word of it.

Sydney

SYD IS A TIGHT-ROPE walker straddling two worlds. One false move and it's over. No one has to tell her this. She just knows.

The first world is a hospital room where the tiny flashing red lights that once endlessly beeped on her monitoring system, have been silenced, thank God. Next on the list of blessings, her IV's have mercifully stopped pumping chartreuse poison into her fragile ecosystem. The chartreuse poison, of course, is intended to kill the putrid disease that also poisons her body. Which will kill her first?

It's a race.

It all came to grief about an hour ago, but, really, who would know since the clocks have stopped. The world has come to a grinding halt. At least this world has—the first world. A code red hospital emergency was issued a while ago, and ever since, no one's monitored her at all. It's as if she isn't there. Maybe

320

she isn't. She doesn't even know what the emergency is, and to be honest, doesn't care. All she knows is that whatever it is, it doesn't involve her for a change. Except of course that it involves leaving her to her own devices.

The lack of medical attention is not what bothers her; that part is a godsend. What bothers her is the unbearable weight of her body. Ever since this morning, a mysterious force has been pulling her down, pulling her under. Right through the mattress springs it feels like, into the floor and straight to the earth's core like a giant magnet. She feels like a chunk of embedded rock. Her head pounds steadily. *Compression.* She couldn't talk if she wanted to. But all around her, children scream. Nurses walk purposefully up and down the halls in what, from Syd's room at least, appear to be slow motion. Or maybe not, how would she know? She herself is in some kind of suspended animation. Only her eyes are alert, hypnotized as they are by tiny glimmering particles of what look like fairy dust floating around the room. Or maybe it's heaven. Maybe heaven has come to get her.

Or maybe she's already there.

On the other side is the second world, the world of nebula. It beckons like the finger of the gypsy queen. *Come to me! Come!* What choice does she have? She's balancing on a string across the canyon of infinity. She collapses in and out of that world, entering it partially then returning to the hospital room with a start. *Where am I? Who am I?* These questions are real. As wary as she is of the nebulous nature of the second world, absence from the hospital room is a blessing. Her heavy body, pounding temples, and burning veins can't follow where her broken body won't go.

Maybe she's had enough.

She tries to keep her eyes from closing in case her family returns, or Dane. *Funny Dane!* But she can't do it; it's impossible. Her leaden eyelids are doors to a secret passage. She enters. Behind her, they seal shut.

She travels back. Back. And further back. As far back as she can go.

More aware now in her second world than she ever was in the first, she drinks it in—the fullness of light, the vibrant, palpable energy, the infinite breadth of space. For some reason, Pandora stands beside her. But why? *Doesn't Pandora belong to the first world?* So maybe Syd is delirious and the wizard seer is sitting beside her in the hospital room as she was this morning. Maybe it's still morning. Maybe the second world is just a psychedelic version of the first.

Both of them suspended in the cavernous sky, Pandora grips Syd's right hand while raising her own left arm into the wind, directing them to a new location. Seconds later they share the summit of a misty mountain in the midst of a majestic range. The Blue Ridge, maybe, or the Adirondacks. But no...these peaks are higher, more remote than any Syd has ever seen. All around them are snow-covered peaks surrounding a crystal blue glacial lake. At a distant point, bands of neon light stack on the horizon like a sandwich of melted crayons.

"Do you see that?" Pandora asks searchingly.

Syd nods. "The magnetosphere," she says, surprising herself. The name just comes to her like that. She knows without asking. Barriers to language and physical motion removed, this world is an altogether easier place to be.

"Exactly," says the gypsy, grinning. Her white hair whips around like a halo of laser lights; her topaz eyes sparkle like a cat's.

This woman is somebody here, Syd thinks—a goddess, maybe, or an angel. Or maybe a witch, she doesn't know. She's being careful. The woman bends down, looks at Syd, and locks eyes. "We're going to get you well," she says pointedly. "Do you hear me? But you have to do everything I ask."

Syd doesn't nod. She doesn't know what will be asked.

"We have to do two things here," says the goddess witch. "First, I'm going to harvest the zeon blue from that storm." She points her elegant ringed fingers at the horizon. At the base of the ribbons of color lies a far-off river of indescribable blue, highlighted with sheens of magenta and emerald iridescence.

"Why?" says Syd, concerned. *It's so far away!*

"To heal you," she says gently. "To heal you of the false disease that consumes you."

"The false disease?"

"Yes," she says. "Like a wounded animal, false disease burrows in at an opportune time. When the host is frail. Every living thing seeks immortality, even disease."

"Disease is a living thing?" says Syd. "I thought it was dead. That's what it feels like. Like I'm carrying something dead inside me."

"No, dear," she says kindly. "It's a living thing whose life depends on consuming yours. Just as the disease seeks to kill you, we seek to kill the disease. It's a competitive world."

"Why?" says Syd.

A wild gust billows the gypsy's rich, blousy silks and she raises her arms to honor its force. "Our enemies hone us," she says. "That's why. They build our strength. Without them, we would be weak. Untested."

Her posture erect, she raises her chin nobly into the air. "But we have allowed this enemy enough life. You are sufficiently honed. It's time to destroy it now and for all time."

324 REA NOLAN MARTIN

Syd's eyes tear in the whipping wind. They are real tears. She touches her cheek to feel them. *Wet!* Everything in the second world is real in a different way than the first, dense and at the same time luminous and transparent. She's surprised to feel anything as concrete as a tear or even an emotion.

"How?" she says into the wind. "How will we destroy it?" Her words echo. "*destroy it? destroy it? destroy it.*"

"Ah," says Pandora. "It has taken me lifetimes to conjure that answer." She looks at Syd earnestly. "Everything has a signal," she says, "even disease. We simply locate the signal for your particular affliction..." She claps her hands firmly. "... and cancel it."

The simplicity of this answer nearly knocks Syd off the mountain. *Find the signal and cancel it. Of course!* Can it really be that simple?

"Zeon holds the precise signal we need to cancel the opposing signal of your disease. Once we cancel it, we will open up the coordinates of time, you and I," she says. "We'll travel back to reclaim your original light. It's the absence of that light that made you vulnerable in the first place."

"No," says Syd. "I didn't give it up. It's right here..." She pats her belly. But closing her eyes, she sees that the light is already dimmer than it was this morning.

"Not that light," says Pandora. "That's the temporary light I gave you earlier today. That light doesn't last forever. It isn't *yours*. It's borrowed from the plasmasphere and can hold a charge for just so long. Instead, we must recover your original light. The power of our intentions will lead us to the exact coordinates of that event."

Syd gazes at the bands of color on the horizon, bewitched. "That's what I've been searching for, too" she says, "every time I play the game."

"The game?" says Pandora.

Syd nods. "The Anesthesia Game. Where I try to remember the answer to a question while I look for the lost light."

Pandora's arched white brows form a deep vee against her polished bronze skin. "This is no game, my dear," she says gravely. "Lives are at stake."

A storm lights up on the horizon and a shiver races through them both.

Pandora regards Syd deeply for what feels like an eternity. When she shakes herself out of it, she says, "It won't be easy, darling child. In order to harvest the necessary signal, I have to sacrifice particle form for a time."

Syd's eyes dart side-to-side. "You have to become a wave," she says.

Pandora holds Syd at arm's length, her eyes glowing. "You know about waves, do you?"

Like an unread book under her mattress whose information she'd absorbed in her sleep, Syd doesn't know how she knows what she knows. *But she knows.* "It's how I survive," she says.

Pandora smiles broadly. "Waves are possibilities. They change everything!"

"But you can't stay one," says Syd.

"No." The gypsy's smile vanishes. "I must be quick. Efficient."

"And there's no guarantee of return..."

Pandora swallows hard. "...to a particle," she says, finishing Syd's thought. "No. It's a risk. And this isn't the only risk, just the first."

"What..." begins Syd, but Pandora raises her index finger in warning.

"One thing at a time," she says.

They shimmy left and right on the summit, jostled from the

second world as commotion surrounds them in the first. Noise, yelps, machines, someone calling out in despair, *"Sydney! Oh Sydney!"* She feels she has to respond.

"Don't," Pandora commands. "Don't do it. Zeon...and even the storm that created it...are ephemeral. If you respond we may lose this window."

But the pull is so strong.

"Sydney!" she hears her mother wailing softly, more and more clearly. "Sydney, please come back! Ohhhhhh, Sydney!"

She can't help herself. She drops down the chute, opens her eyes, blinks. There around her bed is her family—her mom, her dad, Aunt Hannah. "Where's Dane?" she says. "Why isn't he here?"

Crying softly, her mother leaves the room.

Why isn't she answering! Can't she hear me?

"Don't you people have any backup generators in this hospital?" demands her father.

"Even the generators are out," yells someone in the hall.

"Signals are scrambled," says someone else. "Even planes aren't allowed to fly."

Voices whirl around her, above and below. She wants to answer them, but she isn't strong enough to animate her physical body. She just isn't. It won't respond. She tries to push herself into it; make it sit up. Anything.

It's a wall of flesh and bone.

The next thing she knows, she's back on the mountain.

"Oh, thank God," says Pandora. "You *must* stay focused or all will be lost! I'll travel in to get the zeon, but if you're not here when I return..." She brushes her hands together. "That will be that."

Pandora

STARING INTO THE INFINITE chasm, Pandora knows she has no choice. The thing she has avoided for lifetimes must now be done. Do it. She squeezes her eyes shut and wills herself de-solidified, swept into the stream of awareness from whence she derived. She wills herself dispersed, while at the same time in control of her boundaries, her dynamics. To accomplish this mission, she must not lose track of her energy ever. She must hold the signal together well enough to recall it when the time comes.

She reopens her eyes, and in that split second, lets go and abandons particle form.

She is confused, then bewildered, then exhilarated. Loose in the wild abandon, the freedom is chilling, nearly unbearable in its piqued ecstasy. But even her ecstasy must be guarded. She allows herself to be part of it and yet...not. *She is a wave!* Wave properties allow her to shed all predetermined outcomes. She rolls up and down the sea of consciousness freely, still set on the horizon where the blue draws her closer. The zeon has consciousness too, she knows. Everything does. She sees this more clearly now than she ever has. It is one thing to know something with the mind, and quite another to *know* without human intellectual or emotional filters of any sort.

To just know.

She travels through the atmosphere's upper region to the ionosphere into the magnetosphere. Everything is charged; she has to fight to keep her energy from being scrambled. She is nearly there...nearly within reach of the stream of zeon in the river of deep dense plasma. In the near distance, a familiar purple orb radiates before her.

Anjah, she thinks, but tries not to conjure with any depth, because that, too, will deter her from her path and possibly even convert her back to particle form. Everything outside of this single focus is a threat to her existence. Anjah carries too much weight, too much history, though she has to confess ignorance to his precise origin, or even his attachment to her. But he's been a good enough guide. Or informant, really. And she knows that he knows where she is. He knows what she's finally doing. He will guard her, she supposes. He will help. After all, it is he who brought her here in the first place.

When she arrives at the outer reaches of zeon, its signal is so powerful she's pulled to the surface of its pole. She resists. Resistance takes more concentration than she thinks she has, but she knows she cannot fail. Failure would either disperse her completely, or convert her instantly to a particle form so dense she risks losing all wave properties, not just now, but forever. Even as a wave, she has a heart that warns her of the danger. She feels it beat...or really, *thud*, in the center of her awareness. Pa-boom. Pa-boom. Pa-BOOM. Her plan is to gather particles of zeon on the surface of her wave and carry them back. *How much is enough? How much is too much?* She has no idea.

Blocking the distracting presence of Anjah and the danger that lurks everywhere around her, she begins by focusing deeply. She concentrates, setting her intention to *zeon*. She is all about blue. Her consciousness attracts it; pulls it in. She feels it defecting from the plasma river, bouncing up, and moving toward her. One infinitesimal particle and another collect on the foam of her whitecap swell as she pretends to be one of them. *She is blue. She is zeon.* Another particle jumps to her surface. And another. They are one thing. They are family.

She doesn't know how long she's there, how could she? Her human aspect is still bound by time, but the plasma is not. The zeon can take its sweet time gathering or not gathering. The zeon is part of the infinity she resists. It is not individuated. It doesn't fight its nature. *It just is.* Only Pandora fights.

Another particle jumps; attaches. And another.

Though she conjures patience, deep within her soul she knows this is taking time. The minute she thinks this, fear colors her signal and she begins to lose her charge. Now Anjah places himself in her view, separating her from the zeon. "*Get away,*" she wants to think, but can't allow herself to form the thought. Forming the thought would doom the mission, and he knows it. So *why isn't he helping? Isn't this what he's been leading her to for a lifetime at least?*

His interference makes it impossible for her to harvest any more blue, but then again, maybe it's because she's out of time. Or maybe he's telling her she has enough—that any more would be dangerous. Whatever it is, she has to accept it without examination. Examining it wastes precious time and energy.

She returns her focus to the mountain. Equipped with the particles of zeon that singe the membrane of her energy, she remains a wave until she reaches the peak. There, she deposits the zeon particles at a safe distance, instantly returning to particle form.

"Elysha," she says, gasping for air, "these are yours."

The girl instinctively places her arms in front of her and calls out to the radiant blue. The particles are drawn to her bloodstream like yin to yang. One, and then another, and another gather in an orderly row.

Pandora watches, terrified. *Will it be enough? Did she collect enough?* She's in no shape to do that again. She should have stopped all her nasty habits long ago. Should never have started them! She should have listened to Anjah. Notwithstanding his irritating manner, he tried to tell her, didn't he? *A thousand times.*

Pandora checks her thoughts, refocuses, and aligns herself with the process. Watching Elysha now in all her majesty, calling the zeon forth and absorbing it, Pandora's consciousness becomes a dizzying time lapse of so many lifetimes. She is alert and super-conscious. She sees every particle, however infinitesimal adhere to the girl's mutated blood, to her disease. *She sees the disease.* She sees the tiny spinning decagon-shaped molecules consuming the child's blood. She sees the treacherous signal they radiate to each other as they conspire to overcome their host. She sees their shock as the zeon enters; watches them gather in protest, rising up against the intruder. She sees the zeon now, absorbed into the girl's etheric envelope and deeper, into her body temeer. She sees the child nearly collapse from the battle. She watches.

She waits.

Sydney

IT'S FUNNY HOW YOU can suddenly know things that you never knew. How obvious everything is when it finally comes together after years of ranting to the universe, *Why me?! Why!*

The tiny specks of crystal blue, if it can even be called blue—calling zeon 'blue' is like calling the sun 'yellow'. Zeon is not a pigment anymore than the sun is a pigment. *It is light of the highest frequency.* It is light of a nature unavailable before the magnetic storm that produced it arrived. Nature is a constant creation. Syd used to think that the palette belonged to God, but more and more she realizes that long ago, God gave it to us. The palette is ours.

Understanding this finally, she stands with her arms outstretched watching the zeon particles gather one by one, as if called by name. *Joey, Roger, Martha, and Stan, ha ha!* Individually and collectively they are aware of her. Aware of her problem. Her *curse*. They have intelligence. They penetrate her energy with that awareness, attracted like tiny missiles to the dark, ten-sided, spinning weapons of destruction that course through her. She sees them, too, the arsenal. She tries not to worry about the fact that there are many more dark ten-sided weapons of destruction than there are crystal particles of zeon to combat them. Warfare is warfare. All weaponry is not equal. Let's see what the zeon can do.

Scanning the surface of her inner body, she sees the zeon are strategic. Somehow they locate the dissonant signal. They hover then attack. They attack then attach. They cling for dear life. They won't let go. *But are there enough of them?* There is so much disease. Her system is a sea of inky black marauders. There goes another blue, and another. They seek and find. They attack and attach. One by one, they neutralize the signal of the marauders. The invaders weaken to a neutral gray. Their last gasp is a vibration that Syd can feel from head to toe. She shivers and seizes as her brain registers the signal switch of each cluster.

Even here, in this eternal land, on this majestic peak on this infinite landscape where the physical world is subordinate, she collapses into Pandora's arms from the fight within her. It is *too* much. She's endured the physical fight and the personal battle longer than her memory mercifully allows. How long has it been?

Eternity.

While she fights, Pandora holds her, kisses her forehead, strokes the glorious strands of flaxen hair that magically reappear on her bald scalp—in this world, anyway. Pandora watches with her as the zeon continues to zap one after another hostile invader—*attack and attach; attack and attach.* Until finally... *finally*...the zeon is in control. It assumes strategic locations in her blood and nervous systems, like Swiss guards—in the brain, the marrow, the spleen, the liver, the kidney, the colon, the upper and lower tracts—routing out the particles of cowardly disease that dare to hide. *We will find you!*

Her hands shake; her legs jerk; her eyes roll back in her head as the zeon seizes command. Her spirit moves in and out of her physical body as it is first shocked by the battle, then shocked again into a state of wellness she hasn't experienced in so long, it's more foreign to her than the disease itself. She doesn't know which condition is worse.

Mitsy

"GET THE DOCTOR," MITSY commands. "Oh my God, get the doctor, Aaron. She's returning. She's trying to talk."

Aaron rushes out as Hannah rushes in.

"What are you saying?" Hannah mutters almost unintelligibly. "I heard what you said to Aaron! *She's returning!* Are you saying she talked?"

Mitsy shakes her head. "No, but I feel she will. I feel it!"

Hannah sits beside her. "I hope to hell you're right," she says.

Mitsy looks up. "What about Pandora?"

Hannah shakes her head. "She's on life support. Still brain activity, but..." She places her head in her hands. "I'm sorry, Mits. I really am."

Mitsy swallows hard, her eyes darting left and right. "And...and Dane?"

"Cracked skull, broken pelvis, shoulder, arm...you name it. They induced a coma."

"Oh my God."

Hannah nods. "But he's young," she says. "The doctors haven't given up hope. Anyway, we can only focus on one disaster at a time."

"But his family..."

"We called Zelda. She's trying to contact his father."

Mitsy nods faintly, but really, she's too stunned to take in anything beyond the condition of her daughter. All she knows is that if she hadn't returned to the farm, she would likely be dead by now. The rudimentary strength she rediscovered back here is what makes it possible for her to sit upright in the midst of this storm. She is resolved to save her daughter. She can feel Pandora guiding her. *See her in the light, Mitsy! The light! And breathe, for God's sake! Breathe! Find your center and stay there!*

Sydney's leg jerks, breaking Mitsy's meditation. She reaches for it; holds it.

"Have you heard from Jonah?" she asks Hannah. "About Daizee?"

Hannah shakes her head. "My phone still isn't working. One of the techs said the entire electromagnetic field is whacked out by this storm. CME's, he called them. Coronal Mass... whatevers." She shrugs. "She was right," she says, referring to Pandora. "There was something about her I didn't like, I admit it, but the woman knew what she was talking about."

Mitsy dismisses the comment. "It is what it is," she says just as Aaron rushes back into the room followed by Dr. Blanca. The doctor observes Syd closely, takes her vitals, and warns them gently. "The body may show what appear to be signs of life..."

"No," Mitsy says, "no!" She wags her finger. She will not allow anyone to steal her hope.

"You have to decide," the doctor says compassionately.

Aaron steps back in horror. "Decide what?" he says.

She folds her arms. "How far we want to take this when the power returns." She shakes her head sadly. "I'm sorry, but a transplant is no longer an option."

Sydney

SYD FLOATS. SHE HAS no pain. She floats in and out of one world and the next, through past and present without boundaries or fear. She floats through the hospital, through Z's house and barn, through her room in Darien, and back to the farm where she walks right past Hannah and her mother leaving the barn.

Next she's in the house, opening the mudroom door. The Persian cat darts outside before she can close it. On the hill, he jumps at her, startled, clawing the air all around her. He sees her; he sees everything.

"Where's my dog?" she says, and tiptoes back through the house for her puppy. "There you are!" she exclaims, and joyfully chases Godiva out the front door, around the bushes to the back, where she sees the aurora in the southern sky. It takes her breath away. It's here, too, not just on the mountain—so rich and abundant! She's glad to see it; glad it penetrates both worlds. The zeon has given her new life, at least in this form. Her energy is low, but responsive. Wherever she is now, she has freedom to move back and forth. Whether she keeps this freedom or relinquishes it is a question she can't answer right now.

The next thing she knows she's riding Daizee, lost to the lower world, in a gallop across the horizon where she's released to a cot in the Darien clinic awaiting anesthesia. How can she be in so many places at once? She's happy when Roz enters the room. She hasn't seen her in so long. Her heart glows; she loves Roz. She misses her, too, but not enough to stay here.

"Ask me a question," she tells Roz.

"What kind of question?" Roz says.

"You know, The Anesthesia Game. Ask me anything at all. When I wake up, I have to give you the answer."

"Oh right," says Roz. She ponders and ponders. She turns her back, cups her chin and frowns then flips back around. "Okay, I've got it!" she says.

Syd waits in anticipation. This has to be good; it took her long enough.

"Okay, what's the spirit name of the gypsy who took your light?" Roz says.

Syd has to go deep to remember. "The gypsy who took my light?" she says, stalling. "The gypsy who..."

"Your original light," says Roz.

Syd thinks. The answer dribbles in. "She was a queen, I think."

"Whether she was a queen or not, I don't know. But you must remember her spirit name," Roz says. "It's important. Think hard. To win the game, you must know her name."

"I have to win," says Syd.

"Yes, you do," Roz says.

"This is it," Syd says. "The end of the game."

Roz nods. "Yes. Or the gypsy presides."

Seeking the answer, Syd's mind searches lifetimes of events, questions and answers, causes and effects, challengers and allies, until all at once she perceives the answer in a flash of purple light. "Anjah," she says. "Her name is Anjah."

The anesthesia is administered, knocks her out, and she returns clutched between the claws of two eagles to the mountain where Pandora waits.

Pandora

"WE DID IT," SYD says as she's dropped into Pandora's arms by the eagles.

"Not yet," says Pandora. "That was the easy part."

Syd says, "There was nothing easy about that."

"You're stronger now?" Pandora asks.

Syd nods. "Much."

"Okay." Pandora places her hands on the girl's shoulders. "Now we both become waves, open time and slip through."

"Why?"

"To recover your lost light."

"Stolen, you mean," says Syd.

Pandora's lips tighten. "Yes." So much signal enters Pandora's head at once, her head spins. But with the signal, come the bits and pieces of information she requires to complete her task.

She clutches Syd's hand and says, "Focus on the rim of infinity, nothing else. Let nothing interfere. Not one thing. This is a task of quantum faith. There is no room for doubt."

Together, they bear down, split, disperse, and move freely, rolling toward the horizon, up and down.

At first it's easy. But Pandora is wary of changing her focus. Not only hers, but Sydney's. She is in charge of the child. She stays close; her energy enveloping the outskirts of Syd's to keep her contained. They move unfettered into the next dimension and the next and the next until they are stopped abruptly at the end of the continuum. For them, space and time end here. Moving past it is a trick of the karmic wheel.

The wheel spins.

The wheel spins through births and deaths, marriages and children, pageants and battles. They run through wildflowers and killing fields. They celebrate the living and commemorate the dead. They morph gender to gender, race to race, status to status. They are male, female, black, white, aristocrat, peasant. But then the wheel squeaks, hesitates, and pauses. When the wheel pauses, they enter.

Behind it is a tent.

Within the tent is a gypsy queen. Resting on a cypress stump beside the queen is a sparkling crystal globe containing an orb of the purest inchoate light Pandora has ever seen. It is innocence itself; the stem cells of creation. The queen stares at the globe, unable to look away. She stares and stares. She covets the light, wills it within her, but it remains in the globe. Without the child herself, the light is powerless to the queen. The queen knows this. Pandora knows this, too. All of the queen's resources have been spent in search of the child.

At the sight of the queen both Pandora and Syd return instantly to particle form. They have arrived.

Hovering above the tent, Syd says, "She has the light." She turns toward Pandora and blinks. "But she can't use it."

Pandora shakes her head, aghast, as her memory of this

life materializes fully. "After she expelled me from the tribe for saving you and your sisters, I never knew what became of her," she says. She points down. "But I see she never reincarnated. She just sat there, staring, waiting, separated from her own energy, obsessed by yours." Her attention is drawn up and to her left where Anjah pulsates madly.

Sydney bristles when she sees him. "The Taker," she says.

"No, dear," says Pandora. "That's Anjah. He's here to help us."

Sydney tries to talk, but Pandora rushes on. "We're out of time," she says, and darts for the tent.

Anjah blocks her, his violet energy a shield.

"Anjah!" she says, "for God's sake! You're in my way! How do you expect me to do my job!"

Every time she moves, he blocks her path.

"What are you doing?" she says, confused. *Frantic!* "This is what we came for! This is what you led us to, for God's sake! Get out of the way so we can reclaim the light!"

Sydney glides between them.

"No!" Pandora tells her. "Return to the edge of the continuum immediately! I'll retrieve your light and return it!" *For God's sake listen to me!*

"Anjah and the queen are the same," Sydney says fiercely. "Anjah is The Taker."

Pandora knows this is ridiculous, but something in her core freezes.

Anjah glowers at Pandora. "Thank you for bringing her to me," he signals smugly. "Well done, Dorenia!"

Pandora's ghostly screams reverberate across time, depleting her.

"As if you're innocent," he says. "As if you're pure."

"What…"

"All those years—*lifetimes!*—you followed the child, wishing to possess her as much as I. You had her once and lost her through sheer negligence. You pretended to help those women, yet you hoarded my knowledge like I hoarded her light. You shared nothing. You and I are complicit."

Pandora weakens. He's right—or is it *she?* Anjah and the queen are one thing; masculine energy in female form.

Behind the tent, the gypsy queen throws back her head and cackles.

Pandora bows her head. She'll never make it into the gypsy tent now. She knows this. She's too exposed. "Sydney," she whispers. "Circumvent us. This battle is mine, not yours. Get your light and leave. I'll protect you."

"But you'll...he's stronger..." she stammers. "You'll never..."

"Go!" Pandora says. "NOW! You must!"

The girl bolts.

Pandora remains to battle Anjah, blocking his every attempt to pursue the girl again and again and again. She won't let his light merge with the gypsy queen's to reanimate that persona; she won't have it. For the first time in her life, or all their lives together, she will not give in or give up. She will fight this to the end.

Even if it kills her.

Sydney

SYD IS A FLASH of light, a burning torch. She streaks down, down, down into the new continuum, behind the curtain, into the tent where she shimmers boldly before the queen. The queen, delighted from a distance, is literally blinded by her speed. Her twisted scepter flies into the air as she howls in protest. Syd dodges the queen's dense energy, laying her own spirit directly on the globe of what she now knows to be her original light. This light belongs to her. It is hers. She absorbs it. Reclaims it.

Becomes it.

Her center solidifies with vitality and she rises above the smoky scene, above the tent, the inanimate queen, and the now soupy puddle of toxic purple waste outside. Pandora is nowhere to be seen, though Syd feels her presence deeply. *Did she escape? Where are you?*

"Come with me," she calls out to Pandora. "Please!"

Her words echo into a void. But in this void is a peace Syd hasn't felt in a very long time. Still, she must find Pandora. *She must!* She returns to the mountain peak, searching, but Pandora isn't there. She is drawn downward to the pine valley at the mountain base, and from there, to a crystalline beach at the edge of a sparkling indigo lake. There is nowhere else to go. This is it; the end. She must be here.

Where are you?

Nothing. No one.

She whimpers, kicking the heavy sand. "I'm going back now," she calls out. "Come with me! I owe you my life!"

Below her resound her mother's howling cries, the sucker punch gasps of her father's grief, and the sorrowful lament of her beloved aunt. And Dane, sweet Dane calling out to her in silence, a silence that nevertheless lives and breathes. Dane is in trouble.

He needs her.

"I have to go!" she calls out in desperation. "Pandora, come! Please!"

To her left, a gentle wind arises carrying her long hair in its embrace. She can't wait. She has to go. Will she see her friend there? *Her mother? Her savior?* Or carry on alone?

Just as she pivots, initiating her return, she stops and turns back toward the water. Her heart is inscribed with a deep understanding that arrives on the cusp of a glistening wave. She waits with reverence as it rushes in, caresses her feet, and lingers like a kiss. She reaches down to collect it, but before she can cup her hands or beg it to stay, it kicks up a pearl-white froth and retreats wistfully into the blue.

Epilogue

JONAH STOMPS THE TOES of his worn Frye boots against the cement step twice to loosen the dirt then scrapes the bottoms on the edge of the threshold. How many times has he entered this mudroom? *This house that he loves?* And yet never has he been more nervous than this.

"Anybody home?" he calls as he enters the kitchen.

"Oh my God, it's Jonah!" shouts Syd from one of the back rooms. "Uncle Jonah is back, everybody!"

Just hearing the sound of that bright voice, so strong, so confident, is enough to make him weep. All over the world people suffer, he thinks. This household is not the first or the last. Even now, this very minute, it's happening everywhere— grief, devastation—entire families hanging by the thread of a crippling diagnosis. *Will they survive or won't they?* And how? How will they do it? How did we? How did we all keep going? Only in the safety of the floating aftermath can one even contemplate these sinking questions.

But oh, how things change in the wake, he thinks. How they transform. Nothing is the same.

At the end of the open kitchen, Syd flies at him, followed by the 100 pound lobbing, loveable beast they call Godiva. "Rrrrruff!!" she barks, stopping cold and sitting back at Syd's stern command.

Jonah steadies the large package under his right arm as he grabs the feather-light Syd with his left; lifting her, treasuring her powerful life force against him. Breathe it in. It's real! *She survived.* He never knew what it was like to love a child until Syd snuck into his life these last few months, and nearly left.

"Hey darlin'," he drawls. "I missed you out there."

She grins, grabbing his arm and leading him into the living room where Mitsy, in full riding gear, reviews catalogs of what look like tractors. When she sees him, she stands, hands on hips. "How was it?" she asks earnestly. "What did you find?"

Before he can answer, an erratic flutter of footsteps on the adjacent front stairs is interrupted by a long hard slide, followed by an "Oh my God! Oh my God, ouch!"

Jonah's heart skips at the sound of Hannah's melodic treble. How will she take what he has to say? How will she deal with it? He holds his breath as she flies around the corner on bare feet, her lean body dressed in uncharacteristically wrinkled denim; her long hair in a casual braid. She looks like a girl.

"Hey," she says timidly.

"Hey," he replies. "Are you okay?"

She rubs her rump. "Just..." she shakes her head. "I'm fine."

Behind them, Syd jumps up and down like a pogo stick. "Tell us, Uncle Jonah! Tell us!" she says. "Come on! Don't make us guess!"

"Yes," says Mitsy. "The house looked so interesting on the screen, but what was it like to actually be there?"

"As soon as they finish the medical study on Syd, you have

to come out," he says. "You have to see it for yourselves. It's unbelievable."

Mitsy nods. "Soon," she says. "October, they say." She looks off in the distance, drifting. "We'll distribute the ashes then," she adds plaintively.

"I know just where," says Jonah. "The cabin looks out at a peak called Heavenly. It's spectacular. We can sprinkle them from there." He adjusts the cumbersome package beneath his arm and places it delicately on the surface of the antique cabinet.

"What's in the package?" says Syd. She runs her fingers anxiously through her unruly, gold hair, ear-length now and glistening in the late summer light that streams unfiltered through the room.

Jonah glimpses beyond her, out the window, where giant, carmine red Cana lilies border the long fence and wild honey-suckle sways in the breeze. Guru treads the paddock fence like a tight rope walker, his tail high.

"Uncle Jonah?" Syd urges. "The package?"

"Oh," he says, snapping out of it. He reaches into his pocket for the jackknife, and clips the twine that secures the brown wrap. "I found this in her living room," he says.

He bunches the paper in a ball, and tosses it at Godiva who lunges playfully. After pausing a dramatic moment, he turns the portrait in their direction.

They gasp collectively.

"Oh my God, it's beautiful!" Mitsy whispers reverently.

Syd steps forward, reaching. "Can I touch it?" she says.

He nods. "As much as it looks wet, the paint is dry," he says. "But she must have been working on it when she left for Virginia. It's so fresh."

"Like she painted it yesterday," says Hannah in a hushed voice. "And the colors…"

Jonah nods. "I know. The aurora."

"How did she do that with ordinary paint?" says Hannah. "I mean, did she pull the colors right out of the sky, or what?"

"There it is," says Syd. "In the eyes." She points. "The girl's eyes. That...*blue!*"

"She kind of looks like you, cookie," says Hannah. "But not...really."

"But something," says Mitsy. "Something deep. Integral."

Jonah centers the canvas carefully on the top of the cabinet and steps back so they can all drink it in. He points to the neck. "See the tattoos?" he says.

Syd's hand rushes to her mouth. It's a moment before she can speak. "Wings," she whispers.

"Oh my God," says Hannah, "*wings!*" She moves toward Syd, embracing her from behind. "Is that how you imagined them?"

"Exactly," Syd says. And then more quietly, *"Exactly."*

"It's Sydney, but it's not Sydney," says Mitsy. She looks up at Jonah for confirmation.

"Oh, it's Syd all right," he says. "In some form or other."

They all stare ahead until Hannah finally says, "What about the house? Were you able to list it?"

He nods. "It already has an offer," he says. "I didn't want to close the deal without Syd's approval, though. After all, she's the heir, not me."

"I still can't believe it," says Syd quietly. "Why me? Of course I'm honored, but... a whole house!?"

"Such a mysterious woman," says Hannah.

Mitsy says, "Jonah, we gave you power of attorney. Free reign, seriously. If you think it's a good offer, accept it, right? You're the only one here who knows anything about real estate."

Hannah says, "What was the offer?"

He rocks his head back and forth nervously. If they had any idea what a wreck he was, they would sit him down and offer him a shot of whiskey. But he soldiers on. "How does a million dollars sound to you, young lady?" he manages to say.

"What?!" says Syd. "A million...*what*?!"

"I thought the comps were in the neighborhood of $650," says Mitsy. "How did it get to a million?"

"Easy," he says, "the view."

Syd turns to Mitsy excitedly. "Mom, can we buy a new broodmare now? Please?"

Mitsy sighs, still reeling no doubt from the death of Daizee. "We can do that," she finally says. "Or...we can buy Aunt Hannah out of the farm."

Hannah frowns. "I know I want out, but...that makes it sound so final."

"Well, not the corporation, Hannah," Mitsy says. "Just the house. You're still a partner."

"Still," says Hannah. "Where would I go?"

Jonah's heart beats so loudly he can barely hear the conversation. It's a steel drum in the silence of a river in repose. *Paboom!* Can they hear it? He has to sit down. Backing into the over-sized rocker behind him, he leans forward, arms resting against wobbly knees.

"Anyway, we'll take it!" says Syd. "Right, Mom? I've gotta go tell Dane. He won't believe it. Maybe he'll even move down here. Do you think he'll move down here, Mom?"

Mitsy smiles. "We could certainly use the help," she says.

Syd hugs her mother before charging out the door, dancing on one foot then the other, a kinetic sculpture on a windy day. Godiva follows, stopping for a stick she brings to Syd. In seemingly one motion, Syd tosses it down the hill as she pulls out her cell phone to call Dane. So much excitement.

So much life! It would bring Jonah to his knees if he were standing.

Mitsy says, "I've gotta go, too. Jesse's giving me a dressage lesson at the lower barn in five minutes." She gives Jonah a kiss on the top of his head and flees. "Thanks a...*million*..." she says chuckling, as she runs out the door.

And there they are, alone.

Jonah sits quietly, mining courage.

"Well, I guess that's that," says Hannah. She leans against the wall, arms folded. "But it's kind of a shame if you ask me."

He raises his head. "Oh?"

She shrugs. "The cabin, I mean. Just looking at it on a flat screen takes your breath away. Those mountains! Forests! *That lake!*"

His eyes avert hers. "So inspiring, right?" he says.

"Hell yeah," she says. "Anybody could be a mystic up there."

"I would have to agree," he says then pauses, inhaling all the courage he can muster, and stands.

"Well, I'll see you later," she says, pointing upstairs. "I finished two more chapters while you were gone, and destiny awaits." She raises her eyebrows. "Up to ten now," she says. "Ten out of probably twenty, I don't know. But I'm doing it, Jonah. I'm really writing this thing."

"That's terrific, Han," he says. "Before you go, I have something for you." He reaches into his pocket and retrieves a small velvet envelope. "If you want it. No obligation, of course."

He can't even look.

"For me?" She frowns. "*What...?*"

"Just open it," he says in a voice he barely recognizes.

Her slender hands, fingernails neat but unpolished, grasp it uncertainly.

"Go on," he says. "Open it." He shrugs. "If you want to."

She unsnaps the tip of the envelope and pulls out a silver key that tumbles to the floor. "Oh," she says. "What..." She looks up, her eyes a question.

"It's yours," he says. "I don't know if you'll want it forever, but I thought it might be a good place to write a book."

Her eyes sparkle. "You mean...what? The cabin!" She squints. "In Tahoe?" As it seeps in, she says, "Pandora's...?"

He nods, smiling. "It's not what you're used to," he says. "It's small; plenty rustic. But the ceilings are high, and the view..."

"*Your* million dollars?" she says in disbelief. "*You're* buying Pandora's cabin? For... me?"

He holds her at arm's length and searches her eyes. This is the moment he fears most. After all, everything has changed. No one is the same, least of all Hannah. The independence she's gained in these last few months is staggering.

"Not for you exactly," he says. "For us." He blinks, waiting as she catches her breath. He can't tell which way this will go.

"For us?" she says, incredulous.

"I could use a change, too," he says. "Just being there... practically in the clouds..." He shakes his head. "And then that lake. I don't know. It's transformative." He shrugs. "And there's certainly no shortage of real estate there. We wouldn't starve."

At that, Syd flies through the door, her thin arms raised in victory. "He's coming!" she says jubilantly. "Dane's coming! Just for a week, but you never know. There are plenty of colleges down here." She looks from Hannah to Jonah and grimaces, "Oh," she says. "Sorry. Is, uh...everything okay?"

Hannah swipes her arm across wet cheeks, shaking her head. "Oh cookie," she says, arms outstretched. "Come here, baby, I've got to hold you."

Syd moves willingly into a tight embrace. "Because you love me so much?" she says with a toothy grin. "Or..."

Hannah nods. "Because I love you so much, yes." She turns her head slightly toward Jonah, winking. "And because I'm gonna miss you like crazy."

THE END

Acknowledgments

MANY THANKS TO MY beta readers and supporters, including Mary Lou Alter, John Nolan, Leslie Wolfe-Cundiff, Polly Bardagy, Karen Sirabian, Tom Martin, and Janet Denlinger. Much gratitude to Leyane Jerejian for her friendship, help and professional advice. Finally, hats off to my new cover artist and designer, Victoria Colotta, for a job well done!

About the Author

REA NOLAN MARTIN IS the award-winning author of *The Sublime Transformation Of Vera Wright* (2009) and *Mystic Tea* (2014), as well as essays, short stories and poetry published in national literary magazines and anthologies. *Mystic Tea* is the recipient of the 2014 Independent Publisher's IPPY gold medallion; 2014 US BEST BOOK award for visionary fiction; 2014 PINNACLE gold medallion for literary fiction; and a Finalist in the 2015 IBA International Book Awards. Her inspirational essays are published regularly on The Huffington Post and The Charter for Compassion. *The Anesthesia Game* is her third novel.

Readers can access author info, blogs, discussion questions, book signings and other inquiries, such as requests for signed copies at www.reanolanmartin.com.

Made in the USA
Middletown, DE
27 September 2015